KINGSBLOOD

SINCLAIR LEWIS

KINGSBLOOD

ROYAL

Introduction by Charles Johnson

THE MODERN LIBRARY

NEW YORK

LIBRARY OF CONGRESS CATALOGING-IN-PUBLICATION DATA
Lewis, Sinclair, 1885–1951.
Kingsblood royal / Sinclair Lewis; introduction by Charles Johnson.
        p.   cm.
ISBN 0-375-75686-8 (alk. paper)
1. Racially mixed people—Fiction. 2. Race awareness—Fiction. 3. Middle
West—Fiction. 4. Bankers—Fiction. I. Title.
PS3523.E94 K5   2001
813'.52—dc21   00-049616

Modern Library website address: www.modernlibrary.com

Printed in the United States of America

2 4 6 8 9 7 5 3 1

SINCLAIR LEWIS

Sinclair Lewis, the first American novelist to be awarded the Nobel Prize in Literature, was born on February 7, 1885. The son of a country doctor, he grew up in his birthplace of Sauk Centre, Minnesota, the prairie village that inspired many of his acerbic portrayals of American life and manners. In 1903 he entered Yale University, where he wrote for the *Yale Literary Magazine*. Lewis briefly interrupted his studies to live at Helicon Hall, Upton Sinclair's abortive utopian community in New Jersey, but graduated from Yale in 1907. Afterwards he roamed the United States working as a freelance editor and journalist, eventually settling in New York City to search for employment in the publishing business. Lewis's earliest fiction—*Our Mr. Wrenn* (1914), *The Trail of the Hawk* (1915), and *The Job* (1917)—seemed to announce the appearance of a new and original talent on the American literary scene. But reviewers were disappointed by his other apprentice novels, *The Innocents* (1917) and *Free Air* (1919).

The publication of *Main Street* in 1920 brought Lewis immediate acclaim. An extraordinary critical and commercial success, this sardonic novel about life in Gopher Prairie, Minnesota, exposed the complacency and provincialism of small towns everywhere. "What

Mr. Lewis has done for myself and thousands of others is to lodge a piece of a continent in our imagination," said E. M. Forster. "Whether he has 'got' the Middle West, only the Middle West can say, but he has made thousands of people all over the globe alive to its existence, and anxious for further news."

Lewis enjoyed an even greater triumph with *Babbitt* (1922), a lampoon of middle-class values as championed by an archetypal businessman, the robust but pathetic George F. Babbitt. "I know of no American novel that more accurately presents the real America," remarked H. L. Mencken. "As an old professor of Babbittry I welcome him as an almost perfect specimen. Every American city swarms with his brothers. He is America incarnate, exuberant and exquisite." Writing in the *Saturday Review,* Virginia Woolf judged *Babbitt* to be "the equal of any novel written in English in the present century."

Lewis won the Pulitzer Prize for *Arrowsmith* (1925), a best-selling exposé of the medical profession. It was regarded by many as his most mature and well-rounded picture of American society. But he refused to accept the award, claiming it was intended only for champions of wholesomeness. Lewis further enhanced his reputation as national gadfly with two more popular satires: *Elmer Gantry* (1927), a controversial attack on the hypocrisy of fundamentalist religion as practiced by flamboyant Bible Belt evangelists, and *Dodsworth* (1929), the tale of a Babbitt-like businessman abroad. "Sinclair Lewis could in one sense be considered the first American novelist," observed Alfred Kazin, "for in his unflagging absorption of detail and his grasp of the life about him Lewis caught the tone, the speech, of the pervasive American existence." But his other novels of the period, *Mantrap* (1926) and *The Man Who Knew Coolidge* (1928), failed to reach a wide audience.

In 1930 Lewis was awarded the Nobel Prize in Literature "for his powerful and vivid art of description and his ability to use wit and humor in the creation of original characters." In his acceptance speech titled "The American Fear of Literature," which he delivered before the Swedish Academy in Stockholm, Lewis spoke for a whole generation of writers involved in the revolt against gentility in literature. He stated: "I had realized in reading Balzac and Dickens that it was possible to describe French and English common people as one actually saw them. But it had never occurred to me that one might without indecency write of the people of Sauk Centre, Minnesota, as one felt about them. Our fictional tradition, you see, was that all of us in Midwestern villages were altogether noble and happy; that not one of us would exchange the neighborly bliss of living on Main Street for the heathen gaudiness of New York or Paris or Stockholm. [Once] I discovered that Midwestern peasants were sometimes bewildered and hungry and vile—and heroic—I was released; I could write of life as living life."

Critics agree that Lewis's subsequent novels are uneven and often undistinguished. Alfred Kazin noted: "As his characters became public symbols, he came to seem more a public influence than a novelist [and] some part of Lewis's usefulness seemed to be over." During the 1930s he turned out *Ann Vickers* (1933), a flawed feminist saga; *Work of Art* (1934), a novel about the hotel business; and *The Prodigal Parents* (1938), a disappointing satire that pokes fun at the radical offspring of another Babbitt-like hero. *It Can't Happen Here* (1935), his most celebrated novel of the decade, imagines a fascist takeover of America. Clifton Fadiman deemed it "one of the most important books ever produced in this country." In addition Lewis brought out *Selected Short Stories of Sinclair Lewis* (1935), a collection of short fiction originally published in *The Saturday Evening Post* and other magazines.

In the final decade of his life Lewis managed to write six more novels. In *Bethel Merriday* (1940) he told the story of a stage-struck young actress, and in *Gideon Planish* (1943) he skewered organized philanthropy and the activities of liberal do-gooders. *Cass Timberlane* (1945), a bestseller about American marriage, landed Lewis on the cover of *Time* magazine. "The book ... made me realize that Sinclair Lewis, in spite of his notorious faults, is one of the people in the literary field who do create interest and value," wrote Edmund Wilson in *The New Yorker.* "He is, in fact, at his best—what I never quite believed before—one of the national poets." *Kingsblood Royal* (1947), another bestseller, addressed the subject of race relations in the United States, and *The God-Seeker* (1949) formed the first part of a projected trilogy about labor intended as a history of America.

Sinclair Lewis died of heart disease in Rome on January 10, 1951, two months before the appearance of his last novel, *World So Wide*. *From Main Street to Stockholm*, a collection of his letters, was published in 1952, and *The Man from Main Street*, a compilation of essays and other writings, came out in 1953. "Like his master, Dickens, [Lewis] created a gallery of characters who have independent life outside the novels, with all their obvious limitations, characters that live now in the American tradition," wrote Mark Schorer in *Sinclair Lewis: An American Life* (1961). "In any strict literary sense, he was not a great writer, but without his writing one cannot imagine modern American literature."

Contents

INTRODUCTION

Charles Johnson

In "A Note About *Kingsblood Royal*," a 1947 essay published in *Wings*, the Literary Guild review, Sinclair Lewis, the first American to receive the Nobel Prize in literature (1930), made the following observations:

> I don't think the Negro Problem is insoluble because I don't think there is any Negro Problem.... There are no distinctive colored persons. The mad, picture-puzzle idiocy of the whole theory of races is beautifully betrayed when you get down to the question of "Negroes" who are white enough to pass as Caucasians.... There was a time in our history, and ever so short a time ago, when the Scotch-English in New England thought all the Irish were fundamentally different and fundamentally inferior. And then those same conceited Yanks (my own people) moved on to the Middle West and went through the same psychological monkey-shines with the Scandinavians and the Bohemians and the Poles. None of the profound and convincing nonsense of race difference can be made into sense.[1]

Lewis's twentieth novel, published that same year, reads like a raging dramatization of this declaration: namely, that what we have always had in America is a White Problem, not a Negro one. In his story, set in 1945, Neil Kingsblood is a thirty-one-year-old former infantry captain and a junior bank officer living a comfortable, privileged, and blind life in a segregated community, Sylvan Park, in Grand Republic, Minnesota. Like all his relatives, neighbors, and friends, Kingsblood is a digest of racial misinformation, prejudice, and white arrogance, although his ignorance seems almost innocent—a *received* bigotry picked up from others, like a cold. That is, until his dentist father confides in Neil that their unusual last name is possibly a sign of royal blood and asks him to look into the matter. Neil does, researching his father's lineage, but finds no English kings. Then he traces his mother's roots to an eighteenth-century ancestor, Xavier Pic. Thus begins the unraveling of Neil Kingsblood's life. Pic, he learns, was "a full-blooded Negro." Psychologically, Neil lurches from horror, fearing especially for his daughter's future, to questioning everything he'd heard about blacks, to the decision of saying nothing about his 1/32nd inheritance from Pic, and finally to a full unlocking of his perceptions of the social world. Being "black" suddenly forces Kingsblood to develop a complex inner life, a rich, questioning subjectivity that reads all the objects and others of his former "white" world with a critical acuity he did not before possess. For this ontological liberation, this apostasy from whiteness, Neil is thankful: "What a clack-mouthed parrot I was! I think God turned me black to save my soul, if I have any beyond ledgers and college yells."

His soul is soon tested when Kingsblood announces his new identity to black friends he makes after his self-discovery, Negroes who are (except for one Uncle Tom and a few called "bad medicine") the very portrait of dignity, individualism, decency, intelligence, and compassion—hitherto unknown residents of Grand Republic whose company Neil comes to *prefer* when his own family (except for his wife, Vestal, his daughter, Biddy, and his sister, Pat) reacts hysterically to the uncovering of their black ancestry, and his erstwhile friends, each revealing a foulness of spirit, make him a pariah. Kingsblood learns racial oppression firsthand, enduring insults and unemployment. But when a racist organization called

Sant Tabac ("Stop all Negro trouble, take action before any comes") begins driving blacks from Grand Republic and Kingsblood's execrable neighbors attempt to evict *him* from their community, he and his new black friends take up arms against a white mob in the novel's final scene. Race traitor Captain Kingsblood has, in effect, returned to "the great gray republic" from fighting one war in Europe to find himself again battling fascism, but this time right in his own backyard.

All in all, *Kingsblood Royal* is a perennially astonishing book, for Lewis, a chronicler of American life since 1912, deploys the full range of his satirical and mimetic gifts, his naturalist's fidelity to detail, and his amazingly careful research into black life to exhaustively catalogue the entire gamut of WASP practices and toxic, sociological fantasies. To put this bluntly, Lewis absorbed more African-American history than most blacks knew in 1947 (and probably know today). And, as if this were not enough, he writes with such devastatingly accurate insights into the absurdity of what W.E.B. DuBois called the twentieth-century's central problem, "the color line," that after fifty-four years *Kingsblood Royal* reads as if it might well have been written yesterday—and by someone with a master's degree in black studies. No less noteworthy is the fact that this savage novel appeared at the very moment Americans concluded, with much self-congratulation, a world war to stop the greatest "race man" of all time, Adolf Hitler, and a full generation before the color-blind civil rights movement inspired blacks and whites to challenge northern enclaves of bigotry and middle-class banality like Grand Republic (also the setting for 1945's *Cass Timberlane*).

Yet while this book follows a template Lewis developed in earlier novels such as *Main Street* and *Babbitt*—the story of an idealistic "insider" gradually transformed into a nonconforming social rebel who exposes some form of hypocrisy in American culture—it must be judged, in the final analysis, as less a novel than a corrosively effective polemic. Composed in roughly sixteen months, with a first draft done in only five,[2] *Kingsblood Royal* has the feel of a barnburning tract, a crusading indictment of the racial rot festering just beneath the deceptively placid surface of any American community. His characters are one-dimensional caricatures, the plot is more episodic than energetic, and Kingsblood's "coming out" is risible because he has so little African blood a mosquito might extract all of it with one bite. But even though it is flawed and failed as a fully realized work of fiction, it succeeded in shocking the million and a half readers of *Kingsblood Royal* from their mid-century racial slumbers (*Ebony* magazine awarded Lewis a plaque for the book of the year that did the most to improve interracial understanding), and it added a new dimension to the novel of "passing" established as a literary subgenre by two generations of distinguished black American authors.

Critic Robert E. Fleming, in his 1986 article "*Kingsblood Royal* and the Black 'Passing' Novel," discusses Lewis's book in terms of several important literary antecedents that explored this subject, among them William Wells Brown's *Clotel, or The President's Daughter* (1853), James Weldon Johnson's *The Autobiography of an Ex-Coloured Man* (1912), Jessie Fauset's *Plum Bun* (1928), and Nella Larsen's *Passing* (1929), as well as works by white authors: William Dean Howells's *An Imperative Duty* (1892) and Mark Twain's *Pudd'n-head Wilson* (1894).[3] According to Fleming, Sinclair Lewis knew both Johnson, with whom he sometimes corresponded, and novelist Walter White, an executive (like Johnson) of the National Association for the Advancement of Colored People, who introduced him to "prominent black intellectuals" and supplied him "with material from the files of the NAACP when Lewis was working on *Kingsblood Royal.*" In addition to this direct debt to black authors and activists, Fleming refers to an article by critic Charles F. Cooney, who speculated that Neil Kingsblood may "to a limited extent ... have been based on Walter White, who once was referred to by Lewis as a 'voluntary' Negro." (In *Great Negroes Past and Present,* White is described as a "blue-eyed, pink-skinned Negro with reddish hair," a description identical to Kingsblood.[4])

Fleming notes the striking similarities between *Kingsblood Royal* and *The Autobiography of an Ex-Coloured Man;* indeed, he finds the influence of Johnson's classic work to be "pervasive" insofar as both novels begin in the supposedly less prejudiced North, both feature protagonists who trace their black ancestry through their mothers, both hold blacks in contempt before their moments of racial revelation, and both have "an intellectual acquaintance whose worth is recognized only after the protagonist discovers his own black heritage." Despite his clear indebtedness to black literature, Lewis's book, concludes Fleming, is "a thorough updating of an important theme in American literature."

One final observation by Lewis deserves our attention. "Actually," he wrote in his 1947 essay, "the 'race question' is only a small part of *Kingsblood Royal*, but it is the part that will stand out." When Lewis, whose earlier works critically examined a variety of twentieth-century institutions such as the medical profession (*Arrowsmith*), organized religion (*Elmer Gantry*), big business (*Dodsworth*), American fascism (*It Can't Happen Here*), and social welfare (*Ann Vickers*), thought about Neil Kingsblood, he saw a young man whose "romantic and rather terrifying courage" had not been blunted by "the banal slickness of electric refrigerators and tiled bathrooms and convertible coupes," in other words, all the detritus of contemporary lives mired in conformity, lies, materialism, hatred, and anti-intellectualism. He believed "it makes sense to see and try to understand a young man like my hero, kindly, devoted to bridge and hunting, fond of his pleasant wife and adorable daughter, who flies off the handle and suddenly decides that certain social situations, which he had never thought of before, were intolerable. In order to fight those situations, with a grimness and a valor probably greater than that of any fancy medieval knight, not hysterically, but with a quiet and devastating anger, he risks his job, his social caste, his good repute, his money, and the father and mother and wife and child whom he loves."

That "terrifying courage" of the individual confronting the tyranny and torpidity of the tribe is constantly held up for admiration in his oeuvre and, for Sinclair Lewis, is the deeper—and perhaps truly universal—meaning of *Kingsblood Royal*.

Notes

1. All quotes from Sinclair Lewis's essay "A Note About *Kingsblood Royal*" are taken from *The Man from Main Street*, Harry E. Maule and Melville H. Crane, eds. (New York: Random House, 1953), pp. 36–41.

2. Mark Shorer, *Sinclair Lewis: An American Life* (New York: McGraw-Hill, 1961), p. 748.

3. All material from Robert E. Fleming is from "*Kingsblood Royal* and the Black 'Passing' Novel," in *Critical Essays on Sinclair Lewis*, Martin Bucco, ed. (Boston: G. K. Hall & Co., 1986), pp. 213–21.

4. *Great Negroes Past and Present*, Russell L. Adams, ed. (Chicago: Afro-Am Publishing Co., Inc., 1969), p. 122.

———

CHARLES JOHNSON is the author of many books, including *Middle Passage*, which won the National Book Award. He lives in Seattle.

To S.S.S.,

WHO FIRST HEARD THIS STORY

KINGSBLOOD
ROYAL

1

Mr. Blingham, and may he fry in his own cooking-oil, was assistant treasurer of the Flaver-Saver Company. He was driving from New York to Winnipeg, accompanied by Mrs. Blingham and their horrible daughter. As they were New Yorkers, only a business trip could have dragged them into this wilderness, and they found everything west of Pennsylvania contemptible. They laughed at Chicago for daring to have skyscrapers and at Madison for pretending to have a university, and they stopped the car and shrieked when they entered Minnesota and saw a billboard advertising "Ten Thousand Lakes."

Miss Blingham, whom they called "Sister," commented, "Unless you had a New York sense of humor, you would never be able to understand why that sign is so funny!"

When they came to their first prairie hamlet in Minnesota, six cottages, a garage, a store and a tall red grain elevator, Mrs. Blingham giggled, "Why, they've got an Empire State Building here!"

"And all the Svensons and Bensons and Hensons go up to the Rainbow Room every evening!" gurgled Sister.

Their laughter buoyed them for a hundred miles, till it was time to think of lunch. Mrs. Blingham looked at the map. "Grand Republic, Minnesota. That seems to be about forty miles from here, and it's quite a village—85,000 people."

"Let's try it. They ought to have some sort of a hotel to eat at," yawned Mr. Blingham.

"All the best people there eat at the Salvation Army Shelter!" yelped Mrs. Blingham.

"Oh, you slay me!" said Sister.

When, from the bluffs of the Sorshay River, they looked down to the limestone shaft of the Blue Ox National Bank Building and the welter of steel and glass sheds that had been erected for the Wargate Wood Products Corporation since 1941, Mr. Blingham said, "Fair-sized war plant they got there."

Since the beginning of World War II, Grand Republic had grown from 85,000 to 90,000. To some ninety thousand immortal souls, it was the center of the universe, and all distances were to be measured from it; Moscow was defined as a place 6,100 miles from Home, and Saudi Arabia as a market for Wargate wallboard and huts and propellers. The Blinghams, who knew that the true center of the solar system is the corner of Fifth Avenue and Fifty-seventh Street, would have been irritated to find out how many of the simpletons in the valley below them believed that New York contained nothing but hotels, burlesque shows, a ghetto and Wall Street.

Mrs. Blingham urged, "Come on. We can't waste all day looking at this dump. The hotel-guide gives the Pineland as the best place for chow. Let's try it."

They did not notice them, but on the way to the Pineland they must have passed scrollwork palaces of 1880, an Italian Catholic Church, a pawn-shop in which a Lithuanian lumberjack had recently pawned the Lüger pistol with which he had murdered a Siamese mining-camp cook, the best women's dress-shop between Fort William and Dallas, a Victoria Cross aviator, and a Negro clergyman who was a Doctor of Philosophy.

In front of the tapestry-brick, nine-storied Hotel Pineland (designed by Lefleur, O'Flaherty, and Zipf of Minneapolis), Mr. Blingham said doubtfully, "Well, I suppose we can get *some* kind of grub here."

They thought it very funny that the more choosy of the two restaurants in the Pineland should presumptuously be named "The Fiesole Room," though they would not have found it funny if they had known that locally it was pronounced "Feesoly," because that was how the Blinghams pronounced it, also,

The Fiesole Room had, for cinquecento atmosphere, Pompeian-red walls, majolica dishes, a Spanish wine-jar on either side of the doorway, and a frieze of antique Grecian runners done by a local portrait-painter.

"My, my, don't they put on the dog in—what's the name of this town again?" mocked Sister.

"Grand Rapids," said Mr. Blingham.

"No, that's the furniture, where Aunt Ella comes from. This," said Mrs. Blingham authoritatively, after looking at the map, "is Grand Republic.'

"What a silly name!" pronounced Sister. "Sounds like Fourthajuly. Oh, God, these hicks!"

They were elaborately escorted to a table by the headwaiter, a dignified, erect colored man whose head resembled a brown billiard ball. They did not know that he was Drexel Greenshaw, the leader of the conservative wing of the Negro Community. He looked like a bishop, like a general, like a senator, any of whom he might have been if he had chosen another calling than tablewaiting and another color.

Mr. Blingham had the Hungarian goulash. Mrs. Blingham was bold in the matter of roast lamb. Sister took the chicken salad, snapping at the colored waiter, "And do try to have a little chicken in it, will yuh?"

They found it highly comic that the waiter bowed, and said, "Yes, Miss." They could not have explained why they found it comic. As they said, "You have to be a New Yorker to understand our Sense of Humor. A nigger hash-hustler in a dump like this making like he was at the Ritz!"

It is true that in New York, on their evenings of festival, they did not dine at the Ritz but at a Schrafft's.

Toying delicately with her chicken salad, but finishing all of it as well as all the rolls, Sister looked cynically about the Fiesole Room.

"Mm, mm! Respected parents, will you look at the table to my right? Please buy him for me—the young one."

The person whom she had thus favored was an amiable man of thirty with solid shoulders and freckled paws and the clear skin that often goes with red hair like his. You thought of football, later tempered by tennis. But what you most noticed was the singular innocence of his blue eyes and the innocence and enthusiasm of his smile.

"He looks like a Scotch army officer," approved Sister. "He ought to be wearing kilts."

"Sister! And he looks to me like a shoe-clerk," sniffed Mrs. Blingham.

With that, they forgot the young man, who was neither a shoe-clerk nor more than a quarter Scotch. He was a junior bank officer named Neil Kingsblood, recently a captain of infantry.

On their way north, after lunch, the Blinghams got off their proper route. They were too proud to ask questions of the barbaric natives, and they circled through the expensive residence district of Ottawa Heights and a new, gray-shingle and stucco and asphalt-roof and picture-window real-estate development called Sylvan Park. As they turned from Linden Lane upon Balsam Trail, they did not note a "colonial cottage," new and neat and painty, with broad white clapboards and blue shutters, on the northwest corner; nor did they look at the brisk and handsome young woman and the four-year-old girl, all pink and pale gold, who were coming out of the cottage. Yet this was the house of Captain Neil Kingsblood, and these were his wife, Vestal, and Biddy, his lively daughter.

"I guess we'll have to ask the way. Do you s'pose the folks out here speak English?" said Mrs. Blingham irritably.

That evening, as they were approaching Crookston, where they were to spend the night, Mr. Blingham mused, "What was the name of that burg where we had lunch today—where we got lost, leaving town?"

"Funny, I can't remember it," said Mrs. Blingham. "Big River or something."

"Where the good-looking young man was," said Sister.

2

Neil and Vestal Kingsblood were having an amount of servant trouble that seemed improbable with so tolerant a couple, and it was not entirely a comedy of domestic mishaps. Tragedy in wry forms may come even to the Colonial Residence of a Young Banker.

You would have said of Neil Kingsblood that he would not encounter either tragedy or remarkable success. Red-headed, curly-headed, blue-eyed, stalwart, cheerful, and as free of scholarship as he was of malice, Neil was, in November, 1944, an assistant cashier in the Second National Bank of Grand Republic, of which Mr. John William Prutt was president.

He was devoted to his family, his friends, his job, to shooting and fishing and golf, and to the guns, rods, canoes and other enchanting and childish objects associated with those sports. But he was now unfitted for excursions among the forests and lakes of Northern Minnesota. A year ago, when he was a captain of infantry, his right leg had been wrecked in the capture of an Italian village.

That leg would always be half an inch shorter than the other, but he could limp briskly now, and by spring of 1945, he was sure, he would be able to hitch about the court in a sort of tennis. The limp did not damage his position as one of the best-looking men in town; it gave an almost humorous lurch to his gait, and his chest and arms were as powerful as ever.

Last Christmas he had spent in agony at an army hospital in England; this Christmas, he would be with his beloved Vestal, a tall, gay, affectionate but sensible matron, and his daughter Elizabeth, aged four and always known as "Biddy"—the enchanting, the good-tempered Biddy, with her skin of strawberries and cream, her hair like champagne.

Neil was born in 1914, during the fever-symptoms of the First World War; he had believed in the sanctity of the Second World War; and over highballs at the Sylvan Park Tennis Club, he stated bravely and he almost believed that there would not be a Third World War arriving just in time to catch the son whom the benevolent gods (his God was Baptist and Vestal's was Episcopal) might send them.

His father, still blessedly alive and in practice, was Dr. Kenneth M. Kingsblood, the popular dentist (office in the Professional and Arts Building, Chippewa Avenue at West Ramsey Street) and his maternal grandfather was Edgar Saxinar, retired telephone official living in Minneapolis. He had, thus, a scientific and industrial background, very solid, but it must be owned that for wealth and social standing, his family could not touch the gentility of Vestal's father, who was Morton Beehouse, president of the Prairie Power and Light Corporation, brother of Oliver Beehouse, chief counsel for the Wargate industries. In Grand Republic, we say "Beehouse" as you say Adams or Cecil or Pignatelli.

Vestal had been president of the Junior League, women's golf-champion of the Heather Country Club, top war-bond sales-woman of the county, secretary of the St. Anselm's Altar Guild, chairman of the Program Committee of the Women's Club, and winner of the after-dinner coffee-set at the Cosmopollies' bridge-tournament. She was, however, human.

She was a graduate of Sweet Briar College in Virginia, and it was understood that she was possessed of rather better taste than Neil, who had had a boarding-house and beer existence at the University of Minnesota. But she said, "I'm no highbrow. At heart, I'm a Haus-frau."

Her face was narrow, a bit long, but lightened by humorous gray eyes, and her hair, of an average chestnut, was remarkably thick. Her hands were squarer than Neil's, which were strong but tapered to slender fingers. Vestal laughed easily and not too much. She loved Neil, she respected him, she liked him; she often held his hand at the movies, and in the bedroom she was serious about him. She had, before his leg was injured, enjoyed canoeing with him all through the lonely Border Lakes; and she shared with him his Sound Conservative Republican Beliefs about banking, taxes, and the perfidy of labor unions. They were truly a Happy Young American Married Couple.

———

Though she had been reared in a Beehouse mansion of gray stone, in the old faubourg of Beltrami Avenue, Vestal liked coming home to the artful simplicities of Sylvan Park. Here were forests ancient as the hills enclosing sunny spots of greenery, all laid out in curves and crescents, regardless of expense, by Mr. William Stopple, Real-tor and Developer.

Vestal was friendly with her own white cottage and the smart semi-circular stoop and its slim pillars. Inside, the living-room was modest enough but bright as a gold purse, with barrel-chairs in dark-blue corduroy, maroon curtains, a ship's-clock, an ardent hearth-fire (electric, with glass coals), and on the mantel a German helmet which Neil was supposed to have captured in combat. But even more indicative of their prosperity was the "sun-porch," with green wicker furniture and red-tile floor and a portable bar and, for grandeur, a view of the mound on which was "Hillhouse," the fabulous residence of Berthold Eisenherz.

No ordinary bank teller could have afforded such richness, and Neil had been only a teller until a couple of months ago. His father-in-law had helped to make this splendor possible, and to enable them to have a maid of all work, that last and dearest luxury in a pattern of American civilization in which you own a Cadillac but black your own shoes; and a sound civilization it is, too, in which you may bully only the servants that are made of steel.

In Sylvan Park there are none of the brick-walled gardens and brick-faced chauffeurs which adorn Ottawa Heights. Neil's neighbors rejoice in Cape Cod cottages, seven-room chalets, and plain wooden boxes with fake half-timbering. Along the halfmoon Lanes and Trails are fountains, and the chief square, named "The Carrefour," is surrounded by smart shops with illegitimate Spanish arcading. But all over this plaster Granada children are passionately running, mothers are wheeling baby-carriages, and fathers are raking leaves.

Mr. William Stopple (and remember that not long ago he was mayor of Grand Republic) privately advises you that Sylvan Park is just as free of Jews, Italians, Negroes, and the exasperatingly poor as it is of noise, mosquitoes, and rectangularity of streets. Publicly, he announces:

———

"WHERE are boyhood's dreams and the maiden's fancy, where are old-time romance and the lily-white maid beside the mirroring pool under the shadow of the castle tower flying its gallant gonfalon? YOU can recapture that dream today. Sylvan Park is where gracious living, artistic landscaping, the American Way of Life, and up-to-the-minute conveniences are exemplified in Dream o' Mine

Come True, at surprisingly reasonable prices and liberal terms, phone or write, two offices, open 'til 'ten P.M. Wedns.'"

———

Neil and Vestal jeered at this true modern poetry, but they did consider Sylvan Park a paradise and a highly sensible paradise—and their house was almost paid for.

Back of their own double bedroom (it had a tiled bathroom adorned with seahorses and lotos blossoms) was Biddy's apartment, bunnies and Mickey Mouses, and behind that a coop, all angles and eaves, with things tucked behind other things, which they called Neil's "den," and which could serve as guest-room. Here Neil came to gloat over his rods and clubs, the Arrowhead Rifle Marksmanship Cup, which he had won in 1941, and his beloved collection of guns. He had a Hudson's-Bay trade rifle, a .45 automatic pistol which had belonged to the Royal Mounted, and half a dozen contemporary rifles. He had always wanted to be a frontiersman, an Astor Company trader of 1820 on the Minnesota border, and he liked calendars portraying canoemen and the habits of the moose.

And here were his own not-very-numerous books. The set of Kipling, the set of O. Henry, the set of Sherlock Holmes, a history of banking, and the bound volumes of the *National Geographic Magazine*, with Beasley on tennis and Morrison on golf. Among these solid wares, pushed back on a shelf, was a volume of Emily Dickinson, which a girl, whose name and texture he had now forgotten, had given to him in college, and sometimes Neil picked at it and wondered.

———

The rooms to which they gave the most nervous care were at the end of a constricted hall: the bedroom and private bath of their maid, Miss Belfreda Gray, a young lady of color.

In the hope of keeping a maid at all in these war days, they had made Belfreda's suite as pretty as they could afford. The bedroom was complete with radio, candlewick spread, and copies of *Good Housekeeping*, and in an entirely insane moment, Vestal had bought a real English loofah for the bathroom. Belfreda had considered it some form of mummified bug, and had almost quit when Vestal presented it to her.

Also, Belfreda declined to use the cake of pink bathsoap, in the shape of a duck, which Vestal provided, explaining that her dark skin was delicate and she could tolerate only Gout de Rose, at a dollar a cake.... Vestal got that for her, too, and still Belfreda thought about quitting. She was a good cook, when she wanted to be, but just now she did not want to be.

Belfreda was twenty-one, and beautiful in her slim elastic way. She firmly preferred not to wear stockings, even when waiting on table, and her voluptuous legs of warm, satin-finished bronze, not much concealed by her flirting skirts, bothered Neil and his masculine visitors continually, though they didn't do anything about it.

It is to be feared that, after putting more spiritual agony into holding a maid than it would have taken to do the housework themselves, Neil and Vestal had a distinct anti-Ethiopian bias in the matter of Belfreda, along with no very remarkable pro-Semitism or love for the Hindus, the Javanese, or the Finns.

3

"No," Neil said to Vestal, "I've always considered Mr. Prutt too conservative. He thinks that only people like us, from British and French and Heinie stock, amount to anything. He's prejudiced against Scandinavians and the Irish and Hunkies and Polacks. He doesn't understand that we have a new America. Still and all, even hating prejudice, I do see where the Negroes are inferior and always will be. I realized that when I saw them unloading ships in Italy, all safe, while we white soldiers were under fire. And Belfreda expecting to get paid like a Hollywood star—and still out, at midnight!"

They were having a highball in their wondrous kitchen, with its white enamel electric stove and refrigerator and dishwasher and garbage-disposer, seated on crimson metal chairs at the deep-blue metal table—the Model Kitchen that had replaced the buffalo and the log cabin as a symbol of America.

It was one of Vestal's nights for being advanced and humanitarian.

"I don't see that, Neil. I don't see that Belfreda is any more demanding than these white bobby-soxers that are only fifteen years old and have to have the family car every evening. I wouldn't like it if I had to spend all day in somebody else's kitchen, in the grease and cabbage-smell. Would you like it, you bloated financier?"

"No, I don't guess I would. But still: private bath, and no six in a room, like I hear there are in the nigger quarter, on Mayo Street; chance to sleep quiet and alone. At least, I hope Belfreda sleeps alone, but I always wonder about those back stairs. And a rest every afternoon from two to four-thirty, just when we're going crazy in the bank over the books. Free board and room and eighteen dollars a week to put away."

"Well, you make eighty!"

"But I've got to support you—and Belfreda!"

"But she tells me she has to help her granddad—you know, that old colored bootblack at the Pineland, old Wash."

"Oh, I know." Neil was reasonably tender-hearted. "She probably doesn't have much fun, always taking care of some other girl's baby. Charley Sayward claims the time will come when nobody will do domestic work for strangers except as a specialist, at fifty dollars a week, and go home every night like a banker—or a plumber. But I wouldn't like it! I liked it when the hired girl worked all week for eight dollars and did the washing and baked cookies for the little massa—that was me. Won't it be a hell of a joke on the re-turned heroes if all the subject peoples that we fought to free, *get* free, and grab our jobs? Oh, Vestal, this world is getting too much for a poor rifleman!"

She had been inspecting a cupboard. She wailed, "That dratted girl has gone and made two pies again, to save herself trouble, and the second one will get soggy before we eat it! I swear, I'm going to fire her and do my own work."

"Aren't you busting down in your defense of the downtrodden?"

"Grrrr! Let's take a look at her room, while she's out."

Feeling like spies, they tiptoed upstairs and into Belfreda's boudoir. Her bed was not made—it never was made—and over it were scattered shoes and pink-ribboned underwear and movie magazines, and the pillow was black with hair-grease. Upon her

Bible, on the night-table, was a pamphlet labeled, "High John the Conqueror Magic Catalogue: Lodestones, Hoodoo Bags, Jickey Perfume, Mo-Jo Salts, Adam and Eve Roots, Ancient Seal of Shemhamforas." An odor of incense and perfume was solid in the room.

"And it was such a sweet room when we gave it to her," mourned Vestal.

"Let's get out of this. I feel as if we were in a conjuh den and somebody's likely to sneak out from under the bed and start cutting."

As they came to the head of the back stairs, Belfreda was skipping up. She stopped to stare at them, malevolently.

"Oh, uh—good evening," said Neil, with a sound of guilt and idiocy.

Belfreda's face was very dark, with round little cheeks and a mouth of humor, but it was rigid as she looked at them, and they fled to their bedroom.

Neil mumbled, "She was plenty sore at our snooping. Do you suppose she'll burn a wax image of us? The lives and ideas of these niggers are certainly incomprehensible to our kind of people."

"Neil, I think they like you to say 'Negro,' not 'nigger.'"

"Okay, okay! Anything to oblige. These Negresses, then."

"But Belfreda says that 'Negress' is the one word that you must never use."

"Oh, for God's sake! Why are all these—uh—Negroes so touchy? What difference does it make what they're called? As I say: we don't know where Belfreda goes or what she does—rug-cutting or witchcraft or maybe she belongs to some colored leftwing political gang that's planning to take this house away from us. One thing is obvious: the whole biological and psychological make-up of the Negroes is different from that of white people, especially from us Anglo-Saxons (course I have some French blood, too).

"It's too bad, but you have to face facts and it's evident that the niggers—all right, the Negroes—don't quite belong to the same human race with you and me and Biddy. I used to laugh at the Southern fellows in the Army who said that, but I guess they were right. Look at that trapped-animal glare that Belfreda gave us. Still, I'm glad that in the North there's no discrimination against 'em—going to the same public schools with our own white kids. Some day I suppose Biddy might have a desk right next to a little pickaninny."

"I don't know that it will hurt that little snob particularly!" sniffed Vestal.

"No, no, sure it won't, as long as it's only in school, but how would you like it if your own daughter married a Negro?"

"Well, so far, even at the enticing age of four, I don't notice that she's bothered by any very big gang of dusky suitors!"

"Sure—sure—I just mean—I mean——"

The struggle of the honest and innocent Neil to express his racial ideas was complicated by the fact that he had no notion what these ideas were.

"I mean, up North here, we been proceeding on the idea that a Negro is just as good as we are and has just as much chance to be President of the United States. But maybe we've been on the wrong track.

"I met a doctor from Georgia in the Army, and he assured me—and good Lord, he certainly ought to know, he's lived down there among the darkies all his life, and him a doctor and a scientist—and he told me that it's been proven that all Negroes have smaller brain-capacity than we have, and the sutures in their skulls close up earlier, so even if they start well in school, pretty soon they drop out and spend the rest of their lives loafing, and if that isn't inferior—Oh, nuts! I guess the fact is I hate to hate anybody. I never hated the Italians or the Krauts, but I do hate Belfreda. Damn her, she's always laughing at me, right here in our own house. Doing as little as she can and getting as much as she can out of us, and sneering at us for giving it to her; never taking any pride in cooking decent meals, but just thinking how many evenings she can get off, and always watching us, and snickering at us and trying to get something on us, hating us!"

He meditated, after Vestal had gone to sleep:

——That colored fellow in my class all through school—what was his name?—Emerson Woolcape, was it?—he always seemed quiet and decent enough and yet it always irritated me to see that black face of his among all the nice white girls.

———Come to think of it, his face wasn't black. It was as fair as mine; we'd 've all thought he was white if they hadn't *told* us he was part Negro. Still and all, when you knew that, you *thought* of him as being black, and it made you sore to see him showing off and answering questions when Judd and Eliot had failed on 'em.

———Those black roustabouts in uniform in Italy—I never really talked to any of 'em, but they always seemed so different—the standoffish way they stared at us—I wouldn't 've stood for a three-star general looking at me like those boogies did. Yessir, if we want to preserve our standards of civilization, we got to be firm and keep the niggers in their place. Though I guess I'm not so hot in being firm with Belfreda, the little monkey!

———

The great young banker-warrior, legitimate heir of the sword-swallowers of Dumas, the princely puzzlers of Tolstoy, the brave young gentlemen of Kipling, twisted in bed, not altogether happy.

4

They were finding again the Christmas spirit that had been lost through the war years. All of his intimates were still fighting in Europe or the Pacific, and it was as much for the thought of them as for Biddy that Neil and Vestal bustled all over town, buying a Christmas tree a full month early.

They hoped to have Belfreda as a sweet and trusting member of the Yuletide family, and Vestal throbbed at her, "Mr. Kingsblood and I have already found the jolliest tree, and the expressman is bringing it here tonight. We'll keep it in the garage. Wouldn't you like to help us—you know, make a little ceremony of it? The tree is just as much for you as it is for us, of course."

"We got our own tree, at home."

"Oh, do you have Christmas trees on Mayo Street?"

"Yes, we got Christmas trees on Mayo Street! And we got families on Mayo Street!"

Vestal was more furious with herself than with the girl. She perceived that she had been assuming that Christmas was a holiday invented by the Pilgrim Fathers at Plymouth, along with Santa Claus and yule-logs and probably the winter solstice, and must all be delightful novelties to persons of African descent. She stuttered:

"Yes, I meant—I didn't mean—I just thought it might amuse you——"

Belfreda said airily, "No, thanks. I'm going out with my boyfriend this evening," and she departed, leaving Vestal and Neil flat in the kitchen which they had once loved, but which Belfreda had turned into an alien and hostile cave.

"Oh, let's get out of here! The place reeks of her," Neil raged.

"Yes, I've got so I hate to come in here. She acts as if I were an intruder—as though I was going to snoop into the refrigerator and see if she keeps it clean."

"Well, you do. And she doesn't."

"What gets me is the way she just looks at you, if you ask her to do anything unusual. She always does what you tell her, but she always makes you think she's going to refuse, and then you wonder what you'll do—fire her or apologize. Oh, dear!"

Neil boasted, "I've got so I can laugh off that look, but what gets me is the way she never empties all the ash-trays. By God, she'll leave one of them dirty, even if it kills her. I'll bet she makes a memo to do it."

"That doesn't worry me as much as that sullen look, as though she's going to get out a razor."

"I believe the ice pick is preferred now, by the better smokes," said Neil. "Oh, I'm sorry. That sounds snooty. Poor Belfreda—dirty dishes all day. We've got a phobia on the dinges."

But after dinner, the next evening, Neil again viewed with alarm:

"We've got to do something about our Topsy. Maybe it's time to fire her. That was the worst meal she's ever given us. She managed to fry the meat hard as leather and—I thought all zigs were wonderful at sweet potatoes, to which they're believed to be related, but she does something to them that makes 'em taste like squash. And I swear, this is the fourth time this week she's given us that same pudding."

"Second. But I do hope I can persuade her to do something different for the Havocks tomorrow evening. I dislike Curtiss so much that we simply have to give him a wonderful spread."

For the preparation of that wonderful spread, Belfreda did do something different. She failed to appear at all.

—

Curtiss, son of the lusty contractor, Boone Havock, had always been a mistake. He had probably been confused in the cradle by the boisterousness of his father, the screaming humor of his mother. He was a large lout, good-looking in a sulky way, and he had a large allowance, but he had never been popular with the girls whose love he had tried to buy or the boys with whom he sought companionship in boozing.

In the single month of January, 1942, Curtiss had married Nancy Pzort, who came from a family of inconsiderable market-gardeners, their daughter, Peggy, had been born, and Curtiss had run off to join the Marines. When he was invalided out, as a corporal, his father, though he noisily disapproved of *his* son's having married a dollarless Slav, arranged for Curtiss a makeshift job in the Blue Ox National Bank, and bought for the young couple a fancy villa of stucco and green tiles, next-door to Neil.

As a veteran of four, Biddy considered the Havocks' Peggy, at two and three-quarters, a mere child, but they played together all day. Curtiss assumed that as a fellow-banker and old schoolmate, Neil must love him and desire to listen to his damp stories about chasing stenographers. Curtiss was, in fact, a nuisance.

He dropped in at any time from before breakfast to after midnight, expecting coffee, expecting a highball, expecting an audience, and Neil and Vestal were so annoyed by him that they were extra careful to be cordial. And they were sorry for little Nancy Pzort Havock, that poor child of nature inducted into a family of bankrobbers.

The Kingsbloods were having the Curtiss Havocks in for dinner, this mid-December evening.

Vestal looked forward to it calmly and resolutely. She went to the market for squabs, chestnuts, and mushrooms, and on the morning of the ordeal, she begged of Belfreda, in the manner of a new captain addressing an old top-sergeant, "Look, uh, honey, I'll be away for lunch—just give Biddy her cereal. Now see if you can't run up a dinner that'll knock the Havocks' eyes out tonight. You'll have all day for it. Use the good silver and the lace tablecloth."

Belfreda only nodded, and Vestal went off merrily. Neil would come home by bus; it was her day to have the car; and she was a gallant spectacle as she sped to the Women's Club for bridge-luncheon.

She won.

She went with Jinny Timberlane out to the Judge's smart house in the Country Club District. Jinny had a new moleskin winter suit that was a sight worth traveling for, and Vestal did not go home till after six. She hoped that Belfreda would have the table set as well as the squabs cleaned, and that Biddy would be lenient with a tardy mother.

She bounced into a curiously still house that smelled empty. No one answered her "Oo-hoo!" and there was no one upstairs, downstairs, in the kitchen. The squabs remained nakedly in the refrigerator, and on the kitchen table was a note in Belfreda's writing, which was the smooth machine-made script of a business-college:

"My grandpa sick, I had to go to him, I took Biddy to Grandma Kingsblood's, maybe back this evening, Belfreda."

Vestal said one brief and extraordinarily unladylike word and went into action. She telephoned to Neil's sister, Joan, to bring the baby over, she vaulted into working dress, she cleaned the squabs and mixed the dressing. When Neil came in, she said only, "The dinge has walked out on us for the evening. I knew she was a tart. Set the table. The vulgar lace cloth and all the agony."

His long and freckled hands were deft, and he did a worthy job, calling to her, "When I get fired, we can hire out as cook and butler."

"Yes, and don't think we may not have to, if these Democrats and Communists keep on jacking up the income tax."

Curtiss and Nancy Havock came in, screaming, at five minutes to seven. If they were late for everything else, they were always a little beforetime for drinks. That good-natured wench, Nancy, dipped the French-fried sweet potatoes into the kettle of fat, while Curtiss volunteered to mix the cocktails, which was unfortunate, as his favorite recipe was ninety per cent. gin, five per cent. vermouth, and five per cent. white mule. By the time they sat down, not later than twenty-five minutes past seven, Curtiss was already full of jollity and viciousness.

"You got to fire that nigger tonight. I always told you they were dogs. If you don't whip 'em, they don't respect you. God, I hate the whole black mess of 'em. I know a fellow from Washington that's right on the inside, and he claims Congress is going to bring back slavery. That would be the smartest thing they ever done. Wouldn't I like to see one of these nigger college professors sent back to making cotton, and laid over a barrel and getting fifty lashes if he bellyached!"

"Nuts, you got mixed up," said his wife genially. "What the fellow said was, the big guns in Congress are thinking about moving all the darkies to Africa. That would be a dandy idea."

Curtiss was sufficiently plastered now to scream at his wife, "So I'm a liar, am I, you little Polack bitch!"

Neil heaved up his great shoulders, preparing to remark, "Havock, I'd like to have you shut up and go home," but Nancy was rather pleased by such ardent attention, and she crooned, "Why, dearie, I don't think that's a nice way to talk." She beamed on Vestal with, "Yeh, why don't you can the zig?" (In English, this meant discharge the Negro.) "I know where I can get you a hired girl—my cousin, Shirley Pzort. She's been working at Wargate's and they fired her for just necking the least little bit with a foreman."

That wounded Curtiss's ever-present pride of gentility, and he observed, "Bad enough for you to have a manure-shoveler for a father and a chippy like Shirley for a cousin, without having her work as a hash-hustler right next door to us—for the son of a tooth-jerker!"

Before Neil could say anything, Vestal had them all out in the kitchen, washing the dishes, and neighborhood amity was preserved, even at the cost of a platter which Curtiss broke.

It must have been by voodoo and clairvoyance that Belfreda came flirting in at the second when Neil had wiped the last saucepan. "Howdy!" she chirruped, and it seemed to Neil that she winked at Curtiss. "My granddad was sick. Sorry. Well, good night, folks!"

If there was gin on her breath, and there probably was, none of them was in a condition to know it. She frisked off to bed without so much as breaking out the ice-cubes which would obviously be needed, if Curtiss was to be kept in the state of imbecility demanded by the Havock idea of hospitality—in their house or anybody else's. Neil stared after her, but Vestal warned him with, "Hush! After all, she does save me a little work."

"But she expected us to fire her! She was waiting for it! She had a good come-back all ready. Shame to rob her of the chance. The way she gloated—I've got to crack down on her."

"You leave her alone till after the Christmas cheer, if any, and then I really will hustle and find somebody else," promised Vestal.

5

Always Neil felt that the malign small presence of Belfreda was in the room, making his large, ruddy, Caucasian strength seem bloated. When he was shaving, he fancied that she was standing behind him, snickering. When he learnedly answered Biddy's questions and explained to her that God wants us to go to Sunday School (up to and including age eighteen), he could hear Belfreda's tiny jeer.

And it was this time, when her flea-like insignificance had reduced his St. Bernard bulk to quivering ridiculousness, that Belfreda picked out for being a race-conscious crusader.

For years they had had a black cocker spaniel which they had named "Nigger" without any thought except that black dogs *do* get called Nigger. He was an imploring, mournful-eyed hound, and Biddy's best friend—next to Belfreda.

On a snowy evening, with Christmas close, Neil came home from the bank with cheerfulness. When Vestal let him in, she stood on the stoop calling, "Nigger, Nigger, here Nigger, here Nig!" The dog dashed up in a complicated and happy waltz and almost upset Biddy in an excess of affection, while the young parents looked on fondly. It was altogether a model family scene, until Belfreda, a black rose, much too pretty in a much too short black skirt, remarked from behind them, "I guess you folks just despise all the colored people, don't you!"

It was the first time that either of them had ever heard a Negro mention the race; and there was feebleness and embarrassment in Vestal's plaint, "Why, what do you mean?"

"Calling Nigger, Nigger, Nigger at the front door that way."

"But my dear, it's the dog's name. Always has been."

"Makes it worse, calling a *dog* that. We colored people don't like the word 'nigger,' and when you act like dogs and us are just the same——"

Neil was angry. "All right, all right, we'll change it! Anything to please you! We'll call the mutt 'Prince'!"

Untouched by the effort at sarcasm, blissful in her missionary zeal, Belfreda granted, "That'll be nice," and sailed off, while the prancing Biddy, a flitting white moth of a child, yelped, "I don't want his name to be changed! Nigger, Nigger, Nigger!" Her chirp made the word so enchanting that her correct parents were betrayed into smiling, and that was enough; the little prima donna had a hit, and she knew it.

Though they called after her, she went through the house screaming "Nigger, Nigger!" while the spaniel followed her fondly, a little surprised by all this attention to his name but considering it an excellent idea.

An expressman came with a Christmas package, and Biddy greeted (and offended) that high Caucasian with a hearty, "Hello, Mr. Nigger!"

"Oh, now, darling, you mustn't use that word!" said Vestal.

Biddy was always willing to co-operate, but this seemed to her a lot of nonsense. "Then why do you and Daddy use it? Why did you call Nigger 'Nigger'?" she said reasonably, looking friendly but firm.

"We don't, any more. We just decided that maybe, after all, it isn't a pretty word." Vestal was rather too sweet about it.

"Oh, I think it's a lovely word!" Biddy said with enthusiasm.

Uncle Robert Kingsblood, Neil's older brother, dropped in then for a free drink, and Biddy yelled at him, "It's Uncle Nigger!"

"What's the big idea!" protested Uncle Robert, while Vestal insisted, "Biddy! You stop it now!" But, thoroughly excited by this attention, and slightly hysterical, as all good and energetic children are bound to be at the wrong time, Biddy flashed off to the kitchen, and in horror they heard her address Belfreda, "Hello, Miss Nigger!"

To make disaster utterly distraught, they heard Belfreda cackling with laughter.

They had to explain everything to Brother Robert, who was as curious as a cat, and about as literate.

He commented on the crisis from his experience as Vice-President in Charge of Sales of the Osterud Baking Corporation, Makers of Vitavim Bread, Crisp Crunchy Crusts Jammed with Health and Yumyum:

"You kids want to know how to handle the niggers and not have any trouble? I'll tell you how to handle the niggers and not have any trouble. At My Firm, we never have any trouble with the niggers, and we never have to fire them, because we never hire any of 'em in the first place! That's the way to handle 'em and not have any trouble. See how I mean? Same time, I don't know as I blame Belfreda much, getting sore when you called her a nigger right to her face."

"But Bob, we didn't call her that. It was the dog that we called 'Nigger,'" Vestal clarified it.

"Well, same principle, ain't it? The girl got sore, didn't she? She wouldn't of been here to *get* sore if you hadn't never of hired her in the first place, would she? That shows the difference in what we call the inherent mental capacities of the two races. I wouldn't never get sore if somebody called *me* a nigger. See how I mean? That's the trouble with you two, going to college instead of getting right into a business career, like I done. Never hire 'em in the first place. So now do I get a drink?"

That was Brother and Uncle Robert Kingsblood, v.p. in c. of s.

At dinner, the Belfreda who had laughed at Biddy's "Miss Nigger" looked evangelical and unforgiving again, but toward the end of the meal they heard boisterousness from the kitchen: the giggles of Belfreda and a masculine barking.

"My, my, what's all this! I'm going out and get a glass of water," alleged Vestal, who had a full glass of water in front of her. She scouted into the kitchen. There, by the gay metal table, standing upright yet seeming to lounge, was a Negro of perhaps thirty-five. His color was dark, his hair frizzly, his lips not thin, yet his nose was a thin blade. He did not suggest cotton-fields but the musical comedy, the race track, the sweet shooting of craps; and he wore bright-blue trousers, a sports-jacket in wide checks, and a shrimp-colored bow tie. He had fine hands and the poised shoulders of a middleweight prizefighter; there was in him an animal beauty made devilish by his stare at Vestal, a bold and amused stare, as though he had known every woman from Sappho to Queen Marie and had understood them all perfectly. His eyes did not merely undress Vestal; they hinted that, in a flustered and hateful way, she was enjoying it.

She was at once saying to herself, "I've never in my life seen such a circus-clown get-up," and wishing that her substantial Neil could wear clothes like that and still look romantic.

Belfreda smiled as though they were just girls together, and cooed, "Oh, Mis' Kingsblood, this is Mr. Borus Bugdoll. He owns the Jumpin' Jive Night Club—it's a lovely place. He's a friend of mine. He come to see how I was getting along."

Borus spoke with only the smallest musky taste of Southern Negro accent. "I have heard of Mrs. Kingsblood, often. This is an honor. May I hope that it will be repeated?"

"He's laughing his head off at me!" Vestal quaked, and with a mumbled something which did no especial credit to her intellectual superiority, she bolted from the kitchen—without the glass of water. She grinned at Neil and quavered, not displeased, "I've just been insulted, I think, and I think the gentleman got away with it."

"Who's this? Curtiss?"

"No, a person of color named Borus or Boreas Bugdoll, Mister Bugdoll, and don't leave out the Mister, or else. Borus and Belfreda!

I tell you, the darkies *are* comic! And what a lie *that* is! Don't look now, but I imagine I've just been privileged to gaze upon the most attractive and horrid heel I ever saw."

"What *is* all this? Some one in the kitchen?" Neil said mildly.

"Now for Heaven's sake, don't be your brother Robert!"

"But who is the brash boy-friend? I'm going out and take a look."

With Vestal following and in a lively way wondering whether Neil or Borus would do the murdering, he marched into the kitchen. But Borus was gone, and so was Belfreda, and so was the red coupé that had been parked behind the house, and the dishes lay there in the sink, miserable and untouched.

—

Neil's sister, the pleasant Kitty, three years older, had always been closest to him of the whole family. She was married to Charles Sayward, a very decent young lawyer who for a term had been city attorney. Kitty and Charles came in this evening, to further their lifework, which was contract bridge.

Serenely playing, forgetting the horrors of domestic insurrection, Vestal looked up, late in the evening, to see Belfreda crooking a finger from the half-darkness of the hall. Behind her was the sardonic Borus Bugdoll.

"You back? What is it?" said Vestal crossly.

"Oh, Mis' Kingsblood, I'm sorry but I got to quit. Right away. We got sickness in the family."

The grim warrior-woman snapped, "You mean quit now, for good, at this hour, with the dishes unwashed?"

Borus said smoothly, "You might dock her four bits for failing to do the dishes."

Not Vestal alone but all the others felt uncomfortably that Borus was laughing at them.

"Oh, I'll wash 'em," Belfreda said sulkily.

"No you won't! I want you to get out right now, and get out quick. I'll pay you at once." Vestal stalked to her little cream-colored desk and slammed open her efficient small account-book. "With what I've advanced you this month deducted, I owe you $63.65, Belfreda. Oh. I haven't got that much."

To the bridge-table: "Anybody got any money?"

From Neil and Charles Sayward, she was able to garner sixty-four dollars, but they had not enough silver for change.

"You might make it the even sixty-four," purred Borus.

Neil sprang up, full of the most romantic notions about ordering this bandit out of the house, but as he looked at Borus's amused ease, it was revealed to him that, for his own sport, this was what Borus hoped for.

"Good idea. Make it even," said Neil. "Good luck, Belfreda. Good-bye, Mr.—Bugdoll, is it?"

He resolutely moved over, like a small but very select company, to shake Borus's hand. There was a moment's trial of strength, Borus's steel claw against Neil's fist, and then Borus smiled. Neil liked that smile so much that half a minute passed before he remembered to be a superior white man and to say, with the grave courtesy which is the essence of insult, "Would you care to sit down in the kitchen, Mr. Bugdoll, while Belfreda packs?"

"Yes, thank you, Mr. Kingsblood. Yes, I'll sit down in the kitchen ... while Miss Gray packs." And vanished.

—

Vestal came back with laughter from supervising Belfreda's packing.

"Damn those tramps, they win!"

"How come?" they all said.

"I was simply delighted that Belfreda had up and quit. I felt so free. And I thought I'd show 'em what a grand white-lady I am by being cordial and forgiving. I thought they'd slink off repentantly in his car (which is quite a bus, by the way; I wish we could afford one like it). But they didn't. They drove off yelling 'Good-bye, honey' like hyenas. Because while Belfreda was up packing, Borus washed all the dishes and put 'em away, neater than I ever saw, and he's left for us, right in the middle of the kitchen table, a jorum of champagne! My God, I never saw a jorum of champagne before, outside of an advertisement!"

"What a man!" admired Kitty Sayward. "I thought he had the most stunning build I ever laid eyes on."

"Yes, quite a man," murmured Vestal absently.

But Charles Sayward, most genial of husbands, protested, "What kind of white women do you two think you are, falling for a notorious, booze-peddling, slot-machine-owning, white-slaving black gangster! At least half of this country has plumb gone to hell—the women!"

6

The breakfasts were better, now that Vestal made them, and there was always an ash-tray on the table, and the morning *Banner.* Now and then Neil danced a jig on the kitchen floor, and gloated "This is all ours again!"

But, with the perversity of children and animals, Biddy and Prince kept mourning for Belfreda, coming in to search for her, looking reproachfully at Neil and Vestal, and saying, if only with their eyes, "What did you do to our friend?"

Within a week Vestal engaged Nancy Havock's cousin, Shirley Pzort, as maid.

Shirley was highly willing to share the cheer of the coming Christmas; she was even friendlier than Vestal desired, and always addressed her as "sweetie." She was what at that period was known as a "bobby-soxer"; an almost pure young woman, innocent and graceful as a kitten, devoted to bubble-gum and dancing.

As December grew colder, Neil's injured leg began to ache again, and he thought of the war, of companions who had been killed, of the lonely hospital Christmas a year ago. The English women had been so kind, but he had longed for the voices of the Middlewest, for his mother and Vestal and Biddy, his sisters Joan and Kitty. He had them all now; it would be their first Christmas together in three years.

He wondered what effect the war had had on him. Had there been any at all?

Lying in the hospital, he had been certain that all of the young soldiers would get together when they returned and shut up that one single revolving door called "the Republican and Democratic

Parties," and vote for righteousness and prosperity and no more wars. But when he had been in the bank for six weeks, as he heard nothing from the bankers and lawyers and merchants except the prophecy that That Man Roosevelt would be dictator of the country by 1950, he slipped back into his normal faith in the security of zeros.

But lately, at the Federal and Sylvan Park Tennis clubs, he had found himself irritated by the frequent sneers at "kikes." He meditated:

——I don't suppose the Jews like being called "kikes" any more than my French-Canadian ancestors liked being called "frog-eaters." I admitted that fellow Lieutenant Rosen who got killed by the land-mine. Sure, lots of Jews are just like us—I guess. I ought to get the liberal point of view while I'm still young, and then hold onto it, or I might turn mean, when I'm fat and middle-aged and president of this bank—or maybe of the First National of St. Paul.

——

These meditations were conducted at his desk, under the marble vaulted ceiling of the Second National's banking-room. He had been busy with Small Loans all morning, particularly with returned soldiers who wanted to start businesses, and he had tried to combine generosity with caution. It is not true that every banker lies awake days plotting to ruin all establishments belonging to small indignant men with crippled daughters. The banking business is usually not so good in a community with no money whatever.

He had before him a pile of folders with complicated financial statements, and as he recalled his dawn-thoughts during the war, the folders looked dreary. He sighed over a cigarette and glanced suspiciously at the fine brass plate with "N. Kingsblood, Asst. Cashier."

When he had graduated from the University of Minnesota, in 1935, he had planned to study medicine. But in the summer he went temporarily to work as a messenger in the Second National. Nothing happened that would blast him out of that smug mausoleum, and when he had married Vestal and begot Biddy, he was caught, and not at all unhappy about it. He read books on banking; he rose to be teller; he was popular with women customers who saw his smile and his red hair through the bars that he did not know were there. He was a favorite of President John William Prutt for his steadiness and good-humor and honesty, and this year, after his return from the service, he had been made an assistant cashier.

Mr. Prutt believed in training his young men in all branches of banking, and Neil, even now, was shifted about from "contacting prospects" and the nursing of old customers through overdrafts to book-work, to signing cashier-checks, and the transfer of funds, and Prutt kept him familiar with the depositors by having him sit in as teller for an hour or two every day.

He was as much in favor with the cashier, S. Ashiel Denver, who was a neighbor in Sylvan Park, as he was with Mr. Prutt.

There were eight banks in Grand Republic, of which the largest was the Blue Ox National: Norton Trock, president, Boone Havock, chairman of the board, Curtiss Havock, general nuisance. But Mr. Prutt considered that institution and its twelve-story building merely utilitarian. He felt that the Second National (there was no First) was in the true Morgan or Tellson's tradition. In its two-story marble temple, with massive bronze gates, at Chippewa Avenue and Sibley Street, there were no offices to rent, and it did not house alien chiropractors and machinery-agents.

In the banking-room, under the arched ecclesiastic vastness of its ceiling, which was upheld by ponderous pillars of green Italian marble, upon the glossy sea-shining floor of black marble inlaid with squares and diamonds of polished granite and pink quartz, where there was lacking only a robed choir of High-Church book-keepers to complete the spell of sanctity and of solvency, Neil considered himself a minor canon.

Actually, he was another schoolboy in a row of schoolboy desks.

For all its slanted brass name-plate and its onyx combination clock-inkstand-calendar-thermometer-barometer, his was a small desk, a leg-cramping desk, and his only personal treasures were the silver-framed photograph of Vestal and Biddy, his pipe and tobacco pouch, a copy of *True Detective Stories*, and a begging letter from his alumni secretary.

If Neil had any singular virtue, it was his loyalty to his friends.

He was thinking that at Christmas most of the dozen or so men whom he called his "close friends" would still be in peril abroad, his three intimates, Eliot and Judd and Rod, among them.

Eliot Hansen, the flashing, the dance-mad, the party-giver, was the inheritor from his plain Norwegian father of the Sweet Scent Dairy and Ice Cream Company, of which the symbol, to be seen on billboards along every highway into Grand Republic, was a pot of honey and a penny-piece.

Judd Browler, the sturdy, the careful, son of Duncan Browler who was the first vice-president of Wargate's, had sold prunes and biscuits in carload lots before the war.

The great man in that gallery was Rodney Aldwick.

Five years older than Neil, Princeton *cum* Harvard law-school, now a well-decorated major in the tank corps, Rod Aldwick was the Great Gentleman, the High Adventurer. He was a polo-player, he was a ski-stunter, he was a quick-memorizing genius who had only to look at a page of print to know it. He had the standard Anglo-Prussian specifications for a hero: crisp hair, broad shoulders, slim waist, and 6′2″. Major Aldwick would never seduce any woman in the limbo between countess and chambermaid, and if he had had slaves, he would have hacked them to death, but he would never have nagged them. Probably he will some day be found dead in bed, not necessarily his own bed, with either a dagger in his lungs or a laurel-wreath, slightly twisted, on his fine white brow.

Neil reflected that if these intimates were here, he would be able to discuss such personal puzzles as why he had recently enjoyed hating Belfreda. Then he admitted that all three of them had shied away from any subject more spiritual than the legs of their stenographers, any topic more embarrassing than the Republican Party. Only once in his life had Neil possessed a friend with whom he could talk about fear and love and God, and that friend he had known for only two weeks.

He had been young Captain Ellerton, whom Neil had met on the transport to Italy. All day, all night, they had talked. Ellerton was a designer of machinery, with a taste for Mozart and Eugene

O'Neill and Toulouse-Lautrec and Veblen, and he had not seemed to be impertinent when he had asked, "Do you ever think about personal immortality?" and "Do you love your Vestal out of love or out of loyalty?"

Ellerton was killed by a sniper, forty-two minutes after they had landed in Italy.

Neil had forgotten, by now, just what he had answered when, under the Mediterranean stars, Tony Ellerton had speculated, "Since you have only one life that you know of, do you enjoy devoting most of it to banking?"

7

"We'll have an honest-to-God traditional Christmas, carols and bellyaches and everything. We'll celebrate, because the war will be over by next year, and the boys will be coming home ... and we'll get more butter," Vestal rejoiced.

Their tree was a tall spruce from a northern swamp, but when she came to decorate it she protested that the war was indeed terrible, for in the Five-and-Tens and Tarr's Emporium there were only a few silver balls and twisted sticks of colored glass.

She resolutely explored her father-in-law's attic and in a lurching pasteboard carton, like Captain Kidd's treasure in a shoe-box, she found the trinkets remaining from the good old days of 1940: a great silver star, a silver-and-gold angel, glass oranges and grapes and cherries, a handful of tinsel rain, and a jocose little plaster statue of Santa Claus with a red coat and a red nose and a lighted pipe.

She came home like a walking Christmas van, and that evening the tree was ridden from the garage into the living-room on Neil's stout back, and Vestal, Neil, Biddy, Prince, and Shirley danced round it, squealing.

It was Neil's turn, this year, to entertain the whole Kingsblood tribe on Christmas Day. So, with all of her womanly genius raging, Vestal coursed through Tarr's, allowing herself a strict budget of seven presents to every ten dollars, and she accomplished a fabulous wonder by finding, at Bozard's, a four-strand almost-real pearl necklace for Mother Kingsblood for eleven dollars. With a not-even-almost-real diamond pendant attached to it.

It was at Tarr's that Vestal snatched up the gifts for Biddy: the lovely, old-fashioned, starry-eyed, flaxen-headed doll which resembled a plumper Biddy, and the lovely, new-fashioned machine gun which, in the 1940's, had become just the right token of the Christchild for a nice little girl. And at Tarr's she got the new collar and the rubber bone for Prince, the scarf for Shirley, and the rosewood pipe for Neil's father, which the good dentist would admire extravagantly and never use.

For themselves, Neil and Vestal put Biddy to bed early and spent Christmas Eve dancing at the Pineland.

"It's a crime that you have to feed my whole hungry tribe tomorrow," murmured Neil.

"Sweetie, anybody that you manage to get related to, even if it's that second cousin of yours that runs the filling-station in Hiawatha, Wisconsin, is my pal, and always will be."

"And I love you very much, and I'm praying that we'll have fifty more happy Christmases together."

"I drink to that!" cried Vestal, holding up her tiny glass of the white crême de menthe, frappé, which in Grand Republic is considered the most elegant cordial.

Drexel Greenshaw, the dark-brown, stately headwaiter of the Fiesole Room, with his small white mustache like that of a Haitian general trained in France, smiled to see his young people still so much in love. It elevated his feudal soul to hover near Captain Kingsblood, future president of the Second National, and his young wife, a real lady, daughter of the Prairie Power and Light.

Drexel thought to himself, "It's just as I told that little fool, Belfreda: if she didn't get along with a fine lady and gentleman like that, it was all her fault. My race will never have any trouble with high-class white people. I keep telling these colored agitators like Clem Brazenstar that they do more harm to my race than any mean buckra, and then they laugh at me and call me an 'Uncle Tom'! Those radical scum don't know nothing about aristocratic society.

I'm tickled to death to serve a gentleman like Captain Kingsblood, that couldn't never be nothing but a gentleman, nohow."

Thus did the magisterial old Tory take his triumph all by himself, though he seemed to be considering nothing profounder than napkins. When Neil and Vestal rose, Drexel humbly shadowed them to the door, and chanted, "We always feel it's a great honor to have you here in the Feesoly Room, Captain and Madam, and we hope we shall be privileged to serve you again soon."

Drexel was almost hurt when Neil answered the tribute with a dollar, but he controlled himself.

—

Back home, Neil telephoned a Merry Christmas to his father and mother, at midnight, and they brought out the presents. Vestal had dug up wrinkled wrappings from pre-war Christmases, scarlet and silver and crocus-yellow, and ironed them out, and the odd-shaped boxes under the tree were a sparkling heap.

"It's so pretty!" she exulted. "Oh, my dear lover, it's been Christmas now for seventeen minutes, and you're back from the war all safe, and everybody loves us, and we're going to be happy forever."

They clung together and trembled.

They were a handsome, confident and parental couple, in flannel dressing-gowns and purple scarves, when they came down before breakfast on Christmas morning, to help open the presents; and Biddy was a shining butterball in her tiny blue-and-white robe, Shirley a small dark Eskimo, and Prince a barking whirligig of excitement as they dragged the bright boxes out of the pile under the tree. Vestal was pleased by her own major gift, the fur-piece, because it was handsomer than Nancy Havock's. They had waffles for breakfast, all of them—including Prince, and what a mistake that was—and Christmas carols on the radio, and they dressed and bustled into preparations for the family feast at two o'clock.

—

Head of the family was Neil's father, Dr. Kenneth M. Kingsblood, whom the community esteemed equally for his bridgework, for his Adult Bible Class at the Baptist Church, for his trap-shooting, and for the jig-saw puzzles which he cut out on a private lathe. He was a ginger-colored man, tall and thin and kindly and hesitating.

Neil's mother, Faith, was small and slight and brown-haired, and she always seemed to be a little afraid of life, a little surprised that the four powerful children were really hers. Yet her dark eyes were as hot as those of her own mother, Julie Saxinar, that piquant and bawdy Frenchwoman, who lacked only a scarlet kerchief and a tambourine to become a gipsy. Faith's eyes seemed to have a life of their own, while all the rest of her was gentle and entirely vague, and she never listened to anybody at all.

Next in the family were Brother Robert, the Vitavim Bread salesman, the joker and total-recaller, and his wife Alice and their three children, including Biddy's pal, Ruby. But it must be understood that Alice was not merely the wife of Robert Kingsblood. She was nothing less than sister of Harold W. Whittick, the poetic bullfrog of advertising.

After them were Neil's sister, Kitty Sayward, with her Charles. And youngest of Dr. Kenneth's children was Joan, who was still living at home. Joan was ten years younger than Neil; reasonably pretty, reasonably intelligent, reasonably uninteresting. She thought that she wanted to go to Chicago and study dress-designing and she knew that she wanted to stay here and be married, preferably to her fiancé, an affable young man who was now a lieutenant in the Navy.

The tribe gathered, nine adults and six children—not to include Shirley and Prince—and though they talked about Russia and chemotherapy, they gave the feeling of the farmhouse-kitchen from which none of them was ancestrally far distant. The younger women all bustled about the stove and set the table (including the cut-glass dish of brandied peaches), while Neil elaborately served cocktails to the men, and Mother Faith was throned in the blue wing-chair by the fireplace, smiling and vague.

Dr. Kenneth took the head of the table of fifteen. (Under the linen table-cloths, there were concealed two cardtables, eking out the mahogany.) He looked down the two robust lines of people, loving them all, surprised at how beautiful and buoyant they were. He bowed his head, and in his thin kind voice he said grace:

"Dear Father in Heaven, through all these perilous days Thou hast preserved us, to celebrate again the birthday of Thy dear son.

God keep us together all this wondrous coming year, and bless these, my children, bless them, oh, bless them!"

Neil remembered the hospital ward of a year ago. He looked past those beloved faces to the worn face of his father, and his breath caught sharply.

"Gee, two turkeys!" reverently whispered Robert's Ruby.

——

After dinner, children and dogs and aunties were sleeping all over the house. Vestal's father, Morton Beehouse, accompanied by his brother Oliver—they were widowers and they had dined at Oliver's—honored the house by dropping in, bearing unnecessary things in leather and synthetic ivory. Dr. Kenneth was pleased to see how easy his son Neil was with the fabulous Beehouses.

"He's a sterling young man," gloated Dr. Kenneth. "He will go far. Maybe it's time to tell him The Secret."

He watched his son through the quiet supper, the games of Monopoly and gin-poker and charades, and in mid-evening he said to Neil fondly, "Young fellow, you seem to think so blame well of your trifling house and family, but your old man has to take you up to your den and tell you the facts of life."

He was a man whose fancies sometimes ran away, and Neil followed him upstairs with a degree of nervous surprise.

8

Dr. Kenneth M. Kingsblood (the M. was for his Scotch mother, Jennie McCale) had puttered contentedly through life. He was proud of having once seen Ex-President Herbert Hoover on a train, and of having bought a new X-ray machine, and to him each of his four children was a golden filling. He was more often tired than he should be, at sixty, and his heart fluttered, and he thought that perhaps Mother and he ought to go to Florida next March, when it would be raw in Minnesota.

He was particularly pleased that Neil, the miracle child, was going to be a financier and a civic leader, who would carry out all the reforms—larger schools and a new water-reservoir—of which

Dr. Kenneth had dreamed, but which he had been too busy with dentistry and gardening and scrollwork to carry out.

As they sat with knees close together in Neil's "den," smoking cigars that harmonized only with Christmas or a dinner for the Governor, Dr. Kenneth puffed:

"Boy, it's curious, your changing your dog's name to Prince, because our family might have a special reason to be interested in princes."

"How's that, Dad?"

"Well, maybe it's all foolishness. I like to call it The Secret to myself and here I am acting mysterious—guess the fact is, I don't quite believe it myself, and I'll only tell you and not the rest of the family, because you're the only one that's got enough imagination so you won't laugh at me. Just the same, there's one chance in ten thousand that the story might be true, and if it was, I guess the Beehouses would be mighty proud to be intermarried with the Kingsbloods, and not the other way around."

"Dad, what *is* this big mystery?"

"Son, my dad and his dad before him believed that we have sure-enough royal blood in our veins."

"How do you mean?"

"Just what I say. Maybe we're kings. No joke. And not any of these French or German rulers, either—Looeys and Ferdinands and that lot, but real royal *British* kings. Some people think the name Kingsblood is kind of unusual. Well, it is, and for a very good reason. According to my dad's theory (if he ever really believed it, of which I ain't too sure), 'Kingsblood' was originally a kind of nickname for our forbears, indicating that they had the blood of kings—as you and I have! Now what do you think of *that?*"

"I don't know as I'd care so much, Dad. I'd rather live in Grand Republic than in a drafty old palace."

"Well, so would I, for that matter. I bet none of them have automatic furnaces. But I just mean it would be kind of nice if, while we went right on sticking to business here, we could know that by rights—maybe—we're really the kings of England. It would tickle your mother and Joan and Vestal and some day Biddy. And I don't guess it would hurt your position in the bank one bit if Mr. Prutt realized what kind of a high-born guy he had working for him. *If it's true!*

"The theory is that by the true line of descent, I'm the king of Britain, and you would be my successor. Of course I suppose your brother could claim to be Prince of Wales, but (if the thing were true), I don't know but what I'd ask Robert to step aside, as he certainly ought to, fellow with no imagination like that, and I do wish to God he would quit referring to my really very fine collection of Florida seashells, as 'that junk'!

"Well, here's the dope. I was told about it by my father, William, who may not have been any great shakes as a royal monarch but he certainly was the smartest farmer and horsetrader in Blue Earth County. He had the story from *his* father, Daniel Kingsblood, the Civil War one, and he had it in turn from *his* father, Henry Aragon Kingsblood, who was born in Kent, England, in 1797, and emigrated to New Jersey, after having been arrested for publicly claiming, at a state fair or whatever they had in those days in England, that he was the Legitimate Monarch of Great Britain and Ireland—and I suppose all these Realms Beyond the Sea, whatever they are. He'd of been King Henry the Ninth. And born right there in England that way, maybe he knew—maybe it's true! How's that?"

"Well, it's interesting, but I don't suppose we could prove it, even if it was true."

"That's what I'm coming to. I notice that, now your leg keeps you from going out for sports, you read a lot more than you used to. So maybe it would amuse you to look into this. I'd kind of like to know about it, before I pass on.

"We haven't a scrap of written proof. I always intended to try and check the facts, but I've been awful busy, and household cares and so on, and all of us dentists overworked, with so many of the profession in the armed services, and here lately it seems as if people have no consideration about a dentist's schedule and think you can work 'em in any time, especially these young punks home from school on vacation. If you let 'em, they'd simply work a dentist to death, and *then* never pay their bills, and so—I never got the time. But here's what happened, the way I got it.

"This Henry Aragon Kingsblood claimed he was descended from a son of Henry the Eighth and Catherine of Aragon, who would be the real heir. But when Henry got sore at Catherine and kicked her out, he concealed the existence of this son, who's supposed to have been named Julian, Prince Julian, and who was brought up by faithful cottagers who called him 'Julian of the King's Blood'—hence our name.

"Now of course, him being the son of Catherine, that makes us part Spanish, and I don't know as I like that so much—I've always been proud of our English and Scotch blood; you know my mother was very distantly related to Bruce and Wallace and all those famous kilties, and *that's* a *real* fact! But still, when you think that Catherine's folks were Ferdinand and Isabella, that told Columbus to go and discover America, that makes her just about as high-born as the English, and you can see from our red hair, yours and mine, that the Spanish blood hasn't done us any harm.

"Well, there's the story. Maybe there isn't a word of truth in it, but do you suppose you could make a little effort to find out, boy?"

He looked so wistful. Neil was fond of his gentle father, and he vowed, "You bet I will, Dad."

"I'd appreciate it. Just remember that it's not plumb impossible. There was this fellow out West, in Alberta, I think it was, or it might have been Wyoming—I don't believe he was a Mormon, but very likely he was—and he found out he was the rightful earl of something or other—just a plain ranchman! So you see."

"Anyway, be kind of nice to know," Neil agreed. "And you may think it's a joke, but when Biddy put on that gilt crown in front of the tree, she sure looked like a real queen. Yes, I'll take a shot at it."

And in January of the new year, he did.

9

He had read enough of pretenders to titles and lands to be certain that his father's claim was fool's gold. But the arrogant nonsense of it amused him, and he wanted a new hobby.

Since his leg would not let him ski, or go wallowing through the snowdrifts after rabbits, swimming at the Federal Club was his only sport. He had bored himself with bridge, with crossword puzzles, with an aimless reading of travel and biographies and the novels, the spiritual flowering of the war, in which Elizabethan tarts delighted several million respectable readers by doing things which would be considered undesirable in a young lady of Elizabeth, New Jersey.

He was glad that it was England of which he was to be king. He had seen little of it beyond docks, trains and a Tudor manor house which had been turned into a hospital, but he had felt that the kind and weary Englishwomen who had nursed him had been veritably his own people. From his room of convalescence he had looked out all day at a flint church with a battlemented tower and long harp-strings of winter-bleached ivy, and coming and going through its pointed door he had seen Tess and Jude and Little Nell and Lorna Doone—and J. G. Reeder and Henry Baskerville. There was no building in Grand Republic, not even the bit of log stockade from 1862 which was built into the Fashion Livery Stable Garage, which was to him so admirable a proof of the enduring courage of mankind.

He had a much shrewder notion than his father of what would happen if the London newspapers were to be informed that an American banking gentleman had decided to be their king. Yet if there were that one-millionth chance, if it could be true——

Why not look into the history books and find out whether his father's Secret was completely absurd, or only ninety-nine per cent. so? It would be exciting for Biddy to be able to say that she was the king's daughter. From what he knew of that dictatorial young lady, he would not think it beyond her to round up all the neighborhood children and yelp, "Oyez, oyez, you canst now approach my royal person." He remembered the Christmas crown of gilt paper, which she had worn proudly though sidewise.

At the kitchen table, over gin-and-ginger-ale, he explained it all to Vestal. It was on a winter Sunday afternoon. They had gorged on turkey, napped, listened to the broadcast of the Philharmonic Orchestra, studied the sports and fashions in the *Sunday Frontier-Banner*. On the sun-porch, Biddy, with her cousin Ruby and Peggy Havock, was playing with the debris of her Christmas presents. As children of the final Anglo-Saxon civilization, they were machine-gunning a sad-eyed brown woolen pup and a doll with a glass necklace and a broken nose.

"So look who's a king!" Vestal jeered. "Your dad certainly is an old darling, and the craziest dreamer in town. Isn't that nice! If we ever save up enough money, which with the present price of meat is highly unlikely, we might go over to the Old Country and look at Our palace, and then get the hell back here, where we understand the dialect. But may I say, Captain, that I couldn't love you better if you were not only King of Britain but Exalted Ruler of the Elks. Anyway, I bet I play a sharper game of gin-rummy than any other queen living. Come here."

In the sun-room she dug Biddy's crown out from the Christmas ruins and gravely placed it on Neil's brow, adjusting it as she would a new hat, and she demanded of the three delighted babies, "Now tell me, chicks, what is he?"

"He's a king!" they all shrieked.

Vestal curtsied to him.

"You are both very silly," said Biddy.

In that world of war-widowed wives and of babies who had never seen their fathers, Biddy was proud of having a visible and proven father.

"How would you like it if I were a sure-enough king?" asked Neil.

His daughter admired, "I think you'd be a dandy king, and then maybe you could be an actor in the movies!"

It was Shirley's Sunday night off. As Neil and Vestal got the supper, she meditated, "I love trying to think of you as a king, but I can't do it. You're so obviously just what you are: a one-hundred per cent. normal, white, Protestant, male, middle-class, efficient, golf-loving, bound-to-succeed, wife-pampering, Scotch-English Middlewestern American. I wouldn't believe that you were anything else, not if you brought me papers signed by General Eisenhower to prove it. Oh, didums want to be a king, in a castle? Well, you shall be king in my heart."

"Maybe there's a lot of girls that would like me to be king in their hearts."

"Are there now! Isn't that lovely. Slice those potatoes as fine as you can, will you, sire?"

———

He would never have begun the great genealogical research if his father had not twice begged, "Started to look up our ancestors yet?" Suddenly, on a Saturday afternoon when Vestal had the car and was off playing bridge, he determined, "Why not? At least it would be nice, now that I'll never get much credit in golf or tennis again, if I got to be known as a good historian. Why not?"

He went up to his den, and sat down at his table, a scholar, dedicated and immovable, the vows taken, his lifework clear and vigorously begun, while Vestal and Rod Aldwick and Mr. Prutt and his one-time professor of European History all stood behind him, in awe.

There was one trouble: Now that he had begun his research, just how did you begin a research?

His head slowly turned as he peered speculatively about the room. There seemed to be no very relevant material except Dickens' *A Child's History of England,* a *World Almanac,* and *The Yankee Universal Cyclopedia,* in four volumes.

Resolutely he opened the cyclopedia to look up Catherine of Aragon. All that he learned was that she had been married to Henry, had had a daughter but no son, and that it had taken the destruction of the True Church to get rid of her.

———Well, if she didn't have a son, then her son could have been our ancestor. No, that doesn't sound right.

A Child's History was no more helpful.

What *did* you do with this research stuff?

Probably, you first wrote and bothered some authority. But which authority? His university history professor had never indicated that he longed for correspondence with tennis players. Was there some fellow in the Government whose job it was to explain how you got historical facts? And who was this writer who knew so much about all kinds of history and wrote these great, big books— five dollars a throw?

How did all these professors chase out and get all this information about some guy who had been dead for a couple hundred years? In the university, he had had no singular respect for professors; they had seemed to him oppressive and full of nasty tricks to catch a fellow who had been out on a bock-beer party last evening.

"Those guys may have it harder than I realized. How do you suppose they decide what Shakespeare meant in some line when chances are he was cockeyed when he wrote it, and didn't know himself? I probably missed a lot of chances when I was in college. I'll make up for them now."

It is to be said for Neil Kingsblood that the hardness of a task did not repel him. Now that he saw the disinterring of his royal ancestors as arduous digging, he really began to work.

He hobbled rapidly to Sylvan Circle, took the bus down to Rita Kamber's Vanguard Book Shop, and bought Trevelyan's *History of England*. In the second-hand bins he saw two treasures which could not help him greatly, he knew, but which he could not resist: Lady Montressor's *Memoirs of Court, Camp, and Stately Residences of Our Fair Isle*, two volumes, bound in white buckram with heraldic stampings, extra-illustrated, a great bargain, marked down from $22.50 to $4.67, and *Metaphrastic Documentation of Feoffments under Henry VIII*, a doctoral thesis by J. Humboldt Spare, Ph.D., published at $2.50, now fifteen cents.

His arm ached as he lugged them back to the bus, and he wondered, "Will I ever really go through them?" He was having the first, great, gloomy disillusionment in his career as a scholar.

He also bought *Hard-Hitting Hockey,* by Sandy Gough, and this, later, he actually read.

—

When his father heard that the research was begun, he hunted through old trunks and gave Neil a holograph letter from Daniel Kingsblood, the carpenter-farmer who had been in the Civil War, son of the Henry Aragon who had been driven out of England. Neil tasted it avidly:

Agst 7, 1864

My dr wfe:

I take my pen in hand to tell you all well so far hope Wm & you same. We are somewhere in Va or Car not sure which the sarjent will not tell us. Food is very bad am not complaining I suppose somebody has to fight this damn war but no place for man of almost 40 officers very mean and stuck up reumatism comes back when damp do not like these mts too hard to go up & down much prefer our Mich farm even if in wild & wooly west well there is no special news camp was attacked other night but halfharted do not think the graybellies like this War any better than us so getting along alright hope you all well. Must close now, your affct husband

Daniel R. Kingsblood

Dr. Kenneth, nervously trotting his fingers in air, urged, "Wonderful letter, eh! Can't you just see the old boy? Golly, those fellows were patriotic! Took things like they came—endure anything for the sake of preserving the nation. Wonderful letter. I bet a historian would pay a lot to see that letter, but I'm not going to let one of those fellows even take a look at it, and don't you ever show it to 'em if they come snooping around. Well, that ought to be an inspiration to you, eh?"

"Oh yes—yes—sure, Dad."

"Well now, this is going to be a great surprise to you. I think I know where there's a lot of letters from not only my father and old Daniel but maybe Henry Aragon himself! Think of that! My cousin, Abby Kiphers, was a great hand to save papers, in Milwaukee, the hardware-dealer's wife, and I've already written to her. How'll that be for honest-to-God treasure-throve, eh?"

"Grand," said Neil feebly. "Original documents. I guess they're what you want for research."

———

From Cousin Abby came the letters from William, Daniel, and Henry Aragon Kingsblood, and Neil fell upon them like a kitten upon a catnip-mouse.

He learned a good deal about the price of wheat in 1852, the voraciousness of pigs in 1876, and the health of a whole gallery of Emmas, Abigails, and Lucys, but all of it was singularly unilluminating about royalty. Even in Henry Aragon's letters, written in New Jersey between 1826 and 1857, there was only one sentence that might be of guidance:

"These Jerseyites can never seem to decide whether they prefer a Fool or a Scoundrel for Governor, and if I were King of this ignorant Land, I would hang the whole pack of them."

Neil unhappily concluded that his father's ancestors were an industrious, sober, and dreary lot, and that if he ever did reach back to the putative son of Catherine, the fellow would probably prove to have become a pious gravedigger. He sighed, "I never did think I'd have much luck at getting to be royal. It was just a chore I promised to do for Dad. I believe I'll chuck it and think about Biddy and the future, not about Lord High Prince Whoozit. Hell with him."

But he had been aroused to enough interest in his family to consider now his mother's line. He hoped that they would be spicier.

He knew little of them, though as a student at the university he had often seen his mother's mother Julie Saxinar, who was still living. His mother and Gramma Julie had never been harmonious, and for five years now Neil had not seen her, but he remembered her as a spark-eyed, tiny, scoffing old Frenchwoman, whose childhood had been struggled through on the Wisconsin frontier. The next time he saw his mother, late one afternoon, he suggested:

"I've been reading about Dad's family, Mom, but what about yours?"

They were in the "back parlor" of Dr. Kenneth's lean and aging house, an ill-ventilated room, all brown and dark-gray, jammed with a decrepit roll-top desk and imitation-ebony chairs carved with dragons. Faith Kingsblood was small and flexible, and in her there was a curious stillness. She said little; she seemed always to be waiting for something of which she was apprehensive. Her eyes were bead-black, but her face pale and her lips a faded pink. She trusted Neil and approved of him, and she never gave him advice nor anything more demonstrative than a pat on the arm.

She mused as though she was trying to remember something pleasant but dusty with time.

"I don't really know much about my folks. My father's folks, the Saxinars, were about like your father's: Scotch and English stock, good steady farmers and little businesses. All I know about Mama's family is, they were French, and I understand that in the old days they were in the fur trade in Canada. But those frontiersmen, I don't suppose they ever wrote down much about themselves. One time when I asked Mama about them, she just laughed, and she said, 'Oh, they were a terrible lot of boozy canoemen—nobody for a clean little girl to hear about.' You know, Mama is a funny woman. I think she always kind of objected to my having so much Saxinar in me, and being so neat and orderly, and clean pinnies. Ain't that strange!"

She slipped back into her silent waiting, and the quest of his ancestors became to Neil slightly absurd.

———

In so vast a universe as Grand Republic, with nearly a hundred thousand people, there are many worlds unknown to one another. One of the worlds least known to Neil was the feverish one of music: violin teachers giving lessons in the "front parlors" of red-brick houses in rows; little girls learning the saxophone; the Symphony Association which, once a year, managed to bring the Duluth Orchestra to town.

This year, with the local Finnish Choral Society, the orchestra appeared at the Wargate Memorial Auditorium, in late January. Along with such ordinary citizens as Neil and Vestal, the fabulously great appeared at the concert: Webb and Louise Wargate,

Dr. Henry Sparrock, Madge Dedrick with her daughter, Eve Champeris, Oliver and Morton Beehouse, Greg and Diantha Marl, Judge and Mrs. Cass Timberlane—she a frail, excited sparkle. Even Boone and Queenie Havock were there, both slightly drunk, as that was the only state in which they could endure the enjoyment of music.

(There were also present, but unmarked by the *Frontier* society reporter, a number of people who liked music.)

It amused Neil to think of how they would all turn from the mild magnificence of Hannikainen on the podium to *him,* if they knew that he was a Royal Personage.... He might wear his crown and ermine down to work on the Sylvan Park bus, and set up court at his desk at the Second National.

He forgot these splendors as the orchestra and the chorus marched into Beethoven's Ninth Symphony. He was borne into a place he had never seen. It was a spacious prospect across ornamental waters and oak-shadowed lawns to the pillars of a great house whose windows were wreathed with stone flowers. Behind it was a hill of heather, and over all a tower, broken and ancient. And it seemed to him that this was all his own.

"Is this some ancestral memory?" he wondered. "Did some great-great-something, that is me now, own that once? Is it maybe true that I could be a king?

"Or duke?

"Oh, settle for a baron!"

10

He was developing a new idea in banking, and it had been gratifyingly approved by Mr. Prutt and Cashier S. Ashiel Denver.

He was establishing a Veterans' Advisory Center where, as they were discharged from the Army or Navy, Neil's former companions in arms could come for information about finding jobs and renting houses, about Government compensation and educational grants—and it would be all right if they started new accounts in the Second National, or took out wholesome mortgages.

Neil was to be in charge, with a salary increase to three hundred and fifty a month, and if the Center grew enough, he was to have an assistant. Now, in that Northern April that was not spring but a dilution of winter, he was certain that the war in Germany would be over in a few months, and he hastened to get ready the Center's corner, which resembled a handsome mahogany horse-stall, with Neil's desk and two velvet chairs and a considerably less velvety bench, all fit for heroes.

He bustled all day and bubbled every evening. Vestal was pleased with his achievement and his advancement, and Biddy started a bank of her own, in which her cousin Ruby, Uncle Robert's daughter, deposited six pins, the very first day, and Prince a damaged dog-biscuit. This bank came to no good, however, because Ruby, whose ethics were not up to Prutt banking standards, managed to withdraw eleven out of her six pins, and Biddy, after counsel from Uncle Oliver Beehouse, declared bankruptcy.

Mr. Prutt was cautious in his hopes for the Veterans' Center, but Neil saw no limits to it, and late in April he went by train to St. Paul and Minneapolis, to consult bankers, state officials, and the heads of the American Legion and the other organizations of veterans.

———

As a banking expert, he took the chair-car *Borup*.

To the chronic globe-trotters of Grand Republic and Duluth, the *Borup* had for many years been an ambulatory home. It was so old that its familiars insisted it was not constructed of steel but of wood hardened by winter storms and the prairie July, when the thermometer goes to a hundred and ten. Its interior was decorated with inlaid woods, olive-green and rose and gray. It had been laid out with such pleasant irregularity that you might have known it for years before you opened a door and discovered another compartment with a table for card-players and four aged chairs covered with prickly green hair-shirting.

On the *Borup* Old Mr. Sparrock, Hiram Sparrock, Dr. Henry's father, still alive though somewhat retired at ninety-four, keeps spare sets of his five pills and three tonics and two dentures, with a comb and a stick of mustache-brilliantine. Hiram, that genial old cut-throat who knew John D. Rockefeller, Sr., and Cecil Rhodes, still has, despite the properties he made over to his son, a million acres of land in the United States, and his holdings in Mexico are measured not by miles but by airplane time. It is generally believed in Grand Republic that Hiram is richer even than the Wargates or the Eisenherzes, but he invariably talks about his poverty, and he never gives Mac, the colored porter on the *Borup*, more than a quarter.

His son, Dr. Henry Sparrock, keeps on the *Borup* a Modern Library edition of Karl Marx, which for five years he has been trying to read, in the hope that he will find out "what all these leftwing congressmen and these radical labor leaders are up to," but for five years an invitation to play bridge has always interrupted him just as he has started to read page two again.

And on the *Borup*, Madge Dedrick keeps her pack of monogrammed cards for solitaire, and Oliver Beehouse a crossword-puzzle book, and Diantha Marl a book on psycho-analysis, a book on etiquette, and a bottle of brandy.

Mac the porter, fat and very dark and nearly seventy and professionally genial, knows all of them. He shepherds the college-going daughters of couples whose wedding journey he remembers, and calls them "Miss," even though all through younger years he has known them as "Toots" or "Kay." He finds their lost compacts and candy-boxes, and tries to keep them from being too chummy with handsome strangers met on the train. He knows which husbands say farewell to which wives at one end of the run, and which husbands meet and kiss them at the other.

Mac is the Almanach de Gotha, the sexless maid-valet, the fichuless chaperon of Duluth and Grand Republic and all the towns along the D. & T. C.; it were better socially to be cut by Dr. Sparrock and ignored by Mrs. Dedrick than to be unrecognized by Mac; and to call him "George" instead of "Mac" is to be admittedly an outer barbarian; and so far as Neil or his friends had ever known, he has no surname.

He greeted Neil with, "Mighty nice to have you traveling with us, Captain Kingsblood, sir. I hope to hear your injured limb is ameliorating, sir."

"Yes, thanks, it's a lot better, Mac."

——Kind of flattering to have Mac remember me. Mustn't forget to tip him two bits.

"Would you like to see the Minneapolis morning paper, Captain, sir?"

"Oh, thank you, Mac."

——No, four bits. There's an old darky that knows his place. Why can't these young fools like Belfreda be considerate that way? Be just too bad if I hand Mac fifty or even seventy-five cents!

——And of course it would go on my expense-account.

———

At the end of the journey, when Mac had brushed him off as though he was brushing him off, and had caressed him with, "Hope we're going to have the honor of having you with us on your return trip, Captain, sir," Neil solemnly handed him a dollar.

Farther down the car, as they came into the station, Old Hiram Sparrock growled at Mac, "Hey, you Machiavellian bastard, aren't you going to hope you'll have the honor of my riding back with you?"

"No, *sir*, General. You always make too much trouble—you and those ole pills."

"Why, you gold-digging, uncle-tomming, old, black he-courtesan! Here's a quarter, and you're mighty lucky to get it."

"I sure am, General. Big lot of money for doing nothing but look at you. Usually ain't but fifteen cents. You make another stock-market killing, General?"

"None of your damn intrusive business. How many newspapers do you spy for?"

"All of 'em, General. See you soon."

Neither of them mentioned the fact that Old Hiram gave Old Mac fifty dollars every Christmas. The two relics of the lumber-land-iron feudalism of 1900 grinned at each other, and young Neil Kingsblood looked approvingly at their stock-company performance.

11

Neil had fancied that the vague estrangement between his mother and her parents had come from Gramma Julie Saxinar's habit of diminutively managing every one within range of her cackling and cheery voice. There had never been real hostility, but the family coolness had kept Neil from any great custom of intimacy with his grandparents.

But he did take one evening during his four-day official mission in Minneapolis to go out to Lake Minnetonka and call on the Saxinars.

At sixty-five, when he had retired from the telephone company (he was still living, at eighty-five), Edgar Saxinar had purchased something very tidy in the way of a one-story house. He had admirably described it in a letter:

"We have settled down in a stone bungalow right on the romantic waters of old Lake Minnetonka, with views. There is no city as large as Minneapolis that has as large not to say lovely a lake as Minnetonka within so small a comparable distance. Mrs. Saxinar and I often talk about the romantic Indians who used to canoe on these romantic waters."

The bungalow was not actually of stone, but of cement blocks so pressed as to look somewhat like stones, and the Saxinars' view did not actually include the justly celebrated expanse of Minnetonka, three blocks away from them, but only an eight-flat frame apartment house, a Seventh-Day Adventist chapel, and a grove of cottonwoods. But it was as snug a refuge for two happily querulous old parties as could have been contrived, and Neil felt content as he sat on a tufted yellow plush chair in the small living-room, whose yellow wallpaper was bedecked with a pattern of cat-tails and water lilies.

Though he had had a steak dinner at the Hotel Swanson-Grand, Gramma Julie insisted on taking him out to the kitchen and stuffing chocolate brownies into him. Hers was no glass-and-enamel magazine-advertisement kitchen. She cooked on an aged, not-too-well-polished coal-stove, and kept her treasures in a series of broken-nosed blue teapots and tin cracker-cans and her china came out of an antique shop and should have stayed there. Neil remembered that while his mother and Grampa Edgar had always insisted that they were neat (usually it was pins that they were as neat as), the gay little black beetle, Julie, was a genius of gipsy disorder.

But he noted that in this mess of crockery Gramma Julie could find anything she wanted, while his mother and Grampa, proud of arranging everything geometrically, of properly filing away addresses and letters and laundry bills and not-quite-wornout shoelaces, could never remember their own systems.

He returned with Julie to the living-room, to be grand-filial to that squat, bald, cheerful and complaining patriot, Grampa Edgar Saxinar.

He dutifully made the regulation queries about Edgar's views on the state income tax, the last-season Minneapolis baseball team and future models of telephone instruments. (Edgar thought very little of any of them.) Then Neil demanded the one thing he really wanted to know:

"Gramma Julie, something Dad told me has got me interested in my ancestors. Tell me about your family, and Grampa's."

The little, odd, old lady, eighty-three now by the calendar and forty-three by the clock of her taut slim throat and the obsidian eyes that needed no spectacles, half gipsy and half Irish fay with a trace of Yankee stringency for preservative, knitting and rocking in the untidy old cane-seated chair that her husband detested, while he, with old-fashioned half-moon eyeglasses clerkly in his round red face, smoked a long stogie and constantly grunted in disbelief—Gramma Julie clucked like a nesting hen:

"Your Grampa Saxinar—that solid object there, smoking the stinkeroo—was born in Wisconsin and he worked for a sawmill, as bookkeeper, and he was a clerk and a telegrapher for the Chicago, Milwaukee before he got a job in the telephone office. And his folks, as far as he knows 'em, were like everybody else: cheese-makers and mouse-trap salesmen—nice stupid people."

Edgar spouted like a pond-sized whale. "Now that's all right now! Saxinars good people, and so was Neil's father's folks. I had good, solid antecedents, Republicans and Calvinist Presbyterians, almost without an exception, thank God!"

Julie snickered, "That's what I said. Nice and stupid. But my own folks, they were French. The women all wore ribbons and the men all took 'em off!"

Neil cajoled her, "Now Granny, I learned in the Army that the French aren't a bit wicked, as their funny papers make out. They're the carefullest farmers in Europe, and the tightest shop-keepers."

"Maybe one kind of French are. But my ancestors were the light-footed breed that skipped off from Europe because it was too tame, and settled in Quebec, and skipped off from there, too, because it was too pious, and they drank high wines and wouldn't have any truck with anybody that was tamer than the wolves and lynxes and Assiniboins."

She looked inward on a red-lit girlhood, and mused aloud: "I was born in Wisconsin, too, in Hiawatha, and my, it was a tough lumber-town, then, and I danced with the raftsmen—I could dance awful light and they wore red caps."

Edgar snorted, "Isn't that kind of mixed-up?"

"Well, it *was* mixed up—more 'n you'll ever know, old man! Even then, when it was all tarpaper shanties and pine clearings, you Saxi-nars read your *Sabbath Extracts for Little Christians.* But my folks—— My father, Alexandre Payzold, he died when I was ten, and so did my mama, it was a small-pox epidemic."

Neil was wondering how Vestal, Old Bay Colony out of Dorset, would accept this torch-glaring wilderness origin, as Julie clucked on, in tune to her knitting-needles:

"Yes, Alexandre Payzold. I don't guess I recollect him very good, except he was a fine, big man, with a huge, enormous black beard—it tickled!—and he sang lots. He was a mail-runner and he worked some in the Big Woods and he drove the first coach—oh, he spoke English good, I remember that, but he'd yell at the horses in French. When him and Mama died, I was only ten, and I was raised by Mama's brother, Uncle Emil Aubert. He was a fur-trader. He never told me much about Papa's folks, the Payzolds.

"But I know my Papa's papa, Louis Payzold, was a farmer and a trapper and he dug some copper on Lake Superior, and he married a girl named Sidonie Pic, and *her* father was Xavier Pic—let's see— Xavier would be your great-great-great-grandfather.

"Uncle Emil knew a little about Xavier, because Xavier was a wonderful fellow that got around all over the frontier. I don't suppose there's anything about him in history—he never got rich, and of course they never kept many records or had any newspapers in the wilderness. From what I recall of what Uncle Emil told me— oh dear, it's maybe seventy years ago now since I heard his stories!—Xavier was the best kind of French *voyageur*. Maybe there was some bad things about him, too, but I guess Uncle Emil wouldn't tattle about them to a little girl like I."

"I don't think I'd talk about Pic," urged Grampa Edgar.

"I will so! I'm proud of him. Well, Xavier Pic, he must of been born around 1790. Uncle Emil said that some folks claimed he was born on Mackinac Island and some on Lake Pepin and some in New Orleans or even back in the Old Country, in France, and they all said Xavier wasn't a tall man, but awful strong and brave, and he could sing fine and he drank too much, and languages, my! they claim he spoke all the languages there are—French and English and Spanish and Chippewa and Sioux and Cree—Xavier spoke them all, Uncle Emil told me, and my Uncle Emil was a truthful man, except about furs. Oh, Edgar would have hated Xavier Pic!"

"Always did. If you didn't just make him up," explained Grampa Edgar.

"Yes, like I said. So Xavier—they say he was a *voyageur* for the Hudson's Bay Company, but afterwards he was a *coureur de bois* for himself, a free trader and a fur-buyer. He was slick at shooting the rapids. Prob'ly when he was young, he wore a sash, like the *voyageurs* did, and he sang—

"Why, Neil, I think I must of told you a little about Xavier when you were only as high as my kitchen stove. You would forget it now, but do you remember the little song I taught you of the *voyageurs, Dans Mon Chemin?*"

"Yes, by golly I do begin to remember it now, Gramma."

———

From his anecdotal Minnesota history in high school, from lost tales of his mother and Gramma Julie, Neil could see the outlines now of his ancestor, Xavier Pic.

While Gramma Julie nodded in silence, he sketched that robust and jovial French adventurer.

Xavier was not plowing dun English fields, like the worthy forbears of Dr. Kenneth, who were doubtless as rustic as they alleged themselves to be royal. Xavier belonged not to evening and mist and gossiping cowbells but to alert morning on the glittering rapids of unknown rivers. Neil saw him coming out of Montreal on a spring morning, with the squadron of canoes bound away for the pine-darkened fort at the mouth of the Kaministikwia.

Xavier Pic. He would be a pink-cheeked and ribald roisterer with a short and curly golden beard, and he would be wearing a blanket-cloth capote of morning blue, thrown back, with his tobacco pouch and his agile knife swung from his scarlet sash. His moccasins and leggins were of elkskin, and in his knitted cap was the feather of a Nor'wester.

Challenging the rapids and the wolf-haunted night in the immense loneliness of the Northern forest, laughing back at the monstrous storms of Lake Superior, scoffing at cold and hunger and the malign Indians, Xavier would be singing with his mates, at the gay start of the journey:

> Dans mon chemin j'ai recontré
> Trois cavaliers bien montés—
> Lon, Lon, laridon daine.

Thus, not in words but in images, bright and strong, Neil recalled the springtime hero who was his source.

———

All that would have been when Xavier was young. When Gramma Julie roused from her catnap and went on, she surmised, from the shadows of great legends she had heard in girlhood, that Xavier became an independent trader. She knew that he lived on till 1850, always a mover, and she was certain that he had been the first white man to explore dark leagues of wasteland where now there are farms and villages that were founded on the rock of Xavier's skill and bravery.

It was unquestionable, she stridently maintained against her husband's grunting, that this pioneering Frenchman had been one of the builders, the primitive warrior-kings, of the new provinces of the Americans and the British: Minnesota and Wisconsin, Ontario and Manitoba.

But, Neil improvised, Xavier's service to the Anglican visky-guzzlers must have been involuntary. He must still have borne in his heart the Lilies of the Sun, not the beef-red banner of the British nor the candy-striped bunting of the Yanks. Might not this valorous Gaul, more than some lanky English lordling, have been the ancestor who established for him a valid claim to the blood royal?

This would not gratify Dr. Kenneth, who had none of Xavier's fire in his brittle veins, but some day it would enchant a Biddy who was as venturesome as Xavier.

Why not? Who could tell? Perhaps this singular Xavier Pic was the exiled offspring of some half-royal Duc of Picardie!

But the ducal banner was instantly taken from Neil's hand.

———

"You understand," said Gramma Julie, "that Xavier may not have been pure French? I wouldn't wonder if he was part Indian. We may be part Chippewa ourselves, you and me."

"Chippewa?" said Neil, not very brightly.

"Why, you haven't got any prejudice against our having some Indian blood?" said the old lady, with a foxy glance at her husband.

"No, no, certainly not!" declared Neil, with an extraordinary lack of conviction. "I haven't any prejudices against any race. After all, I was in the War Against Prejudice!"

Grampa Edgar complained, " 'Tain't a question of the boy having prejudices against being a nekkid, baby-scalping Indian. You just don't have to advertise everything you know!"

Julie eyed her man. "Don't talk like you got the simples! I ain't afraid to advertise what *my* folks were! They never peddled wooden clocks, like some! If anybody came up to me and asked, 'Are you a tomahawking Indian?' I'd say, Sure. And tomahawk 'em!"

While the old ones bickered, with the skill of sixty years' practice, Neil was in a small state of shock. In a general way, he believed that Indians were very fine people—they were good at canoeing and the tanning of deerskins. But it was a tumble from the castle of a Duc de Picardie to a bark lodge, smoke-encrusted.

After some spirited notes on Edgar's ancestors as Yankee skin-flints, Julie was going on:

"Anyway, the only time that I ever heard of Xavier's getting careless and marrying, the girl was a Chippewa squaw, so I guess we got Indian blood from her, even if Xavier wasn't part Indian himself. And me, I'd rather have kin that et berries and fresh pickerel than Edgar's folks, that never had anything but codfish—dried—and that's how they all come to look so dry themselves."

"Mine didn't eat boiled dog, like you Chippewas," said Edgar. "And far's Neil's concerned, my folks are *his* folks, codfish and all, just as much as your folks is, ain't they?"

"That's what you think! Anyway, if you like it or not, Neil, whether you're a wild Injun or not, you're descended from Xavier Pic, the smartest man on the frontier, and that's pretty good, hey?"

"Oh, yes, Gramma, that's fine!"

But his new-found Indian blood impressed him more than M. Pic's "smartness."

He was recalling that, as a small boy, from some forgotten hint or other of Gramma Julie, he had for a while considered himself to have a warlike Indian streak in him. He had boasted of it to Ackley Wargate, and that pale scion had been envious. Yes, a royal heritage, Chippewa bravery; a people unafraid of rocks and nightfall and creeping enemies.

But still—

That might be fine for most people, but not for the conformable husband of Vestal Beehouse. And he was unhappy to suspect that his rare Biddy, that bright being of crystal and rose and silver, was less certainly cousin to English princesses and to demoiselles in robes broidered with the golden lilies than to unbathed squaws in shirts of branded flour-sacking.

———Wonder how many Indian kids running around reservations and picking nits out of their hair can claim to be Biddy's cousins?

———Oh, let 'em claim it! Might be good for her and me to have some honest-to-God primitive American in us!... Mr. and Mrs. Neil Injunblood announce the engagement of their daughter, Elizabeth Running Mink, to John Pierpont Morgan Wargate, and damn lucky that little prig would be to get her!

He remembered a Christmas grocery calendar and the portrait of an Indian maid with whom, in boyhood, he had been in love: a slim maid complete with riband, beaded doeskin jacket, canoe, waterfall, pine forest, and moonlight, and she seemed not too feeble a symbol beside the fair but weak-minded Elaine simpering over the Camelot traffic.

At last he spoke, and briskly.

"Okay, Gramma, I'm a Chippewa. Do Chippewas get a drink?"

Grampa Edgar cackled, "They do not. They ain't safe, after firewater, and they get nothing but fried beaver-tails. But any grandson of Ed Saxinar gets a drink—gets two drinks!"

12

He said nothing about Chippewas when he returned to Grand Republic. What had seemed a cheery topic with Gramma Julie did not go well with Vestal's Junior League airiness. He tried to pump his parents, and he guessed that neither of them knew anything about his mother's ancestry. If Faith had ever known, in her gentle estrangement from Gramma Julie she had conveniently forgotten.

And Julie had given no proof that either Xavier Pic or his wife was Indian, Neil insisted. He insisted a little too often and too strongly.

He kept wondering about the sacred Biddy as a vessel for Indian blood. He had a new, anxious way of watching that Saxon child, and comparing her with her playmates. He decided that Biddy was rougher and more practical than the other children, and in a sidelight, at dusk, he imagined a copper shade on her camellia cheeks.

Biddy, he noted, was abnormally good at playing that the living-room couch was a canoe and paddling it with a tennis racket—with no especial advantage to the racket; she was masterful at walking stealthily, at breaking out in ungodly whoops; and when she and he built a bonfire to celebrate the thaw at the end of April, he noted that both of them were competent with hatchet and bark kindling.

——Maybe this isn't just a game. I really do see Indian traits in both of us.

Then, as he watched Vestal sewing beads on a small pair of moccasins for Biddy, he absent-mindedly observed, "Only an Indian would think up patterns like that." He remembered then it was not the Beehousely Vestal who was to be studied and detected as an Indian, and he saw how sumptuously spurious all his discoveries had been. And he most illogically triumphed, proved that neither he nor Biddy really did have "Indian blood."

But even if they had—well, he now remembered hearing that the admirable Judge Cass Timberlane was part Sioux, and that it was something or other called the "genes" which carried racial appearances, not the blood.

Learnedly summing it all up, Neil decided that (1), he probably had no Indian blood or Indian genes or whatever it was and (2), it wouldn't matter if he had, but (3), he wouldn't mention it to Vestal and (4), recalling Gramma Julie's swarthy gracefulness, he was sure that Biddy and he were as Indian as Sitting Bull, and (5), he had now completely lost interest in the subject and (6), he was going to find out for certain, as soon as he could, whether he did have any Indian blood and/or genes.

———

His second business trip to Minneapolis was on Monday, May 7th, and on that day exploded the premature announcement, confirmed a day later, of peace with Germany. While the motor-horns and the flat-voiced church bells were strident in prairie villages along the railway, the car *Borup* was blazing with jubilation. Strangers shook hands and drank from pocket-flasks together and patted Mac the porter on the shoulder and, all standing, they sang "Auld Lang Syne."

Judd and Eliot and Rod Aldwick would be coming back now, Neil rejoiced. He would no longer be friendless and unadvised. It was only, he assured himself, because he had been lonely that he had "taken this Indian nonsense so seriously."

But Jamie Wargate would not be coming back. No one would find out where he lay in Germany, under an airplane engine, his fine hands a pulp that was one with the battered steel.

Neil's friend of the transport, Captain Ellerton, would not be coming back. He, least prim of all young men, was prim now under a prim cross in a graveyard like a suburban lawn.

———

His talks with the Minneapolis bankers and politicians done, Neil marched himself over to St. Paul, on Wednesday morning, to see Dr. Werweiss, official in the Minnesota Historical Society, whose building was beside the great bubble of the Capitol dome.

Dr. Werweiss was in his office, a friendly and learned-looking man, and Neil spoke to him casually, without quite knowing that he was planning to lie.

"I served as a captain in Italy, and one of my men has returned, wounded, and he's been begging me to ask somebody here about a pioneer ancestor of his—a trader named Xavier Pic, round 1830."

"I don't recall the name just now. Was it spelled P-E-A-K-E?"

"No, P-I-C, I believe. I suppose it could be a corruption of Pi-cardy?" Neil said hopefully.

"Ye-es, I suppose it could be."

"Well, this G.I., this soldier, would like to find out if there's any authoritative record of old Xavier in your documents. He was born about 1790, this fellow thinks, maybe born in France. I gather he'd especially like to know whether Xavier was pure French, or part Indian, also—that is, what race it would make this fellow himself."

"Did you feel that your soldier would be pleased if he proved to be part Indian, Mr. Kingsblood, or is he one of these simple-minded Croix de Feu racialists?"

"A——? Oh, yes, he—— What? Oh, I don't know. I don't believe I went into that with him—not thoroughly, I mean."

"If you'll wait a few moments, Mr. Kingsblood?"

Dr. Werweiss returned with an aged manuscript book. "I'm on Monsieur Pic's trail, I think."

"You are?" It was the second of waiting before the judge's sentence.

Dr. Werweiss was casual. "I've found him here in Taliaferro's diary. Yes. 'X. Pic.' May be the same one—helped arrest a bad Indian, it seems. But Major Taliaferro doesn't say whether Pic had any Indian blood himself or not. Of course, if he was born in France, he wouldn't have, unless his father had brought a squaw wife home from Canada, which did happen, but not frequently."

Neil was relieved, and ashamed of being relieved, and relieved again that Biddy and Biddy's father were uncorrupted Caucasians.

"But," Dr. Werweiss went on, "whether Pic had Indian blood or not, he did marry a Chippewa wife."

——Oh, blast it! I forgot all about great-great-great-grandmama, bless her tanned hide! Why didn't Xavier stay home in France or New Orleans or wherever he belonged, curse his itching feet! What did I ever do to him, a century and a quarter ago, to make him do this to me?

Then, all unconscious and benign, Dr. Werweiss let him have it:

"No, I think it's very doubtful that Xavier Pic was part Indian, because—now I don't know whether you'll consider it wise to tell your inquiring veteran or not; so many people do have vulgar superstitions about race; but the fact is that your friend's ancestor, Xavier, is mentioned by Major Taliaferro as being a full-blooded Negro."

Neil's face could not have changed, for Dr. Werweiss went on, quite cheerfully, "Of course you know that in most Southern states and a few Northern ones, a 'Negro' is defined, by statute, as a person having even 'one drop of Negro blood,' and according to that barbaric psychology, your soldier friend and any children he may have, no matter how white they look, are legally one-hundred-percent Negroes."

Neil was thinking less of himself than of his golden Biddy.

13

He found himself sitting at a lunch-counter, gravely staring at the wet slab of wood, the catsup bottle, the tricky nickel holder of paper napkins. He was vague, but he did remember that Dr. Werweiss was to make further search for him, that he was to return to the Society at two, and that he had not admitted anything.

He was in a still horror, beyond surprise now, like a man who has learned that last night, walking in his sleep, he murdered a man, that the police are looking for him.

He was apparently eating a sandwich. He regarded it with astonishment. How had he ever ordered a thing like that, dirty hunks of bread piled around flat-tasting ham? And the lunchroom was stinking, an offense against God and the sweet May afternoon.

——Why did I ever come in here? But I better try and like it. This is the kind of dump I'll get from now on. Or worse. Probably even this joint thinks it's too elegant to serve us niggers.

It was the first time that he had put what he was into a word, and he was too sick to soften it to "Negroes," and anyway, the word seemed so trivial beside the fact. He was protesting that he should be called a black man or a green man or any kind of a man except the plain human and multicolored kind of man that, as Neil Kingsblood, he always had been and always would be.

But *They* would say that he was a black man, a Negro.

To Neil, to be a Negro was to be a Belfreda Gray or a Borus Bugdoll; to be Mac the porter, obsequious to white pawnbrokers; to be a leering black stevedore on the docks at Naples, wearing an American uniform but not allowed to have a gun, allowed only to stagger and ache with shouldering enormous boxes; to be a field-hand under the Delta sun, under the torchlight in salvation orgies, an animal with none of the animal freedom from shame; to be an assassin on Beale Street or a clown dancing in a saloon for pennies and humiliation.

To be a Negro was to live in a decaying shanty or in a frame tenement like a foul egg-crate, and to wear either slapping old shoes or the shiny toothpicks of a procurer; to sleep on unchanged bedclothes that were like funguses, and to have for spiritual leader only a howling and lecherous swindler.

There were practically no other kinds of Negroes. Had he not heard so from his Georgia army doctor?

To be a Negro, once they found you out, no matter how pale you were, was to work in kitchens—always in other people's thankless kitchens—or in choking laundries or fever-hot foundries or at shoeshine stands where the disdainful white gentry thought about spitting down on you.

To be a Negro was to be unable—biologically, fundamentally, unchangeably unable—to grasp any science beyond addition and plain cooking and the driving of a car, any philosophy beyond comic dream-books. It was to be mysteriously unable ever to take a bath, so that you were more offensive than the animals who clean themselves.

It was to have such unpleasant manners, invariably, that you were never admitted to the dining-table of any decent house nor to the assemblies of most labor unions which, objectionable though they were to a conscientious banker like himself, still did have enough sense to see that all Negroes are scabs and spies and loafers.

It was to be an animal physically, It was to be an animal culturally, deaf to Beethoven and St. Augustine. It was to be an animal ethically, unable to keep from stealing and violence, from lying and treachery. It was literally and altogether to be an animal, somewhere between human beings and the ape.

It was to know that your children, no matter how much you loved them or strove for them, no matter if they were fair as Biddy, were doomed to be just as ugly and treacherous and brainless and bestial as yourself, and their children's children beyond them forever, under the curse of Ezekiel.

——But I'm not like that—Mum isn't—Biddy isn't—old Julie isn't. We're decent, regular people. So there's some mistake. We aren't Negroes, not one drop, and there were two Xavier Pics.

——You know that's phony, Kingsblood. Somehow, you know, way down, that he was your ancestor. Oh, damn him for being black! Poor sweet Biddy!

——All right. If Bid is a Negro, then everything I've ever heard about the Negroes—yes, and maybe everything I've heard about the Jews and the Japs and the Russians, about religion and politics—all of that may be a lie, too.

——If you *are* a Negro, you be one and fight as one. See if you can grow up, and then fight.

——But I've got to learn what a Negro is; I've got to learn, from the beginning, what I am!

Behind his struggle to think rationally there was a picture of the pert and candid face of Biddy—the little Duchess of Picardy, royal heir of Catherine of Aragon—and of her being unmasked by jeering neighbors as a Negro—a nigger, a zigaboo, a disgusting imitation of a real human child, flat-headed and obscenely capering, something to be driven around to the back door.

—She's not like that. We're not like that. Negroes are not like that. Are we?

———

Dr. Werweiss, he informed Neil, had found an original letter from Xavier Pic to General Henry Sibley, and he handed it over.

The paper had turned brown, but the ink was unfaded and the script delicate and precise, the writing of a literate man. Neil wondered if he was not the first, except for Dr. Werweiss and his assistant and General Sibley, who had touched this letter since Xavier had written it, by candlelight or northern sun, on a puncheon table or the side of a birch canoe, a hundred dead years ago:

"When you were here, honored General, and I had the priviledge to entertain you with a little fish and tea, more worthy fare being beyond my powers in the wilderness, I told you I am to all intent a full-blooded negro born in Martinique, though maybe I have a very little French and Portuguese and Spanish blood, too, not much.

"My wife was a good Ojibway woman and now my dear dauter Sidonie has married a Frenchman, Louis Payzold, and while I am proud of the negroes, they are such a brave passionat people, the Southern States have made a curse of life to the dark people and I do not want to have Sidonie or her children to be known as blacks and to suffer as my people do suffer there and planely told they are beasts. I ask for her little ones only a chance. So please always refer to me now as French.

"I am getting a little old for wilderness work and my purposes are almost done and do not want to think of my grandchildren under the lash, so please not say anything about my color and how black it is, honored General Sibley.

"Though Indian ladies seem to admire the color very much and all the warriors say I am first white man ever come to their country. Mes estimes les plus distinguées.

"X. Pic."

Dr. Werweiss spoke:

"He sounds like a grand old fellow—lot nobler than the Sieur de Saint Lusson or any of the other Parisian courtiers who showed up on the frontier. If your soldier friend has the guts to take it, and the imagination, he can be pretty proud of his ancestor.

"You know, it's true, what he says. Only red men and white men were recognized by the Indians on the Northern frontier, and so Negroes like Xavier and the Bongas were the first 'white men' to carry civilization—meaning the bottle, the bomb, and the Bible— to the poor heathen. They were like Perry opening up Japan, and if the results have been just as disastrous, that wasn't their fault.

"What a kingly set of names the whole bunch of them had: Sidonie marrying a Louis, and we found that their son, though we found nothing more about him, was royally named Alexandre!"

It was the chain as Gramma Julie had given it to him: Xavier, Sidonie, Louis Payzold, Alexandre, and, if he told the world of it, that chain bound him, bound Biddy.

If he told.

———

——And I was so certain (he thought on the interurban car back to Minneapolis) that Xavier had a short, golden beard!

——Me, with my red hair, even a drop of blackness? Or Biddy? Still, Gramma Julie is dark enough. O God, even to have to think about it!

——What's this about colored people "passing," if they're light enough? I certainly shall. Why should I be so conceited as to imagine that God has specially called me to be a martyr? And pretty vicious kind of a martyr, that would sacrifice his mother and his daughter to his holy vanity! Everything can be just as it was. It *has* to be, for Biddy's sake. You wouldn't deliberately turn your own mother into an outcast, would you?

——A man couldn't do that!

——But what if a lot of people know it already? Or can detect the Negro in me? I hear lots of Southerners claim they can do that. That man goggling at me down the car—can he see I'm part Negro? Has everybody always guessed it?

14

He crossed the lobby of his hotel in Minneapolis with his eyes rigidly held on the black-and-white marble of the floor, irritably noting that it *was* black and white, careful as a drunk who betrays himself by being too careful in his gait. He was wondering who might be staring at him, suspecting the Negro in him. Wilbur Feathering, who was a food-dealer in Grand Republic but who had been born in Mississippi, frequently asserted that he could catch any "Nigra" who passed for white, even if he was but a sixty-fourth black. If Wilbur did detect it, he would be nasty about it.

Right in the center of the lobby he wanted to stop and look at his hands. He remembered hearing that a Negro of any degree, though pale of face as Narcissus, is betrayed by the blue halfmoons of his fingernails. He wildly wanted to examine them. But he kept his arms rigidly down beside him (so that people did wonder at his angry stiffness and did stare at him) and marched into the elevator. He managed, with what he felt to be the most ingenious casualness, to prop himself with his hand against the side of the cage, and so to look at his nails.

No! The halfmoons were as clear as Biddy's.

——But I know now how a Negro who has just passed must feel all the time, when he's staying at a hotel like this: hoping that none of these high-and-mighty traveling men will notice him and ask the manager to throw him out. Does it keep up? All the time?

———

In the vast hidden lore of Being a Negro which he was to con, Neil was to learn that in many Northern states, including his own, there is a "civil rights law" which forbids the exclusion of Negroes and members of the other non-country-club races from hotels, restaurants, theaters, and that this law worked fully as well as had national prohibition.

White hotel guests snorted, "Why can't these niggers stay where they're wanted, among their own people, and not come horning in where they don't belong?" These monitors did not explain how a Negro, arriving in a strange city at midnight, was to find out precisely where he was wanted. Whenever they had been contaminated and almost destroyed by the presence of a Negro sleeping two hundred feet away, they threatened the hotel manager, who assumed that he had to earn a living and therefore devised a technique of treating the Negroes with nerve-freezing civility and with evasiveness about "accommodations."

Even on this, his first night of being a Negro, Neil knew that the night assistant-manager of the hotel might telephone up, "I'm terribly sorry, sir, but we find that the room we gave you is reserved."

He knew it already. He knew it more sensitively and acutely than he had ever known any of the complex etiquette of being an officer-and-gentleman.

He looked bulky enough and straight-shouldered enough in the refuge of his hotel room, but he felt bent and cowering as he listened for the telephone. He did not hear it, yet he heard it a hundred times.

And if he did not belong in this hotel, he thought, he would be no more welcome on the Pullman *Borup*. They could not arrest him for taking it, but he would not again be able to patronize genially the black Mac, who was now his uncle and his superior. In his hazardous future, it might be he who would hope for a condescending dollar from Mac.

He belonged with the other lepers in a day-coach—in a Southern jimcrow day-coach, foul and broken, so that his simian odor might not offend the delicate white nostrils of Curtiss Havock.

All this he thought, but he did not dare think of going back to Vestal and telling her that he had given her a Negro daughter.

He had planned to get his hair cut at the Swanson-Grand barbershop, this late afternoon.

He sat at the small desk in his room, tapping his teeth with his fingernail, occasionally looking suddenly at that nail again, a study in brooding. Whether or not he needed a haircut to the point of social peril, he had to go down to the shop, as a matter of manliness. He wasn't going to let any barber jimcrow *him*! He was a citizen and a guest; he paid his taxes and his hotel bills; he had as much right to be served in a barbershop as any white man——

He stood up wrathfully, but the wrath was against himself.

——Now for God's sake, Kingsblood, haven't you got enough real trouble in being a Negro, and having to tell Vestal, without making up imaginary troubles? That Svenska barber is no more likely to treat you as colored than anybody else ever has, these thirty-one years! Quit acting like a white boy trying to pretend to be a Negro. You *are* Negro, all right, *and* Chippewa, *and* West Indian spig, and you don't have to pretend. Funny, though, if I'm being too imaginative. Always thought I was too matter-of-fact. Everybody thought so.

——It couldn't be, could it, that what I needed, what Grand Republic needs, is a good dash of sun-warmed black blood?

He found a streak of humor in the astonishing collapse of everything that had been Neil Kingsblood; in noting that a black boy like himself could never conceivably be a banker, a golf-club member, an army captain, husband of the secure and placid Vestal, son of a Scotch-porridge dentist, intimate of the arrogant Major Rodney Aldwick. Suddenly he was nothing that he was, only he still was, and what he was, he did not know.

That the #3 barber in the Swanson-Grand Salon de Coiffeur would actually treat Mr. Kingsblood just as he always *had* treated Mr. Kingsblood was so obvious that Neil scarcely noticed that while he was still wondering whether #3 would refuse to cut his hair, #3 was already contentedly cutting it. But even in the soporific routine of the barber's shears and cool, damp hands, Neil could not ease his disquiet.

The head-barber, the girl cashier, the Negro bootblack, his #3 barber—had they guessed that he was a Negro, had they known it for years? Were they waiting for the proper time to threaten him, to blackmail him—waiting, lurking, laughing at him?

"Mighty hard to cut that curly hair of yours smooth, Captain," said the barber.

Now what was he referring to? Curly hair. Kinky hair. Negro wool.

Was his barber, standing back of him, winking at the barber at the next chair? Why had he yanked a lock of hair that way? Was the inconceivable social night already drawing in, and the black winter of blackness?

With the most itching carefulness, Neil crept one hand out from under the drab sheet covering him, scratched his nose, let the hand drop into his lap, and so was able to study his nails again. Was it this mercury vapor light, or was there really a blue tinge in the half-moons?

He wanted to jump from the chair, flee to his safe room—no, flee to yet-unknown Negro friends who would sympathize with him, hide him, protect him.

It was no elegant green-and-ivory barber chair but the electric chair from which he was finally released. In his room, he quivered:

——Vestal's always loved to run her fingers through my hair. Will she, if she finds out what kind of hair it is? Same color as my dad's used to be, but his isn't curly. What would Vestal think? She mustn't find out, ever.

He thought constantly of new things, pleasant and customary, from which his status as Negro might bar him: Biddy's adoration. The lordly Federal Club. Dances and stag-drinking at the Heather Country Club, where once he had been chairman of the Bengali pool tournament. His college fraternity. His career in the bank. His friendship with Major Rodney Aldwick.

He repeated a slice of English doggerel that Rod Aldwick used to quote with unction:

> All the white man's memories:
> Hearths at eventide,
> The twinkling lights of Christmas nights
> And our high Imperial pride.

What had been his own picture, his own observations, of the Negroes?

——Come on, you high Imperial white man, what are we? Let's have it, Mister!

——Well, the Negroes are all sullen and treacherous, like Belfreda.

——Nonsense! Mac the porter isn't and I'm not and I'm no longer so sure about Belfreda.

——They're all black, flat-nosed, puff-lipped.

He went to the mirror, and laughed.

——What a lot I used to know that I didn't know! What a clack-mouthed parrot I was! Quoting that fool of a Georgia doctor. Negroes not quite human, eh? Kingsblood, Congoblood, you deserve anything you get—if it's bad enough. I think God turned me black to save my soul, if I have any beyond ledgers and college yells. I've got to say, "You're as blind and mean and ignorant as a white man," and that's a tough thing to take, even from myself.

——Oh, don't be so prejudiced against the white people. No doubt there's a lot of them who would be just as good as anybody else, if they had my chance of redemption.

——Captain, aren't you kind of overdoing your glee in becoming a colored boy?

——Okay. I am.

———

Under a decayed newspaper in the desk he found one sheet of Swanson-Grand letter-paper, with a half-tone of the hotel and the name of the proprietor in flourishing 1890 type, but with practically no space for writing, an accomplishment apparently not expected of the guests. He turned it over, took out his bankerish gold-mounted fountain pen, and drew up an altogether bankerish table of one branch of his ancestors:

Xavier Pic, possible French and Spanish elements but counts as 100% Negro

Sidonie, his daughter, who married Louis Payzold, was ½ Chippewa and ½ Negro

Alexandre Payzold, their son, Gramma Julie's father, ¼ Negro

My grandmother, Julie Saxinar, an octoroon, ⅛ Negro

Her daughter, my mother, ¹⁄₁₆ Negro

Myself, ¹⁄₃₂ Negro

Biddy, ¹⁄₆₄ Negro

——Well, I finally do have something interesting about our royal royal ancestry to report to Dad!

15

It was late, but he did not go down to dinner at the Swanson-Grand Coffee Shop. He could not endure sitting there and wondering whether he was being stared at. He had already discovered that the Negroes do not stay by themselves so much because they love the other Negroes as because they cannot stand the sheep-faced whites and their sheep-like gawking.

In a stilled panic he rode out to Excelsior and to the decent bungalow of Grampa Edgar Saxinar. As he came in, the old gentleman, in a voice like the squeak of his patent rocker, greeted him, "Welcome, young man! 'Tain't often we get a chance to see your cheerful face twice in one season!"

It was Gramma Julie who demanded, "What's matter, boy?"

Standing rigid and large in the center of the room, which smelled of pine-needle cushions, Neil said earnestly, "Gramma, are you sure that your forbears, going back to Pic, were just French and Chippewa?"

"I told you not to talk about Pic!" Grampa Edgar wailed.

She looked drawn into herself. She knew!

Neil pressed it, "Are you sure we haven't a little Negro blood, too?"

She screamed, "What do you mean, you young scamp? I never heard such a thing in my life!" But her wrath was too facile, and too facile was Grampa Edgar's fury. He was no longer a comic old griper sitting by the fire. His face was terrible, the unsparing and murderous face of a lyncher. Neil had once seen a German captive look like that, and once, a drunken American military policeman. Edgar raged, "Just exactly what do you think you're hinting at, heh? Mean to say you've got some crazy idea your gramma's folks had nigger blood? Or are you stinking drunk? Are you trying to make me out the father of part-nigger kids—make your Uncle Emery and your own mother into niggers?"

Neil had always been chatty and tender with his grandfather, as he was with all pleasant old people, but there was no chat nor tenderness in him now. "I hope not, but I'd like a little truth, for once. What is the truth?"

Grampa Edgar looked pitifully old, and his passion drained out in futility. "Don't you ever pay the least bit of attention to stories and dirty lies like that, Neil. It ain't true, not a word of it, but even if it was, there'd be no need for anybody but us to know it. For God's sake, boy, let's never mention it again."

Gramma Julie was very shrill. "Absolute lie, Neilly. Some folks in Hiawatha got it up because they was jealous of how well Ed and I done."

It was intolerable to watch the two ancient and withered householders strip themselves naked, and Neil retreated, but with a brusqueness he could not avoid. "All right, all right, forget it. Well, got to be getting back. Night."

On the train into Minneapolis he was irritable.

——I'm sick of all this *Gone With the Wind* and Thomas Nelson Page stuff! massa on de ole plantation—massa in de cold, cold counting-house—swords and roses, and lick the damn nigger. If I'm a Negro—all right, I'll be one.

——I never needed a drink as bad as I do now.

But in the bar at the Hotel Swanson-Grand, he had orangeade, and dared not take so much as one highball. He wondered if he would ever drink another one, though highballs and he had been good friends. He looked at his manly fellow-drinkers and thought of how they would turn into wolves and foxes and hyenas if his tongue were oiled enough to say what he could say.

———

All the way home, on the *Borup,* he resented the attentions of Mac. He wanted to growl, "Oh, chuck it. I belong with you." He was exasperated by Mac's obsequious laughter at the not-very-good jokes of Orlo Vay of Grand Republic, who was a lovely man when he stuck to fitting eye-glasses, but only then.

Neil wanted to demand of Mac, "How can you stand listening to that white flannel-mouth? Our people must have dignity."

Not till he had almost reached home did it occur to him that his twenty-eight hours as a Negro was possibly too brief a training for him to take over all of his people's manners.

———

Vestal usually saw through his blundering efforts to look cheerful when things had gone wrong, but when he came booming into the house with "Your husband has just bought all the banks in the Twin Cities!" when he kissed her and tousled Biddy's hair in the best manner of the hearty young husband, she was not suspicious, and she said only, "Glad you had a nice trip. Isn't it glorious about the end of the war! Can you stand a giddy round of bridge at Curtiss Havock's tonight?"

"Yes, sure."

Curtiss, son of Boone, would be the first to yelp at him.

———

He could decide nothing at all, since he could not decide the one dominant question: was he going to tell the world, would he even tell Vestal?

If he kept silence, it was likely that no one would know, aside from Gramma Julie and Edgar, who most vigorously would say nothing. Dr. Werweiss would have no reason to trace Pic and the Payzolds to the Kingsbloods.

He had no accuser except himself. But that lone accuser was so persistent that sometimes he fancied himself blurting, "Certainly I'm part Negro. Do you think I'm the kind of Judas who would deny the race of his mother?"

But whenever he had agreed to do something bold and immediate, a more cynical self always jeered:

——Listen to the brave captain! Going to be defiant, is he, the little man! Going to put yourself in the clutches of a bunch of Southern deputies, with their fishy eyes and their red fists, when you don't have to, when it wouldn't do any good, when nobody's asking you to? You armchair martyr!

———

It was this slice of hell that Neil was carrying in his pocket as he supervised the arrangement of the Veterans' Center booth at the bank. Mr. John William Prutt coughed his way up to him, having in tow Mrs. John William Prutt, who had an astringent face but what would have been a voluptuous bosom if it had not also been a thoroughly Christian bosom.

The lady gurgled, "It seems to me that Mr. Prutt and you are making a mistake in having this booth so severe in color. As you know, I never intrude on banking business—I know how many marriages have been ruined by the wife's doing that, even with the best intentions—but I do feel I have a real instinct for Decoration—I know how many women claim to have that, with their silly chatter about 'curtains picking up the mauve of the couch,' but I feel I really do have it—and after all, so many of the veterans will be coming in here with their sweethearts or brides or whatnot, and you can appeal to them by a deft dash of color—say, a lovely cushion of crocus-yellow on the bench—so spring-like and appealing. I think that might be very important, don't you—one of these things that's often neglected, but is really important!"

Then Mr. Prutt, in his more jovial mood, rich joviality with just a splash of vinegar: "Now Neil, you don't have to agree with my good lady, you know. Are you really sold on the idea that it's important?"

"I'm not sure that I know what is important, sir," said Neil.

——What would they say if I told them?

—

And "What would they say if I told them?" frightened him and depressed him and devilishly tempted him to speak up whenever he met Wilbur Feathering, that Southerner who was now reconciled to Northern cash-registers and who sang "Bringing in the Sheaves" to the tune of "Dixie." Or whenever, at the Sylvan Park Tennis Club, he listened to W. S. Vander, the lumberman, Cedric Staubermeyer, dealer in rugs and anti-Semitism, and Orlo Vay, the political optician, who agreed, between sets, that our American liberties, including the rights to chew tobacco and to charge customers whatever you damn well pleased, were threatened.

They were all good neighbors, ready to lend Neil the lawn-mower or a bottle of gin, all good customers at the bank, speaking well of his courtesy and steadiness, and they were all lynchers, of the Northern or inoperative variety, who had "built up good businesses by their own unaided industry and efforts, and didn't for one by God second intend to let any sentimental love for the lazy bums of workers stand in the way of their holding onto what they got."

With them, there was no question of what they would say if he told.

—

Vestal had gone up to bed. He was alone on the sun-porch, that bland May midnight, restless in his chintz-and-wicker armchair, trying to read an article on "The Use of Bills of Lading in International Credit under Temporary Post-War Financial Structures." It was very bright and well written, and it had a picture of the Paris Bourse for illustration, but he laid it down, he laid it down firmly, and heard the suburban quiet flow over him.

He looked about the airy room, at the ivy on the indoor trellis, the glass-and-nickel-cocktail shaker on the little green bar. He thought of Vestal's face serene on her pillow, and Biddy curled in a golden ball. Next month, Biddy would have her fifth birthday, and she wanted to know why she couldn't be of age to vote then. She stated that she wished to vote for her father for President, and she would not be put off by her mother's frivolous reason, "Oh, no, dear; your father is much too good-looking to be President."

All this simple happiness——

He would say something that would betray him; some Wilbur Feathering would pick it up; he would be disgraced, lose their modest security, this true home that was his love and Vestal's made visible. He pictured the ruthless second-hand-furniture dealers and grinning neighbors crowding in here to buy this furniture—cheap—while Vestal and Biddy stood weeping like a Mid-Victorian widow and orphan with shawl.

"No! I'll preserve our home with my life!"

——Sounds like old-fashioned melodrama. Well, I feel like melodrama!

It came to him, slyly, shockingly, that he could best preserve that home by his death. From the cold tombs he could say nothing that would give him away. As a Sylvan Park business man would, he carried large life insurance. There must be some way of committing suicide so that it would not be found out—something about a car running off an embankment and burning?

That day in the bank had been hard and fussy with Pruttery and he was tired in a way that he had not known he could be, drained-out by the vision of what might happen to him. If he could quietly pass out, secure Biddy's future——

Then he laughed.

——I seem to be learning a lot of new possibilities. I despised the rich investors who jumped out of windows during the last depression—poor white leeches who couldn't take it unless they had two chauffeurs to bleed. We Negroes don't do that.

He laughed again, not affectedly, not for any audience, not even for his own audience.

——

Randy Spruce, Executive Secretary of the Grand Republic Chamber of Commerce, was a chum of Wilbur Feathering who, though born in Stote, Mississippi, on a red clay hill, was now a citizen of Minnesota and a patron of skiing, a sport which he gave the impression of having invented, though he did not actually practise it. Mr. Feathering was founder and president of "The Hot on the Spot Home Food Supply Company—hot meals in your own dinette—

everything from a sandwich to a banquich—linen & silver if desired—run, rite, or fone."

That was Wilbur Feathering. The meals were not bad, the profits were enormous, and he was popular throughout Grand Republic except among people who did not like race-hatred or noises of the mouth.

He had been useful in giving ideas to the Chamber of Commerce, and Randy Spruce often said, "I often say a man in my position as a professional booster of all forward-looking enterprises and the American Way of Life has ideas as his chief stock in trade. I make a practice of not merely reading the magazines and listening to all the round-tables on the radio, but I am not above taking suggestions from the humblest—as I often say, like a Polack or a union member."

Randy was glad to have from one of the Featherings of Stote the Real Lowdown on the Negro Problem.

The benefit of this Lowdown was felt second-hand by Neil, when Randy and he served on a committee of nine to arrange a citywide welcome to the returning veterans.

Randy was fretting, "Of course there's quite a few nigger G.I.'s, and we got fix it so they don't horn in on the parade of our white heroes."

"Couldn't the black veterans be heroes, too?" suggested Dr. Norman Kamber.

"Hell, no!" Randy explained. "As I often say, all the nigger troops were insubordinate and afraid of cold steel. The high command just handed out a few decorations to 'em to keep 'em from mutiny, so we wouldn't have to shoot the whole bunch. A colonel told me that. But Wilbur Feathering has a fine suggestion. We'll cook up a separate homecoming for the zigaboos, on Mayo Street; parade and fireworks and banners and some portion of a horse like Congressman Oberg to make an oration. We'll tell 'em that we didn't want to have 'em get lost in the white shuffle, so we're honoring 'em special. Those niggers are so dumb they'll believe it."

"Are all Negroes dumb?" Neil wanted to know.

"All of 'em!"

"What about the ones that are just part Negro?"

"My boy, as I often say, if a man has one drop of nigger blood, he's a phony. Uncreative, that's the idee. You don't think a circus dog is intelligent because his owner has trained him to ride a bicycle and act drunk like a scholar, do you? That's why no nigger can hold down a responsible position. Doc, you can call me a liar if you can show me one nigger that could be a United States Senator."

"Hiram Revels or B. K. Bruce," said Dr. Kamber.

"Who? What makes you think those niggers could be Senators?"

"They were!"

"Oh, I get you. Wasn't that in Reconstruction days? Feathering explains that. It was because those niggers were just out of slavery, where they'd been trained in industry and obedience. But since then, with all this loose freedom, the colored folks have simply gone to hell in a hack intellectually, to say nothing of their immorality, and today there isn't one of them that's fit to hold down any appointment higher than cityhall janitor."

Neil was brooding:

——What's the use? I shall never tell anybody. That's settled!

It was as simple as that.

16

June the twelfth was all brightness and lilacs and new leaves, as was required, for June the twelfth was Biddy's fifth birthday. It was fit for the birthday of a little white lady, with white blossoms, white dresses, and all the white children in the block admiring her and the new roller skates and the toy theater, gold and white.

Neil came home early. The half-dozen girls and the four screaming but attentive young gentlemen of Biddy's age were playing hide-and-seek in the back yard, around the cement fish-pond and Biddy's playhouse, of white clapboards thick-covered with vines. All the children, especially Peggy Havock, were fond of Neil, and they danced about him affectionately, crying, "Oh, Mister Capten Kingsblood—oh Mister Capten Kingsblood!"

Vestal came out of the house, tall and benign as an angel, in a long sage-green dress, gold-girdled, and she bore the maple layer-cake of the day, on which, in white on yellow icing, was handsomely engrossed, "Our Biddy—5." The six pink candles (one to grow on) were steady in the calm, happy summer afternoon.

To receive the cake, the histrionic Biddy popped into her playhouse and came out wearing her gilt Christmas crown. But if she insisted on being a queen, she was a popular constitutional monarch, and she cut and distributed the slices of cake with royal justice. Neil watched her, and remembered that not for many days had he thought of the Blood Royal. She had it, clearly, but was it from the old lecher, Henry VIII, or from Xavier Pic, regent of the wilderness?

Biddy romped up to him, her eyes diamonds for happiness. She reached up to hug his waist. "Daddy, I never did have such a lovely birthday, not in all my life. Am I always going to have lovely birthdays like this?"

He kissed her roughly.

Prince, erstwhile "Nigger," who all along had assumed that this was his birthday party and that it was his social duty to welcome his little friends by yelping at them and pushing them over, came hysterically bounding up, licking Biddy's face, knocking off her crown and laughing at her, and Biddy forgot her royal dignity in a shrill, "Now you bad ole dog, you stop it and be good now or I'll rule you right out of my cas-tel, you bad ole dog you, *Nigger!*"

Neil was irritated.

———

To Neil, at his desk in the bank, came Dr. Ash Davis, and Dr. Davis was a Negro, his face the color of dry brown bright autumn leaves in the sun. Neil had heard that one of the dismaying exigencies of the war had been that the Wargate experimental laboratory had had to hire this colored fellow, Davis—oh, a good enough chemist, a Doctor of Science from the University of Chicago, but still and all, just a darky. That certainly showed, didn't it (agreed everybody at the Boosters Club luncheon), how hard-up we were for manpower. Though it was a question whether any conceivable contribution to the war effort could justify a precedent like that, of giving a white man's job to a tough dinge. God knows what it might lead to!

Oh, yes, Neil had heard of Ash Davis.

For the first time in his life he really looked at a "colored man." He had never looked at Belfreda, at the Emerson Woolcape who had been in his class all through school, at Mac, at the Negro soldiers; he had not looked at them but only been impatiently aware of them, as though in Arabia he were searching for a road-sign in English or French or some human language, and found nothing but an absurd sign in Arabic. Certainly he had never looked at the Negro callers who had arranged with him for bank loans. They had been merely dark hands holding papers, dark voices that were over-ingratiating.

He looked now at Ash Davis, but he did not see a "Negro," a "colored man." He saw a curiously charming man of the world who seemed also to be a scholar. He was pricked by the familiar feeling, "Where have I known him before?" He realized that here, plus an extra tan, was Captain Tony Ellerton of the army transport, his one completely ungrudging friend.

Dr. Davis was a man of forty, slim, compact, very easy, not tall, wearing a small black mustache without foppishness. His eyes were steady. He was dressed like any other well-to-do professional man, but he wore his gray lounge-suit with a vaguely European air. Had Neil been Sherlock Holmes, he might have detected in Dr. Davis's accent an Ohio boyhood, three years in England and France and Russia, friendships with tennis-partners and piano-teachers and laboratory-mates. But he knew only that Dr. Davis spoke clearly and pleasantly, rather like Rodney Aldwick, but more accurately.

He was, in fact, deciding, "This Davis is a bright-looking fellow. I didn't know there were any Negroes like him. Well, how could I? I've never even had the chance to see them."

(As a matter of fact, a few months before, Neil had sat opposite Dr. Ash Davis in a bus, had heard him talking to a large Negro with a clerical collar, and had never looked at either of them.)

Dr. Davis had, he said, come to beg.

With the war over, hundreds of Negroes would be dismissed from local factories, and the leaders of the Negro community were working with the Urban League in trying to persuade local business firms to give them jobs. Could the Second National hire one or two? He could produce a number of colored business-school graduates who in wartime had been clerks, bookkeepers. How about it?

"How do you happen to come to me?" fretted Neil. "I'd like to do anything I can, but I'm only an assistant cashier."

Ash Davis had a smile that invited companionship. "Dr. Norman Kamber, who is a good friend of my race, told me you were one banker who could be quite human. I'm afraid that doesn't sound too complimentary!"

"For Doc Kamber it does. Well, I'll see what can be done. I really will!"

He tried to think of something that would hold Dr. Davis in talk. He acutely needed someone who understood this Thing that he had become. And the thoughts that had been growing pallidly in the darkness of brooding became fresh and strong in the clear light of Ash Davis's presence. He reflected, "This seems to be a very agreeable fellow and he has to beg white men for a chance for his people. It makes me mad that he should have to be almost obsequious to a louse of a bank clerk like me. He's a lot smarter than I am. Well, Kingsblood, there is a chance for you, if you can recognize your superiors."

He made talk, so far as he could, about jobs for Negroes, but he shyly did not know whether to say "Negro" or "colored people" or neither. Dr. Davis eased away and, for the second time in his life (the first was Borus Bugdoll), in this hand-mauling land, Neil was shaking hands with a Negro.

He seemed to suffer no injuries from it.

———

He put it cunningly to John William Prutt that, as they had several prosperous Negro depositors, and some day they might have more, perhaps they ought to hire one or two Negro clerks. Prutt looked at him pityingly.

"My boy, I'm pleased that you take a liberal attitude toward the Negro. I long for the day when they'll get a decent education and be able to take their stand right alongside white laborers—in their own Southland. But they don't belong up here, and the kindest thing to do is to let 'em starve till it penetrates their thick heads that they ought to hustle back South.... Besides, our customers would kick like hell!"

———

On his way home, he stopped for a cocktail with his father. That gentle fusser fussed gently, "Got any furtherer on our royal path, Neilly?"

"I think maybe I have, Dad."

———

He thought of Dr. Ash Davis by contrast that evening, for it was Rod Aldwick's great homecoming party—staged by Rod himself, since no one else could stage it so well.

Major Rodney Aldwick of the Tank Corps, in private life lawyer and investor, graduate of Princeton and of Harvard Law, trained in National Guard maneuvers, tanned and tall and lean, with cropped Prussian hair, was a soldier, a gentleman adventurer, a hawk, a handsaw, a hero. To Neil, five years his junior, Rod in high school days had always been *the* hero. Rod could do his algebra, correct his tango step, show him where the best pickerel camped in Dead Squaw Lake, coach him in hockey, reinforce him in wars with gangs of Poles and Italians, comfort him when Ellen Havock turned him down, lend him fifty cents, and explain the mysteries of taxes and the Trinity and why decent men like their fathers never voted the Democratic ticket. Not that Rod did do any of these heroic things for Neil, who had gone through boyhood pretty steadily on his own feet, but Neil had felt fervently that he would do them if he were asked.

In his Eastern college days, as Neil learned from afar, Rod had been equally deft at debating and at polo, and while he sozzled with the rowdies he picked up in New York bars and took the oath of the Brother in Blood in pretzels and in salt, he seduced none but girls of families above or below the blackmail line, and said with the humorous clarity typical of him even in youth, "When I get ready to run for the Senate, there won't be any little bastards on the platform."

Rod lived not in the sweet neighborliness of Sylvan Park but next door to Dr. Roy Drover, in the grandeur of Ottawa Heights. He was now on terminal leave from the Army, a figure of romantic war, given to specially tailored battle-jackets. For his own welcome, the wide oaken floors of his large house had been waxed, his collection of crystal vases and bowls, new-washed and glittering, had been filled with daffodils, and behind a Chinese screen, liberated from the unlawful hands of German looters, a four-piece orchestra played Delius and Copland. It was the first warm summer evening in that Northern land, and the men were out in white-flannel dinner jackets (and damn cold they were, too) and the flower of local womanhood were in white net with Mexican shawls.

Rod moved like a Candidate from admiring knot to knot, and to Neil and Vestal he said simply, "You two—now I *know* I'm home! Neilly, I've heard how gallantly you took your wound, and I heard it from some pretty high-ranking brass on the Other Side. I said to them, 'He's about my oldest friend, that boy, and am I proud of him!'"

Neil's stomach burned with pride, and he was annoyed later to hear Dr. Drover speculate, "Looks to me like Rod is going in for popularity and politics when he gets out of the Army."

Rod's wife, Janet was just a little taller than Vestal and a little better made-up and a little chattier about horse-shows, and Rod's son and daughter were as cool and decorative as the wide house, and Neil felt that he was where he ought to be. When Rod could detach himself from circulating like a first secretary of embassy and exchange with Neil precious recollections of juvenile basketball and of beer in the high-school locker room, Neil decided that they were two gentlemen and officers and responsible men of affairs, standing together, shoulder to shoulder, for the higher ideals and enterprise of America.

The thought of Xavier Pic was but a ghost haunting a ghost, and Ash Davis was a fellow who worked in a laboratory.

—

Captain Kingsblood asked in a high manner of Major Aldwick, "Did you see any colored troops in action? Didn't happen to, myself."

"I certainly did! A black tank outfit brigaded with mine, and they were terrible: sullen and undisciplined and we had to keep pushing 'em ahead of us into combat. There was a colored sergeant in that outfit that was an absolute Bolshevik. Instead of going through proper channels, he was always sneaking complaints to the general commanding, through crooked orderlies—endangering our whole morale with a lot of bellyaching about the Negroes being segregated in transportation and Red Cross supplies. If our staff could have managed it, there was one dusky gentleman that would never have come home to his hot mama in the sweet land of liberty!"

Suddenly, to Neil, it wasn't so; the black soldiers had not been like that; and as to the rebellious sergeant whom Rod had sportingly wanted to murder— "It could be me!" thought Neil.

He was most civil to Rod at parting.

17

If he could not believe that many of his own race were as Rod Aldwick had found them, he had to see something of what they actually were. Where could he look at a gathering of them? In a movie theater? In a church?

There must be a Negro church in Grand Republic, now that it had a couple of thousand black inhabitants; there must be Negroes who went to church, wouldn't you think? (His mother did!)

When he was having his shoes shined in the basement washroom of the Hotel Pineland, he looked down more gently than had been his custom at old Wash, the shine-boy, whose name was not Wash, but George Gray, and who was not a boy but a man aged and tiny and infinitely patient. He was the one Negro whom Randy Spruce most favored, as "knowing his place and taking his cap off to us white gents." He was also the grandfather of Belfreda Gray.

There was something shameful in Wash, bent and spiderlike and more gray than black. He peered up at Neil and out of his ancient dusty memories he picked an unclean one about Belfreda, and he sniggered tinily, "Well, Cap'n, suh, you suttinly done right when you kicked Belfreda's tail outa yo' house. She's a little slut. I can't do nothin' with huh." He giggled. "She sleeps with every no-count niggah in town. Can't do nothin' with these biggity young No'th'n niggahs, no suh!"

Neil said genially, as the young prince, "Oh, Belfreda wasn't so bad. She's just young. Uh, Wash—uh—where is there a colored church in this town?"

Wash turned rigid. He looked up painfully, his filmy eyes were grim and discerning, and most of his "cullud" stage dialect dropped as he demanded, "What you want to know for?"

"I'd like to attend one."

"We don't like white folks coming to laugh at us—not when we're praying."

"Honestly, Wash, I had no idea of laughing."

"What else man like you want to come for?"

"I just felt I ought to understand your part of town better."

"We don't like gang of people slumming."

"I'd be alone, and perfectly reverent, I hope."

Neil was not conscious of how humble he had become to this venerable elder of his race. Wash said grudgingly, "Well, Mister, they's fo' or five, but you might try the Ebenezer Baptist— Reverend Brewster's church—in the Five Points, Mayo Street and Omaha Avenue. I go there. We think Reverend Brewster is real smart."

Neil knew vaguely that the Darktown of Grand Republic was called the "Five Points," and had Mayo Street as its principal thoroughfare. His bank held mortagages there, and he had driven through it, but eyelessly. Of "Reverend Brewster" he had never heard, and with a white man's matey joviality, as Wash returned to shining his shoes, Neil crowed, "Isn't Brewster kind of a Yankee name, for a colored preacher?"

"He is a Yankee."

"Oh!"

"He's what they call a Doctor of Philosophy."

Neil could not but chuckle at this darky malapropism. "You mean Doctor of Divinity."

Something of Wash's professional Dixie dialect crept back

into his humble speech as he insisted, "No, *suh*! He got one these Doctor Philosophy degrees from this Columbia University, in Harlem."

"And *Doctor* Davis. Has everybody on Mayo Street got a college degree?"

"No, suh, there's a few of us come along too early."

The white man in Captain Kingsblood wondered, "Is this old devil kidding me?"

———

He had lied to Vestal.

On that June Sunday morning he had told her that he was going to lunch with a Veterans' Association in the South End. He recalled the fictions he had produced at the State Historical Society, and reflected that he was becoming only too good a liar.

He went by bus to the Five Points, and walked westward on Mayo Street. It was like any other lower-middle-class shopping center, in its flabby look, its tawdry wooden store buildings plastered with home-painted signs. In the block between Denver Avenue and Omaha, there were two drugstores not so unlike the domestic treasure-houses of Sylvan Park in their displays of water-bottles, prayer-books, aspirin, douches, and piles of *Sunday Frontier-Banner*. The Co-op Food Store, the Old English Grocery, the Electric Shop, with "reconditioned radios" in the show-window, all reminded him of that Anglo-Saxon city, Grand Republic, and so did the Lustgarten Meat Market, which was in an old residence with a new shop-front carelessly slapped on the ground floor and family washing still flourishing above. Yet this familiar huddle became strange to Neil as he realized that he did not see one white face on the crowded sidewalk.

In front of shuttered doors, over each of which was the sign "Beds 75¢," were groups of burly Negro workers staring at him as though he was the intruder that he was, and most of them were talking in dialect from the Deep South so thick that he could not understand them. He saw a young blade in a zoot-suit: yellow sports jacket, flaring lavender trousers, toothpick-toed shoes, and a broad black hat edged with white. He saw a couple rolling up the middle of the street, arms entwined, singing, and, as advertised, he saw one "colored mammy," fat ebon face grinning under a red and yellow bandanna.

And when he looked down a side street he saw that behind neat stucco cottages, with tidy small lawns, there was such a diminutive jungle slum as he had not known could exist in the enlightened Northern States: shacks one behind another, three deep, in the center of the block, tilted doghouses such as no truly enterprising dog would have endured, each with a couple of inches of stove pipe for chimney. The whole ground between the shacks was a maggot-heap of dogs, chickens, and bare brown babies.

That frightened him. "How would I like turning black, and having to bring Vestal and Biddy down here?"

And he was more certain that he could never become "colored" when he passed the Beale Street Bar-B-Q and saw the dark cloud of Negroes looking hatefully through the steamy window at the slumming white man; when he came to the Jumpin' Jive night club which, he thought, belonged to Belfreda's friend, the sardonic Borus Bugdoll, who had made light of the Kingsbloods in their own kitchen. It had been a store; the show-window was now filled with a gilded plaster seashell decked with silver pine-cones and poison-green ribbons, framing the blown-up photograph of an almost naked black dancing-girl.

The street was more alien to Neil than Italy in wartime, and it seemed to him that every dusky face, every rickety wall, hated him and would always hate him, and he might as well go home.

But all of this had taken only five minutes of slow walking, and in the sixth minute the sorcery was lifted and he was among people who, though their faces were more beloved of the sun, were like any other group of middle-class church-going Americans.

They were Dr. Brewster's congregation, enjoying their weekly gossip before the church bell should summon them in: placid and well-shaven men, wearing the kind of Sunday clothes that people do wear on Sunday; Mothers in Zion, nervously thin or comfortably buxom, talking about their sons in the service; supernaturally Sunday-neatened small boys restless in tight shoes and little girls flaunting Sunday splendor; elders with a long good life recorded in their etched faces; voluble babies who had not yet heard that they were Negroes and who assumed that they were babies.

The voices of that half of them who were Northern-born sounded like the voices of any other Minnesotans; and while they looked at Neil with a slight doubtfulness, they did not make him feel like an intruder as had the derisive loafers at the Bar-B-Q.

The Ebenezer Baptist Church was a small tidy oblong of brick, with an absurd dwarf steeple. The clear glass windows, rather narrow, with wooden frames rising to peaks that tried to suggest Gothic arches, had inserts of colored glass displaying Bible texts in script. With that, the Gothic revival ended.

The little bell quacked, and the amiable crowd bobbed slowly up the steps, shyly followed by Neil.

Inside, the church seemed to Neil less like a place of worship than a lodge room. It was lined with gray wallboard, neatly fastened with red-topped thumb-tacks, and neat and gray the straight lines of pews. Texts, gold-embossed on black placards, were on the walls, with a portrait of a black St. Augustine of Carthage. On a platform in front was a choir of nine girls in black gowns and mortar boards. Two of them were creamy white.

The surprise to Neil, himself a Baptist and brought up to denounce the heathen gauds of Rome, was that against a pathetic little reredos of wooden latticework stood a home-made altar with a lace-edged cloth on which was an imitation jeweled cross.

He had been standing as awkwardly as a new patient in a doctor's waiting-room. Would *They* resent him, ask him to get out? But the usher who tiptoed toward him, a man black-silk black, with a flat nose and heavy lips, smiled at him as though in the House of God they were friends. He was wearing a blue-gray herring-bone suit exactly like the newest pride of Neil's father. He touched Neil's arm politely, led him halfway down, gravely motioned, and Neil had another First in his career as a Negro. He sat down between two colored people and they seemed to him very much like people.

On his left was a small woman who ignored him, as her lips moved in rapid silent prayer; on the other side was a large man, black as a cellar, who was probably a carpenter or a painter and who bowed good-naturedly in answer to Neil's flustered nod.

He looked over the mimeographed church bulletin, and wondered about the title of the pastor's sermon: "Delivered from Corruption." Would it be something funny and inferior and Negroid, for all that doubtful pastoral Ph.D. degree, or would it be just another of the Baptist sermons that all these years (once a month or so) he had been chewing without tasting?

Then, through a narrow side door to the chancel, the Reverend Dr. Evan Brewster made entrance. For a moment he seemed to be showing off, as he halted to look over his flock, to stare doubtfully at Neil. But the theatricality, if it was such, lasted only a moment; then Dr. Brewster chatted with the choir, muttered something to an usher—Neil was afraid that it might be a scurrility about himself— and moved to the reading stand, a priest in his temple, confident and serene.

Evan Brewster was a large man, black as a japanned deed-box, with the shoulders of a roustabout and just the kinks of hair, the pushed-in nose, bulbous mouth, sloping forehead, thin legs that Neil had seen in every picture of a black dock-walloper, every primeval brute who regularly assaults fatherly white policemen. He was everything that would give a petal-pale white lady a shock, and if Neil was less delicate, still he was disapproving that this bruiser should mock the holy Baptist pulpit by wearing, over his rather shiny blue suit, the canonical primness of a Geneva gown.

Dr. Brewster was silent, looking at them, and Neil slowly permitted himself to see that never, in any human face, had he known such gentleness, such kindness, such honest and manly sweetness, such outpouring love for all living beings and all life. And when he spoke, his voice was that of any vigorous and scholarly man who had gone from a literate family to a shrewd university, the voice of a man who could also be intolerably eloquent.

"Friends—and especially the new friends whom we welcome here this morning—may we start with singing *How Firm a Foundation, Ye Saints of the Lord?* It is a *Battle Hymn of the Republic* for these days of battle."

Evan Brewster—and he really was a Ph.D. of Columbia—had also attended Harvard College and the Union Theological Seminary, where the students believe in a trinity of Father, Son and Sociology—the Father as a symbol, the Son as a poetic myth, and Sociology with a pink halo. But after that, Evan got religion and race.

He had been born in a Massachusetts village of elms and white steeples, his father a tailor with white patrons. He was something over forty now, with a quiet wife, a daughter named Thankful, and a son named Winthrop, who now in high school was showing talent for physics. When he had first come to Grand Republic, as a missionary to his people, his church had been a shanty in Swede Hollow. In his dozen years here he had seen the Negro island expand from three or four hundred to two thousand; had seen over-timid or over-bumptious dark immigrants from the Carolinas and Texas turn into citizens; seen the young people going to college, becoming army officers, writing for the *Defender*, the *Courier*, the *Spokesman*.

Swede Hollow became overcrowded with Finns and Poles and Scandinavians; rents were grossly raised (by favorite customers of the Second National Bank); and Dr. Brewster led his own flock and most of the other Negroes from Swede Hollow to the brick-fields and swamps where the Five Points was to rise. When his new church was built, he worked with his members in laying brick, while his doe-like wife, Corinne, served coffee and brought the hymn-books to the men and lent her lipstick to the sisters.

Judge Cass Timberlane had once said that Dr. Evan Brewster was the most intelligent person in Grand Republic. That was doubtful, when you considered Sweeney Fishberg or Dr. and Mrs. Kamber or a couple of Wargate chemists named Ash Davis and Cope Anderson, or possibly Judge Timberlane himself. But none of these competent people had Evan Brewster's love for all suffering human beings.

Neil Kingsblood's friends had never heard of Dr. Brewster.

During the hymn, which the congregation sang with neither a comic swing nor any of the richness fictionally associated with spirituals, but like any other evangelical Americans, Neil looked at the people about him.

Except for four or five of whom he was in doubt, they all seemed "colored." He recognized only two: Wash, the bootblack-sage, who now, in a double-breasted blue jacket, looked like a tiny, secret, fatherly old Jewish international banker, and Judge Timberlane's cook-general, Mrs. Higbee.

When they had finished singing and sat listening to the gospel, Neil discovered that his sense of their being "colored," being alien, being fundamentally different from himself, had evaporated. Their similarity to one another in duskiness and fuzzy hair was so much less than their individual differences that they had already ceased being Negroes and become People, to wonder about, to love and hate.

Evan Brewster was no longer ugly to him, in his thick virility, but noble as a grizzly is noble, and Neil saw dimly what a piece of impertinence it had been for the Caucasians to set up their own anemic dryness as the correct standard of beauty.

He was not an amused tourist; it was desperate for him to know his own people. His vision was magnified, and he was able to see how these Negroes varied in complexion, from black-glass to vellum and cream and copper and lemon-yellow; and there was one man, pale and heavily freckled and almost as red-headed as Neil himself, about whom you nevertheless felt certain that he was a "Negro."

He began to identify them with the white people he knew. The large and probably bad-tempered woman who had been singing with such powerful unction was unquestionably Mrs. Boone Havock. The dashing lady, slender, amiable but aloof, whose face was shadowed by a tilted black hat dripping with lilac net, with pearl earrings clear against her dark neck, was Mrs. Don Pennloss, and a proud woman who was more white than any white person and yet obviously was not "white," could be no one but the exclusive Eve Champeris.

The workman beside him, who had smiled and offered him an opened hymn-book, was the old Scotch-Irish carpenter who used to give him, as a small boy, the long sweet shavings for use as beards and wigs and kindling for Indian camp-fires.

Neil had never seen how beautiful hands can be till now, when he was sensitively aware of the carpenter's palms. The backs of his hands were dark gray, a weary color, but the palms were worn pink as Neil's own, except in the creases, where there still clung a dark tint, and his nails were pink as Neil's. They were hands competent to rip off old boards, to grasp a hammer, to guide a chisel, to bless a child.

"Maybe hands like that do something better than make figures in ledgers," sighed Neil.

———

He tried to find out whether they *did* smell like that.

Like most Americans, he had always touchingly believed that all Negroes have an especial and detestable savor, and he could be seen now earnestly sniffing. He did catch a distinct odor, but it was the aroma of soap, moth balls, and laundry which is peculiar to all church congregations, white, black, yellow, or magenta, on any warm Sunday morning. Indeed his exploration into the mysteries of his own people was a failure insofar as he expected to find them different from that other caste, equally his own people, who were called whites.

He, the customary even if not very credulous Baptist, felt at home in this Baptist church.

As he had begun to find in Dr. Brewster the harsh beauty of a rough bronze statue and the spiritual beauty of a Coptic saint beneath the desert sun, so he began to relish the leopard beauty in the woman with pearl earrings, and the healthy, flapper-and-bobby-sox beauty of these appallingly typical American schoolgirls about him.

18

The sermon of Dr. Brewster was long and stately. Under divine law and divine love, he lectured, there can be no corruption save by the will of the corrupted.

It did not mean very much to a young man who wanted to know what was the right course for a person whom God had made white but whom the legislative enactments of many God-fearing States of the Union had made black. It was such a sermon as might have been preached in any Rockefeller-Gothic church on Fifth Avenue, Michigan Avenue, or Hollywood Boulevard. In Neil's waxing desire to know how real was reality, it was too collegiate and cultured and generally white. He could have done with more tom-toms and jungle-dancing, more samples of what his darker ancestors might have been, and through the whole sermon, the congregation showed unction with not more than two or three dehydrated Hallelujah's and one "Praise God, ain't it de trufe!"

Neil was rather comforted when the Harvard-Columbia-Union Seminary superiority broke down, and Dr. Brewster was guilty of "My brethrens" and of "cherubims," and not only confided that for one summer he had "pastored" a church in St. Joe, but that its members had enthusiastically "brotherhooded."

That was more like it, Neil thought gleefully. That was getting nearer to the Southern darky sermons reported by the Southern-gent-journalists and joyfully quoted by Rod Aldwick, in which all Tinted Men of God invariably spout, "Mah bretherens and sisterens, Ah absqualulates dat dis-here congoleum of crapshooters is powuhful lakly to perish in dat ole lake of fire."

——If I *am* going to be a Negro, I want my sermons hot. I might as well enjoy getting away from certifying checks and playing bridge, and roll the bones in the jook.

——Quit being sentimental, Kingsblood. If you get caught and publicly turn Negro, you're going to play it just as safe and respectable as you can, and hope that the kind white folks won't mind your nasty little Biddy being in school with their darlings.

——And it comes to me that I've heard my own white Baptist preacher, Doc Buncer, say "cherubims" and "to pastor." This is plain hell, to get myself nerved up to being a Negro and then find there aren't any special Negro things *to* be. Wouldn't it be flat for an enthusiastic martyr to find that the fire just warmed him pleasantly?

——Don't worry. It won't feel flat when Biddy and I get kicked off a Tennessee bus by a Mick conductor and a hillbilly cop breaks my jaw while a Wop detective grabs Biddy and snickers and begins——Oh, stop tormenting yourself. Stop it!

——

If he had criticized Dr. Brewster for an address that was pretentious in that humble chapel, he was stirred when Brewster read the Scripture. Neil was no judge of drama, but he felt a high moment like King Lear's madness as the pastor read, tenderly and movingly, the eternal cry of all dark peoples, all Orientals, all women, all men sick and bewildered and lame with poverty:

"I did mourn as a dove; mine eyes fail with looking upward. O Lord, I am oppressed; undertake for me.... I shall go softly all my days in the bitterness of my soul.... Behold, for peace I had great bitterness, but thou hast in love to my soul delivered it from the pit of corruption.... The grave cannot praise thee, death cannot celebrate thee; they that go down into the pit cannot hope for thy truth. *The living, the living, he shall praise thee, as I do this day.*"

———

The audience were softly moaning, "Were you there when they crucified my Lord?" and they leaped to sudden cheerful jazz in "Just a little talk with Jesus makes it right, all right!" and Neil saw a turpentine camp and men molded in copper and ebony singing slow and stopping to laugh under the chains of the white men as they swaggered, bound, into the swamps, into the sunrise.

——This is my history, thought Neil; this is my people; I must come out.

19

During the sermon, Neil had noticed, in the pew across the aisle, a family of father, who was a man of sixty or so, mother, a son who was in uniform as a captain, a young woman holding a baby who was being extraordinarily good, and a girl of perhaps seventeen. All of them were serious, capable-looking people, and all of them, except for the darkish young wife and her baby, might unquestionably have been taken for white, if they had not seemed so habitual here.

Where had he seen that captain?

He realized that this was the "colored boy" who had been in his class all through school, respected and ignored. Some of the white girls had even pretended to like him, and he had once been elected class secretary. Now what was his name? Oh. Emerson Woolcape.

Neil had heard that the fellow had become a dentist, with an office in the Five Points, with a regular chair and X-ray outfit and even a uniformed girl assistant, just like a regular practitioner. As the son of a real dentist, Neil had found this slightly comic.

He did not, just now, find it so comic, nor the fact that Woolcape should be pretending to be a captain, like himself, and that on his collar there was no suggestion of gentlemanly guns for killing people, but merely the caduceus with a D which indicated nothing more warlike and noble than saving their teeth.

Neil recalled that as a boy he had once seen the whole Woolcape family picnicking on the bluffs of the Sorshay River, about a red and white tablecloth spread on the rocks. They had all been singing, and he had enviously thought that they were having more fun than his family ever had. He was sure that he had seen the Woolcape father around that crazy Mermaid Tavern Building, with its phony half-timbering, as janitor and handyman. But there was nothing apparent of the mop and furnace-dust about him now. His gray suit was easy, his tie was well knotted, and his face of a Roman Senator, crowned with gray-shot sable hair, was proudly back as he listened to the sermon.

Staring at the grave competence of John Woolcape, Neil felt a premonitory chill about his own future in a world, his own world of Pruttery, which had nothing more than a dirty and half-servile job for a man who looked like that. He warmly assured himself that however sympathetic he might be with these Negroes, it would not be a very bright notion financially to announce himself as one. But, "I wish I had that man's dignity," he sighed.

Mrs. Woolcape had an especial look of familiarity that perplexed Neil until he realized that she was surprisingly like his own mother. He denied it, and shivered, and looked again. She seemed older than "Mum," and at once more calm and more resolute, yet in her color of pale honey, her chiseled-down nose, her small shy mouth, her eyes that asked nothing for herself, she was so like his mother that he felt bound to her and to her family by something more than a tale about a moccasined frontier rover. This was a woman whose questions he would answer gladly, and in her smile and tenderness he could find solace.

———

"The Lord be with us, while we are parted one from another, the Lord wash us clean of corruption, the Lord dwell in loving kindness among us———"

Evan Brewster paused, he looked straight at Neil, he had a wonderful smile of friendship, and he ended, "loving kindness among us all, rich or needy, black and white—His children."

The African girls in the choir, who were American girls, were chanting "Blessed be the tie that binds," but the spell was shattered as everyone rose—everyone but Neil, who sat enchanted.

When he moved toward the door with the last of the congregation, he felt their doubt whether he was friendly or just curious; whether they should bow or ignore him. But all of them who had come from the South had learned that it was safer to do both, and get away quick.

At the door, Dr. Brewster was shaking hands, and he spoke to Neil not otherwise than to the others: "It has been pleasant to have you with us this morning, Brother."

The conventionality of it irritated Neil, yet was that not just what his own Dr. Buncer said?

Seen close, as they shook hands—and by now Neil had enough training so that he no longer made a production of it—Dr. Brewster had tiny folds of flesh over the inner corners of his eyes, he was moist as a fieldhand and had the dismaying grip of one, and in his eyes was every sorrow since Golgotha.

When Neil was rather confusedly out on the sidewalk, he was not glad that the ordeal was finished; he was lost and puzzled in a common world where neither the hard-faced whites whom he saw now on the street nor the tough and lounging Negro gamblers could conceivably have any of Evan Brewster's patience for his quandary.

For a long time he stared at the Ethiopia Motion Picture Playhouse, across the way, as though it were Chartres Cathedral. He did not realize that he was standing beside the Woolcape family, who were in after-church gossip with neighbors. Captain Emerson Woolcape looked as though he recognized Neil but did not expect to be recognized himself, and he was surprised when Neil half bowed, and babbled, "I thought that was you, o' man. Haven't seen you since high school."

The Woolcapes stared at him with a silence that could become either welcome or hostility. He rushed on, longing, for reasons not too clear to him, to be accepted by them:

"In fact, years ago, I saw all of you having a grand picnic together, and I wished I were with you."

They all widened their mouths in forbidding politeness, and Neil urged, as one who would be loved even if he had to kill them for it, "Sorry I never had the pleasure of hearing Dr. Brewster before. Uh—did you get over to the other side, Captain—Emerson?"

"I saw a little of the show there." Reluctantly, Emerson did what was necessary. "Captain Kingsblood, this is my wife—I imagine you know her father, Drexel Greenshaw of the Fiesole Room—and our baby. My father and mother, and this young lady is my niece, Phoebe.... Mother, you've heard me speak of Mr. Kingsblood—we were in school together."

The Woolcapes all looked like children who have done their politenesses to the nosey deacon and feel that they may sneak away now and be happy. But, at whatever risk of being snubbed, Neil wasn't having it. This family had become immensely important to him. When a man is born a Negro at thirty-one, he needs a family.

He had never done much in the youthfully-beseeching line; yet, he was solicitious now with Emerson.

"Which way you going, Captain? I don't know this part of town very well."

It was not Emerson but his mother who rose to a hearty, "Oh, wouldn't you like to walk along with us, Captain?"

John and Mary Woolcape lived a block from the church, with Emerson next door. As they trudged, John pointed out the dwarf parsonage of Evan Brewster, and tried, "Did you enjoy the sermon, Captain Kingsblood? We think quite highly of Dr. Brewster."

The Woolcapes were surprised by the ardor with which this

white banker—probably down here on some regrettable piece of financial spying—answered, "Seriously, I thought he had a remarkable combination of power and gentleness. A saint—but smart!"

"He's too good a bowler and much too good a cook to be classed as a saint, but we're very fond of Dr. Brewster," said Mrs. Woolcape, and Neil felt that she was faintly laughing at him and his status of amateur critic. But he would not be smiled down. He studied the parsonage, shabby white, one-story, three or four small rooms, the whole thing not much larger than his own modest living-room. There were prim curtained windows, and on the pocket-handkerchief porch were three jars of geraniums.

"Rather small house for a man as big as he is. And I suppose he's married?"

"Yes, and two children. Dr. Brewster says they manage by sleeping on top of the cook-stove and keeping the bathtub and the cat underneath it, and his library—*both* books!" said Mr. Woolcape.

His wife rose to it. "Now John, you know perfectly well that Evan has a splendid library for a man on his salary—hundreds of books—all the important new ones—Myrdal and Wright and Langston Hughes and Alain Locke and everything!"

They laughed at her like a family who love one another.

Neil found some more conversation to offer: "Small church—don't suppose you can possibly pay him a high salary. Seems a shame."

John said proudly, "No, we can't. None of us make very much ourselves, you know. So Evan—Dr. Brewster—has to work nights in the post office, to make both ends meet, as his children are still young. But he just laughs about it. He says we're lucky to have a preacher that's a civil-service employee and not a panhandler. And," boastfully, "he's a supervisor, and he has quite a few white men working under him!"

"Yet for a man like that," offered Neil, "college degrees and all, to have to waste his time sorting circulars——"

"We don't think so," Mr. Woolcape insisted. "We're glad Reverend Brewster is willing to work with common people like ourselves, and not soak away in dreams in a pastor's study. Especially my son Ryan feels that—he's home on leave from the Army but he didn't come with us today. He's a little leftwing, I'm afraid."

"My, my, my, Captain Kingsblood must be simply fascinated by our family history. Do tell him about the pup we had once that had six toes on each foot!" Mary Woolcape scoffed, and stretched out her hand to Neil in farewell.

He wilfully did not see it.

They were standing in front of the Woolcape house, which was not much larger than Evan Brewster's, one-storied, white, immaculate; they were standing there, and Neil just stood there, till John Woolcape could scarce escape saying, "Won't you come in?" And Neil did come in; he stepped right in after them, like it or not, and he was determined that nothing so petty as good manners should keep him from a chance of enlightenment.

He saw the shared glance of Emerson and his father which meant, "What does this loan-shark from the bank want? What sort of a crooked white-man's trick is he up to?"

He tried to set up an old-schoolmates-together atmosphere with, "Do you remember that funny old hen we had in algebra, Captain?"

Emerson chuckled. "She was a crank, all right."

"But she had a good heart. One time after class she said to me, 'Neil, if you would do your algebra better, you might become Governor of the State.'"

"Did she, Captain?" Emerson spoke with a drawl that was on the insulting side. "What she said to *me*, one time after class, was that she was considering only my welfare, and for a boy of my race to learn algebra instead of short-order cooking was 'my, such a waste of time!'"

All the classmate cordiality was frozen. The Woolcapes were looking at Neil bleakly, they were waiting for his real mission.... Did bank clerks sell burial insurance?

"Please, I don't intend to intrude. I know that you want to get your Sunday dinner, and I'm going to skip right along, but there's a few things I earnestly want to know about—I mean, I don't know much of anything about—uh—about this part of town, and I simply must have a better understanding of—*of this part of town*."

What Neil was trying to say, without offense, was "better understanding of Negroes." But did one say *to* them "Negroes" or "colored people" or "Ethiopians" or that cumbersome "Afro-Americans" or what? What would offend them least? Once, in Italy, he had heard a Negro soldier bawl at another, "Hustle up, nigger," and yet he knew now that they were not fond of the word. It was confusing.

They looked more cordial. "What can we tell you, Captain Kingsblood?" asked Emerson.

(How did they know he had been a captain? Was it true, as some people said, that the whole dark world was a conspiracy planning the destruction of all the white people, viciously clever yet jungle-mad, wild as smoke-blackened midnight fires for human sacrifice; a cabal that spied on every white person's acts and noted them in little books audited by witch-doctors and Communist agents?)

Now the one thing he yearned to say was "Shall I, who am a Negro, become a Negro?" While he struggled to phrase it, he looked about.

There was no reason why a man of average perception should have been astonished that the house of middle-class Negroes with ordinary good taste and neatness should be exactly like the house of any other middle-class Americans with ordinary taste and neatness. What, Neil taxed himself, did he expect? A voodoo altar? Drums and a leopard skin? A crap-game and a demijohn of corn liquor? Or an Eldzier Cortor painting and signed photographs of Haile Selassie, Walter White and Pushkin? Yes, probably he *had* expected something freakish.

But, if they were janitors, instead of lawyers and salesmen, he and all of his friends would have living-rooms exactly like this: the same worn carpet-rug, tapestry chair with foot-rest, love seat, ornamented ash-trays, satinwood radio-cabinet, women's magazines, and not very good reproductions of not very good floral pieces!

——Vestal would approve of this room and point out that Mrs. Woolcape keeps it better than Shirley does ours.

Then he stopped lying to himself and with a pang he admitted how impossible it would be to conceive of Vestal as ever being here and being natural with these, his own people.

Well, they were waiting, and he tried to speak out.

"What I wanted to ask—I don't quite know how to express it, but certain things have happened, and they make me feel that I ought to know you, uh——"

" 'Negroes' is the word," said John Woolcape.

"Or 'colored people.' We don't mind either," said his wife, and they were both suave about it and rather tolerant.

"What Mother means," Emerson explained, "is that we dislike both terms intensely, but we consider them slightly less ruffling than 'nigger' or 'coon' or 'jig' or 'spade' or 'smoke' or any of the other labels by which white ditch-diggers indicate their superiority to Negro bishops. We expect it to take a few more decades before we're simply called 'Americans' or 'human beings.' "

"Don't be so damn smug!" Emerson's father threw at him. "You're right about the unpleasantness of the labels, but when did a ditch-digger get to be so inferior to a bishop? I'm an ash-shoveler myself! But if Captain Kingsblood would like to ask about the Negroes—that's the word that I happen to use—we'd be glad to tell him anything we can."

Emerson hastened, "Of course we will. I didn't mean to be smug. I just don't like being branded as a kind of barnyard animal. But Captain, if you'd really enjoy a red-hot race-talk, wait till my brother Ryan comes in. He's only twenty-three, but he can be as wonderful and wrong as if he were ninety. He's on leave—hopes to be out soon, but he's still in the service, as I am; he's a sergeant, and how he does look down on us captains! Ryan's been out in India, and way he tells it, he was hobnobbing with Gandhi and Nehru, though *they* may not have noticed it. And Burma."

The reference to foreign service sent the two soldiers off on the shop-talk of veterans. Captain and Doctor Emerson Woolcape looked like a soldier, sounded like a soldier, had the very tune of it, and Neil reflected that if Emerson had little of the magic of that great leader, Major Rodney Aldwick, he seemed no less professional, as they traded opinions of B-29's, rations, colonels and sea-sickness.

They were all seated now, though only Neil looked settled and comfortable.

Emerson's niece, Phoebe, who had not yet been explained, was as bored by the droning of these venerable soldiers as any other seventeen-year-old American girl would have been. She was a graceful thing, breathless with youth; she was as gilt-headed as Biddy, as pink-and-white as Neil's sister, Joan, and more restless. She sprang up now as a boy of her own age burst in.

He was thoroughly black, his features Negroid, yet in his blue Sunday suit and his beige sweater edged with maroon at the neck, he was completely the American High School Boy, shoulders proudly back, free and independent—probably too free and too independent, like his white classmates, who were the despair of their clucking teachers.

"This is Winthrop Brewster, our pastor's boy. Phoebe and he are driving to Duluth for lunch," said Mrs. Woolcape, as though that flight, seventy-odd miles each way, were a step across to the park.

Winthrop said How was he, Phoebe said Sorryhaftrunaway, with decently veiled joy at escaping from an old man of thirty-one, and they were gone in a blur, the same blur of gasoline fumes in which two other American children, Neil and Vestal, had flickered, only a dozen years ago.

And in just the tone of Vestal's mother then, Mrs. Woolcape lamented, "I'm worried about that child. Our granddaughter Phoebe. Her mother and father have passed on, and we're responsible for her. I'm sure I didn't act like that when I was in high school and Oberlin. She seems to be simultaneously in love with Winthrop Brewster—he's a wonderful boy; he'll be a great expert in electronics or something after he goes to college, but Phoebe thinks Winthrop is too sober and fussy, and so, if you please, our young lady calmly up and announces that she is also in love with Bobby Gowse, who's a wild stage dancer here, and with our neighboring boy, Leo Jensing. But Leo is white, so of course we wouldn't like that."

"Are you prejudiced against white people, then?" wondered Neil.

Her husband raged, "She certainly is, and I keep telling her that with her education—I only finished grade school, myself—she has no excuse for condemning a whole race. I tell her that if she is patient and looks for it, she'll find just as many kind-hearted and understanding people among the whites as in our own race.... But I'm also somewhat opposed to intermarriage, though only because there are so many people, both white and black, who have been denied the power to love and so they are envious and do all the harm they can when they see a mixed couple who love each other so much that they are willing to stand social exile. Of course this whole color code is nonsense, but it's so tied up with the old aristocratic class myth, like the D.A.R. or the English nobility (so I read), that you can't ignore it any more than you can syphilis, which it greatly resembles."

"John!" said Mrs. Woolcape.

"And so," her husband continued, "I would—well, to tell the truth, Captain Kingsblood, I'm hanged if I know whether, if Phoebe wanted to marry a white boy, I would lock her in, or throw up my janitor's cap and shoot anybody who tried to interfere with her rights!"

"Now John, stop being so racial," said Mrs. Woolcape, but in a strictly routine way.

Emerson's wife had taken the baby and gone home—somewhat pointedly. Neil knew that they were waiting for him to leave.

"I mustn't stay any longer but——Tell me. Is it hard to be a Negro? Here in the North, I mean—in Grand Republic? I'm not just being curious. I want terribly to know."

The older Woolcapes and Emerson took wordless counsel, and Emerson answered for them:

"Yes, it is hard, unceasingly."

His mother corrected him, "Not always. Most of the time we forget we are classed as pariahs, and go about our business without thinking of race, without thinking of ourselves as anything special. But occasionally it is intolerable, not so much for yourself as for the people you love, and I can understand the young men who talk so wildly about machine guns—wicked talk, but I understand."

Neil worried it, "But—I'm honestly not trying to argue, Mrs. Woolcape, but I want to know. I have no doubt it's tough in the South, but here in the North there's certainly no prejudice—oh, maybe some individuals, but no legal bars. Why," with pride, "I even understand there's a Civil Rights law in this state, so Negroes can go into any restaurant! And your son and Phoebe, the way they look, they don't seem to have suffered from any discrimination!"

"Captain," said Emerson, "we were classmates. I thought then, and I see now I was right, that you were a frank, good-hearted fellow. You made a point of being pleasant to most of the boys, and you and I had common interests—track, mathematics, civics—and yet in twelve years, you almost never spoke to me except to say 'Good morning' as if you were doubtful about it."

Neil nodded. "Yes. And too late to apologize. I wish I could. But Phoebe, her generation is different. She seems as unself-conscious as my sister."

The quiet mother, Mary Woolcape, cried out, "That child is just beginning to learn the humiliation that every Negro feels every day, particularly in our self-satisfied North Middlewest. In the South, we're told we're dogs who simply have to get used to our kennels, and then we'll get a nice bone and a kind word. But up here we're told that we're complete human beings, and encouraged to hope and think, and as a consequence we feel the incessant little reminders of supposed inferiority, the careless humiliations, more than our Southern cousins do the fear of lynching. Humiliation! That's a word you white people ought to know about!

"Especially we who look white get humiliated here. We're constantly meeting people who don't know about It and who take to us, so that we drop our defenses—like fools. Then one day they snub us or glare at us or run away from meeting us, and we know that *they* know, and the pleasant times with them are over.

"But those who are visibly black—— No discrimination in the North? No, merely looked at like rattlesnakes by all the mean-tempered people on trains and buses and in stores. Rarely get jobs better than the kitchen, no matter what our ability. Ambitious colored boys becoming gamblers or hoboes because no one will try them at responsible work. Admitted grudgingly to restaurants because of the law, and then insulted or neglected there, so that next time we'd rather go hungry—so that we'd rather walk the streets all of a winter night than ask for a room in what you'd call a good hotel. So that John and I, who *would* be admitted, hate to take a hotel room when we travel, with our own brothers driven to the streets.

"Humiliated till we get broken or else, like John and me, prefer to stay home, always, always, and not take a chance on meeting any white man, any time. And we're not bad, oh, we're not, and when I think how good and courageous my husband is, and my children, and my father, the zoologist that——

"Oh, sorry. Being sentimental. I know you white people think it's very funny for a black woman to praise her men like that!"

"No—please!" Neil was extraordinarily moved and shaky.

"Don't you read the humorous stories about pretentious darkies in the magazines, hear the jokes about Mandy and Rastus at banquets? And Phoebe—you spoke of her new generation. Just the other day, a fifty-year-old white garage attendant, and Phoebe is much whiter than he is, told her that he would be willing to sleep with her, if he could only get used to her being a nigger. That's not as bad as the South, where a friend of ours, a colored woman, was hurt in an automobile accident, bleeding to death, and they turned her away from white hospital after hospital, and she died in the street—murdered.

"But still, when Phoebe went out for the school play, at your own Hamilton High, before she had a chance to read at the try-out, they told her the cast was already chosen, but they told a white friend of hers that nobody had been chosen. And one of her teachers this year keeps looking at her and at the Greek and Italian and Russian youngsters, and then she says something like 'those of us who have New England ancestors will not need to be told that so-and-so is a point of honor.'

"But that won't break her bones, as it did her father's. He was our oldest son, Bayard. He would have become a fine economics teacher. He graduated from Carleton—earned his way through, doing chores, but he was *summa cum laude*—and he married a wonderful girl.

"He was brought up entirely in the North—yes, yes, I know I'm inconsistent; I admit the South *is* worse, even worse! He was brought up here, and he'd never experienced one minute of *legal* segregation, and he just couldn't believe that a decent, educated Negro would ever run into violence in the South.

"He went to teach in a Negro college in Georgia, where his great-grandfather had been a slave. The first time he saw that hideous sign 'For colored only,' he wrote me, he felt so angry and so scared, as if a man were coming at him with a knife, that he had to draw the car up beside the road and be sick.

"But he tried to do what his Southern acquaintances advised and to 'play the game'—a game in which the other side always makes the rules. Then when he'd been there only a month, a policeman stopped his car and acted as if he'd stolen it. This man had seen Bayard around the college—he knew that though he was so pale, he was classed as 'colored.' He was so vicious that Bayard forgot and talked back, and they took him to the police-station and said he was drunk—he never even touched beer—and he got angry and they beat him. They beat him to death. My son.

"They beat him a long time. Till he died there on the cement floor. He was a handsome boy. And they told his wife that she'd better keep still or she'd never get to bear her baby—who was our Phoebe.

"After the baby came, she escaped North, all day and all night in the jimcrow coach, and she died within a year. He really was a handsome boy, and they kept kicking his head, on the cement floor, all dirty and bloody, and he died there."

Mary Woolcape was crying, and it was the more racking that she was not hysterical but hopeless. Neil wanted to make her the greatest offering he could, and he heard himself saying, "I understand, because I've found out that I am part Negro myself."

——Good Lord, I've done it! How could I be such a fool?

20

"You say you're part Negro? That's not our idea of a joke." John Woolcape, who was less ruddy than Neil and therefore more "white," was stern.

"It's not my idea of a joke, either! I never knew it till recently."

He felt trapped. Oh, these Woolcapes were admirable people, but he did not want to be in their power. He urged them, "Maybe I shouldn't have blurted it out. Nobody knows it, not even my parents or my wife, but I'm afraid it's true. Only a small percentage, but legally, so many places, I'm afraid I'm a colored man."

He was surprised that they did not look more surprised. They looked, indeed, rather hard. He tried to be airy:

"Well, I suppose I'll just have to face it."

John Woolcape said evenly, "Don't be so sorry for yourself. Don't be so childish. I've 'faced' being a Negro for sixty-five years now, and my wife and children and a few million other decent folks have managed to 'face it'!"

They glared at each other, but it was Neil's arrogance that was broken.

"You're entirely right, Mr. Woolcape. I guess I'll have to apologize again. It's just that the idea is so new that I haven't been able to get used to it. Not even Dad and Mum know it. I was looking up my ancestry and I ran into a—well——"

"You white folks would call it a 'touch of the tar brush,'" Emerson said sardonically. "Not so easy, eh?"

"Well, God Almighty, you two ought to know whether it's easy or not!" Neil snarled.

"John and you, Emerson, both of you, you quit badgering that boy!" Mary Woolcape's voice had a mother's tenderness and a mother's sharpness. "Of course he's upset. Poor boy!" Her arm was about Neil's shoulder and she lightly kissed his cheek. It was his own mother comforting him.

"How old are you, son?" she murmured.

"Thirty-one, nearly, Mrs. Woolcape."

He had almost said "Mum."

"It's tough to wake up to what the world's really like as late as that. We colored have to understand both our own world and the white folks' world, to be safe. But I tell you what!" Mrs. Woolcape sounded practical and bustling. "You stay and have dinner with us. Will your wife let you? You sit right down and telephone her."

Vestal said Okay, and was he enjoying his spree with the veterans?

He found that Mary Woolcape carried out the myth of the "typical Negress" in one detail: she was an excellent cook. But he was still novice enough to marvel that they did not have fried chicken and watermelon for Sunday dinner, but a quite Aryan roast of beef.

Emerson had gone to his own house for dinner. He had said, "I won't repeat anything at all about—uh—about what you told us, Captain, unless or until you want me to. But welcome to our club. Swell membership, even if we haven't a pool." They shook hands. They were friends, as they might have been twenty years before.

John sighed, "Ryan late again. These young revolutionists are going to be late at the barricades. We'll start without him.... Mary! Let's feed!"

So for the first time Neil sat down and ate with his new friends: that most ancient and universal symbol of equality.

He thought that it was to make him feel at home that the Woolcapes told him their stories.

John Woolcape was a "colored man," and he was entirely "white," which means pink and brown and gray, and he had never in his life been south of Iowa or east of Chicago. He was born in North Dakota, his family the only "Negroes" in their county. His father was a railroad section-gang foreman; his father's father had been a slave in Georgia and, after the Civil War, had been a farmhand in Florida, which he had apparently not viewed as a paradise of roulette wheels and beach umbrellas.

John himself had worked on farms, had hoped for college or school of agriculture, but when he was a freshman in the village high school, his father had been killed by a runaway box car, and he had apprenticed himself to the local barber. As a barber, he had come to Grand Republic, in 1902, and there, at twenty-two, he had first learned what it is to be a Negro.

Till then he had known little more of the diplomatic art of being colored than had a Neil Kingsblood. Perceiving that his father was a good Baptist and a good boss of Irish and Swedish section-hands, John had never heard the news that he was biologically inferior, and his untutored white playmates, boys and girls, had not known that the touch of his hands was pollution.

Especially the girls.

There had been a few people in that Dakota village who had muttered something unpleasant about "tar-brushes," but they had been "cranks" and "grouches," and to John their venom had been incomprehensible.

Accepted in Grand Republic as a white man and a sound barber, he had forgotten the infrequent hints from his father that connected with his family was a mystery called "the race problem." At that time it would have seemed to John just as reasonable for anyone to say to him "You're a Hydrangean Polypus" as to say "You're a black man." Not being black. And not caring a hang whether he was "black" or "white," so long as his customers and his Swiss sweetheart liked him.

But a man moved in from his boyhood village in North Dakota and whispered something to the boss barber, who said to John, "Why, you're part nigger, ain't you?"

"I suppose so. What of it?"

"Don't know 's it makes any difference to me, personally, but the customers don't like it. They'll all kick, and leave me."

"Have any of them kicked yet?"

"No, but they might. Can't take no chances. I will say for you, you're the best barber I got, but can't take no chances."

Back in 1904 they were already using this formula of caution which, unchanged in its massive dignity, imbecility and cowardice, was to go down to the middle of the Century of Democracy and Enlightenment.

John was discharged from shop after shop, and never because he was incompetent or because the customers disliked him—at least, they never disliked him till the Great Fact was whispered to them. Sometimes John himself flung the Fact at them, for he had no taste for the rancid butter of uncle-tomming, and in that two minutes of accusation by the first boss barber who had fired him, he had become "Negro" and "race-conscious."

His Swiss girl, a rosy chambermaid to whom he had been teaching English, had thought nothing about it when she learned the Great Fact, but her Irish and Scandinavian colleagues taught her that if she was to belong to this Land of Democracy, she must drive him away.

John was the first raceman in Grand Republic to hear of the founding of the N.A.A.C.P.—the National Association for the Advancement of Colored People, the Grand Army of the Negroes— and at its convention in Minneapolis, he met Mary, who, like himself, was imperceptibly "colored."

She was a graduate of Oberlin College, the daughter of a prosperous and rather scientific experimenter with turkeys and chickens and geese in Iowa. John and Mary disliked each other when they met, because they were both white and resented the swank of whiteness. But the fact that both of them refused to be anything so tyrannical as white drew them together. What had kept them together since was a common liking for integrity and humor.

John set up his own barber shop, and it failed, not because he was a Negro, since few of the customers seemed to object to his Ethiopian touch, but because he would not jimcrow it and bar out Negro customers, and the whites felt they had a social duty to be nasty about that.

Then, with his natural skill with tools, John had tried to become a mechanic. But he had little training, and technical schools then were distant and segregated. Mary and he wanted to go off to a larger, more mechanized city, where he could learn, but they had been so foolish as to believe the white real-estate men's slogan that a community honors any worker who shows his faith in it by buying his own home and having a nice little family.

They had bought the home, and they had the nice little family in the person of Bayard, and so they were stuck here, and always would be, and John became a janitor and was glad to get the job, and Mary helped him out by baking cakes for sale and by working as extra-waitress at party-dinners.

"Yes, I've seen you several times, Captain, when I've helped wait on table at the Havocks' and Mrs. Dedrick's, but you never saw me, I imagine," she said, and though she was too maternal and sensible to mean it that way, Neil was shamed.

He was certain that with white for a label and some Morton Bee-house as father-in-law, John Woolcape might now be president of the Second National Bank, and that with an equal adjustment, John William Prutt might be a janitor. But while it would work out admirably, in so far as Mr. Prutt would be a methodical furnace-tender and a passionate sweeper and remover of old bottles, Mr. Woolcape would be less happy and certainly less dignified in flattering large depositors than he was now.

Through most of dinner, they discussed, with few reticences, the propriety of the Negro Neil becoming a Negro.

"The only thing I'm sure of is that you mustn't do anything hasty, Mr. Kingsblood," said John.

Neil felt as near to them as to his own father and mother, of whose lives and purposes he now knew less than of the Woolcapes'. He would have been comforted if they had called him "Neil," but they had only softened the Captain to Mister, with an occasional affectionate Son.

"Don't take martyrdom as a game," John insisted. "Before you can know what you ought to do, or at least want to do, you must read the great books about my race, as I've been trying to do, with my defective education, these thirty years. But I reckon I'm lucky. A janitor's chair by the furnace is the perfect place for study.

"When you have read a lot and thought a lot, you may decide you don't want to come over. It might not do any good to our race, and it might be horrible for your mother and wife and little girl. I'm proud of being a Negro. I know so many plain, ordinary folks among my race that are like the great poets and heroes in the Bible. But white businessmen don't like it when humble people are heroic—black *or* white. They claw us down. Anyway, you have no right to expect your ladies to enjoy sharing your sacrifices. I wonder do many women enjoy martyrdom? Maybe they got too much sense."

Mary complained, "I never can make John understand about Joan of Arc—or, to take a much more sensible person, Harriet Tubman. He just won't get the feminist point of view. It's that old barbershop training."

Neil meditated, "As a matter of fact, I never have thought of coming out as a Negro. Do you despise Negroes that give up the fight and pass?"

The elders sighed. John pondered, "No. We're sorry to lose them, but we know how hard they've found it, and I'd say there's a general rule that if your old friend goes by you on the street, with white folks, and doesn't know you, you don't even wink—not public. Just as we'd cut our tongues out before we gave *your* confidence away. So will my younger son, Ryan, if you meet him and feel like telling him. Yes, he'd be the loyalest of us all, even if he is the most leftwing and gets awful ornery, sometimes, with you white folks!

"Maybe you'd like to come here next Friday evening. Clement Brazenstar of the Urban League will be here, and Ash Davis, a chemist——"

"I've met Dr. Davis. In the bank."

"And maybe Sophie Concord. She's a very pretty colored lady, a city nurse, real smart. Those folks are all terrific race-talkers, even worse than I am. Maybe, for an evening, it might be more interesting than pinochle, or whatever game of cards it is you play."

"Bridge!" said the more fashionable Mary.

"I'll come," said Neil.

John went on, "You won't need to tell 'em you're colored. In fact, Mr. Kingsblood, I don't know as I'd go around saying that, except here with us, who feel kind of like your family— Emerson used to tell us about you, when you and him were in school together. He admired you so much.

"If you come next Friday, you'll learn something from Clem Brazenstar. He's as black as Tophet; by birth, he's a real, low-down Mississippi Delta Nigra fieldhand, and he never went to college, but I doubt if there's any of these fancy college professors that reads as much as him.

"And then Ash and Martha Davis, they're kind of betwixt and between. They aren't black and born between the cotton bolls, like Clem, nor yet white and born in a blizzard, like Mary and me. They're high yella in color and border-state by family, and you know how these border white folks, Tennessee and Kentucky, never quite make up their minds. They appoint a colored fellow to the police force one day and lynch him the next and have a lovely obituary about him in the *Courier-Journal* the third."

Neil sighed, "I'm not sure my own record with the Negroes is any too good."

"Hm?"

"We recently had a colored maid, Belfreda Gray, and I got awfully prejudiced against her. I thought she was slovenly and sullen—I almost hated her, almost hated *all* Negroes, because of her. Do you know her?"

"Oh, yes, we know the little tart," Mrs. Woolcape said serenely, and Neil was as shocked as if his official mother had said it.

Mr. Woolcape was equally placid. "Yes, Belfreda is bad medicine, a bad example for our young people. I don't think we'll hold that prejudice against you, except as, like most white folks, you concluded that all of us are like her. And there's some excuse for Belfreda. Her parents are dead, her grandfather, Wash, is pretty weak, and her grandmother is a tough old devil. Belfreda is a real slick-chick. She likes to tell the Polish girls how much smarter she is than they are. Still, that's better than being a Topsy and clowning around and eating dirt to amuse the white folks. Or getting sloppy and lazy and thieving, as the Southerners claim their colored servants do. (Why *wouldn't* they, when they have no hope at all except the kitchen!) Oh, there's a lot of excuse for Belfreda."

"You," said his wife, "make me tired! I'm sick of all these environmental excuses. A cause isn't an excuse. All these murderers, black and white, smirking, 'It's not my fault, because my parents didn't understand me.' Whose parents ever did understand them? Everybody excusing themselves that way for drinking and whoring, even here in the Five Points. I'm sick of it! I don't think Borus Bugdoll, who sells dope and girls, is justified by having been born on a bankrupt farm!"

Her husband flared back, "Even Borus feels the discrimination against him——"

It was the first of the debates, the "race-talks," that Neil was to hear in the Five Points: debates that continued all night, contradictory and emotional, learnedly and sometimes ungrammatically carried on by Negro tailors and waiters and oilers who never, like Oliver Beehouse or John William Prutt, bought a ranked regiment of books and put them up on oak shelves, but borrowed them, one at a time, from the public library.

Neil tried to get into the talk with an offering of "I don't think many white people are really vicious. I don't believe most of them know there *is* any discrimination."

Behind him, an unknown voice, somewhat youthful but somewhat basso, jeered, "Then who are the mysterious guys that start the discrimination?"

"Mr. Kingsblood, this is our son, Ryan," said Mrs. Woolcape.

"Our son Ryan, who is always late," said Mr. Woolcape.

"Your loving son Ryan, who is damn near always right on racial issues, too. And who may our friend be?"

21

Sergeant Ryan Woolcape, in uniform, could have been taken for a typical Anglo-Saxon collegian in the Army. He was six-two or -three, with a proud back and a head rearing as haughtily as his father's. He was snarling, "What is all this junk about you pinks not wanting discrimination?"

John spoke sharply: "That'll do Ryan. This is a friend of ours— Captain Kingsblood, of the Second National Bank."

"I'm aware of that noble fact, Dad. I've seen him captaining in the bank.... Cap, excuse me for my bumptiousness. I have some reason for being in a temper. I've just been in God's holy temple, listening to the Reverend Dr. Jat Snood, that Kansas Fundamentalist Evangelist and all-around bastard. I doubt if I'd ever have gotten in if the ushers had known I'm a spook, blast their worm-eaten souls and slimy handshakes. But I did, and I heard Snood explain that Jesus wants the frozen-toed Christians up here in Minnesota to chase all us niggers back to Georgia. So the Captain must excuse me if I get rough when I find one of the pious ofays here in this low shack."

"Ryan," said Mr. Woolcape, "shut up!"

"Ryan," said Mrs. Woolcape, "Mr. Kingsblood is not a white man, legally."

(——I knew I shouldn't 've told!)

"He is one of us, Ryan. He's just found it out. You're under pledge of complete secrecy, by the way. He came to us for advice and friendship, and then you go and talk like a Texas sheriff!"

Ryan held out his heavy paw to Neil, smiled like a happy giant, and grunted, "I don't know whether to be pleased or sympathetic, but I always thought you looked like a good guy, for an officer, and now I understand why. Welcome! Sure, I'll say nothing, and I'm sorry I shot my mouth off. But in the Army you get to hate all white officers."

Neil demanded, "Why? Did you really run into much discrimination? It happens I didn't serve with any colored troops."

"I'll tell you, Cap. One camp where I was in the South, the white G.I.'s had movies or U.S.O. shows every night, in a big theater, and swell rooms for playing cards and writing letters, and all the buses they wanted into town, and dozens of bars. We had movies only once a week, no place to write letters, and we had to walk two miles to a bus, and not enough buses and no bars, and the white M.P.'s watching you, making you feel like a criminal.

"And our colored officers had no power—they were just token officers, to keep the black vote happy. Colored colonels on shaky old jimcrow cars. One colored captain, in uniform, traveling on official business, was thrown into a civilian jail because there was no phone in the colored waiting-room, so he had to step into the white waiting-room to telephone—to his commanding officer!

"But I did get one thing out of it: a trip to Burma and Java, where I learned what the local boys thought about *their* being jimcrowed and how glad they'll be to join us American untouchables against the whole damn world oligarchy of whites!"

Ryan stopped, a stricken giant. "I've been hypnotized into another race-tirade! Blame it on Reverend Snood!"

He beamed at Neil as at his best friend, while Neil was appalled at so devastating a hatred of the whites. He wanted to get out of this. It wasn't *his* race-problem!

Mrs. Woolcape tried to soothe everybody by purring, "We ran into Mr. Kingsblood at church, this morning, Ryan. He thinks Evan is a fine preacher."

Ryan grinned. "Any dinner left? I will not be trapped into my Number 5B speech—about all the Negro churches being deader than the white ones. The young spooks that would have taught Sunday school a generation ago are working for the N. Double-A. C.P., and all the hot ones, that would have become hell-roaring deacons once, have joined the Communist Party. Brewster is a nice guy, but he's still the favorite of a lot of foot-kissing Uncle Toms, and he's still capable of preaching a sermon where a sinful white man—but smart and rich—is converted by a dumb woolly-head that can't pay his poll-tax. No, Mum, you shouldn't have told me the news about Simon Legree, if you wanted me to stick to Christianity and mild manners."

———

While the affable assassin gobbled cold roast beef, Mrs. Woolcape explained that Ryan's particular hope was to organize a Negro co-operative farm. But Neil could not be interested, could not take any more revolution and race-doctrine that day.

He promised that he would come back on Friday. Ryan said heartily, "I'm not sure we'll let you join us Senegambians. You'll be too shocked when you find out what our real opinions are—the ones we don't tell any white man. Why, we don't even believe in dressing for dinner every evening!"

Neil decided that Ryan was being humorous, and that it was but manners to smile and look gratified. But as he walked to the bus, loathing the Sunday-afternoon colored loafers strutting their stuff on Mayo Street, he was raging.

"So, my fine young sergeant, you're not sure whether you're going to allow me to join your race! Oh, I might've known! Why am I such a fool? Well, here I am back in the unfortunate plight of being a future bank-president—white!"

It was no go. He could not escape. The eyes of Mary Woolcape were sorrowfully rebuking him now, as they had comforted him when he had been a new-found son in tribulation.

He came into his house unknowing what and where and how Neil Kingsblood was going to be.

———

Vestal was easy on him. "How were the veterans? Did you boys all tell one another how brave you were?"

"Now I want to tell you I learned something!" he said stoutly. "The Negro troops never got enough credit—building airfields and driving trucks under fire, and no decorations."

"My, my, did I fall down on that, too, and not give 'em any medals? I'll call in Congress and tell 'em to fix that up right away. The poor darkies! I'll give 'em all Purple Hearts and Rosy Crosses and Orders of the Emerald Watermelon, Second Class."

"You ought to take 'em more seriously, and I'm going to take a nap," he complained.

"Take it seriously?" she jeered.

Before he slept, he had to look at Biddy's new design for a bomb-carrying airplane.

———

He had forgotten to open the windows, that afternoon in early summer, and he slept heavily.

He was running in terror through a midnight wood, staggering through bogs, colliding with tree-trunks, branches slashing at his forward-thrust face. He was panting so that his lungs were seared, and a cavern of thirst was in his mouth. He did not know who were pounding after him, but they loathed him, they would knee him in the groin, smash his jaw, tear out his eyes.

He was stopped by a circle of small flashing lights. He saw that they were the eyes of bloodhounds, on their haunches. Behind the hounds he made out, as torches were kindled, a semicircle of men, such horrible men as he had never seen, wrinkled like the bloodhounds, puckered of neck, snake-cold of eye, and these men were moving toward him, moving, coming, close.

Somebody said, quite conversationally, "God damned raping nigger, I bet this brush-hook will go right through his shinbone, one nip."

He was on the ground, and a big boot—he could distinctly catch its reek of manure—was kicking him in the side of the head, but he was no longer lying on the forest leaf-mold, he was lying on a cement floor, dirty and bloody, and the boot was going thump, thump, and the intolerable pain went through to the center of his skull.

They were lifting him up, while he struggled; a rope was lifting him up, slowly up, choking him; then he was standing in a boggy woods aisle and looking up at himself, hanging and kicking, and he saw that while his face was his own white-man's face, ruddy and freckled, his naked body was iron-black, black iron radiant with sweat in the jagged torch-light, while his black limbs kicked, mechanically, grotesquely, and he and all the other white men stood and laughed, "Look at the nigger kick, will yuh! He looks like a damn frog kicking, black frog, lookit him kick, the black nigger. And they claim to be human, like us! Haw—haw!"

———

He lay in unrelieved terror.

———This could be me. They have lynched Negroes, even in Minnesota. They would hate me even more than they do fellows that have always been colored. I could feel that rope.

———I can't come out and take that. But if it's that urgent with my people, I've got to.

———But I can't do that to Biddy. She mustn't be sick with remembering a murdered father, way Phoebe Woolcape is. But maybe she wants to fight for her own. Maybe even the small girls are like that now, designers of bombers, ruthless.

———Look at the nigger frog kicking, and they claim to be human!

He caught himself wanting to run to the Woolcapes, to Mary Woolcape, but most of all to Ryan.

22

Dr. Kenneth Kingsblood winked at his son, to show that they had a secret from the womenfolks, and led him aside to chuckle, "Got any furtherer with your research? We the rightful kings of Britain?"

The question so belonged to the antiquity of six months ago that he might as well have asked, "Have you finally decided to vote for Rutherford B. Hayes?"

With the oppression of that afternoon's dream still on him, Neil had gone to his father's for Sunday Evening Supper—hot soup, cold chicken, potato chips, drug-store ice cream. Biddy was asleep on a couch upstairs, and Vestal was talking Servants & Children with Neil's mother and his sister, Joan, as nice women must have talked in the primitive caves, in the Norman castles, under the tinkling eaves of China's first dynasty. It was a maid's-night-out evening of sweetness and security and affection.

To his father, Neil could answer only, "Haven't got much farther with the court documents, Your Majesty," and hastily skip it.

He studied his mother and found Negro ancestry in her dark eyes, then reminded himself that he had once found Chippewa traits in Vestal.

He mustn't, in his urge toward Africa, forget that he had Indian bravery in him as well. Tonight, when he was restless, he'd like to be out on a stormy lake in a Chippewa canoe. It excited him to think that he had in him canoes and Kaffir knives as well as account-books and plowshares.

If that bland Sabbath domesticity did not soothe him, neither did the effervescence of the next evening dazzle him.

This was another of the practically incessant series of "Welcome home, Major Rodney Aldwick, well done, sir!" parties which had adorned Rod's terminal leave. He was going back to camp now, to get demajorized, and he would come back a Veteran, with an honorable record; he would let the newspapers announce that he had resumed his practice at the bar.

Through this positively last final party, Neil heard Rod keeping to his high theme:

"We vets must stand together against all the elements which produced the Fascism which we have conquered: that is, the inferior races, which turned disloyal and weakened the British and American and French and Dutch Empires, and so gave mongrels like Hitler a chance to pick on Winston Churchill."

Neil was in an empty daze as he realized that his hero was not only vicious but a bore. No man could have been more miserable than Neil in the unmasking of a friend.

—

He did not lie awake, the two nights after his dream of terror. Very few things could make Neil Kingsblood lie awake. His best period for brooding was during his morning shave, when he was in the thoughtful mood produced by the manifold beauties of his electric razor, the lovely body of nickel and ivory (imitation) which, without the feudal superstitions of soap and shaving-brush, whisked like the hand of love across his solid jaw, nipping off the shiny hairs and proving that there may be something to modern civilization.

He thought that his curly hair, revealed in the round shaving-mirror on a bracket-arm beside the medicine cabinet, was as kinky as Dr. Brewster's. He thought of Evan Brewster, and his earnestness, his simple goodness. And, since Brewster was a Baptist, like himself, Neil contemplated the special wisdom and glory of Baptist preachers and their divine program.

He demanded of himself: What was his actual creed? Did he believe in a definable God? In personal immortality? What, except to remain in love with Vestal and to give Biddy a chance to grow up happily, was his purpose in life? And why had God punished Vestal by making her husband a Negro? Or was it no punishment at all, but a noble revelation?

He held the razor stationary as he admitted that for a dozen years, except with Tony Ellerton, he had given no more thought to theological guesses than he had to Washington and the cherry-tree.

He had an official pastor, the Reverend Dr. Shelley Buncer of the Sylvan Park Baptist Church, a sensible and friendly man. Why shouldn't he for once make himself believe that this learned pastor did actually know things about God and Immortality that were hidden from the common laborer or banker, and assume that the church had hired Dr. Buncer for that reason, and not because he was a companionable golfer, a skillful executive at weddings and children's birthday-parties, and a dependable extemporaneous speaker at bond-drives?

So on Tuesday evening Neil called on Dr. Buncer, and considerably embarrassed him by asking what he knew about God and Truth.

———

It was a pleasant summer-evening walk among the maples and fresh-watered lawns of Sylvan Park. The Baptist Church was a bulky pile of red and gray stone in layers, and next door to it was the parsonage, a hungry-looking old white wooden house which Mrs. Buncer (she came from the East, from Ohio) had made as worldly as possible with blue-and-gold Tunisian curtains.

The pastor's office—he called it his "studio," and sometimes gaily spoke of it as "the sanctum sanctorum," poor fellow—was at once reverent and dashing. On the morose dark-red desk were roses in an etched Swedish vase, and on the wall, between the portraits of Adoniram Judson and Harry Emerson Fosdick, was a print labeled "Kids and Kits."

Dr. Buncer was rotund but enthusiastic, a product of Brown University and Yale Theological, twenty years older than Neil. He had thin hair and an Episcopal voice, he wore tweeds and a red tie, and he gave Neil a good cigar—well, good within reason.

"My boy," he pronounced, "my feeling is that to prefer the pulpy cigarette to the mellow and manly weed is a sign of degeneracy in the age, so sit ye doon and light up, and I shall lay aside my volume of Saki. I must confess I have been escaping from the sordid problems of the day into that treasury of wit and abandong."

And with that he deftly slid into a desk drawer his book— *Murder Most Foul.*

To the pastor's dismay, instead of having come to ask him to address the Boosters Club or the Young Executives Association, Neil wanted to know something, and wanted to know something the doctor couldn't look up in that fine reference-library. He would have gone mad and barked if he had guessed the real purposes of this simple parishioner.

"Dr. Buncer, I've had some letters from a soldier who served under me, and he claims he's learned something that makes him suspect that he has a little Negro blood. So he's asked me about an ethical problem that you can solve better than I can. I understand he's married, apparently fairly happily, and has a couple of sons, and none of them have any idea of this Negro ancestry—which, I deduce, must be very distant. Now he wants to know what's the honorable thing to do. Ought he to tell his family, and maybe his friends, or shut up about the whole thing?"

Dr. Buncer gave an exhibition of thinking deeply, an exercise at which he was rusty. Then, "Tell me, Neil, does anyone suspect his plight?"

"I judge not, from his letter."

"Has he associated much with Negroes?"

"I doubt it."

"And by the way, Neil, have *you* ever associated much with Negroes?"

The chill was absolute.

Neil tried to sound uninterested as he droned, "Afraid I've never known any n——"

No! He would not say "niggers," not even if he was betrayed by it, and he finished up: "——never known any Negroes except maids and Pullman porters."

"Reason I ask is, in that case you can hardly understand this poor fellow's quandary in all its profound and I may even say religious aspects."

——God, what a relief!

"Now it just happens that I've had a good deal to do with the darkies, Neil, one time and another. In Brown, I roomed right near one, and many's the time, oh, half a dozen times at least, when I've dropped in at his room and tried to act as if he were my equal in every way. But those fellows, even the ones that go through the motions of getting a college education, are uneasy with us whites, who've inherited our culture and so take it naturally.

"We know and rejoice that they too are the sons of an all-merciful God, and maybe some day, a hundred years from now or two hundred, they'll be scarcely distinguishable from us, psychologically. But now they all feel so inferior, no matter how small a share of the taint they have in their veins, that unfortunately it's impossible for us to sit down for even half an hour and talk frankly and manfully with them, as you and I are doing.

"Then here in Grand Republic, I've served with darkies on several different committees, sat at the council table with them and so come to know them intimately. But where I really learned to understand the darkies was in the South, on their home heath. As a sort of a—ha, ha—internship I spent an entire month working in a settlement house in Shreveport, Louisiana, where I learned that segregation in the South was instituted not to discriminate against the Negroes, but to protect them, from the evil-minded men of both races, until such time as they grow up mentally and are able to face reality like you and I and other white men do.

"Understand me, I don't condone it as a permanent arrangement. There is no reason under heaven why American citizens should be compelled to travel in jimcrow cars and have to eat separately, *provided* they are Americancitizensinthefullestsense-oftheword, and that, I am very much afraid, none of even the more intelligent among our colored friends would even pretend to be!

"There is no one more eager than myself to recognize any slight advances toward civilization on the part of the darkies—like rotating their crops and more hogs and diet—but a parson has to deal with the profoundest reality—and how folks do hate us for being so honest and forthright; well, let 'em, I say; it's really a compliment to us, I always say, ha, ha!

"Now to come back to your soldier and his problem. If he never has been taken for a Negro, I don't see that he would be committing any moral offense if he just kept silent and remained technically a white man. After all, none of us has to tell *everything* he knows, ha, ha!

"I do think, though, if you're well enough acquainted with him to tell him this without hurting his feelings, you might advise him to stay away as much as he can from the white folks because otherwise the cloven hoof of his genetic mutation would be sure to show its hand. With my Southern training, I'm sure I'd spot him at once.

"So, in all solicitude, tell him to go slow, lay low, keep his own counsel, and play the game! Ha, ha. See how I mean?"

"Yes, I guess that might——" Neil was uninterested now in any doctrine that Buncer might have. But he fell into the temptation, that menaces all of us, to ask priests and judges and doctors and senators and traffic policemen what they really think when they are in their baths, unfortified by their uniforms.

"Dr. Buncer, I suppose you serve on committees not only with Negroes but with Jews?"

"Often! I've even had a rabbi here for dinner once, with Mrs. Buncer and Sister and Junior at the table. I think you may say I'm an out-and-out Liberal."

"But you take a Negro, Doctor. Would you feel that it was wise to have a Negro for dinner, if he was a qualified preacher?"

"Now, now, Neil, don't try to pin me down! As I told you, I belong to the New School. I wouldn't in the least mind, say at a Convention, sitting down with Negro intellectuals. But to have one for dinner in my house—oh no, my friend! That would not be kind to *them*! They aren't used to our way of living and think-ing. Can you imagine any Negro, no matter what theological train-ing he might pretend to have, being comfortable with Mrs. Buncer, who is highly interested in Scarlatti and the harpsichord, and who studied at the Fort Wayne Conservatory of Music? No, Neil— no!"

"What do you think of this local colored Baptist preacher, Dr. Brewster—some such a name?"

"I've met *Doctor* Brewster. Oh, he seems a very decent, humble man."

"Why is it that we don't seem to have any colored members in our church, and so few even drop in for services?"

"When they do drop in, as you somewhat lightly put it, I've told our ushers to explain that while any darky is perfectly welcome to fellowship with us, still we feel that he would be much happier with his own people, down in the Five Points. I imagine the ushers make that point quite clear—as, indeed, they should.

"There are some young ministers who disagree with me. They act as if they were the paid agents of the labor unions and a lot of Jewish and Negro organizations. Even birth-control! Well, we are told that Our Lord broke bread with thieves and sinners, but there is no hint that He sat down with doubters and trouble-makers and destroyers of the Christian home and self-seeking agitators, white, black, or yellow, do you see, my boy?"

"I see more clearly now, and many thanks, Doctor," said Neil.

23

Mr. Prutt noticed his mooning at the bank, and in his joky, pecking way he tittered, "You look so absent-minded, you must be in love, Neil." Yet through these days of wandering destiny, Neil was still one of our most trusty young executives, and the Veterans' Center was bringing in desirable new accounts of discharged soldiers, who might be wearing greasy tunics now, but later might become obstetricians or juke-box lessees or manufacturers of candy bars.

An unexpected number of the veterans who consulted him were Negroes, and Neil wondered uneasily if Ryan had sent them, and what Ryan had told them, and just how safe he was. But he dared ask nothing.

All this meditation was prelude to his Friday evening among the colored intellectuals.

———

He insisted on Vestal's taking the car that evening, because "he was going to another veterans' organization," and by bus and foot, he went to John Woolcape's.

Emerson had gone back to army duty, but Neil was greeted by John, Mary, Ryan, and by Ash and Martha Davis. To the surprise of everybody, including himself, he hailed Dr. Davis as a friend long trusted and eagerly found again.

With his fluid way of moving, with the woven gold chain of his wrist-watch against a skin dark-brown and smooth, Ash Davis had more an air of Parisian boulevards than of anything American, and his small black mustache suggested the French artillerist. You saw him in horizon blue. If his fellow laboratory-workers considered Ash a somewhat fancy fellow in his tastes for tennis, the piano, and amateur botanizing, they admitted that he was a solid research chemist, with a respectable knowledge of plastics. He had had three years in laboratories in Paris, Zurich, and Moscow, and in Europe he had almost forgotten that he was a Colored Man and come to consider himself a Man.

If he had hated to return to the great gray republic, yet he had returned resolutely. He was no rhapsodist about the joys of being an exile among the tables of the Café Select and the white hobohemians. The shortage of chemists in the war had given him the chance of a superior job at the Wargate Corporation. He had naively believed that he could stay there permanently, and instead of going on living out of a trunk, Martha and he had bought an ugly cottage on Canoe Heights and remodeled it.

His was a busy, useful and innocent life, and, except for Martha and their daughter Nora, he was a little lonely. He respected the Woolcapes and Evan Brewster as fighters and solid citizens, but they had no liking for the frivolous and learned conversation that was his cake.

Martha, the plump and lovely Martha with the radiant, dark-brown skin, was Kentucky-born, daughter of a Negro lawyer. In college she had been earnest about the drama, and her Nora was named in memory of *A Doll's House.* Martha never could understand that her husband was a Fresh Nigger Who Didn't Know His Place. To her he was the most exact scholar, the most honorable man, the gayest companion, and the tenderest lover of whom she had ever heard.

She gave some effort to trying to keep the poorer members of the Negro Community from considering them as just another family of social climbers. For this suspicion the poor had some precedent. In every city they had seen too many Negroes who, prosperous with hair-tonics or portentous with jobs in the court house, forgot the cabins of their grandfathers and chased something called the Best Colored Society, with its coffee-colored debutantes and coffee-colored limousines, its sweetmen and kept poets and white pansies in the salon of Mme. Noire-Mozambique, and its hunt-breakfasts complete with red jackets and mention in the society columns (colored).

But Neil did not know that there was any Best Colored Society for Martha Davis to dislike. He was making the inevitable mistake of all converts and assuming that Negroes cannot be as smug and trivial as the whites. Why, bless their souls, they can put on frilled shirts and a thirty per cent. solution of a London accent and be just as tedious as Park Avenue any time. Neil had so much to learn about colored people and then, under this revelation, about white people.

———

The Woolcapes and the Davises and Neil sat around and sat around and picked up pieces of conversation and looked at them and dropped them. Everyone was being too polite for comfort when the door banged and into the room came a man like a skilled and enchanting little comedian, and they all yelled, "Hey, *Clem!*"

Clement Brazenstar, the notorious field-agent of the Urban League, was the son of a dirt-common, black, Mississippi Delta sharecropper, whose very surname came from that of a plantation. Clem had had no college. He snatched his books (but so many of them!) out of the air when, as a youngster, he had flashed all over the country as bell-boy, cook, fertilizer-salesman, newspaperman, organizer. His mission now was to find more tolerable jobs for Negroes, to denounce black farmers who were too lazy to study gas motors and co-operative buying and (the office did not assign him to this; it was just his own notion) to bedevil white college presidents who approved of jimcrowing. He was a lover of whisky, peanuts, Tolstoy, and prizefighting. His French, which he got in Marseilles during World War I, was fair, but his Italian and Yiddish were only utilitarian.

If the Woolcapes were de-ebonized Northerners and the Davises just pleasantly brown, suggesting Arabs and the Alhambra gardens, in Clem Brazenstar the astonished Neil saw everything that the missionaries of hate meant by "a little Delta nigger clown." He was a small man, grinning, monkey-faced, popping up like a jack-in-the-box. He was midnight-black; he was black and lustrous like a fresh sheet of black carbon paper; he seemed to be black not just on the surface, like Evan Brewster, but clear through to his bones. His lips were almost purple, there was a shine of black inside his ears, to his eyes there was a tint of yellow, and even the palms of his hands were darker than pink. His face was always comic, especially when he was serious, because then he laughed at himself as well as at the world.

His small but puffy mouth was always moving in derisive parentheses, his forehead was an agitated whirlpool of wrinkles. He was as enchantingly ugly as a Boston bull, yet his skin was so darkly brilliant, he had so gay and confident a manner, that he was as beautiful as a blackbird airy on a swaying reed.

His accent was a mixture of Mississippi, Harlem and the twangy Middlewest. He frequently used the word "nigger" for himself and his friends, but he never let the enemy use it without reprisals. To most people he seemed unbelievable, because he was a perfectly natural and normal man who had never been fettered by an ambitious family, a busy school or any kind of a bank-book.

—

"This is Captain Kingsblood, a new white friend, and a good one," said John Woolcape.

Clem greeted Neil with the smile of a friendly workman, but he give little effort to it. He was as accustomed to soothing or denouncing whites as he was to spurring or slapping down blacks.

"How are you, Captain? Well, my battling breathren, it's always good to get back to Grand Republic, the Development Dainty with no Discriminations. Coming up on the bus, I sit down next to a handsome gal from Miteuropa, with her fine young Nazi boy, and he studies me and yells, 'Maw, lookit the funny dinge!' and she says in one of the warmest coloraturas I ever heard, 'Id's an outraitch and I'm goink to write to the bus company how ve Americans get crowtet in vit all kinds riff and raff.' Mr. Riff, meet Mr. Raff!"

Clem was beaming, he was laughing audibly, at his own discomfiture. The astonished Neil was to learn that this was a habit of the most incorrigible of race-champions. They found nothing quite so funny as their own defeats.

—

They were merry enough, but inevitably they told the "new white friend" about certain trials in being a second-class citizen. Talking of his own Border States, Ash Davis said cheerfully:

"It's the inconsistency of discrimination that gets the poor Sambo down. In one town in the South he can shop in any department store and ride on the front elevators and his wife can try on the clothes; and in the next one, forty miles away, he isn't allowed to enter any decent white store at all, and gets pinched if he tries it, and the elevators are jimcrowed even in twenty-story office buildings. For years we pariahs may buy magazines in the white waiting room of a station, then suddenly we're arrested by a big peckerwood cop for going in there at all.

"Captain Kingsblood, it isn't only the humiliation of segregation that riles us. It's the impossibility of telling when the simplest thing, like raising your hat to a nun, will be considered criminal, and you'll get slugged for it. It's that doubt that makes so many timid fellows go grab a razor.

"Oh, some cullud brethren praise the South because, under segregation, a certain number of sepia merchants get rich on the rest of us chosen people. In fact there's a controversy now in the colored press about whether to go North and get frozen out or stay South and get burned out. Well, either way, there's always fine conversation about being rooked."

Clem Brazenstar raged, "Say, for God's sake, are we going to start another all-night race-discussion?" and settled comfortably on the couch for same.

"Not for me. I never want to hear about our blasted race again!" proclaimed Ryan Woolcape, also making himself comfortable.

Neil said hastily, "Before you get entirely off the subject—" Somebody laughed. "—I would like to have your comments on a letter I got, months ago, from a classmate serving in the South Pacific. May I read part of it?"

Their grunts apparently meant Yes, he might, and he droned:

"I've been having a sticky job as an army criminal investigator lately and I've been surprised to find how differently I feel now about Negroes. They are very unpopular. The white G.I. has more friendliness toward the members of any alien race, because the Negro does not extend to white soldiers the same cheerful courtesy that the whites extend to one another, and that is important where men live so close together. No doubt there are excellent Negro soldiers. But in every stockade the Negro prisoners outnumber the whites three to one, on a percentage basis, and they are in for AWOL, disobeying direct orders, sex crimes, stabbings, and stealing from other soldiers, and in all these cases they are given to lying, freely and volubly. So our boys who before the war had no contact with Negroes will go back into civilian life with a great deal of prejudice."

———

Neil expected rage, but he was answered only by a silence with no particular emphasis in it, and the belligerent Sergeant Ryan Woolcape commented uninterestedly:

"Your friend is a typical cop. He isn't interested in finding good soldiers, only bad ones. He doesn't know one thing about the innumerable colored outfits—like, say, the 761st Tank Battalion—that had great records. But I will hand it to him he probably knows the effect of the story that guys like him spread all over Asia and Europe—that all of us colored fellows have tails! Did *that* make us cheerfully courteous!"

They laughed, and Clem Brazenstar ruled, "Come off the soapbox, Ryan, and let a professional talk!... Cap, what that fellow said is part true, and the truer it is, the more you whites have to do something drastic, for your own sake.

"The old Uncle Toms lifted up their voices in hallelujahs if they got treated as well as the livestock, but not the young tribesmen. They've read a book. Get it clear—the New Negro demands every right of the New White Man, every one, and he doesn't whine for them now; he'll fight for them. You white Iagos have built up a revolutionary army of thirteen million Othellos, male and female. Of course the colored boys are impolite to the white gemmuns, in a war they never wanted to fight. Their own war was closer.

"The boys that were brought up as I was, in shacks beside cricks where dead dogs and human waste floated, shacks without even a privy, where the plantation storekeepers or the cotton-buyers all stole from us and wouldn't even let us look at our accounts—some of these boys steal back. What a haunt you whites have built up!

"Segregated! John and Mary, Ash and Martha, segregated just as much as an old boot like me. Segregated! Told that we're like hogs, not fit to mix with human beings, and then your military gumshoe friend expects us to be obedient—and chummy!

"Segregated! 'Separate but equal accommodations'—new coaches for the whites and pest-houses on wheels for the happy jigs! New brick schools for your kids—see pictures in the Atlanta Sunday paper—and unpainted barns for us, and benches without backs and no desks, no desks at all, for our pickaninnies, as you would call 'em. Let the little bastards write on their knees, if they have to write—which sensible folks gravely question.

"Segregated! School buses for your darling chicks, but ours can hoof it five miles. Marble-floored hospitals for you and slaughter-houses for us. No jobs excepts the hard work, the dirty work, the dangerous work, and the white cops making their own laws to use against us and acting as provocateurs and our judges and our executioners all put together. And then your classmate complains that we won't whisper our secrets in his dainty ears! I'll say!"

And Clem yelled with laughter and looked at Neil affectionately. And affectionately Martha Davis crooned at Neil:

"Mr. Kingsblood, the Southern white man invariably tells you that when he was a boy, his best friend was a lil black rascal who was his guide and bootlegger and pimp and pal. Good Ole Jim! He never tells you he was friendly with a black boy who was studious and sober. He didn't know there *were* any colored boys like that— he still doesn't!

"And really kind, sweet Southern women who give the tenderest care to a cullud wench if she takes typhoid but are offended if she takes psychology.

"It isn't merely the major horrors that oppress us in the South— the fear of being lynched, burnt, beaten. We can forget those things, except on sultry nights with heat lightning like the flash of guns. Then you lie rigid in the dark and listen and you're terrified when you hear a car, a footstep, a whisper, terrified that the whites may be coming, and they never come for any good.

"But it's not that fear so much as the constant, quiet slaps. It's the little things, in a South that cherishes the little things—roses and Grandfather's sword and Lanier's verses and the joyful controversy between bruising and crushing the mint for a julep. It's the signs 'For colored only,' that tell a pretentious Negro female like me that she's unclean.

"I taught for a year in the Deep South, after college. I believed the story that the whites likes to have the colored teachers be extra clean and neat as an example to the children. I had a funny, rickety little old car, and I painted it white, myself. One Saturday I was coming into town, and I washed the car—it was like glass—and I was so proud of my new white suit and white shoes. And new white gloves! I got out at a drugstore, and there was a horrible old peckerwood farmer—yellow as an angleworm—and he walked over and deliberately spat a huge gob of tobacco juice right on the door of my clean car. And the other white men all laughed. Then I knew that Hell has the sign 'For colored only.'"

24

Clem Brazenstar insisted that if they spoke only of these trivialities, if they did not mention the more lusty violence in the South, such as a returned Negro soldier's having his eyes gouged out with a policeman's night-stick, their new white friend would be bored, and Clem's own virility as a Southerner would be slighted.

They all laughed again, but now Neil shuddered.

He insisted, "But there's no such violence against the Negroes in any Northern state."

"Sure there is, in race riots," Clem said placidly. "But the job-ceiling is more important; trained brownskin teachers and stenographers flatly told they can't have the job, not because they're incapable but because they're beige. And restaurants that, in this state, are compelled by law to admit Negroes, so a lot of them either keep the smokes waiting or else salt their food so much that they can't eat it. And Negroes doing war-work in factories not allowed to drink from the same bubbling fountains as the sacred whites. It certainly makes an ardent patriot out of a guy who happens to like bathing every night to be told he can't even share the same running stream of water with a Yankee farmer or a Tennessee hillbilly who earnestly believes that a bath-tub was invented to keep angleworms in.

"No, get it straight, Little White Father; in this democratic Northern town, they don't lynch Negroes—not often—but they tell us every day that we're all diseased and filthy and criminal. And do they believe it? Hell, no! But they make themselves believe it and then they make other people believe it and so they get rid of us as rivals for the good jobs that they'd like themselves.

"But what inspires us here in Grand Republic is that the vile Ethiope is not allowed to join the Y.M.C.A., the very well-endowed association to spread the example of Christ, so that his brown body won't contaminate the swimming pool and poison the feeble little sons of sons of so and so of white contributors to African missions. The Y.M.C.A.! The Yes-Men's Crawling Arena!"

"I didn't know there were discriminations like that in Grand Republic," said Neil meekly.

———

"The thing that got me most," said Ryan, "was that when I was a little kid in school here, I was friendly with all the whites, boys and girls; swam with 'em and built mud forts and skated and went on the same toboggan, and so I came to believe they really were my chums, and then when we got to puberty, they discovered I was 'colored,' and said so frankly, and when I went to see a girl with whom I've played for years, right in their front yard, I was told she 'wasn't home,' and then I saw her come out of the house with a white pimple-face that we all despised. Segregation here, Cap? No. Just quarantine!"

———

John Woolcape said gently, "Mary and I don't run into much discrimination. It does irritate me sometimes, in my basement, to have some twelve-year-old white child bellow, 'Here you, Johnny, where the hell are you?' But that's what any janitor expects. And as far as having our feelings hurt in restaurants and movie theaters goes, we just feel it's better not to take a chance on them. We stay home evenings and read or listen to the radio or play cards with our friends, and never, never go outside. Mary and I don't like squabbling and screaming, and we feel it's safer so. Then nobody can say we're bad people, and try to run us out of our home. Yes, we love our home, and here we're safe."

"So far you are!" said Clem rudely. "But the South is getting better—less lynching, more of us voting, equal pay for teachers in some places. So the North is getting worse, very obligingly, just to keep my job going."

"Yes," said Ash Davis, "the Northerner has a great future as a synthetic Lee. Take Mr. Pete Snitch, of the Snitch Brothers Steel Company of Illinois. He buys a winter home in South Carolina, and inside of two years he is more Southern-born than any born Southerner.

"He's been an iron-puddler but now he has a million, and so he and the little woman long for an aristocratic tradition, the real Walter Scott pawing charger and ivy. And there in the South he has it—magnolias and mocking birds and white columns and the glen where the gallants used to duel and the respectful poor—at least they sound respectful. The only known living descendant of the family whose house the Snitches cuckooed into is working on a newspaper in Birmingham, so Mr. Snitch feels he's taken over the family ghosts, in crinoline, along with the title-deed.

"He's a gent by purchase and a Southerner by linguaphone. But he has to prove his gentility, and the best way to do that, obviously, is to be insulting to his inferiors, and as we Africans lack his fine, Anglo-Saxon beer-flush, we're elected as the inferiors, and he yells at us even louder than a Carolina jailer, and in any conversation at Bollington Hall, Colonel Peterborough Snitch will be the first to be heard screaming, 'You wouldn't want your daughter to marry a nigger, would you?' Oh, yes, you Northerners have a great future in the chivalry and blacksnake business.

"And I have revised the old rule, to read, 'In Rome, do as the Romans do, but you don't have to claim that you invented it.'"

———

Then the race-talk became a little hysterical, to Neil a little confusing. It was broken by the arrival of Sugar Gowse, with lunch-pail.

Sugar had been born to the Louisiana canefields, but he had picked up a knowledge of tools and lathes. He was on his way now to the Wargate plant, where he was a machinist on the graveyard shift. Since his work was faultless, he believed that Wargate's would keep him on in peace time and, as naive as Ash Davis, he had bought a two-room shack where he "bached it" with his motherless son, Bobby, the fleet-footed and antic dancer, the boogie-woogie wizard of the Five Points.

His Black Belt accent was like blackjack molasses and Neil could but half understand him. He looked like an Indian, with thin lips, thin black hawk nose; tall and straight; an impression of Judge Cass Timberlane cut in basalt. He was wearing now the blue-denim blouse and overalls that were romantic as all work-clothes are.

When they tried to drag him into the race-talk, Sugar said, no, he knew nothing about discrimination, except that here or any other place, the colored folks were always the last to be hired and the first to be fired, so why worry?

Neil wondered, "But can you stand our cold winters?"

"Mister, it's colder in a Louisiana shack, full of holes, at forty above than it is here in my plastered house at forty below."

"Sugar just wants room to rest his hat. He's sensible enough not to have the constant feeling of insecurity and futility that gets Martha and me down," said Ash.

"You educated fellows are too touchy, Doc. You don't know how a worker feels," said Sugar.

"Worker!" Ash protested. "When I got out of college, I was cook on a private car—that ineffable official and his booze!—and when I finished graduate work in chemistry, my first job was in a patent-medicine dump, where I packed boxes and loaded 'em on trucks when I wasn't making up formulae."

Clem Brazenstar argued with Sugar, "You get touchy, too, when some woman changes her seat because you sit next to her in a bus. Sophie! My eagle!"

A brownskin girl had slipped into the room, and Mary announced to Neil, "This is Sophie Concord. She's a district nurse.... Mr. Kingsblood, a new friend."

"I've seen Mr. Kingsblood in the bank," said Sophie, and added,

as though she was trying not to, "being efficient and handsome!"
She looked at him with no signs of anesthesia, and he was certain
that she was the most beautiful young woman he had ever seen and
the least frigid.

———

Sophie Concord, Alabama-born and Neil's own age, was tall, like
Vestal, and frank-faced like her, but more endowed with curves and
long sweet lines that interested even a sober carthorse like Neil.
She had a generous mouth and a skin nearly as dark as Ash Davis's,
a rich brown skin that was incredibly satin-smooth, and her bare
arms were the color of a polished dry fig against the white rayon of
her rather ancient party-dress.

Sophie had once been a torch-singer in minor night clubs in
New York; she had been accepted in sequin and champagne circles
in Harlem; but she had resented having to clown for gap-mouthed
white patrons. She had turned flippantly pious, taken a knight's
oath sung to jazz, and after three hard years had become a nurse,
well trained, patiently consecrated, and very pert.

She preferred, she mockingly asserted, the care of infants af-
flicted with nits to the care of white gentlemen patrons with leers.
The exacting Ryan Woolcape admitted, "Sophie is a hardboiled
nurse even if she does look like Cobra perfume and lace pillows."

———

"Our new white friend seems to be a good guy," Clem explained
publicly to Sophie. "We've been giving him Second Year Subversive Doctrine, and he hasn't blinked yet. He must have a little drop
of chocolate in him, I guess!"

Everybody laughed—except the Woolcapes, and Neil, who felt
frozen.

"You *would* drag out the propaganda, to entertain a poor man
that wants to know about Joe Louis. He must by this time be as sick
of your racial soapboxing as I am," protested Sophie, climbing on
her own soapbox. "Tell me, Mr. Kingsblood, are you another white
slummer, or a real friend of our race?"

"You have no idea how real!" said Neil.

"He is a sweet, fine man," insisted Mother Woolcape.

"Goody, goody!" Sophie's voice, Neil thought, even when she was lamentably trying to be cute, was like summer dusk quick with fireflies. "Lots of white people think we're suspicious and hard to get acquainted with. And maybe we are. We've all had the most shaming experiences with apparently friendly whites who come around and tell us 'You're just dandy' and then go home and make a funny story out of it.

"For one white like Sweeney Fishberg or Cope Anderson, that never even notices your color if you're a friend, any more than he especially notices whether you're black-headed or red-headed, there's ten ofays who pretend they want to be chummy but are either on the make, trying to sell us something—a sewing machine or a church or Communist doctrine—or else they're taking up Social Equality for the Poor Colored Brethren, in between Bundles for Britain and Thomas Wolfe, between Dali and Monsignor Sheean. Or else they're failures in their own white world, frustrated women and reporters without a job and preachers without pews, who believe they can be important and get loved hot in our world, which they think is just panting to be patronized by some gray that once read a life of Booker T. Washington. They make us awful leery of our dear white friends. So you see, Mr. Kingsblood, we'll be examining you as cautiously as you will us."

While she was lecturing as a missionary, Neil was looking at her as a woman. She was a soft-moving cat, a bronze cat whose bronze would turn into soft flesh under the fingertips. Her breasts were firm like bronze and softer, he speculated, than the sides of a cat.

Then he shook his head fretfully.

——Don't you think you could love the race without wanting to pet its representative, Kingsblood, you frustrated white man?

Sugar Gowse got up, lunch-pail in hand, and drawled, "I reckon I like the white fellows I work with better than the biggety guys Miss Sophie talks about. At the factory, they either divvy their beer and bolony with you, or they hate you and tell you so with a crowbar. Good night."

Sugar's pronunciation was as thick as gumbo; he said "excusing" for "except," and he remarked that when the foreman "lowrated him," he had "paid him no mind." But Neil saw that Sugar had ceased to be a Nigra, a half-human creature who, had he remained in the South, would by even the kindliest whites have been rated as "pretty decent, for a darky." He had become a human being here, like Webb Wargate or John Woolcape. Only, more gay!

Neil noticed that he had not heard tonight the wild picturesqueness of speech that he had found in fiction about Southern Negroes, nor the gilded perversions of the stories about Harlem and dope and creepers. Except for an occasional self-consciously used word like "ofay," these people—it was another shock—talked like the people he knew, like all the people he had ever known, in the bank or the army or the university. Only, more gaily!

—

Clem was holding forth:

"Uncle Bodacious—I want to tell Mr. Kingsblood about Uncle Bodacious. He's the guy—he's white but he has some cullud cousins across the tracks—he's the clothhead that first invented 'Some of my best friends are Jews' and 'I'm all for unions but I hate these outside agitators.' And Uncle Bodacious is the authority who explains that the reason for segregation is that otherwise the blues would marry all the white women, and with a jackass like that, there's no use pointing out that most of us sables would rather marry a gal like Sophie than a chalkette.

"My own frau, bless her, is none of your high yallas. She's a high patent-leather. But if I wanted to marry a pink who wanted to marry me, I sure would.

"When anybody hollers that there's any importance to the amount of marriage between blacks and whites, you can be sure that he's trying to find a good, pious, obscene reason for low-grading his colored help, so he'll feel virtuous in underpaying them.

"But Uncle Bodacious's prime cackle is, 'There is no solution of the Negro Problem.' That sounds learned and ethnological as hell, but all it means is that there is no solution, this side of a nice tomb in Forest Lawn, for Uncle Bodacious!... And now, for the Lord's sake, Mary, do we get coffee and doughnuts?"

And coffee and doughnuts were what Mary did serve. They were wonderful.

———

Holding his cup and leaning over a youngish colored woman, Neil may not have appeared as a man in a dramatic crisis, but Sophie Concord and her sliding eyes and her tawny voice embodied for him all the tempting strangeness of a mythical Africa, and he felt that she should be chanting a voodoo charm instead of being emphatic about funds for the treatment of infantile paralysis.

As a recent convert, Neil longed to be close to these initiates; he wished they would call him by his first name as they did one another, but they went on gravely Mistering him. Even when he slipped and absently spoke to Dr. Davis as "Ash," he was put in his place by a Mister. He politely said "Miss Concord," but that way of addressing her seemed like the damp saucer of a women's club teacup, as he watched her throw back her head, shake her dark hair, and mutter "De Lawd!" He longed to see her in the steaming lushness of her Broadway night-spots, not eating doughnuts on Mayo Street.

Talking to her alone, he got out, "How do you feel about the future of the race?" and was fairly proud of himself for being professional.

Sophie was as crisp as Vestal. "Just what does that mean, Mr. Kingsblood? That's one of those insurance-man-on-the-telephone questions, like 'How did you sleep last night?' or 'Well, well, well, how's every lil thing this morning?' "

"Maybe it is, except I do want to know."

"Why?"

"It's——Miss Concord, I have such a liking for your friends here—and you."

"Mister, I haven't had a white banker so attentive since I worked in the Tiger Divan, in Harlem, and an ofay high financier, a jig-chaser from Bismarck, wanted to come up to my flat and look at etchings, and he was willing to bring the etchings, done by the Government, and——"

"Stop that!"

"What?"

"I really want to learn about Negroes. I'm a humble student."

"Laws amassy, listen at the man!"

"What was your college, Sophie?"

"Hm?"

"You're just another educated Alabama girl trying to be African."

"Mister, you're learning! I only had a year, and I spent all my time studying French history, God help me!"

"I didn't expect tonight that I'd find quite so many of your race that are better-read than I am."

"Don't get fooled. Mostly, they ain't!"

"The bunch here are. Don't make fun of the poor dumb whites like me. Tell me about yourself."

"Mister, don't you realize what I am? I'm that beautiful convent trained New Orleans octoroon, that passionate slave-girl with the lambent eyes and long raven tresses, standing on the block with hot blushes, and practically nothing else on, before the leering planters (or theatrical agents) with their beaver hats and beaver watch-chains. But one young man there, young Nevil Calhoun Kingsblood of Kingsblood Corners, Kentucky, pities her, and soon, along the gal'ry of a mysterious old mansion nigh Lexington, there is to be seen a veiled figure gliding—lookit her glide, lookit her, the *nebig*!

"Now, dear Mr. Kingsblood, don't try to find any of us romantic. We're a bunch of hard-working people who believe in just one thing—getting the job ceiling raised for the whole race, so that a highly competent colored girl will have a chance at a $32.75 job as a filing-clerk instead of working in the laundry all her life. That's all we are!"

But as she said it, they were friends.

He was at last noticing what she wore: a white long dress with a barbaric gold jacket, a huge topaz ring that questioned her plain-talk.

"I must be sure and remember what she has on, to tell Vestal," he had dutifully recorded before he realized that he was unlikely to tell Vestal about Sophie's costume or anything else regarding that statistical hoyden.

When the race-talk, which was resistless to them as a ball of paper to a kitten, started all over again, Neil learned that whenever a well-meaning white asks, "Wouldn't the Negroes be satisfied with——" the answer is No. He learned that a Southern Liberal is a man who explains to a Northern Liberal that Beale Street has been rechristened Beale Avenue.

He heard of colored judges, surgeons, war correspondents for the Negro press. Odd things he heard of: black Buddhists and black Orthodox Jews, colored Communists and colored Masons and Oddfellows and Elks and Greek-letter fraternities, lowly Negroes who hated all Jewish shopkeepers and Negroes so highly placed that they hated all lowly Negroes.

They came, inevitably, to the Second Question, and Neil said awkwardly to Dr. Davis, "It's probably old stuff to you, but what about this argument that the Negroes must be inferior because they didn't build a lot of cathedrals and Parthenons in Africa?"

Everybody laughed, but Dr. Davis answered gravely:

"Did you ever try building a Parthenon among the tse-tse flies? As a matter of fact, our people have built their share—along with the other slaves in Egypt and Rome. And who do you suppose built our plantation houses? The owners? And do you know how many young colored architects there are now?

"Mr. Kingsblood, you can't count on the Negroes remaining less architectural than the whites, despite the eloquence of the pecker-wood preacher who talks, in an unpainted plank chapel, about 'The Nigras that the myster'ous han' of God done fix so they cain't nevuh build no Pa'thenonses.' It's one o'clock! I'm going home!"

He felt that he had come on a new world that was stranger than the moon, darker than the night, brighter than morning hills, a world exciting and dangerous.

"I love these people!" he thought.

25

I wouldn't know about you millionaires, but I'm a working woman and I have to go home," said Sophie Concord.

——I've heard Vestal say that!

Martha Davis was to drive Sophie home. Ash suggested, "I'll walk over and put Mr. Kingsblood on a bus.... Just as well not to wander around here alone, after one in the morning. Some bad actors—not all colored. I'll promise to keep off the race-talk, though there is no complete cure for it. The other day, in the bathroom, I read a label 'facial tissues' as 'racial issues.'"

To Mary Woolcape, Neil said privately, "This evening has been exciting but I still don't know that I can tell even our friends here that I am a Negro."

"I'm not even sure you ought to, not sure at all. Why risk the humiliations we've been talking about tonight?"

There were late-burning lights behind dark curtains along Mayo Street, and from the rooms over a store came a high cackle of laughter. The alleys were filled with shadows—they may have been men lurking and they may have been barrels, but in neither case did Neil like them. Ash had nothing to say, and Neil saw how attentively he watched every sliding alley cat, every dusky loafer squatted on his heels on a grating.

Neil insisted on their walking from the bus stop up to Canoe Heights, and Ash's house.

It was a small house and low-roofed, but Neil saw from its great window, which made one whole corner a cage of glass, that this was what was called a "modern house," in revolt from all the Cape Cod and Tudor of Sylvan Park. He had heard Mr. Prutt condemn such structures as anarchistic, but he had never been inside one.

Ash murmured, "You must come in for a drink," and Neil entered a room that repelled him and fascinated him by its conscious bareness, its freedom from all silver-boxery. It had two centers: the huge corner window, through which he could see a net of pale lights far down below them in the Five Points, and a severe fireplace, of polished stone, without a mantel. The few chairs, covered with rough-woven material, were of unconventional shapes, more attentive to the human form than to Chippendale; and on the wall, which was lined with something that seemed at once to be wallpaper and metal, there was just one picture, an orgy of reeling triangles. On the small piano was a lump of awkward black sculpture.

"Well—so this is a Modern House," Neil marveled, as Ash mixed a highball at a competent closet-bar.

"So they call it."

"Who was your architect?"

"Me, so far as there was one. This was a kind of shed, and Martha and I made it over. But you know, I think this house is the symbol of my shame. I'm afraid I really did it to spite Lucian Firelock, and keeping up with the highbrows is worse than keeping up with the Joneses. You know Firelock?"

"Advertising manager at Wargate's—Southern guy? Yes, a little."

"He's a Southern Liberal—Vanderbilt University—the kind that wants both to keep us evil darkies in our place and get credit for being very tolerant—wants us to study the same things as a white man, but do it under the table. Firelock lives two doors from here in a dreadful old Noah's Ark with trimmings like fungus— only place he could get, in the war shortage, poor gentleman!

"He was agitated when he found I was a neighbor. He's used to having 'darkies' in the neighborhood, only they're supposed to remain poor and humble and grateful. He looked down my nose at me when he first saw me. Then his kids got to playing with my Nora, and we got half acquainted, and the worst of it is, the poor devil likes me better than anybody else around here, and he can't admit it.

"When I made over this place, I didn't realize at first that I was going out for this Modern Style, which is, of course, a Freudian form of Puritanism, just in order to impress Firelock. The worst of it is, I succeeded, and every time I see him go by, he's looking envious. Can you beat that for a low human motive on my part? And this room is so blasted chaste that I long for a golden-oak rocker under a picture of the old church by moonlight. I'm a Rotarian in professor's clothing.

"No, that's not true. (God, I am talking so much tonight! That's because almost every evening I stay home.) I'm not in the least either an affable businessman or a heated race-agitator.

"I'd like to live in an ivory tower, play Bach, read Yeats and Melville, be an authority on the history of chemistry and alchemy instead of a plodding laboratory hack. But the white scholars won't accept me, so I try to become an ardent race-crusader. But it's a role, and I'm not a good actor.

"I have an affection for our friends tonight, but I find Clem too emphatic, Ryan too ridden by Communist Jesuitism, Sophie too imitative of the white Talking Women, and John and Mary, whom I honestly love, too smug. My notion of an agreeable evening would be to sit by the fireplace with George Moore, saying nothing. Oh, it's not easy for me to bellow for our 'rights'—even though I do emphatically believe that they *are* our rights.

"I think I'm telling you this so that you may know that neither we nor our propaganda are as simple as we seem. Nor are you!

"I think you have some quite special interest in the race. You certainly are not a philanthropic dabbler. What is it?"

——Here's the man that really might have something to tell me, that might become the friend I need. I don't want to go on blabbing this, but——

"Ash, I think possibly I have some Negro blood myself, way back."

There was no sympathy from Ash nor surprise but only a quiet, "Oh. Well, perhaps it's something to be proud of. Perhaps you're in a better war now."

"But I'm scared of being found out—and by people for whose opinions I don't really care a damn."

"If you need a refuge, at least verbal, Mr. Kingsblood, I shall be glad if you'll come here."

"I certainly shall. Good night, Ash."

Dr. Davis distinctly hesitated before he said, "Good night—Neil."

—

As he tramped on home, a good-looking but stolid-looking youngish man, through streets where clerks and foremen lived, streets like the aisles between boxes in a dark warehouse, there was more hope than apprehension in him. If he was still nervous about a conceivable future as a Negro, he no longer hated anything in it; in spirit he was on the side of the bars with Ash and Sophie and Ryan and Clem.

When he came dubiously into the bedroom, Vestal woke only to jeer, affectionately, "Some evening you vets must have had!" and went back to sleep.

It was astonishing, he thought, that his beloved wife did not instantly perceive that this evening had been the most critical in his history. Would Sophie have seen it?

—

Vestal and Neil were off for their two-weeks summer vacation in a rented cottage on the North Shore of Lake Superior. Before they went, Mr. S. Ashiel Denver, cashier of the Second National, gave them a dinner at the Pineland Hotel, to celebrate the glory and profitableness of the Veterans' Center. In the pink glow from the rose-shaped wall-brackets against the Pompeian frescoes of the Fiesole Room, they were ushered to their table, handsome with silver and roses, by the senatorial Drexel Greenshaw, with his dark-brown dome, his clipped white mustache.

As they toyed with sardines lying exhausted on little couches of cold toast, Vestal looked after Mr. Greenshaw's majestic back, and admired, "He's quite the old-fashioned darky, isn't he! I bet he loves pork chops and watermelon and shooting craps."

Mr. Denver agreed, "Yes, he's a fine old fellow. Never gets fresh or tries to act like he was white. He knows his place and does just what he's told and says 'Thank you,' instead of trying to make you think he owned the hotel, like some of these flip young niggers would."

But Mrs. Denver was not quite sure that she could grant Drexel a license to live. "He gets a little *too* friendly, for my taste. I do think one has to keep up standards in these critical days, with the breakdown of morale and all, and I can't say I enjoy seeing a colored waiter acting like he belonged to the family. I don't see why they don't get rid of all the nigger help, in a place that claims to be so highclass, and hire some nice waitresses—but American ones, not all these thick Scandinavians."

"Oh, I think all these darky waiters mean well. Only thing that bothers me about them is, I simply can't tell them apart," Vestal said broadmindedly, looking at the three waiters now in sight, one squat and black, one slim and coffee-colored, one very tall, very pale, and spectacled. "Can you, Neil?"

"Oh, yes, they seem like individuals to me."

Mrs. Denver wheezed on—there was always a sound of corsets in her voice—"But Neil, even if you can tell 'em apart, you don't like that old fussbudget of a headwaiter, do you?"

"Yes, I do. I think he's a fine old gentleman."

"Gentleman? My, what a funny word to use about a darky!"

After the festal dinner, they drove to the Denver abode, just back of Neil's house, and in came a spate of neighbors: Don and Rose Pennloss, and Cedric Staubermeyer, the much-traveled dealer in paints, wallpaper, linoleum, and other objects of art, with wife. There was pleasant but intellectual conversation, and Neil was able to compare the prosperous white man's range of cultural interests with the primitive outlook of the Negroes to whom he had listened, three evenings before, at the house of a colored janitor:

"I think it's getting quite a bit warmer."

"Yes, but June was awfully cold."

"Oh, did you think so? I didn't think it was colder than usual. Not especially, I mean."

"Wasn't it? Well, I felt like it was colder."

Flashes like that, thrown off without effort.

But Mrs. Cedric Staubermeyer was more studied and, it might be said, educational:

"My, my, doesn't seem like ten years ago, just seems like yesterday we were in Rome. We saw the Eternal City through and through, and the ruins, very ancient, and the Vatican and the airfield, and the lady at the English teashop, she was English, and she said my! we seemed like old inhabitants to her, and of course we had a great advantage, not staying at a hotel but at a pension where we met the native Italians, we met several, and they explained everything to us, and such an interesting Frenchman, my! he spoke the most beautiful English, just like Cedric's and mine, and imagine! he told us he had a cousin living right here in Grand Republic!"

But Mr. Staubermeyer put in a sour note:

"We never looked his cousin up when we got back here, because I suspect this French guy was a Jew, and you know what I think of Jews, and so would you, if you had to do business with them, and so I said to my wife, 'Oh, the hell with him! I can stand foreigners in foreign parts,' I said, 'and I like the natives all right, except for the way they live and do business, but let's just keep 'em abroad, where they belong.' "

———

Their range of interests was by no means limited to travel. They went thoroughly into the prospects for pheasant-hunting this coming fall, the crookedness of their congressman—for whom, however, they would continue to vote, lest a Farmer-Labor-Democrat get in, and the facts that Mr. Jones was buying the house of Mr. Brown and Mr. Brown was drinking too much. They skillfully compared the prices for women's stockings in Tarr's Emporium, the Beaux Arts, and the shops in Duluth, Minneapolis and St. Paul, until Mrs. Denver cried, "My gracious, we've been chatting away so that I never realized it was so late, but you don't mean to say that you're going home, Neil?"

He was.

26

The waves of Lake Superior splashed among the bare dark roots of the birch and cedar and white pine, and their log cabin smelled damp and fresh. They dived into the cold water and came out blissfully screaming, and on the warmer small lakes, back in the solid forest of the Arrowhead, they canoed, they fished for small-mouth bass, and made a whole warfare of shooting at tin cans floating. And in all this peace, Neil never stopped fretting.

This was old Chippewa country. Xavier Pic must have driven his canoe through the shadow of these cliffs on his journeys to Thunder Bay. There was, indeed, still a Chippewa Reservation near their cabin, and Neil had prickly ideas about getting his Biddy to love the redskin brethren and gradually becoming able to tell her that she—though, of course, a very sweet little white girl, too—was part Chippewa, part Negro, and wasn't it all nice and natural!

Like every thoughtful parent in every age of history, Neil consoled himself, "My generation failed, but this new one is going to change the entire world, and go piously to the polls even on rainy election-days, and never drink more than one cocktail, and end all war."

He sat in the car with Biddy at a small encampment of Chippewa women and children, who were lodged in bark huts for the summer, selling baskets and toy canoes of birchbark to the tourists.

"Biddy! Look at the Indian pickaninnies, or whatever they call 'em. Aren't they cute! Wouldn't you like to play with them, play scouts and make campfires and everything?"

"No."

"Why not, dear?"

"They're dirty."

"The little Indian children? Dirty?"

"Yes."

"Well, maybe they are, but think of beaver-dams and, uh, war-bonnets. Aren't they wonderful?"

"No."

"But why do you object to their being a little dirty? It's just smoke from cooking. After all, Daddy's little girl gets pretty dirty, too, sometimes!"

"They look like niggers."

"And what's the matter with—Negroes?"

"I don't like 'em."

"Did you ever know one?"

"Yes."

"And just who, now, besides Belfreda?"

"Little Eva."

"She wasn't a Negro. She was white."

"I didn't like her."

"May I put it to you, Elizabeth, that you are being a horrid little girl?"

"With a curl in the middle of my forehead?"

"Oh, hell!"

"Oh, Daddy, you said it, you did—you said 'Hell.' Hell, hell, hell, hell, hell!"

In the midst of her feminine seizing of an advantage, Biddy was so enchantingly pink and white and gleeful that he loved her despairingly and realized, like cold dough in his brain, that all the cheerful little viciousnesses of common belief among nice people are more devastating than bombs and great wings.

Because he had a fortnight of leisure, because it occurred to him that Vestal was "the white wife of a colored man," he studied her as they loafed on the lichen-cushioned rocks. She was less intelligent and worldly-wise than Nurse Concord, he thought, less warm and beautiful, but possessed of more clarity and control. She was a "fine type of young American matron," clean, athletic, well read—well, well-enough read—and Interested in What Goes on in the World. She had a piety adequate for Sylvan Park, and derision of sentimentality. She had, indeed, everything, except any individuality whatsoever.

In a matter of weeks, he had learned that without suffering and doubt, there can be no whole human being. Vestal had never known suffering except in child-birth, nor any upsetting surprise and doubt except on her wedding-night.

In one thing she was clearly superior to a good many virtuous women: she did not enjoy intentional cruelty. But Neil was discovering that unconscious cruelty can be very effective.

Vestal, remembering old days, kept singing, "Coon, coon, coon, how I wish my color would fade."

——That's what I am. What Biddy is. A coon. A moke. A boogie. Something so grotesque that a fine lady like Vestal couldn't imagine hurting its feelings.

Prince trotted up, shaking off a shower of mud, and Vestal

scolded him, "We shouldn't have changed your name, dog! You're no prince. You're nothing but a dirty, good-for-nothing nigger!"

And smiled at Neil so trustingly.

———

He saw that, to Vestal, his devotion to the Negroes would be half insanity and half naughtiness, if she knew. Why take on such a silly character? And two weeks can do an extensive healing, in a Northern magic of gray rocks and orange lichens and sweet pines and sliding red canoes and blade-blue distances across the tremendous lake. He bathed with her in shock-cold water and, for all his hobbling, they raced like children, and he came back to town cured of his frenzy.

He came back to it an energetic young banker—white.

27

That Neil was going to be a bank-president, but with a salary ten times that of Mr. Prutt, was too obvious for Vestal to talk about it. What interested her was the house that would then dignify their position. Neil was amused by her ambition to buy half of The Hill from Berthold Eisenherz and build the perfect house that every woman wants.

Could he, Neil teased, interest her in a "modern type" house, all windows and plaster, such as he had seen when—oh, well, he'd seen one some place.

He could not! She would patronize nothing so cold and queer. She had decided on a stone Norman manor house, only with sleeping-porches, a pine-paneled Rumpus Room with a built-in bar, and a doll's-house for Biddy which should have—or am I too crazy? Vestal wanted to know—a doll's-bathroom with real running water!

"Is that important for her?" Neil asked.

"Nothing could be more important, because she'll be a little girl only once, you know."

They had gone so far toward the assemblage of this Norman dungeon as to have planned to buy a new gas-stove.

The war with Japan had ended, and while Vestal was properly glad that their friends would be coming home from the South Pacific, she confessed to an equal delight that now the manufacturers would turn from arms to unimaginable domestic treasures: plastic dressing-tables and crystal coffee-pots and automatic dishwashers. She was already thinking of the wardrobe, in fabrics still uninvented, which she would prepare for Biddy when she went to Bryn Mawr, a dozen years from now.

At breakfast she suggested to Neil, "I'll come downtown today, and you buy me a lunch and we'll look at the gas-stove that I've set my girlish heart on. It's a jewel of a stove, a rose, an eagle, a Bedlington of a stove, a stone, a leaf, a door, and I love it more than I do virtue—at least, it's more practical."

When he saw it, the stove did possess most of the splendors that Vestal had advertised, and she gloated, "That'll make even our present dump of a kitchen look like the manorhouse of our destiny."

He sighed, "But you still do like our house, don't you?"

"Oh, Neil, no matter how I rave about future palaces, I love our little shack violently—our own place, that not even a crazy, wild-haired Democrat government can take away from us. Comes the depression, we'll retire there and grow onions in the bathrooms and be happy as grigs—how happy is an average-size grig, do you suppose? Oh." She nodded toward the arm-folded and wearily back-tilted salesman. "I think you can jew him down five dollars on the price. Try it."

——I wonder if a Jew likes that phrase, "jew him down," any better than my people like "sweating like a nigger"? Oh, quit it! You're the possessor of a beautiful wife, a beautiful gas-stove, and you were going to forget all this race-hysteria.

It was on that same afternoon that Ash Davis came to sit by his desk and say formally, lest anyone be listening, "Mr. Kingsblood, may I disturb you for a minute?"

"Nobody around, Ash."

"Neil, again I'm here begging. Bad news. Several colored returned soldiers arrested in South Carolina for a murder they couldn't have committed. Sophie and I are raising a fund for lawyers. I want all the money you can spare. And I warn you that if you're so simple as to give me one cent, it will be only the beginning of the leech's daughters yelling 'Give, give!' "

Neil decided what he could afford, and made out a check for slightly more than that. He was longing for the cool, humorous, devastating talk of Ash and Clem and Sophie.

"When can I sit in with all of you again?" he urged.

"Clem won't be back in town for weeks. But would you like to have dinner with Martha and me at my place—maybe Sophie, if I can get her? What about tonight?"

His lie to Vestal was almost automatic, this time. But he felt pitifully that he would not again be able to glow with her over her beloved gas-stove. She was a great lady in her assumptions; she was a poor child in her trusting heart.

When he sat with the Davises and Sophie at the table which had popped out from beneath a bookcase and turned all that end of the severe room into a dining-room, he had nothing to say. They belonged to a world that was closed to Our Mr. Kingsblood of the Second National; and the more taboo Sophie was, the more tempting were her soft, sealbrown hands, moving surely as a cabinet-maker's or lying in peace.

He played with his food (which was plain hamburger steak, after excellent mushroom soup), and he demanded, "What are you three arguing about? Who is 'the Turk' and why is he a stinker?"

Sophie said, rather wearily, "He's a colored fellow named Vanderbilt Litch—a usurer—the only suspected colored Quisling in town. But you wouldn't be interested."

"Why wouldn't I?"

"How could you take any interest in the fussing of us local busy-bodies? Our sign is 'For colored only,' and that let's you out, Captain."

——Don't say it! Don't tell her you're colored! Shut up! Don't say *anything*! You've already told Ash and the Woolcapes—too many. Wait now, wait!

And with that he babbled, "That lets me in, Sophie, because I've discovered, here recently, that I'm part colored."

Her mouth stayed open, her fingers, like brown reeds, stayed motionless in air, holding a cigarette, her breast pulsed, and then her astonishment deepened into a look of tragic commiseration for him. The nurse who had been a small-town-neighborhood girl was tenderly concerned for him, but it was the Broadway singer who spoke:

"No foolin'?"

———

He heard himself discussed, genially but firmly.

"Why, you smart little devil," crowed Sophie, "to think that you passed and got away with it, and I never guessed!"

"But I didn't know till just recently, I tell you!"

"Really he didn't," said Ash, like a schoolmaster.

"Come off it!" Sophie gloated. "How could you help feeling that rhythm, little Neil? Why, I tell you, when you're black, you're in the groove, you're in the grove, you got reet, you got meat, you got feet, you can feel that ole mumbo-jum right out of Africa zizzing right through you!"

"That's enough, Sophie!" from Ash.

"Well, you get the idea, anyway. Maybe I was trying to strut a little Harlem stuff, but honest to God, I don't see how anybody could have Congo genes in him and think he belonged to those hot-fisted, cold-hearted freaks that call themselves the white race! Anyway, congratulations, pal!"

"Stop it!" said Ash. "Neil, her jungle blood is pure fake, and so is her aversion to the whites—a heterogeneous group with many virtues. Sophie is a conscientious uplifter and record-keeper. But———"

There was a "But" in everything Ash and Sophie said—not in what Martha said, because Martha didn't say anything. The nearer Neil came to them, the more complex they seemed in their dual attitude toward him as a friend to be protected and as a convert to be exploited as publicity for the race. Without much reference to his feelings, they speculated whether "Even though it might be hard—just a little hard—just at first—might it not be a good thing if you did come out frankly as a Negro?"

But they thought they might let him off for a while.

It had not occurred to him that the news that he was a Negro, with its public branding or crowning, could come from anyone save himself. He realized that the words had gone out of his mouth, swift and unrecapturable, and that it depended only on the whim of these three and of the Woolcapes—any Woolcape—whether he should be betrayed. But if he was slightly in fear, he was also relaxed in accepting Sophie and Ash and Martha as his own people. When Sophie rose, he said, "I'll trot out to your car with you."

He sat with her in her shaky coupé and held her hand, warmer than any hand he had ever known, with the curious warmth that has nothing to do with the thermometer, that is cool and smooth while it is hot and seamed.

But the Sophie who had just been advertising the unrestrained joys of the jungle was reluctant. When he urged, "If I do get known all over as a Negro, can I count on you to make up for the people I'll lose?" she burst into shrill scolding:

"Damn it, you won't lose anybody that's worth keeping! Man, don't expect us brownskins to be *sorry* for a person who's lucky enough to become a brownskin!" She relented: "There, there, mother's baby!" It was too exactly the wifely tone of Vestal. "Didums get crestfallen—crest shot to pieces? Mother make it well!"

She kissed him. He had not known a kiss like that, the closeness of it and the softness and the frankness of what it said. But she hastily drew back.

"Sorry! I don't kiss white men, and even if your heart is good and black, your poor brains are still white, like a baby's. Good night!"

He looked after her car as it rattled off.

——I can't do this to Vestal—so excited about her little gas-stove! I've got to get out of this African world. It's too complex for country-folks like Vestal and me. Prutt, I'm coming home!

28

They were all back from the wars, all his friends: Rod Aldwick, the sturdy Judd Browler, "Elegant Eliot" Hansen. They were back, and they powerfully assumed that no matter how rackety the rest of the world, Good Old Neil would not have changed.

Day on day he never saw Ash or Sophie. Vestal and he had Judd or Eliot and their wives for dinner, and insensibly he again became the Sterling Young Banker in every part. His racial adventure had been a dream, perhaps a nightmare. The good sense of The Boys made his fancies seem sentimental, and he suspected that the Rodney Aldwick who had been his model in dancing-class, in hockey, in the display of loose silk ties, could not have been as vicious about colored troops as he remembered.

At the Federal Club, he heard Rod debating those colored troops with another returned officer, Colonel Levi Tarr. Now Rod was only a major, but he seemed to Neil so much more of a major than Tarr was of a colonel.

Levi Tarr had been assistant general manager of his father's department store, the Emporium. He was tall, scant, spectacled, and while he was reported to have led a great counter-attack in the Bulge, no one could see this professional ribbon-seller waving a sword or doing anything else with a sword, while you pictured Rod Aldwick eating his shredded wheat with a dirk, scratching himself with a bayonet, writing love-letters with a saber.

Neil had to agree, however uneasily, when Rod laughed at Colonel Tarr's nervous praise of the black soldiers. Then he was confused all over again when he found a partisan of the Negroes in his own cousin, Patricia, daughter of his mother's brother, Uncle Emery Saxinar, the energetic dealer in pumps and valves. Pat had always been a comely girl but peering and withdrawn. Back now after serving as ensign in the WAVES, she was noisy and interested. She praised the colored sailors, and one evening she astonished Neil by extemporizing:

"I want to deny this rumor that the Daughters of the American

Revolution are the women's auxiliary of the Ku Klux Klan, because there are no Negroes in the Klan, but there must be a lot of them in the D.A.R., since the first man killed in the American Revolution was a Negro."

Vestal protested, "A fine, ribald barroom louse you got to be in this woman's war, Pat!"

Neil was troubled.

———

Rod Aldwick came to dinner, with his handsome, fresh-faced wife, Janet. Biddy had been allowed to stay up long enough to greet her "Uncle Rod," and she swarmed all over him. She made a proposal that if she was allowed to stay up half-an-hour longer to talk things over with him, she would not be naughty at all for two and a half days.

"You're wonderful with children, and I bet you were with your troops," said Vestal to Rod.

At dinner, Rod volunteered his plans for the whole future of his son, Graham, aged nine but already doomed. Graham would, like his father, go to Lawrenceville with a couple of summers at Culver Military Academy, go joyfully on to Princeton and Harvard Law, enter his father's firm, enter the National Guard, be a gentleman, marry a lady and, when his time came, defend Anglo-American Civilization and the Bar Association against Spigs, Wops, Kikes, Chinks, Bolos, and the Pan-Islamic Union. And with any luck, he ought to be not just a major but a major-general.

———

The emotions have their own logic, swift and incomprehensible, and it was by that logic that Neil thought of Winthrop Brewster, son of the Reverend Evan. Winthrop was lucky; he would not be sent in a plush-lined coffin through Princeton and the officers' club; he could honorably be independent and poor.

And by that same logic, dismissing his promise to himself that he would play safe, next afternoon Neil drove down to the little house of Dr. Brewster, off Mayo Street.

He had not thought out the whole reason for his going; he had nothing pertinent to say when he walked in on a surprised Evan, his wife Corinne, who was less dark and a good deal less cordial, and the children, Winthrop and Thankful, those true Yankees whose family had been in Massachusetts ever since a very black Pilgrim ancestor had fled there, if not by the *Mayflower*, at least by the underground, which is the same thing.

He had not lied to Vestal, this time; he had telephoned Shirley to explain that he might not be able to get home for dinner.

Business.

29

It was not that Winthrop and Thankful were much less black than their father, or had straighter hair or beakier noses, but they had even more assurance as American citizens. The easy confidence with which they looked at Neil, the straightness with which they carried their shoulders, made them seem not like products of the slave-block and the cotton-field, but like what they were— American school children, unusual only in unusual gentleness.

You cannot hear constantly at school that Americans are the bravest, richest and most generous people in history without absorbing a certain pride, which is not too objectionable if it be tempered by a more serene and informed culture at home.

Neil lumbered in, explaining that he had never forgotten Dr. Brewster's sermon. "Just thought—coming past this way—might drop in and say hello." Winthrop took to him as to a robust older brother, and Thankful rather considered him the type of man she had been thinking of marrying but hadn't noticed around here anywhere.

Out of pulpit clothes, in a brown jacket, a soft white shirt and an insignificant blue bow-tie, Dr. Brewster was as much the post-office worker as he was the clergyman, and if his grammar persisted in being more accurate than Neil's (or Rod Aldwick's) and his vocabulary more flexible, he was much jollier. His laughter came from a huge chest, a large mouth, a tolerant heart. His wife was more watchful of the intruding white man, more suspicious, less willing to risk the security of the family. She was a more delicate image than Dr. Brewster, with a thin nose carved in brown agate.

Neil suspected that both of them nervously wanted to know what he had come for, and he understood that very well, since he rather wanted to know it himself. They chatted about the weather and city politics, in that small room that was the more cramped with a venerable typewriter sitting on a homemade and unpainted table, and books of history and theology and anthropology on seismographic old chairs.

Winthrop was glad to see a male visitor who might know something about electricity. He demanded, "Were you ever a radio ham?"

"No, but I used to sit in with a friend who was."

"Come down to the basement and see my set."

Neil regretted that to him the collection of wires and tubes in that tiny cellar looked like a junk pile, and when Winthrop boasted, "I get Miami, right along!" he was impressed.

"Have you any favorite ham that you talk to?"

"Yeh, a fellow in Dallas, Texas."

"Is he colored?"

"I've never asked! I guess maybe he's white—anyway, he's silly about the Civil War. But what difference does it make?" Winthrop rebuked, and Neil felt humble.

"What do you and he chat about?"

"Mostly about *jai alai*. I want to learn it, some day. But naturally, what I'm really interested in now is radar. Don't you think that's the coming thing?"

"I certainly do," said Neil, who knew of radar only that it had something to do with fooling icebergs.

Winthrop rattled, "I want to get into electricity as soon as they'll let me, at the U. I'm going there this fall."

"I went to the University, too," said Neil.

"Swell!"

"Aren't you a little young for it?"

"Golly no! Why, I'm seventeen! Did you know I was salutatorian in high school this spring?" Winthrop spoke not priggishly but with artless pride. "But of course I was lucky, having Dad to coach me. We did four years math in two. Say, look, Mr. Kingsblood, you must do a lot of fishing in the Arrowhead country."

"I used to. Northern pike in Sawbill Lake."

"If I could only do that—camp and swim and fish—zowie! Instead of having to sit around and listen to all this race-talk. What's the use of it? These days, everybody except a hillbilly knows that colored and white folks are exactly alike, same as black and white kittens are. Didn't you always know that?"

"No, not—uh—not entirely." Neil hastily tried to get out of his examination with an enthusiastic, "Why don't you spend a summer in the Arrowhead? I could tell you some fine places."

The boy turned his face away, and muttered, "You forget. None of these summer places will take in colored folks. Not even Dad and Mother. Oh, gee, I guess we still do have to go on with this race-business and all the talk, talk.... And then, we haven't much money. I have to work all summer, and save for the U."

"What are you doing, Win?"

"Well—it was all I could get—I asked at the electric company but they turned me down hard—same at the radio stores. I'm scrubbing floors in the waiting-room and the men's toilet at the railway station."

———

Neil had to knock together some explanation of his intrusion. When he came up with Winthrop, he said to Mrs. Brewster, "Will you let me tell you something you already know? Win has most unusual talent. I'm proud to know him. And he represents something I'm trying to find out, on behalf of both the bank and myself: the progress of all the so-called minorities here—the Finns and Poles and Negroes and, uh, the Lithuanians and———" His geography was running out. "And everybody! I hope you'll accept me as a student."

Evan Brewster had accepted him before he was born. Corinne Brewster began to look as if she might accept him after he was grown up.

"I wish you'd let me do something: get hold of Dr. Ash Davis and Mrs. Davis and maybe Miss Sophie Concord, and let me take you all to dinner at this Bar-B-Q place I've noticed. I'm afraid it's a little impertinent to ask you so late, but if you could manage it——"

They could but encourage so earnest a disciple.

On their way to the Bar-B-Q, Winthrop and Thankful, the raceless and young, each clung to an arm of their burly new banker friend, and interrupted each other in stories about their collie pup, Algernon C. Swinburne.

——But what would happen if we met Rod Aldwick on the way?

The Bar-B-Q was almost filled with a long lunch-counter, but there were tables, like card-tables, with twisted-wire chairs. The napkins were of paper. The bill of fare featured spare-ribs, ham, hamburg steak, and tenderloin—which was out; and the waitresses were young women with good will, gum, and no training. It was like any other cheap restaurant in the entire land, where democracy has begun with food and clothing and adjectives, and often promises to end there.

Most of the diners were black workmen, a few of them in overalls. But, with a feeling of having neighbors now in the Negro world, Neil saw John and Mary Woolcape and greeted them more readily than he ever had S. Ashiel Denver & wife. And in the village talk with the Brewsters and Sophie and Ash and Martha, over the ham and cabbage, he could join more familiarly now.

It is not, perhaps, a remarkable fact that a good deal of that talk should have been concerned with the woes of Negroes. Well, and if Neil had heard a good deal of it before, he had also repeatedly heard everything that Mr. Prutt and Mr. Denver had to say about the woes of bankers and Rod Aldwick about the woes of serious lawyers and duck-hunters.

The liveliest topic tonight was the Reverend Dr. Jat Snood, who was probably the nastiest piece of goods in Grand Republic.

With the drifting of the great denominations, the Methodists and Baptists and Presbyterians, from moaning and hallelujahs to indirectly-lighted Gothic and pulpit book-reviews, the job-tortured masses in America had dribbled into new churches which promised that they should have salvation if they could not have larger paychecks, and which encouraged them to howl publicly at the Devil, the Pope, and Wall Street, in recompense for not daring to howl publicly at the Boss. In lofts and empty store-buildings there had been organized such wondrous new creeds as The Church of God in Christ Through Bible Salvation, and The Assembly of the Divinely Appointed Saints, which signified ten tired men and women, eight hymn-books, and four benches.

With true American enterprise, spiritual leaders who in less cultivated days would have been Indian-medicine showmen or itinerant lady milliners had seen that they could make a tidy living by appointing themselves ministers or even bishops, renting a hall and setting up a church, with no annoying work except yelling loud and mourning low, and taking up three collections at every meeting.

Among these latter-day Barnums in Grand Republic was one Jat Snood, who had not finished high school but who was a Doctor of Divinity. He was the owner and chief ballyhooer of a vast shed down on South Champlain Avenue and East Winchell Street, in the South End, and he had romantically named it "God's Prophecy Tabernacle: Founded on the Book: Christ for All and All for Christ."

It is true that the Reverend Doctor had never been able to stay in any one town for more than five years, because he knew only fifteen sermons and fifty vaudeville tricks, and even his faded and gnarled and gum-chewing audiences got sick of him. But while it lasted, he did very well financially, because he titillated his crowds with ginger and hell-fire and made Swedish hired girls and German grocery-clerks and Yankee linemen feel that if they could not meet Hiram Sparrock at the Federal Club, they could meet God and His angels and the souls of the elect at God's Prophecy Tabernacle: contributions voluntary (but frequent). Jat screamed at them, in high-toned polysyllables flavored with jazz and slang, that if they were ill-used by the snobs among the Old Americans, still they could be snobs themselves, and he invited them to look down, contemptuously, upon all Jews, Negroes, Catholics, and Socialists.

Ash Davis explained to Neil, at the Bar-B-Q, "There's two or three Snoods in this town, though Jat runs the biggest crap-game of them all, and they've trained their congregations as perfect recruits for the Ku Klux Klan. They aren't so comic when their gangs of Christian knights beat up frightened little brownskins and burn their houses. As a friend of our race, do you think there's anything you can do with Mr. Snood?"

"I'll certainly try," said Neil.

And knew that he certainly would do nothing at all.

———

A young man in uniform as captain in the army air corps, cinnamon-colored, erect and smiling, joined their table. He was, they explained, Captain Philip Windeck, who had been a senior in the University of Minnesota engineering school when he had enlisted, and who had flown on many missions over Italy.

"You know," he said to Neil, "I really haven't the right to be wearing this uniform any more, but I had a reunion with the fellows tonight. Tomorrow, I go back to overalls."

"What doing?"

"I'd like to earn a little money and get married and take my wife back to school with me. I thought, with some engineering and a little aviation experience, I might get a job. Well, the airfield here and the automobile dealers all turned me down, but I've been lucky enough to get back the job I had before I ever went to engineering school—washing and greasing cars at the O'Toole Cut Rate Garage. Drex Greenshaw—I'm engaged to his daughter—thinks he could get me on as a bus-boy. But I feel it's better for my martial vanity—the returned hero that was going to be so modest when he was greeted by the mayor and two bands—to have white ex-privates yelling at me, 'Here you, boy, get a hustle on, you black bastard!' "

As always, all of them, including Phil Windeck, roared at his plight. It was better to laugh at the Thankless Republic than to grow faint and whining. Only Neil looked angry. He was rather gratified when he was accepted by this fellow veteran of the Italian campaign as a friend, and it was as a friend that he greeted Ryan Woolcape when he came in—out of uniform, out of the Army.

Neil was in deep now, deeper than he knew.

———

Like any good woman pleased that her new beau is welcomed by the family circle, Sophie Concord watched Neil in his approach to Phil, to Ryan, to Evan's children, and looked proud. It was Sophie who suggested to Neil, "The Brewsters and Davises have to go to a committee meeting—naturally. They couldn't get through a night without one. Committees are the most habit-forming drug that exists. But let's Ryan and Phil and you and I go to the Jumpin' Jive and see the brownskins at their most uncommitteeized. You're a typical good-hearted slummer. You meet Ash and Evan and conclude that all of us are intellectuals with pure hearts, who just lead hell out of the race. Let's go take a look at the ones that get led—and do they hate it! I don't know whether the dumb fieldhand or the city hepcat or the rich sepia professional man like Dr. Melody most hates getting taken in hand and being led into the Ethiopian spiritual commonwealth. Anyway, let's go see the flick-chicks."

———

The Jumpin' Jive was noisy enough and tinseled enough, but it was not as evil as the romantic heart of Neil had hoped. It was a large, L-shaped room decorated with pink and gilt lattice-work with artificial orchids. An orchestra of drum, piano and clarinet, manhandled by three fat merry Negroes in plum-colored dress-coats with gold derbies, gave Grand Republic versions of Duke Ellington. Colored sailors and soldiers were dancing, some of them with white factory girls, as close-packed as though this were the most expensive resort of gaiety and sweat in New York. With dark or ashen colored girls, laughing but not talking much, danced young Negroes with the elegance and suavity that seem natural to them.

Neil belatedly realized that at another table was Borus Bugdoll, proprietor of the Jive, and that the girl with him, pert in filmy green tulle, was Belfreda Gray, and that they were grinning at him. He complained to his table, "There's a girl that used to work for us and that hates me—Belfreda. She's a tough baby. Now don't go and get socialistic on me, Ryan, and tell me she's a victim of environment."

"Why not? Let's all go over and talk to her. I've known her since she was a kid. You've probably never had the cultural advantage of being slapped by a hired girl."

And Neil, vastly surprised, found himself really looking at the Belfreda who for months had slept just down the hall from him, and discovering that she was a Nell Gwyn in ebony, eyes and smile and ruffles and spirited flexibility of morals. With the languidness of that lovely orange-seller insulting a lord, she drawled:

"Why, if it isn't Mr. Kingsblood! I'm surprised, seeing you in a dump like this. I thought you never went no place except to teach Sunday school."

"You know I never taught a Sunday-school class!" protested Neil, his manhood as a duck-hunter insulted.

"I heard diff'rent."

"What are you doing now, Belfreda?"

Belfreda and Borus glanced at each other as though this was a very funny question, but she took pity on the untutored white burgher, and condescended, "I sort of got my own beauty-parlor. Me and another girl are partners. We only got choosy customers— high-class ladies and preachers' wives—and there ain't a bit of use your trying to date 'em up just because you know me. They already got sharp fellows, with real dough."

She looked at Neil with defiance, she looked at Sophie with dislike, she looked at Borus and giggled.

Neil begged, "I hope you don't remember us too badly, Belfreda."

Airily, "Oh, that's all right. You were dumb, but *Mrs.* Kingsblood, she was swell. She's got savvy. Nobody can blame a white man like you for being slow, but her, she's so smart she could almost be colored. Well, glad to seen you, Mister."

"Uh—Belfreda—I'm sorry we didn't get along better. Maybe a good deal of it was my fault."

"Yes, it was! You always acted like you was expecting me to be mean, and so I'd *get* mean. Jesus! I wasn't raised in no parlor! I was raised in a shoeshine dump, with all the white guys trying to make me when I was thirteen. First, at you folks' house, I thought I had such a nice room, but you and Vestal used to sneak in there and laugh at my stuff and the way I kept it. Listen, Mister, when you make enough beds for other people, you're so sick of it you ain't got much pep left for making your own, and you figure there's *one* place where you ought to be allowed to be just as God-damn sloppy as you want to. But even there I wasn't safe. And whisper about me— whisper, whisper, whisper!"

"Belfreda, I'm extremely sorry."

"Okay, forget it. Well, glad to seen you."

———

Our Mr. Kingsblood had the sensation of having been dismissed, and he choked and meekly followed a muted Sophie, a smiling Phil Windeck, a derisive Ryan back to their table. But before they could voice the "Well?" that was arching their lips, he burst out, "She's magnificent!"

Miss Sophie Concord did not tease him for having been snubbed by his ex-cook. Quite the contrary. She snapped matrimonially, "Just how intimate were your relations with Miss Belfreda Blackbird, my friend? Eh? That's what I want to know!"

———

In an alcove of the Jive was a table at which gathered habitually the sardonic sires of the colored colony: Drexel Greenshaw, Wash the bootblack and, when he stopped over in town to see his sister, Mac, the porter of the *Borup*. Sugar Gowse, the machinist, was with them tonight. Since Drexel was to be his father-in-law, Phil Windeck tolerated the handsome old Squire of the Damask Tablecloths, and he lured Neil over to the Uncle Toms' *Stammtisch*.

They looked uncomfortable at having one of the people who tipped them intrude on their private conversation as gentlemen.

"Mr. Greenshaw, Captain Kingsblood is getting to be a real friend of the race, and he wants to know whether Mac and Wash and you, who have such a chance to study the white man when he's showing off, really think all white men are stupid."

Drexel glanced cautiously at Neil, and hemmed, "No, no, Phil. They just don't have much chance to get on the other side of the swinging door."

Mac the porter stared at Neil almost as at a fellow man, and held forth:

"I'm sure Captain Kingsblood will excuse me if I say—he's one of the few *smart* people that can afford to travel on the *Borup*—and the way I look at it, as the fellow says, white folks are awful nice, but of course they're all babies, and have to be taken care of. They never look things over real sharp, way we colored folks have, since we were knee-high to a traveling-man. They're like some Delta colored fellows that we all know—believe what the preachers and the law tell 'em. You can't blame 'em, poor things."

Drexel commented, "I think higher of the whites than you do, Mac. Now take a man like Mr. Hiram Sparrock. No colored fellow ever made as many millions as he has, and that takes brains.... And he give me a five-dollar tip once!"

——Already they've almost forgotten that I'm white. Only, I'm not! Can they see the colored blood in me?

Mac said scornfully, "Mr. Sparrock? He's the worst baby of all. Why, them pills he takes all the time, they ain't nothing but sugar—his doctor told me so, Dr. Drover—and he said I could give him all he wanted."

Sugar Gowse ventured, "You older gentlemen got to excuse a machine-hand for butting in, but way I see the white gentlemen, they're always playing big. My foreman, he asks me can I fix a machine, and I does, and then he takes hisself a chew of tobacco and struts hisself around like a turkey gobbler and he says to the super, 'Look what I done!' But they ain't so mean to you and don't lie about you so much if you help 'em. I'm always studying on how to handle 'em, the bastards—oh, excuse me, Captain, sir."

They looked at Neil like solemn black owls in a circle; they shifted to politics; but presently, fascinated by the unforgettable topic, Drexel went on. He had been magnificently trained in servility to white men, but also he had seen too many of them drunk and lecherous in his restaurant to have any awe of their Mumbo Jumbo; and if a white man deliberately asked for the truth—let him have it!

"Handle 'em? Ain't but one way to handle a white man: uncle-tom him. Be humble, tell him how smart he is, tickle his shoulder-blades and pick his pockets.... I mean, that's what *some* fellows says, Captain!"

Mac protested, "I don't like this uncle-tomming. Course I *can* do it——"

The venerable Wash cackled, "You can and I does! They's just like babies—got to have a sugar-tit. Only they's got awful big shotguns and awful strong ropes, so I says, 'Uncle-tomming, here we is,' and I uncle-toms their silly, grinning heads off.... Course I don't mean *you*, Mister!"

"Oh, we darkies are all notorious for humor and humility!" said Captain Philip Windeck, U.S.A.A.F. But with his smile he looked to Neil for forgiveness.

—

He walked with Sophie to her tenement, two blocks from Mayo Street. He said, "Lot of life and color there tonight. It makes me feel more like a real member of the race. They're so—I don't know anything as brave as the way they laugh at themselves."

"My benevolent but sophomoric friend, there isn't any They among human beings, only We!"

He was not quite sure, at her door, whether or not he was to kiss her. She was. He was not. As he limped away, for a time he thought less about Sophie than about Winthrop Brewster *versus* the favored son of Rodney Aldwick. Which side was he on, which side demanded the loyalty he had once sworn as a soldier? With a purpose definite but not admitted, he marched back to Evan Brewster's parsonage. Through a window, he could see the huge shoulders humped over a desk.

Dr. Brewster came to the door looking, in his dressing-gown, like Othello played by Paul Robeson. Inside, Neil said evenly—you didn't lie to a man like this as you did to a Buncer—"Something I would like to tell you, Dr. Brewster. I must get it off my chest quick, or I'll turn prudent. I've found I have some Negro blood in me, way back. I've told Ash, Sophie, the Woolcapes—no whites. In your opinion, is it my duty to come out and acknowledge it to the world?"

He expected Evan to snarl, "Certainly!" whereupon he could turn angry and defend himself, but Evan gasped, "I don't know—I don't know." He stared, looking more like the warlike Moor than any neat Doctor of Philosophy, in that small house of learning and post-office jobs, while Neil told about Xavier Pic, and ended with a curt, "Now how does it strike you I ought to act?"

"I'm not sure at all." Evan was moving his vast hands curiously, as though he wanted to give a blessing. "I *believe* I'd say that there is no reason at all for your acknowledging something that doesn't really exist but is just an American superstition—a theoretical kinship to my people."

"Oh." Neil was disappointed that no one wanted him to volunteer, disappointed and markedly relieved.

"But Neil, when I think of the growing attacks on my people by swine like Jat Snood, when I picture men lighting our torture fires with the cross of Christ, then I'm moved to say, 'Yes, certainly, you must give up wife and father and ease and good repute and join us.' But I don't *know*!... Confound it, let me think, before I butt in on your life, will you! Come again in a few days and—you might try praying, mightn't you?"

Neil attempted to look as though he piously agreed, but he could hear Ryan Woolcape chuckling.

When he was safely back in Sylvan Park, where monsters of holiness like Evan Brewster were as improbable as lizards like Jat Snood, Neil tried to be defiant.

——That was the silliest thing I ever heard of: a man with some responsibility going to a black religious fanatic to whimper, "Please sir, may I give up my wife and my daughter and my home, in order to hoist gin with Belfreda at the Jumpin' Jive?"

It did not work. He recalled, from university days, attending a storefront church and hearing a white Okie preacher shout, "When the Lord ketches holt on you, you can kick and scream and holler, but He ain't never going to let you go!"

30

He would hear this Reverend Dr. Jat Snood and see whether the fellow was as eloquent or as evil as the admiring world declared, and he would take Vestal with him into this obscure suburb of the dark city of man. For however jumpily Sophie might attract him, it did not occur to Neil that his devotion to Vestal could ever diminish—a phenomenon which has been the cause of rage to free women in their contest with secure wives throughout history.

When he suggested the spiritual slumming, the joke was that Vestal protested, "Why, I'm surprised at you, wanting to hear a vicious Ku Kluxer like Snood and his race-prejudices!"

"Oh, I'm all against him. I have a considerable respect for Negroes," said Neil, affably.

"Since when?"

——Could she really stand it if I came out and told her? Oh, don't be a fool, Kingsblood!

His cousin, Patricia Saxinar, former officer of the Navy, was about the house that evening of early fall, and they took her along. "Though," said Pat, "I never did like to hear little dogs yap."

"God's Prophecy Tabernacle" was as humble as the stable in which the Savior was born, but much better publicized. It was a shed holding eight or nine hundred people, built of secondhand boards so cheaply painted over that you saw the old nail-holes. As you crossed the weedy and stinking waste-lot, scattered with ancient tires and decayed shoes, on the side of the tabernacle you read a sign in three-foot letters, "Low-down on the international conspiracy, revealed by God's Word & Dr. Snood."

The unplastered walls inside were scrofulous with red signs depicting both the Soviet premier and the Pope as demons leering through the flames—"which seems fair enough," said Pat Saxinar. Hung at the far end was a diagram indicating that Napoleon, Tom Paine and all the Rockefellers and Vanderbilts were in hell, which promised a highly diverting show, lasting through eternity with tickets free, for the poor bakers and butchers and factory-workers who filled the hall. They gave the place a pleasant domestic flavor: hard-working fathers and mothers, in Sunday best, with children sucking lollipops. They were the salt of the earth; also, when used by dictators, they could become the saltpeter of the earth.

Pat fluttered, "Nice, plain folks, and my word, how they would enjoy a nice, plain lynching to break up the monotony. As a worshipper of Abe Lincoln, I love 'em, but I'd be terrified of this Old Testament gang, led by a Snood, if I were a Jew or an Italian or a Negro."

Neil remembered that Pat's relationship to Xavier Pic was of the same degree as his own. He could see these neighborly faces, these worn, bleached faces, horrible in the torchlight of his dream.

Before the service, the audience strolled at the back of the tabernacle, gossiped, agreed that the rain and the machinations of the Vatican had been somethin' fierce here lately. Children ran after dogs and dogs ran after black beetles. Mrs. Jat Snood, a scared and shriveled woman, stood behind a book-counter, which had formerly been an ironing-board, selling copies of a magazine called *Trumpet on High*, which was illustrated with half-tones of Jerusalem and Colonel Charles Augustus Lindbergh.

The ushers, solid men who looked like stone-masons, wearing solid blue suits which looked like stone, affably patted the human mortar into vibratory folding chairs, and on the platform, the All for Christ Silver Trumpet Orchestra played "Hello, Central, Give Me Heaven," and mounted frantically to "Hark, the Herald Angels Sing" as that modern version of a herald angel, the Reverend Dr. Jat Snood, bounced across the platform, knelt center-stage, with head bowed but not so bowed that he could not count the audience, and raised his tremendous voice in prayer, assuring God Almighty that if He listened this evening, He would hear a lot of extremely perplexing mysteries solved.

Snood leaped up then, as brisk as though he had not just been engaged in the presumably startling experience of chatting with God, and skipped to the pulpit, on which were a Bible, a pitcher of water, and a bunch of Russian thistles. But before he got down to the sermon of revelation which (except for the collection) was the chief business of the evening, he led them in three hymns, flapping his arms as though he were scaring away crows, and he gave them the devil for not coming through better with the hard cash (his phrase) in the collection box.

Snood looked like neither a mystic priest, a dangerous demagogue, nor a scoundrel, but like an ambitious small-town businessman who is ingenious about window-displays and a little hard on delinquent debtors. He could be dynamite to his followers, yet he was a short, square, bushy-haired merchant with the latest thing in octagonal rimless spectacles.

He was droning, he was illiterate, he was dull. But he had two gifts of genius: a magnificent voice, on which he played as on a mouth-organ, and a yet more magnificent lack of scruples. He was indifferent as to who got lynched, so long as he made six thousand dollars a year. He had a very sweet, natural little pride in making so much, for in the barbed-wire line, to which he had been trained, he had never got above $22.75 a week, and plenty of the barbed-wire fraternity had laughed at him and insisted that he never would make good.

He often said playfully, after private prayer-circles, "Mother and me have no yen for caviere and champagne wine, but we do want to see Atlantic City and make a trip to the Holy Land before we die, and stay at the best hotels."

He has often been compared to Abraham Lincoln and Huey Long, as a potential leader of the Common People. Jat is young yet; he was born in the early 1890's, and he may still have some very interesting things to show the cynical journalists who think he is funny and unimportant.

He began his gospel with the zest of a man who takes cold showers:

"This ain't any sermon that I'm going to give you! It's a plain bellyache! I'm getting good and sick and tired, and God Great Almighty is getting good and sick and tired, of having the gang of Jew Communists that run our Government in Washington hand over our wages and the education of our dear prog-geny to the hell-hound agents of Rome and Moscow!"

He explained things. Essentially, he explained them just as the fastidious Major Rodney Aldwick did. He explained that there was an International Conspiracy of Jewish bankers, British noblemen like Sir Cripps, Soviet plotters, Mohammedan priests, Hindu agitators, Catholics, and American labor leaders ("though not the union rank and file, my brethren, for you and me belong there; it's the big bums of grafting leaders that I'm gunning for").

He explained that the English are the lost tribes of Israel. He explained that the dimensions of the Great Pyramid can be used to prophesy almost anything you want—though probably not whether it will rain tomorrow and spoil the picnic—he did not *think* the Pyramid would do that for you, though he certainly had heard some awful amazing things about that ole Pyramid.

Even handier for prophetic use, he said, were Revelations and Ezekiel, chapters thirty-eight and thirty-nine. The Biblical Rosh, he told them, is clearly Russia, and Mesheck is Moscow. He rasped:

"The United States Senate, the old boys there fuss and fume and get in a sweat under the arms, not on their foreheads, because they ain't got anything behind their foreheads, and all because the old goats are trying to figure out what's going to happen between Russia and Uncle Sam. Well, if them Senators would come to me and say, 'Doctor, what is going to happen?' I would say to them, 'Boys,' I would say, 'I'll just open the old Book and tell you just exactly what will happen!'

"But do you suppose the people would have the sense to elect *me* a Senator? Not on your tintype—not them—though there is a dear old lady out here on a farm in Tamarack County, a dear old Christian lady who is a regular contributor to our work, God bless her, and she writes me that she gets down on her knees every night and prays that I will be nominated and elected to the Senate and go to Washington and so give God a chance to take a hand in running the Government.

"But I wrote back and told her, 'No, Sister,' I wrote her, 'I think maybe my work here in dear old Grand Republic, with its gamblers and agnostics and pimps, is more necessary, and God willing, and providing some of you milk-and-water Christians, that keep your hearts and your pocket-books buttoned up so tight, will occasionally come across with something sweeter unto the Lord than a dime or two-bits, we will get the devil and the Jews and the radicals on the run, and start the Kingdom of God right here in this small city, like once it was started in the hick town of Bethlehem—in the Holy Land, I mean.'"

Toward the end, after a happy interlude devoted to the collection, Snood's voice became hard, rhythmical, deep, like a brazen clock striking:

"I haven't said so much about our colored friends tonight, but you come tomorrow night and I'll reveal something about those black and accursed Sons of Baal, whom God turned black for their ancient sins and made into the eternal servants of the white man. I'll tell you about the Jewish plot to put all of us under the black heel of these degenerates—something the newspapers are afraid to print, and that'll make you sit up in your seats and shiver.

"The time hasn't come yet to revive the Klan, but when we do, I want all of you, my dear saints in Christ, to realize what it means to erect in high places the cross that regenerates, the fire that purifies, the Book that gives wisdom, and the whip and rope that were used by our Lord himself upon the money-changers in the Temple, and that we shall use upon the fiends, in the black image of Satan, who have run away from the kindly Southland to force themselves, by the thousands, into our factories, our restaurants, our very homes and beds! You bet! You come tomorrow night, and you'll learn something!

"And now, O loving master, gentle Jesus, send that our message tonight shall, not by our power and eloquence but by Thy grace, have touched the hearts of all suffering mankind let us pray."

———

On their way home, under the generous September moon, Neil drove in silence, Pat was silent, after grumbling, "As an issue-confuser, that Snood is a magician; he managed to make me simultaneously love the Communists and the Roman Catholics."

Vestal rambled, "I didn't like him, did you? I thought he was very vulgar—as ignorant as these clowns of nigger preachers that Rod Aldwick is always taking off—you know: 'Brebben, you is done been stealin' moh watuh-melonses dan is rightfully comin' even to Massa God's black chilluns!' "

She laughed boisterously, and Neil thought that it was less the horrors of Snood than the pleasantries of wives like Vestal that would make him join forever that "clown of a nigger preacher," Evan Brewster.

———

When, after banking-hours, he went again to the Brewsters', he had to wait till Evan came home from his post-office job. In an old sweater, he looked like any other working-man. His hand rested quietly on Neil's shoulder, and his eyes had the look, tender and unwaveringly steady and not entirely sane, of a saint of Byzantium.

"Please sit down, Neil. I ventured to do something—to slip out to Sylvan Park and walk past your house a couple of times. I saw Mrs. Kingsblood and your little daughter in the yard. I'm sure they never noticed me. I was careful not to disturb them. They just saw another darky who probably had a girl in some neighborhood kitchen.

"I thought they were both unusually fine people—indeed, since they were yours, I ventured to love them. And I asked myself, have I the right to do anything that would help drag them into the Battle of Humiliation?

"I don't think so. It's my battle, but I can't see that it's theirs—or yours either! Maybe you owe that child and that bright, lovely, confident-looking young woman something more than you owe the race—if you owe it anything. I can't even tell you that the Lord will guide you. Either you believe that already, or you will never believe it. Neil! Don't tell!"

Winthrop galloped into the room, which was his normal gait of entrance anywhere, and he yelled, "Hey, will you teach me gin-rummy, Captain?"

"Sure I will, if you'll call me Neil!"

"Well, okay. But couldn't I call you 'Captain'? I'm nuts about military titles!" said the reactionary young American scientist.

31

It was accident—there had been no conscious plan in it. He met Sophie Concord on the street, invited her to lunch, and she nodded Yes. He did not feel that they were "compromised" till he had hesitated, "Where do you suppose we can go?"

Then he saw all that his question meant, and it was horrible to him to have said, to a woman more intelligent and better-bred than any he knew, what amounted to, "You must not forget that you are a colored wench, and what dive is so slatternly that it will admit a monstrosity like you? And it is probable that even my asking you amounts to rape."

But there was no guilty coyness in her matter-of-fact "We might go to the Shaker Shicken Shack. That's a sepia joint—out on the Old North Military Road—on the left-hand side just after you turn away from the Big Eagle River. Meet you there? One o'clock tomorrow?"

There was no reason why he should have been as jittery as though he were going to be married or hanged the next day. He was a steady man, a married man, and a banker *sans peur*, and he was merely going to take lunch with a high-minded district nurse. Yet all afternoon, all evening, he felt guilty toward Vestal, he felt that he would probably be fired if he were seen at a colored resort, he felt as sickeningly loose as Curtiss Havock.

When he put it to himself frankly, "Just what are your intentions toward this young woman, if you can get away with them?" he had no answer except a shaky explanation that if he ever did come out as a Negro, he would need some one more friendly than Ash Davis, more courageous than Vestal.

Would, in fact, need Sophie.

———

The Shicken Shack was a streakily whitewashed shanty of old boards, low and unsteady, and when this white man parked his car and ventured in, the small old Negro proprietor, the two bulky Negro waiters, the half-dozen Negro guests, all stared at him, waiting for something unpleasant. To their primitive experience, the white man's burden always consisted of bills, writs, and trouble.

"Uh—I'm to meet Miss Sophie Concord here," he tried.

"You know Miss Concord?" the proprietor said grudgingly.

"Why, yes."

"The nurse?"

"That's it."

"Dark-brown girl?"

"Yes, I suppose———"

"Never heard of her. You got the wrong place, Mister!"

There was a hissing of small laughter around him, behind him, all through the place, but before he had time to get angry at this gross instance of race-prejudice, Sophie blew in, panting with being late, throwing "H'are you, Punty?" at the proprietor, and having for Neil nothing more compromising than "Wonderful September day."

Punty reluctantly gave them a table in a distinctly segregated corner at the far end of the bar, in an alcove with portraits of Count Basie and Kid Chocolate, and assumed, "You'll have the Fresh Southern Terrapin, folks?"

"Two Maryland fry and beat it, Punt," said Sophie. To Neil, then, "This is a horrible little hole, isn't it?"

"It's not so bad."

"Oh, yes, it is. It's worse. But I'm used to it, and anyway, this is the sort of place where you white gentlemen expect to work your will on us poor, beautiful girls."

"Sophie! I know you're being highly humorous and so on, but you don't seriously mean that you think I invited you to lunch with any—uh——"

"Evil intentions? I have some such skittish idea."

"Honestly, you make me sore! Why should you think that?"

"Isn't it the only thing that would bring the two of us together? We don't belong in the same room. Oh, I don't mean any nonsense about difference in shades. Only a bumpkin with a mental age of ten thinks anything about that, nowadays. I mean, I'm the working woman and I'm the uplifter, worse than a nobody—I'm the pest that constantly buzzes around and annoys the prosperous somebodies like you. We don't harmonize. Any more than a cat and a dog."

"Cats and dogs do sometimes like each other and even lie down together, Sophie."

"Hey, less of that discussion of lying down together, my worldly friend!"

"Worldly, hell! I'm a back-street suburbanite, with much less experience of the bright lights than you have. I'm so unworldly and such a backwoodsman that, I give you my word, I hadn't thought about it till now. But I see no basic reason why I shouldn't fall in love with you, and make all the low gentlemanly proposals. What reason is there?"

"Let's see. One: you don't know me."

"You and I knew each other five minutes after we'd met."

"Two: I don't especially like you."

"That's another lie. You look right now as if you liked me."

"Oh, that? That's just playing the game—sort of expression a good-natured gal is expected to put on, in a fly-by-night joint like this."

"Oh, God, Sophie, you know I'd much rather take you to the Fiesole Room——"

"Or to your home?"

A metallic silence, before he said, rather coldly, "You know that would take me a little time—entirely aside from the ethics of introducing one's love to one's wife. I can't jump from being a cash-register to being a raceman on a soap-box in six months. It took too long to build the register. I can't take you home till I can take my own self there."

"And how would Vestal like it? Aah, you see! You wince when I call that woman 'Vestal!' Of course you do, Neil. Poor baby, you've been brought up to the strongest superstitions since Feudalism. I think maybe I could be reasonably in love with you, because you're broad and red and white and meaty and honest, just as I loved my last man because he was slim and dark and devious. But no more hole-and-corner loves for me. I'm a nurse, and a good one. And I'm an American and blatantly proud of it. When I look at Lake Superior or the Root River Valley or the Mississippi bluffs below Red Wing, I get all trembly, and I mutter, 'Breathes there a girl with soul so dead!' And I remember that I've been an American for eight generations! And we Old Families are very snooty about our loves.

"If you did have the courage to come out as a Negro, and so got turned down by that ice-water woman, Vestal—oh, I've seen her, at public-health meetings, at a distance—and if you came running to me, hurt, then I might love you—hot, baby! But you'll never do it. Something will give you a scare, and you'll yell for Mother Vestal, and go back to being a super-banker and whiter than Stonewall Jackson on Sunday."

"You may be right—you may be right, Sophie."

He was staring at her dark-red lips, at the curve of her bosom under the jacket of her utilitarian suit. He thought of her as a woman, warm and enveloping; he thought of her as a fiercely competent human being who knew the evil of the world and fought it with laughter. He admired the humor of her mouth, which was never tight with meanness, admired the cinnamon of her cheeks, which made the women of Sylvan Park seem washed-out sacrifices. But more than her bodily magic, he admired her resoluteness.

"No," he was grumbling, "I don't know that I can come out. The cards are stacked against me. And you're right. I do love Vestal."

"You're telling *me*!"

"But maybe she won't be able to stand by, if I get in trouble. How could she? She's been educated to believe that God's purpose in creating the universe was to lead gently up to the Junior League. But—so—when—if I need you, will you be there?"

"I doubt it."

"Hm?"

"Darling, the loyalty to the good white massa during his critical struggle to get elected representative from Plantagenet County is clean gone out of me. I could love you like a lady Casanova—I even like to contemplate kissing you and having those Norse God arms around me—but I don't get any farther with such unworthy thoughts than you do with a like fancy for Nurse Concord. Our last great kiss has done been kissed. Oh, Neil, darling, darling one-per-cent-solution lover, you might have been a grand New Negro if you hadn't been brought up as a suburban Christian white gentleman! But as it is—farewell forever, for maybe a couple of weeks."

"Rot!"

"I beg your pardon, Mr. Kingsblood!"

"The fact that we've been honest—and I think quite caddish—about Vestal has pulled down the blinds between you and me. You'll always have me on your conscience now."

"No, just on my phone-list. Dear Neil, good luck.... Hang it, I wonder if I ever *will* fall in love with you, you blasted Yorktown drill-sergeant!"

———

Fondness for Sophie and Ash had fixed in him a partisan view of the whites' mouthings about the Negro, and he heard plenty of such mouthings now, with the increasing dislike among the citizens of Grand Republic for the colored factory-workers who, during the war, had been tolerated as patriots.

These were the great days of gold and crimson October weather before the long Northern winter set in. Once, Neil would have devoted the enchanted season to golf and shooting, but now he seized the last free afternoons before the invasion of ice to hobble rapidly about the courts of the Sylvan Park Tennis Club with Vestal, the fleet and silver-armed.

There was no real clubhouse but only a cabin like a white country schoolhouse, for balls and rackets and lockers of liquor.

That afternoon gave pure zest of living—the white flannels and shorts of the players, the twang of the rackets, the lively scoring, sun and air and motion and the autumn leaves. After the game they sat beside the courts on camp chairs, attentive to highballs: the veterans Eliot Hansen and Judd Browler, with wives, Curtiss Havock, Neil's brother, Robert, and his Alice, Rita Kamber, wife of the cranky doctor, and Lieutenant-Colonel Tom Crenway, who had recently returned to his printing-business, with his Violet, who took her melting eyes into all sorts of reforms and charities and then froze them.

They were generous friends and neighbors, reflected Neil, and he was grateful for the loving kindness with which they had let his lameness cramp their games. Nowhere in the world was there such neighborliness as here in the Middlewest. There was none of the obsequiousness of the humble toward the gentry, of the fight for precedence among the wives of doctors and lawyers and merchants that staled the air of Europe and Great Britain and the British colonies—including New England. These were his affectionate friends, and the standard-bearers of democracy.

They mentioned the newspaper account of a mild stabbing at

the Jumpin' Jive, last evening, and the increased Negro migration to Grand Republic. Colonel Crenway said that he wanted to define the present place of the Negroes in our civilization, and they were glad to help him. Curtiss Havock had learned "the real truth about the niggers" from fellow-marines who came from the South, and Colonel Crenway, invited to dinners at plantation-houses near his training-camp in Mississippi, had acquired such secrets as are rarely divulged to Northerners.

Most of the neighbors accepted the Crenway-Havock report, though Rita Kamber and Neil Kingsblood said nothing at all, and Violet Crenway flirtatiously questioned a few clauses. Violet often observed, looking into the bulging eyes of philanthropic and otherwise guilty old gentlemen, that she just couldn't help being a liberal and a highbrow. She was on all known committees, for and against practically any Cause, though she was not distinguished so much for action as for displaying her neat little bust and drowning eyes. Violet also explained that she "knew the Negroes first-hand, thoroughly," which meant that she had once had a colored cook.

Thus the group worked out an American Credo about the Negroes which is here presented in summary:

No person has the right to judge or even to talk about Negroes except a born Southerner or a Northerner who owns a winter home in the South. But all Southerners, whether they be professors at Chapel Hill or pious widows in Blackjack Hollow, are authorities upon all phases of Negro psychology, biology and history. But the term "all Southerners" does not include any Southern Negroes.

As infants, all (white) Southerners, including cotton-mill hands, had colored Mammies, of whom they and their fathers, all of whom were Colonels, were almost excessively fond.

All Negroes, without exception, however pale, are lazy but good-natured, thieving and lecherous and murderous but very kind to children, and all of them are given to singing merry lyrics about slavery. These are called Spirituals, and they are beautiful but funny.

All Negroes so revere the godlike white man that no Negro wants to be mistaken for a white man, and all Negroes (which is pronounced Nigras) want to pass and be taken for white. This is called Logic, a favorite subject in Southern (white) colleges.

Any Southern white man, upon meeting any Negro, including judges and congressmen, invariably says, "Here's a dollar, Jim, you black rascal, and you go around to my back door and get a big meal of vittles." Indeed, Negro welfare is the sole interest of all white Southerners, and since it is also the chief desire of the Negroes, we have the agreeable spectacle of the Southern Negroes as the best-paid, best-housed, and most extensively and intensively educated group in all history. This is known as the New Industrialism in the Sunny South.

Negroes are not human beings but a cross between the monkey and the colonel. This is proven by their invariably having skulls so thick that, as experiments at the University of Louisiana have conclusively shown, cocoanuts, sledge-hammers and very large rocks may be dropped upon their heads without their noticing anything except that they have been kissed by butterflies. This is called Science.

(But what it really all comes down to is, would you want your daughter to marry a nigger?)

All Negroes, including college presidents and bio-physicists, spend all of their lives, when they are not hanging around white folks' kitchens, in drunkenness, dice, funny camp-meetings, and the sale of marihuana.

Persons who maintain that, psychologically, socially, industrially, Negroes are exactly like the whites are technically called "trouble-makers," and their heresies are "a lot of confused, half-baked ideas," and all pretty women should answer them by saying, "If my husband were here, he would horsewhip you for trying to give the Nigras a lot of false ideas." This is officially known as Loyalty, or The Heritage of Our Gallant Defenders, and is particularly prized by the Lees and Jacksons who produce our patriotic Confederate films in Hollywood.

Even if these cranks that go round criticizing the white attitude toward the darkies are partly right, they don't provide any Solution, and I make it a rule to never pay any attention to these cynics that don't Furnish a Practical Solution to the Whole Problem. "You're very smart," I always tell them, "but what do you expect *me* to do?"

All Negroes constantly indulge in ferocious fighting with knives, but all Negro soldiers are afraid of and abstain from ferocity, fighting and all forms of cold steel. This is the branch of wisdom called Folk Ways.

Since they are all indolent, no Negro ever earns more than eleven dollars a week, but since they are all extravagant, out of that sum each of them spends eighty dollars every week in the purchase of silk shirts, radios, and the premiums of the Big Creek & Hallelujah Burial Society.

(It ain't a question of prejudice; it's just a matter of freedom to choose your own associates; and let me ask you this: would you like your daughter, sister or aunt to marry a colored man, now answer me honestly.)

All Negroes who move to Chicago are perpetually chilly there, especially on July afternoons in the rolling-mill, and they are ceaselessly homesick for the warmth, cotton blossoms, pecans, magnolias, grits, black-eyed peas, pork chops, watermelons, corn bread, banjos, jails and congressmen of the Southland, and whenever they see any real Southern white man, they rush up to him and volunteer a confession that they should never have left the South and their God-given, natural, Caucasian, meridional guardians.

All Negro males have such wondrous sexual powers that they unholily fascinate all white women and all Negro males are such uncouth monsters that no white woman whatsoever could possibly be attracted by one. This is called Biology.

All Negroes who reside in swamps are extremely happy, and laugh their heads off at the pretentiousness of Negro would-be doctors, lawyers and them phony highbrows in general.

(And just what would you do if some big black Nigra breezed up to you and said, "I've been necking with your daughter, and so what?" And believe me, that's what we'd have, if them mokes made just as good dough as you or me.)

All mixed breeds are bad. This information we owe to the British, to whom we also owed the original importation of a good share of our slaves. Thus, a mulatto invariably lacks both the honor and creativeness of the whites, and the patience and merriment of the blacks. So, the reason why so many mulattoes display talent and high morality is because they have so much white blood, and the reason why so many extremely dark Negroes show just as much talent and morality is because it simply ain't so. This is called Ethnology, Eugenics, or Winston Churchill.

The Nigra press is full of lies about injustices to the darkies, and down my way we would correct the editors by gently showing them a rope. This is called Good Breeding.

All Negroes, including Walter White, Richard Wright, and Brigadier-General Benjamin Davis, have very funny names, like Sim Sowbelly, Cleopatra Gutch, and I Will Arise Pipsqueak, which proves that all Negroes are ridiculous, and how would you like your daughter to become Mrs. I. W. A. Pipsqueak? This is called Genealogy.

Any writer who portrays any Negro as acting like a normal American is either an ignorant Northerner or a traitor who is trying to destroy civilization.

In discussing the education of Negroes, it shows both profundity and originality if you start by saying, "They got to learn to walk before they learn to fly," and, later, when the matter of Heredity has breezed into the conversation, to look pretty profound and explain "Water can't rise higher than its source." This is a branch of Dialectics called Argument-by-Metaphor, as favored by women and clergymen.

All Negroes are inefficient, which is the reason why, during the war, they were able to organize so efficient a movement to jostle white persons every Wednesday afternoon at 3:17, and to drive white women into the appalling horror of doing their own housework, that it was the envy of the German General Staff. For seven months, all Negro women incessantly shouted at white ladies, "You'll be in *my* kitchen, by Christmas." I know that this is true, because my Aunt Annabel, a woman of probity, told me so.

There may be a little discrimination against Negroes in backward sections of the South, but nowhere in the North is there any discrimination whatever.

In fact, to be authoritative about it, *the Negro Problem Is Insoluble.*

Did I ever tell you the story about the nigger preacher that was bawling out his congregation——

——

When the American Credo had thus been outlined, Judd Browler doubted, "I think some of that goes a little too far."

But Vestal Kingsblood, who had gone to college in Virginia, insisted, "No, I think it's a fair picture generally."

Brother Robert, great-great-great-grandson of Xavier Pic of the islands, exulted, "I'd be for a law to make it a crime for any man with a single drop of nigger blood in him to pass for a white man. If one of my girls was deceived into marrying a fellow like that, I'd kill him with my bare hands!"

But the hands that Robert held up were better fitted for signing letters than for garroting.

Neil silently looked at him, looked at his neighbors, good and kind and generous and literate.

Violet Crenway piped up then, with some enthusiasm for herself as a thinker:

"All of you miss the point. The darkies aren't really so bad. Some of the educated ones are just like us—practically. But where they are all going haywire is in wanting to rush their advancement too fast, instead of taking it naturally and depending on their own honest, unaided efforts to so develop that eventually, *some* day, they'll make us whites recognize their evolution.

"I always say to my colored friends, 'Yes, yes, I know there are some talented members of your race who don't get their due. I'm a regular rebel myself, and I believe in you coons grabbing all you can get. But let me remind you of something maybe you haven't noticed. There's just been a war on. Europe isn't settled yet, and there's a lot of labor trouble and so on and so forth in the United States, and so, while I'm all for equal rights and maybe social equality some day for you darkies, when the time is right, can't you see that *now isn't the time for it?*"

Neil knew, without having been instructed, that this was the most vicious thing that had been said, and the most foolish.

32

The gold was gone, the streets were mud, and November was near, when Neil lunched with Randy Spruce of the Chamber of Commerce, Lucian Firelock, who had come from a Georgia newspaper to be advertising manager of Wargate's, and Wilbur Feathering, who had also migrated North, but more after the fashion of Morgan's raiders.

Wilbur was the newest business sensation in town; small, trim, forty-five and full of twenty-dollar bills. He had been born in Mississippi, the son of a bankrupt grocer, but he thought that it would be much nicer if you supposed him to be the scion of a plantation-owner. Randy said, in a Boosters Club speech, "Wilbur may be as Southern as a hot tamale but he's also Northern as a blizzard and as streamlined as a flying torpedo."

After six years in Grand Republic, Wilbur had added to his Delta accent the virile phrases of Chippewa Avenue, and he was now more likely to say "That's for sure" than "Ah declare," and not Randy himself more often crowned a sentence with "Or what have you."

Wilbur had a mission, even aside from the nurture of his bank-account, a mission to enlighten Grand Republic about the danger of race riots that, he said, was inherent in the growth, since 1939, of its Negro colony from eight hundred to two thousand—to nearly two and a quarter per cent. of the total population, which, by Wilbur's arithmetic, was ninety-eight and a quarter per cent.

Neil met them in the maple-paneled Green Mountain Cocktail Lounge of the Pineland for a quick one, and they lunched in the Fiesole Room. The presence of the colored waiters started them talking Negro Problem.

"Where you boys got it wrong," said Mr. Wilbur Feathering, "is in looking on the Nigras here as a reservoir of labor to use in breaking strikes and busting the unions. Used to could, but the damn unions are some of 'em beginning to enroll the niggers just like human beings."

"I believe he's right," said Randy.

They heard their friend, Glenn Tartan, manager of the Pineland, asking a waiter, "Where is Mr. Greenshaw?"

Wilbur wailed, "That's exactly what I mean about you Northerners! *Mister* Greenshaw! For a nigger headwaiter! None of you know how to treat the black apes."

Lucian Firelock objected, "On committees, I've often said 'Mister' to Nigras."

"Aw, you're just trying to show off, Firelock," said Feathering. "Me, I have never in my whole life called any colored person Mister, Missus, or Miss, and I never shall, so help me God! Here's what you might call the philosophy of it. The minute you call one of the bastards Mister, you're admitting that they're as good as you are, and bang goes the whole God-damn White Supremacy racket!"

Lucian Firelock, once highly thought of in Georgia university circles, protested, "Do you always have to talk of the Nigras with hatred?"

"I don't hate the shines. Fact, they tickle me to death. They're such sly, thievish monkeys, and they all dance good, and when they find a white man that's onto 'em, like me, they just laugh like hell and admit they'd all be a damn sight better off under slavery. But you're one of these New Southern Liberals that claim it's okay to have niggers right at your house for dinner!"

Lucian said earnestly, "No, I believe thoroughly in Segregation. It prevents conflicts. But I also believe in scrupulously seeing that the Nigras get accommodations exactly as good as ours. For example, there is a Nigra chemist here named Dr. Ash Davis, and while I don't want to intrude on his home or have him intrude on mine, he deserves the best of everything."

Feathering snorted, "I've heard of that guy, and I wouldn't worry about his equal accommodations being so damn equal! Fact, his having his appointment at all is a stinking injustice to some young white scientist that's toiled and sacrificed and prepared himself for a good position, and then he finds this fat, greasy, four-flushing nigger has plotted and connived and grabbed it! Don't that make your blood boil?

"And take this nigger headwaiter here. Does he have the decency to ask Glenn, 'Please, boss, don't mister me no misters! It makes me ashamed befo' de white quality'? Not him! You Yankees——"

And then he said it, he really did say it: "Iwastwelveyearsold-beforeIknew damnYankeewastwowords."

"You Yankees have spoiled him and he'll stay spoiled till he gets a little kind-hearted flick of the bull-whip."

Neil was saved from bursting out by Lucian's abrupt, "Oh, don't talk like a Mississippi Senator!"

"Now that's all right now! Those Senators may be hicks, but they talk sense on this *one* subject! Say! I hear this headwaiter has a daughter that's married to a nigger dentist! Can you imagine that—poking around in people's mouths with his big black fingers! He ought to be run out of town. Yes, and maybe we'll do it. Some day you boys may be glad that one man come here and stirred up a little action before any nigger trouble could start!"

Neil was choking inside.

——God curse all white people, all of them! When shall I speak up? When shall I come out?

Uncle Bodacious Feathering was going on, "Used to be in the South we had a lot of dignified colored waiters that said 'Sir' to every white man even if he was a night watchman or what have you, but we had to kick out a good share of 'em and put in white waitresses, because those anthracites were getting corrupted by hearing the educated Nigras talk about what they called 'the wrongs of the race'—lot of stuff that never happened. I'd like to hang every buttinsky that helps any nigger to go to college, and deep down in your heart, Firelock, so would you."

"I would not!"

"Oh, I'm naturally a tolerant guy, myself. I love dogs. But when my dog has been rolling in manure and comes parading in and claims a right to sit right down at the same table with me——"

Neil heard nothing more. He had risen and walked out.

———

He sat in the Green Mountain Cocktail Lounge, with its hand-pegged maple furniture, its glass icicles on cartwheel chandeliers.

He attentively drank one glass of water, throbbing, "I must come out—I must come out," in a rhythm that beat and beat on endlessly. As he cautiously went back into the lobby, he saw that a Negro, dark-brown, handsome, slim, in tweeds, was standing at the desk. Neil guessed that he was a doctor or a teacher, and that, with his dove-like brown wife, he had been daring to motor and look at his own country.

The room-clerk was yelling, "Oh, Mr. Tartan, could you step this way?"

A year ago, Neil would certainly not have stopped, would have seen nothing, would have heard nothing. Now, he heard Glenn Tartan explain to the unknown, "Yes, sure, Doc, I know it's the Minnesota law—and a most unjust and discriminatory law it is, and the legislators who passed it would be sore as goats if there were a law compelling *them* to shelter people they don't like in their own homes. It's the law, but I want you to understand—you look fairly intelligent—that there has been a lot of complaint among our decent guests at you people horning in. So if you could go some place else, we would be very much obliged."

The husband and wife turned away, silent. Neil caught them at the door, with, "I think you can find fairly clean accommodations at the Blackstone, at Astor and Omaha, in the Five Points."

The man answered, "If it's not rude, may I say that my people don't ordinarily expect such courtesy from a white man!"

"I'm not white. I'm colored, thank God!"

He heard himself saying it.

33

He saw his father sweeping up the last of the fallen leaves, only a block away. He strolled over, with his mind blank, as though he had been saying good-bye to a number of people.

Dr. Kenneth Kingsblood's house was an antiquity in Sylvan Park: thirty years old! It was of brown wood, faded, and it had a lot of assorted architecture that you could never remember, though you might recall the flying balcony on the third story, and a fern in a glazed brown jar between the lace curtains of a plate-glass window looking on the front porch. It was as homelike as the minor poems of Longfellow.

Dr. Kenneth puffed briskly, "Well, my boy, glad to have you drop by and report that you're still alive. You living up North there, in Grand Republic?"

"If you can call it living, with the thermometer dropping this way."

"Somebody said you were in the banking line now. You must write and tell me about it."

"I don't think you could stand the scandal."

"Seriously, what you been doing with the research? I don't take the royal business too much to heart, but I do feel there's certain duties inherent in your blue blood—your red, white and blue blood. *Noblesse oblige!*"

Neil spoke tonelessly, with no desire to be cruel but no particular passion to be kind.

"Dad, maybe you have red, white and blue blood, but, according to your own classification, my blood is plain black, and I want it that way."

"What the——"

"I find that Mom's family was part Negro, and I've decided that goes for me, too."

"What is this joke? I don't like it!"

"Mom is descended on *her* mother's side from a frontiersman who was a full-blooded Negro—incidentally, married to a Chippewa. Do you mean she's never told you?"

"Your mother has never told me a word of any such a cock-and-bull story, and I never heard such a vicious charge in all my life, and I don't want to hear it! She's descended from a fine French family, on her mother's side, and that's all I want to know. Why, good God Almighty, are you trying to make out your own mother—my wife—is a nigger?"

"I'm not trying to make her out anything, Dad."

"The whole story is a dirty libel, and if anybody but you dared to repeat it, he'd get himself clapped into jail pretty darn quick, let me tell you, and you can quote me on that. There's not one drop of blood in you that's either Chippewa or nigger!"

"Can't you say *Negro?*"

"No, I can't and I won't and I don't intend to, and I'll tell you right now—— My God, boy, your own father ought to know *something* about your ancestors, and I can tell you, you haven't one iota of inferior or barbaric blood in you and I ought to know, hadn't I— I've studied bacteriology! Oh, Neil, my dear boy, in the name of all that's holy, try to understand the ghastly seriousness of this! Even if it *were* true, you'd have to conceal it, for your mother's sake—your daughter's. *Got* to!"

"Dad, I've been trying to, but I don't know how much longer I can do it. And I'm not sure I entirely want to. I'm not sure but that I have more affection for a lot of supposed colored folks than I do for most of the whites."

"You can't say that! It's insane, it's treachery, it's treason to your own race and country and religion—and it would be very bad for you in your job at the bank! Say, uh— Who was this frontier impostor?"

"Xavier Pic. P-I-C."

"How did you ever get the idea this fellow was colored?"

"From Gramma Julie, from the Historical Society, from Xavier's own letters."

He wanted to spare this kindly, rustic man, his father, but he had to enlist against Wilbur Feathering, and he could not see that his mother would do ill to consort with Mary Woolcape more than with Mrs. Feathering.

Dr. Kenneth was shaky, at the end; he begged of Neil, "You've simply got to keep all this dark till I can think it over and get my head around it."

This, Neil realized, meant Forever, but he gave what sounded even to himself like a promise.

———

On that cold fall evening in Neil's living-room, a room dark-blue and maroon, with the formal ship's-clock that was the denomination of Grand Republic respectability, Biddy cut out paper dolls and stayed up much later than was allowed—as usual, Vestal wrote letters and listened to a hockey game on the radio, and Neil looked at the Business & Finance notes in *Time* and perceived, in the flushing and paling quiver of the electric fire, that none of this Negro nonsense need exist, none at all, and that he had been monstrous not to have known better how his father would take it.

The doorbell. Vestal answered. She came back with a casual, "There's a colored woman here wants to see you—something about some relief committee." She went back to her letters with no instinctive fear in her, though she had let in Sophie Concord.

Sophie was urgent:

"No, we'll just stand here in the hall. Speak low. I've been talking to Evan Brewster. We—your friends—we don't think you should come out as a Negro, and we're scared you're up to something melodramatic. With us, it's been ground into us from birth, but we don't see why you should have to take it, and as a white man you can do just as much for the race. How we will milk you for contributions! Neil, don't say anything! I could have telephoned you this, but I did want to see your house and your baby and see your wife again. She's beautiful, like a race-horse. They're your sort, all right. Good night, my dear, *and shut up!*"

Sophie was gone, into a filtering of gray snow.

In the living-room, Vestal mumbled, "Who was the gal?"

"A city nurse. Miss Concord."

"Oh.... Oh, Neil, did I tell you that Jinny Timberlane has the cutest embroidered blue-wool suit from an Austrian shop in New York? I think I'll get one like it."

That seemed to Neal altogether reasonable.

And so, without communicating his reason, without consulting Neil, Dr. Kenneth Kingsblood in mid-November summoned a council of the entire family.

34

Neil was at an evening meeting of the financial committee at the Federal Club when his father telephoned, "Your mother and I want to see you immediately. It's important. Can you stop by at the house in not over forty minutes? Good."

That there was to be a council, even that Vestal was to be there, Neil did not guess. He came into the narrow, Brussels-carpeted hall of his father's house, into the "front-parlor," whistling, and stopped at the spectacle of the entire family, beneath the pictures of Pilgrim Fathers and sleigh-rides and Venice, sitting on the imitation-petit-point chairs, on the egg-yolk-yellow couch, on the floor, looking at one another and at souvenir ash-trays and an Album of the New York World's Fair.

Including Vestal and Neil and his parents, there were fifteen worriers gathered, none of them except Dr. Kenneth knowing why they had been summoned: Brother Robert and Alice, with her brother, who was none other than Harold W. Whittick, the entrepreneur of radio and advertising; Sister Kitty and her husband, Charles Sayward, the attorney; Joan, Neil's unwed sister; the tribe of Saxinar—Uncle Emery and Aunt Laura and Pat. To make it all legal, Dr. Kenneth had also gathered in the portly presences of Vestal's father, Morton Beehouse, and his brother Oliver, dean of the Grand Republic bar and the only connoisseur of Napoleon brandy and of the odes of Pindar in town.

Oliver Beehouse was short and solid, with a fringe of fine, sand-colored hair about his huge freckled tonsure. He was always pouting all over his pale but freckled face at the contemplation of the perfidious attacks on capitalism. Brother Morton, taller and four years younger, substituted a small liver-spot on his right cheek for Oliver's freckles.

Pat Saxinar and Vestal and Joan giggled together, thinking how old-fashioned were the house and their elders, who were muttering about the reason for this parliament, while Neil's mother sat reserved and frail, and Dr. Kenneth ambled about with mystery and lemonade.

Such was the grand jury when Neil came in.

They smiled upon him, for if there really was trouble ahead, no one could be more depended upon for common sense than good old Neil.

Dr. Kenneth, fluttering his hands, looking frightened, cried, "Now you young people please get up off the floor and all be properly seated. Oliver, you take that big green-plush chair. Now please let me have your close attention.

"My son Neil, who hitherto has been a boy to be proud of and with a lovely wife and daughter, has astonished me by wanting to do something of which I violently disapprove, in fact you might say it appals me, something of which, as I understand it, even Vestal hasn't the slightest idea, and which I shall certainly not tolerate without his first asking all your advice, and which he will now confess to you. Neil!"

Dr. Kenneth sank on a frail gilt chair, and Neil was sick with pity for his father, but he stood out and spoke gravely, like a man on the scaffold with no more hope of reprieve:

"I have learned that my mother—she may not even know it—is descended from one Xavier Pic, who lived from about 1790 to 1850, and who was a brave and honorable pioneer on the Northern Minnesota border, an ancestor to be proud of, and who was also a full-blooded Negro. Which makes every one of us, technically, either a Negro or the close relative of one."

He got only so far before he was whelmed by the fury, the denials, the shouts that he was insane. Vestal was burning with an unspoken astonishment that he had told her nothing, burning and rigid. Only his mother and Pat were altogether quiet. He held up his hand and the hecklers slowly stopped. He chronicled the story of Gramma Julie, the discoveries of Dr. Werweiss, and he wound up:

"A few months ago I would have been scared or apologetic about telling you this, but now I see that the only apology is to the Negroes, the Indians, the Orientals, for the wrongs that have been done to them for hundreds of years——"

Oliver Beehouse, not even rising, took charge:

"So, young man, you propose to correct those wrongs by hideously wronging all of us, your friends and family, who have never given you anything but loving assistance—to ruin even your wife, my own niece! Will you kindly stop your self-pity and your self-dramatization? I think you've been shameless enough, for one evening!"

Neil suggested, "Will you go to hell?"

"What?"

"You heard me. Quit acting supreme court. Maybe I would have shut up and never told, if Dad hadn't summoned this inquisition and you hadn't appointed yourself referee, but since you have, the question is, shall I be plain honest and tell the world the truth about what we are? Oh, Mom, I'm so sorry you got dragged into this!"

———

The comments of the distressed tribe did not come so clearly and patly as they are here given, but together, and all mixed with wails, curses, protests, interdicts from Oliver, something like laughter from Pat Saxinar. Dr. Kenneth asserted, "Neil, I think we are all agreed that if you continue to say nothing to outsiders, we'll try to ignore this whole business."

Since he had already told the Woolcapes, Ash, Sophie, Evan, Neil had nothing handy with which to answer, and his father soared on, "You claim you revere the truth, but do you call it the truth to make your own mother, that bore you, into a nigger, when obviously she isn't?"

"I don't——"

"Why, her and your daughter and your grandmother and your brothers and sisters are the last people living that any intelligent man would ever call niggers," Dr. Kenneth insisted. "I suppose it would tickle you to see your own Biddy a low-down nigger tramp!"

"*Negro!* And she wouldn't be low-down; she'd be just what she is now. She won't change; it's your ideas that have to change. And will you please quit saying nigger? Least you can do!"

"And the least *you* can do, that want to torture your own family, is not to be frivolous and quibble about mere words!" snapped Oliver Beehouse.

Dr. Kenneth was laboring on, "Boy, none of us has to tell all he knows. Suppose I were a dope-fiend. I wouldn't expect you to go around blabbing that I——"

Pat Saxinar piped, "But you aren't, Uncle Kenneth. Or are you?"

"Shut up!" contributed her father, Uncle Emery, son of Gramma Julie, who was in no exhilarated mood at having been nominated a Negro. Pat's mother (a Pedick of Winona) added, "This is no time for you to be impertinent and saucy, Patricia. I wish I'd never let you join the WAVES."

Neil's brother, Robert, simple-heartedly denied the whole thing.

Neil, he ventured to say, had gone batty from his war-injury, and even if this disgusting story could be true—but it was merely the addled recollection of an old woman like Gramma Julie—there was no proof. Nobody could pin it on them. A letter from Xavier Pic? Why, a forgery!

Charles Sayward suggested, Forget the whole thing. Cheer up. There was no law that they had to incriminate themselves. He led thus to a set speech by Oliver Beehouse:

"Neil, I've been thinking it over, and I was wrong and you were quite right, my boy, in insisting upon our having the courtesy to refer to this nation's darker wards as Negroes, not niggers. We appreciate the finer qualities of the better class of Negroes, and have since long before you were born! Didn't T.R., when he was President, have Booker T. Washington to lunch? (That's more than F.D.R. would've done, let me tell you!) But hot-heads like you, by demanding more for these unfortunates than they're able to digest, more than the decent ones would even think of asking for, are merely interfering with the orderly processes of evolution, and ——And so shut up about the whole thing, Neil, and try to have the sense of a moron at least! And while, as an illegal act, none of us would take any personal part in it, I think some day those documents about Xavier Pic may be found missing from the files of the Historical Society, and then none of us need worry!"

Oliver's cheery smile urged, "Have courage, my young friend," and Neil expected to hear an archangelic judge say, "Motion granted." But the court-room silence was ruined by Harold Whittick, brother of Robert's wife. He was screaming, "The hell with Neil and his 'truth'! It's outrageous that my own sister should be dragged into this and wake up and find she's married to a nigger like

Bob. And what the scandal may do to my advertising business, I hesitate to even contemplate!"

Alice yelled in agreement, "Outrage is right!" She turned upon Robert a glare of extreme dislike, and hissed, "I see now why you always make such noises in the bathroom!"

Robert, a dull man but fond of home and slippers, mourned, "Great God, it's not my fault if I have some queer blood. Besides—you heard me—I deny the story, lock, stock and barrel, and I think Neil has gone plumb crazy!"

"Something worse than crazy," said Morton Beehouse.

Aunt Laura Saxinar looked sniffy at all this vulgarity, and stated, "This is a vile mess, with which I simply do not care to be associated. My husband will tell you whether or no he considers himself a black man. But as for my daughter, Patricia, I have not merely a mother's heart to feel but a mother's eye to see that she is most certainly no—no Negro, or whatever you prefer to call those freaks—and I am told that none of them can ever learn to speak a foreign language, whereas Patricia speaks French like a native!"

Her husband, Uncle Emery, looked at her with no tenderness, and snarled, "Very kind of you to allow me to define my own racial status! Well, Neil says that his mother, his own mother, is a coon, but it just happens that she is also my sister, and let me tell you right here and now that she is no nigger, or me either, and if I'm descended from any Xavier Pic, and who the hell he was I don't know a thing about it, but I can tell you beyond the peradventure of a doubt, he was no nigger, and unfortunately that goes for Neil, too, though just now nothing would give me more pleasure, you young stinker, than to have you exposed as the blackest shine in Christendom, if it wasn't that it dragged in all the rest of us, you hear me? But as for my family——"

He was cut off by Neil's young sister, Joan:

"Oh, for God's sake, Uncle Emery, shut up about your family. They're has-beens. You're married, and Aunt Laura has *got* to stand for you. But what about me—what about me? Johnny will never marry me now, and he'll bawl me out plenty for deceiving him about my race, and I never meant to, I never did!

"Oh, Neil, what made you do this to me? I've never hurt you, never! You've turned me into an outcast for my whole life, just to satisfy some silly idea of justice. Why? How could you deliberately make me queer like this, hiding from people all my life, never daring to have a friend, not one boy-friend, not my whole life now, when I was so happy with Johnny? Oh, why—how could you?"

But his sister Kitty Sawyard, his loyal playmate all through childhood, was intent on him with unspoken horror that he should have destroyed her when she had loved him so.

He was frightened, ready to cry out that it had all been a maniac joke, when defense came from the still woman who was his mother.

They had been particularly tender of her, because she was so fragile and out of the common world. Her husband had been keeping a hand of affirmation and love on her shoulder, Joan had been smoothing her hair, Neil had peeped at her wretchedly. But she spoke more clearly than anyone else in the room. They stopped squabbling as she raised her hand, and so they got it full:

"Please! I think maybe Neil is right."

The chorus was tremendous, but it ceased in agonized attention.

"I never could see why there is all this fuss about whether you're 'white' or 'black,' so long as your folks love you, but you all seem to be so worried about it, so I must tell you.

"Once or twice when I was very little, there was an uncle of mine, my mother's brother, Uncle Benoit Payzold, that used to come calling on us, but only when Daddy was away. I always thought he looked like a light-complected darky. My mother never talked about him. He was a gambler, and he drifted off somewheres and I don't know if he's alive today or dead.

"I asked my mother wasn't Uncle Benoit a colored man, and she slapped me and told me to be still, and I went and forgot it till just now. I guess maybe I made myself forget it, and I think my mother did, too. I think she knows about us, about our being—— You know.

"She had a voodoo lodestone that, she told me one time, came from Martinique, maybe a hundred and fifty years ago, and then long afterwards I couldn't find it, and I asked her where it was, and she got mad and said there never had been such a stone. I don't know. Maybe I just imagined it. But you mustn't punish Neil if he tried to tell the truth."

Dr. Kenneth was triumphing, "There, you see, Neil? Your mother's had the sense and the magnificent will-power to simply forget evil and only look upon the good, like the Bible says.... Mother, I want you to simply *forbid* Neil to go around trying to convince himself and everybody else that this miserable business is true."

His wife wondered, "I don't know, Kenny. If it *is* true———"

Robert turned hysterical then. "Mother! God is going to curse you for making a nigger out of me, when I'm really white and decent, and I'm getting so successful——— I'm going insane! You and Neil have driven me absolutely dotty, and it's a dirty fake, and all because of a damn-fool lodestone that could of come from anywheres and you don't even know for sure it existed!... Alice! Don't you *see* I'm white, darling? It's a lie and I'm white and our kids are white! They are! I'm not going to be ruined by any lunatic like Neil! I'm white, and God help any bastard that comes around trying to prove different. Look at me, Alice!"

She did.

———

Pat Saxinar's voice was precise and frigid.

"All of you are assuming that you are superior to the 'colored people,' which isn't obvious to me at all. I've been infuriated by discrimination against extremely nice colored sailors, and I've wanted to do something about it, and now that I'm colored myself, I shall!"

The chorus, this time, was catastrophic, and it lasted for many minutes, while Neil turned toward Vestal.

She had ardently said nothing at all. When he had a chance to mutter "Well?" she answered, "I must think it over. Naturally, I'm a little surprised."

After one o'clock, her eyes told Neil that it was time to go home, and, with nothing whatever settled, with even his father determined to stay up all night and exclaim, it was hard for Neil and Vestal to break away.

They did, by the admirable feint of sudden deafness, and now the unknown Negro, Neil, faced his white wife, and he had no allies.

35

There was but a three-minute walk to their own house. Vestal was silent, her hand trustingly on his arm, till they were on their doorstep, and she spoke then naturally, not angrily nor too carefully:

"My dear, why didn't you tell me before? I'd 've tried to understand and help."

"I was going to. Dad sprang this on me before I'd worked out what I wanted to say. Now you can help me. The biggest question is: must I admit this publicly? It is the truth!"

"Hush now. Be quiet. I know what you're going to do, because I know you!" She touched his lips to silence, and drew him into the house. Holding his hand as though they were young lovers again, she led him up the pink-and-white room where Biddy was sleeping, curled tight, very earnest about it, and Prince curled and asleep at the foot of the low bed.

"Look at her, Neil. I know you wouldn't let anyone hurt or shame *her*, and even if the story about Pic being a colored man were true, you wouldn't tell the world, you wouldn't torture her, to satisfy your vanity about being so truthful. But I'm as sure as I ever can be of anything, as sure as I am of your love or of our immortality, that the story is not true! There's some mistake in what Gramma Julie told you—she's old and forgetful—and she always was a malicious old pixie, curse her! We'll find out there was some other Xavier Pic or Pick or Peake or whatever his horrible name was—and how I hate him! So! You'll see! It'll come out all right. Neil! Will you look at that child—all rose and sating and gold. There's no Negro blood in *her*!"

But Neil remembered Phoebe Woolcape, all rose and satin and gold, and a Negro.

"We'll wait and see," was all he could manage.

———

Next morning, his father telephoned that, under the chairmanship of Counselor Beehouse, the family had Resolved that it was the sense of this assembly that Neil would please shut up.

It was weeks later when Neil received from Dr. Werweiss of the State Historical Society a copy of a letter from Xavier Pic to Major Joseph Renshaw Brown which had been found in the society's files:

"The castors you ask about are not plentiful this winter. The white men have been stripping our forests. I have been thinking about you whites. Of course to the Ojibways I am white too as they recognize only white & Indian, but I think I would rather be counted as Indian then.

"You said to me, 'Why don't you defy them all and wear your black visage as a badge of honor?' But why should I explain it or excuse it or think about it at all? Why should a man with red hair excuse it to men with black hair & brown & straw color?

"You white men set yrselves up as the image of God, but which of you have seen Him? You have seen Genl Sibley & you have seen Govr Ramsey but which of you has seen God? Maybe He is dark, like the Indians and me, and maybe He is all colors, or no color at all, like a rock in the moonlight.

"I have been reading the Scriptures a gd deal lately & found a text to tell you whites, He that hateth Me hateth my Father also. Excuse writing as my hands are stiff I froze them last week getting a missionary out of some rapids when his canoe upset, he asked me, Can you or the heathen Indians read & write?"

———

Neil admired, "There is blood royal for Biddy to be proud of." Then he laughed. He could hear Clem Brazenstar jeering, "That's the trouble with all you mulattoes. You got to be so high and biggety, while the rest of us only want good jobs and a good seegar!"

———

As December froze its way toward Christmas, the family avoided Neil except for urgent private conferences at which only Charles Sayward seemed quite human—and firmly hostile. The rest of the tribe were either touchy or desperately respectful.

Pat Saxinar was constantly running in. To an extent which did not at all please Vestal, Pat assumed that Neil and she were under-ground conspirators, and she had tales for him of how frantically Harold Whittick and Alice were sniffing at Brother Robert to see if he really had done the foul crime of getting himself born a Negro.

Vestal did not again speak of "that other Xavier Pic," and Neil guessed that while consciously she would not believe in his piebald origin, deep down and hopelessly she was certain. She held Biddy on her lap and looked at her so long.

He remembered how she had skipped through the sacred chores of Christmas a year ago, while now she sighed, "There's still such a post-war shortage of all the pretty things; let's not try to get any new Christmas-tree ornaments this year, but use the old junk." In pity he saw that her zest in life was being wiped out, saw that he and his social justice had done this to her.

They did try to make a festival of Christmas shopping. They lunched togethed at the Fiesole Room, looking at the unconscious Drexel Greenshaw as at an unwelcome relative. They struggled through the human surf at Tarr's Emporium. Levi Tarr, who had been a colonel four months ago, was now trying to learn again how to rub his hands and be piously attentive to women who wanted an electric refrigerator for forty-nine ninety-five. He shepherded them through the toy-department, calling them Neil and Vestal, and when with slightly heavy secrecy they parted, to shop for each other, he murmured to Neil that he could get a very fine thing for Vestal in the way of matching bracelet, earrings, necklace, in bril-liants.

When they came out of the store, they plodded to the grim parking-lot, and Vestal's cheeriest Yuletide comment was, "My, the traffic is thick! I thought the cars were all worn-out, but seems as if these dubs have just as many as ever. Look at that lavender sports-job. My, my, and who is that driving it but that awful nigger, Borus Bugdoll. Oh! Sorry! Honestly, darling, I *am* sorry! I forgot that—— Well, it's hard for me to realize."

———

It was tacitly understood by the whole family that he was to say nothing *until.* Just when *until* would arrive had not been mentioned.

He was constantly afraid, meantime, that the news of his honorable state would sift out through Brother Robert's confusion or Uncle Emery's fury or Pat Saxinar's excess of courage or the conniving site of Harold Whittick. How many people actually knew It? Fifteen in the family, eight or ten colored people—oh, too many! And who else knew, who suspected, who was watching and leering, holding a match to blow him up?

At Eliot Hansen's buffet supper, when Violet Crenway tittered at Neil, "Oh, you red-heads are always peculiar," what did she imply? How could she possibly know of Xavier's letter about red hair and black?

At Ackley Wargate's annual snow-party, what was Pomona Browler getting at when she sang the voyageur's song, "Dans mon chemin"? That whole fiesta gave Neil a depressed feeling of leaving forever the easy white-man's life: the cheerful guests driving in cutters through the great stand of white pine to Ackley's enormous log lodge on frozen Lake Riflestock; old friends, pine torches, the frail afterglow at the end of a forest trail, girls, hot rum punch, rapturous singing of traditional songs like "Seeing Nellie Home" and "I've Been Working on the Railroad."

Yes, that was all very nice, but wasn't Ackley watching him in a curious way?

Neil felt safer when he went down to the Five Points, one afternoon just before the holidays, with small gifts for the Brewsters, Davises, Woolcapes—but not for Sophie, lest he slip.

He talked for an hour with Mary Woolcape, as he had every week or two. With her he had the comfort and reassurance of sharing in little things that once he had treasured with his mother and Vestal: meditatively gnawing a doughnut, really getting right down deep into a discussion of whether the thermometer had gone down to seventeen above this morning or only eighteen.

"Don't worry too much, son," said Mary, the eternal. "You have more people that love you than you know."

———

At the Brewsters', that afternoon, only Winthrop, back for vacation from his first year in the University, was at home. That typical bright-young-college-man in sweater and moccasin-shoes was full of yells and welcome.

"Neil! I just heard you've come over to my race! Oh, boy, am I glad!"

"Where did you hear that?"

"Listened to Dad and Mother doing a fine job of worrying about you."

As, with overstrained cordiality, he shook hands with his youthful admirer, Neil was fretful. So many others could have been listening. It could all pop out so easily. His "Okay—let it!" was not highly spirited. But he was proud that this ambitious boy turned to him as a friend with whom he could drop the parboiled cynicism with which his kind protected themselves against a dull and extremely advisory adult world.

"Neil! Maybe you'll really get into the race-struggle and be able to give us some new slants. I wish you could do something with the racemen that are too touchy, and insist that the colored press spell That Word as n-blank-r, and have a cat-fit when they hear a bunch of innocent white kids doing some corny old song like 'You could hear those darkies singing.' I'll bet some of 'em insist that Niggardly ought to be pronounced Negrodly. Couldn't you make fun of them? Gee, you know, you could maybe become one of the leaders of the race."

Neil was gratified by such faith, after days when he had been creepily conscious of the Family muttering, secretly telephoning to one another late at night.

The Family stood there looking at him, no matter where he was.

The Charles Sayward who had always been the most cheerful and reasonable and decent of his in-laws was most firmly alienated. He had quietly abolished Neil along with any silly rumors that Kitty might have "Negro blood." Charles had the simple-hearted immobility of the small man who knows his small job perfectly, and Kitty turned to him now for the sweetness she had once found in a brother named Neil, who had died here recently—very regrettable, but let's not talk about it.

He found a measure of sympathy only in his mother and Vestal and Pat. And his mother, though she was tender, though she was not retaliatory, was now asserting that she had thought it all over and received a new revelation, to the effect that Uncle Benoit had been neither colored nor a gambler, but a respectable Caucasian in the bill-collecting line.

So they came to a Christmas that was a caricature of Christmases past, with more Topsies than Tiny Tims. No Saywards or Beehouses appeared at the holiday dinner, held at Robert's this year, and the rest of the Family poured a horrid sweetness upon a self-sufficient young woman to whom they could not help referring as "poor Biddy."

Snow was falling all day, and from time to time somebody would say brightly, "Fine! It's a real *white* Christmas," and every time he heard it, Neil thought, "So even Christmas gets jimcrowed."

The Family did not, as of old, stay on for a rackety supper, but managed to get themselves gone by three. When he had escorted Vestal and Biddy home, Neil muttered, "I think I'll get a little fresh air," and hastened to Ash Davis's for a taste of security.

Not only was Sophie there, patting his hand, placidly fond of him, but also there was that jittery and courteous Southern Liberal, Mr. Lucian Firelock, of Wargate's, discussing the part of Negro sculptors in a black world that had once seemed to Neil a mass of dark pathos or of dark poison but that seemed now as lively and multi-colored and unpredictable as a tropic aviary.

Lucian was apologetic: "The Davises and Nora have been so nice to my kids that I thought I'd drop in and—and so I'll be running along."

Neil wanted to stay with Sophie in the warmth, but he could feel Vestal and Biddy alone at Christmas twilight. As he limped home through the snow, he meditated that he could conceivably have for Sophie a love that was altogether spiritual, but that he had for Vestal a fleshly love, and that of the two, it was the flesh that was likely to endure.

Sophie was his sister, his other self. As he had once shared toys and all the small rebellions against their father with Kitty, so with Sophie he shared the greatest rebellion he had known. But Vestal—

she was his love. Every thought that the brownskin Alabama girl might have was natural to him and familiar; every thought of the woman with whom he had gone to high school, played tennis, shared a bedroom for seven years, was exotic and amazing, and so he loved her most of all and hoped some day to captivate her and even to understand her.

Oh, he had understood her once, had known everything that she would do and would say, but that had been in a day when she had nothing to do that was not perfectly scheduled, when she had not been called upon to say anything upon the topic of a man who seemed prepared to ruin her and ruin himself for the love of a God in whom he did not very ardently believe.

Vestal looked bright as a candle at his return. She seemed to Neil little older than Biddy and more defenseless. That child would always attack life and scare it into obedience; the humble and unexacting Sophie would always get along, in hospital or nunnery or low cabaret; but the brisk Vestal, pride of the Junior League, would always be forlorn and bewildered without a man: a father, a husband, a son, a priest.

He kissed her fairly, and they were happy cooking their supper. Shirley had gone off to a Balkan carnival. They put Biddy to bed and sat at the shiny kitchen table, eating scrambled eggs and agreeing about the viciousness of Curtiss Havock and the virtues of Father Kenneth, and the putative cost of a "picture-window" in the living room.

Yes, they really might get the new window, they said joyfully, on this black night after a black Christmas.

36

No Jew, no musician, no teacher and very few Democrats had ever belonged to the Federal Club. Not that there was any by-law against them. There was no need of one.

Here the veteran millionaires of Grand Republic, like Hiram Sparrock, played bridge or backgammon every evening, with a hot toddy exactly at eleven. If the club servants were not English by origin nor baronially trained, the Tudor architecture of the members' faces turned them so within six months, and when any old-enough member saw a stranger in those crypts, he would summon Jeems and puff, "Who's that fella? Throw him out." The inner ring of the club regarded the coming of new industries to town as vulgar, and felt placidly that there was enough money in Grand Republic already.

They owned most of it.

No one had ever dared propose the names of Randy Spruce or Wilbur Feathering for membership; Curtiss Havock had been ignored, despite his father's solidity; and Neil Kingsblood had been elected chiefly because he was the son-in-law of Morton Beehouse. It was only by a rare slip that his brother Robert had been elected also.

Nothing in the higher social events of the year in Grand Republic was more significant than the Federal Club's Auld Lang Syne Holiday Stag, holden annually between Christmas and New Year's, which enabled the members to escape from the young relatives who are so especially present and flippant at Yuletide, and to bask in the clear sun of male conversation. Dinner-jackets were obligatory, mutton chops were regulation, and they were never affronted by salads or ice cream. The whole affair resembled a bachelor-dinner given by J. P. Morgan the Elder to King Edward VII, but it was called Supper, and spread in the Pillsbury Grill, which had a bold atmosphere of oak tables, Flemish tiles and pewter mugs.

The Stag this year had a distinguished array of Sparrocks, Wargates, Beehouses, Grannicks, Tarrs, a Havock, a Timberlane, a Drover, a Marl, a Prutt, a Trock, a general, a commander, and an Episcopal bishop.

Neil, with his feeling of walking constantly on an icy roof-slope, did not want to go, but he had to please Mr. Prutt. He carefully brought his gold cigarette case and carefully left outside his new opinions. During the conversation before the supper, he had to skate around somewhat rapidly to avoid Brother Robert and Hal Whittick, and he took refuge with Rodney Aldwick.

After supper, they worshipped with church-warden pipes and

with tankards of old bitter ale, which most of them disliked and changed for highballs as soon as it seemed reverent. Then—feet upon the table, which was also obligatory except for the sixty per cent. or so of members with arthritis—they began the canonical Auld Lang Syne Hy-Syne, an annual presentation of short, funny talks, occasionally with an important financial announcement, to be held confidential. This secrecy was almost guaranteed by the presence and the consent of Gregory Marl, the large, quiet man who had inherited both of the two newspapers published in Grand Republic.

The president of the club, Dr. Roy Drover, introduced Rod Aldwick as speaker.

Usually, Dr. Drover was humorous, but tonight he said with emphasis, "I'm not going to guarantee that we'll get to any short Hy-Synes this evening. Major Aldwick, our friend Rodney, has something so important to say that I've given him the green light to take as long as he wants."

Looking at Rod's curt hair, wide shoulders, shaped waist, you thought of all sorts of Kipling words: sirdar, sahib, polo, tiffin, pukka—duty, power—beggar, native—pure breed, outcast, blood—lightly answered the colonel's son, I hold by the blood of my clan; your son I'll take and we shall make a Quisling of the man. And Rod's voice, as he spoke, had the true parade-ground bark, with legal refinements.

He was very happy, or so he said, about the behavior of all our white troops in Europe. "The commonest commodity in our outfit wasn't beans or bullets but sheer courage!" But he had to tell them that there had been one disappointment: the behavior of our Jewish and Negro soldiers.

He devoted ten spirited minutes to the Jews, and carried on:

"Those minority laddies like to dish it out, in their seditious press, but on the field of honor, those bellyachers can't take it, especially the darker brothers. If you will permit a rude soldier to use the expression—they stink!"

(Neil looked at his wincing brother; at Webb and Ackley Wargate, who employed Negro skilled labor. Webb was an eyeglassed, medium-sized bookkeeper worrying about the balance, and Ackley a small-sized bookkeeper who had not yet learned to worry.)

Rod grew measured and firm:

"I have no prejudices, the Army and Navy have no prejudices, I presume God has no prejudices. We had hoped that these tinted gentry had learned their lesson of playing the game in the former war. We gave them every chance in this—even made a Negro general and a number of colonels! And if there was any segregation, it was always and only at the request of their own colored leaders, who frankly admitted that their black lambs were not up to the strain of associating with the whites.

"I have seen a mild-mannered and spectacled little Caucasian sergeant keeping a gang of black soldiers, headed by a big buck with the nerve to wear two bars on his shoulders, from running away during an assault, and when that 'captain' saw me, he just snickered foolishly. But they were all brave enough when it came to forcing their ill-odored attentions on ignorant French peasant girls!

"The worst incident connected with the Negro monstrosities and atrocities that I saw personally, however, was when one of them, and he must have been drunk, had the nerve to say to a big Irish-American sergeant of M.P.'s, 'I'm going to get invalided home, and when I do, I'll service your girl for you.' Now I don't know how legal it was, and I shall never inquire, but *that* buck had a funeral without honors!"

(Laughter and applause.)

"What's the answer? Well, I think our new friend and member here, Lucian Firelock, has the only answer, *complete segregation*, so successful in the South and some day soon, God willing, to be universally demanded throughout the North. In the next war, I'd like to see the Negroes not even called soldiers, not given any uniforms except overalls, and kept by force in a work corps."

(Neil looked at Lucian Firelock, who sat next to Duncan Browler, vice-president of Wargate's. He did not think that Lucian was comfortable over either Rod's compliments or putting his feet up on the table.)

"But now," said Rod, "I have a few things to tell you about the Negroes right here in Grand Republic. When we citizens-in-arms went off to fight for our homes, there were only a few of the black folk here, and the predominant element among them were well-trained old-timers like Wash, who has blacked all our shoes since we were kids, and enjoyed it, bless his dear old ebony hide, and whom we all loved and respected!

"But we G.I.'s came back to find that hundreds of the worst type of colored men have forced their way in here, and are being followed by all their unwashed and unwanted and lice-infested relatives from the South—which is powerful glad to get rid of them—and so we are on our way to accumulate such a sinister darktown that race-riots are going to be inevitable—and all because of a false liberalism, an ignorant tolerance of the Negro."

(Major Rodney Aldwick never said "nigger." He would not have said it even at a lynching.)

"We already have approximately two thousand of these Sons and Daughters of Mumbo-jumbo here, and soon there will be twenty thousand, and a fair city will be fouled and smirched and ruined—*if we don't do something about it!*

"On my own initiative, I have been having an investigation made of some Negro agitators who are trying to corrupt our labor picture, and I'm going to tell you about these fancy fellows, of whom most of you have never heard, but who are getting ready to take over your own business, gentlemen, and have a pretty fair chance to do it, too, if you don't wake up and get very, very busy!"

(At this line of the spy-melodrama, all their heads went up.)

"They are plotting to compel the unions, most of which have hitherto barred out black members, or hamstrung them by keeping them in phony auxiliary unions, to open their ranks, so that any ignorant, black ditch-digger can come in and even take office.

"Soon you will have the spectacle of a big, black union official coming into your private office and sitting down with his hat on, puffing a fifty-cent cigar in your face and telling you how to run your business, that you've given the best years of your life to building up. Yes, and you'll have coal-black wenches demanding the 'right' to share the toilets with your own daughters and delicately bred secretaries!

"And you professional men, you doctors and my fellow-lawyers and even the clergy—don't think that *you* will escape! If you don't *do* something, there will be pressure to compel you to hire swarthy secretaries and cashiers—and all of you clever leaders of the community have been letting this plot go on under your very noses!"

(It was a sensation. They had known that Rod Aldwick was a good fellow, a swell soldier, a smart lawyer, but not that he was a thinker and orator like this. Say! How about him for Governor or United States Senator some day?)

"And now, confidentially, so that you may defend yourselves and your most sacred honor and businesses, I'm going to give you the names of the ringleaders in this plot—educated Negroes with soft jobs and none of them having the smallest show of right to intrude on labor organizations.

"The worst of them is one Clement Brazenstein, a professional agitator with shady antecedents. He does not live here, but he comes sneaking in here by night to pour his devil's brew of sedition into the, I must say, highly capable local traitors. These include one Ryan Woolcape, a veteran who was kicked out for insubordination, and Susan, sometimes known as Sophia, Concord, who is actually a city nurse, paid out of taxes, out of your money and mine, to sow subversive propaganda in every decent Negro shanty in town!

"Plotting with them are a fly-by-night black preacher and spellbinder known to his dupes as 'Evangelist' Brewster, who uses the sanctity of his pulpit to spread the red doctrines of slave revolt, and a former handy-man in a patent-medicine joint who got in here on the pretense that he is a qualified chemist, and calls himself 'Doctor' Asher Davis.

"All these delightful playmates are in constant touch with the Jewish bureaucrats in Washington, who are secretly scheming to make the F.E.P.C.—the Future Enemy Power Conspiracy—the basic law of the land, to replace our American Way of Life and to force every industrialist to employ a gang of black men, whether or not he needs anybody at all. All over America they are organizing this titanic revolution, from the fish-canneries of old New England to the studios of Hollywood—and don't take my word for it, gentlemen, but read the Negroes' own outrageous weekly newspapers!

"But here in Grand Republic they are particularly insidious, and meeting nightly with certain white men—and not Jews, not tramps and crooks, but actually of our own class!"

(As Rod's triumphant glance swept over the listeners, it flickered on Neil, who answered it with an unspoken, "All right, Rod. I'm ready.")

Rod pounded on, "The Wargates and Dunc Browler, who are with us tonight, deserve our heartiest applause for their generosity in affording a vast number of black gentlemen a chance to show what they can really do.

"Now the starry-eyed leftwing boys in Washington maintain that the colored brethren have made just as good a showing as white machinists in punctuality, discipline, and quality of work done. But I am authorized to state that Webb and Ackley and Dunc have arrived at an entirely different conclusion, and at Wargate's we shall see from now on an economic picture in which there will be a lot less of grinning slaty faces!"

(Neil looked at Ackley, in whose forest camp he had had so lively a party, two weeks ago. Ackley and his father seemed self-conscious, but they were not contradicting anything.)

"So, gentlemen, I have not given you the traditional comic Hy-Syne, because those of us who faced the enemy guns cannot feel very comic until we are assured that you are going to preserve for us what we fought to preserve for you—the pure, clean, square-dealing, enterprising, freely-competitive America of the Founding Fathers!"

———

They pounded their tankards on the tables and broke their clay pipes in applause.

Neil was thinking, "This is it. Come on. That's the warden and the chaplain coming."

Dr. Drover was asking for silence, to thank the speaker, when Neil stood up. He spoke as unemotionally as an official making a routine announcement, and they all listened. Nice, sensible boy, fine future, young Kingsblood—you know, in the Second National—son-in-law of Mort Beehouse.

"I was junior to Major Aldwick as an officer," Neil said, "but I must correct him."

He saw the eyes of Rodney shrewd upon him.

"Gentlemen, what Aldwick said about Negro soldiers was half fireworks and half fake. It was poisonous nonsense."

Rod was rising to interrupt, but Neil insisted, "You've had your chance, Rod." Dr. Drover made sounds like a chairman, but Dr. Henry Sparrock yelped, "Let the boy talk!" Through the room there were mutters of "Give him a chance," and a more sinister "This sounds interesting!"

But Robert Kingsblood, on his feet but hunched over, was wailing, "Shut up, Neil! Oh, God!" as Neil lumbered on:

"Aldwick never mentioned Negro gallantry, nor the seditious efforts of officers and non-coms from the Deep South to corrupt our army by prejudice. I wouldn't expect that, from a political climber. But I will say that his statements about Dr. Davis and Dr. Brewster and Miss Concord are plain untrue—and he didn't even have their names right. I'm ashamed of myself for having sat and listened, because——"

Robert's agonized voice—perhaps he did not know that he spoke aloud—was beseeching, "Don't do it, boy!"

"——because," Neil went on, "I have some of what you call 'Negro blood' myself."

They were paralyzed and still.

"I am only one thirty-second Negro, but according to the standards of Lucian Firelock and his friend Mr. Wilbur Feathering——"

Lucian's voice was even: "No friend of mine, Neil!"

"Well, according to the general Southern myth, which they have sold to simple careerists like Aldwick, that makes me one hundred per cent. Negro. All right! I accept it! And I have no friends whom I honor more than Dr. Davis and Dr. Brewster and Miss Concord and Mr. Brazen*star*! I'm very cheerful about being a Negro, gentlemen, and about the future of our race, and I think that's enough."

Boone Havock drawled, "I'll say it's enough—plenty!"

In the babble, Neil heard Prutt's scream that this was all an ill-advised joke, caught Robert's hysterical denials, and part of an argument between Firelock and Dunc Browler about Ash Davis's competence. All such chatter was crushed by the fury of Boone Havock, the vasty railroad-contractor, who was roaring at Browler:

"You boys talking about whether some nigger knows a test-tube from his finger, while this terrible thing has happened: a member of this club confesses he's a nigger and covers us all with shame! Who cares anything about nigger soldiers——"

Colonel Levi Tarr began, "I care! The discrimination against them——"

Dr. Roy Drover blanketed him: "The hell with that! As president of this club, I suggest that we accept Mr. Neil Kingsblood's resignation right here and now—this minute."

Neil looked not at Drover but at Rod Aldwick, relaxed, smiling, malicious.

Greg Marl was standing. "Roy! Before we do that or anything else, I suggest that we go home and think about it, and tomorrow you can appoint a committee to talk this over with Neil. Meantime, I can promise that nothing will appear in my papers, nor in the press services, if I can help it—and if all of you will keep quiet."

Judge Cass Timberlane insisted, "Whether he was wise or not, Neil has been courageous, and we must keep our heads."

Ackley Wargate—Neil used to play checkers with him—and win—Ackley shouted, "Sure we'll keep our heads, but I know what my attitude is, right now. I have always considered Neil a good friend and been glad to entertain him in my home. I think I have always been nice to him. And I resent his having pretended to be a white man—sneaking in and meeting my wife and children on a basis of equality. I just want to assure him and all of you that that will not happen again."

Judd Browler, bless him, solidest and oldest of friends, stood up to proclaim, "I think that's nonsense! We all of us know that Neil is the swellest guy and the most loyal friend in town. What's a mere thirty-second part Negro blood? He's the whitest man here, and I stand by him."

There were controversial rages, and Neil walked out on them.

He was tired. He could no longer hear their voices. A curtain had been lowered between him and these white men. To have resigned from the white race was more important than to have resigned from the Federal Club.

Judd Browler caught him in the lobby, and grunted, "God, I think you were an awful fool to spill the beans like that, old man, but we'll back you up. You and Ves come in for dinner—say next Tuesday, New Year's Day—and we'll talk it all over. Okay? Swell!"

37

When he walked into their living-room Vestal was in fluffy negligee and was knitting, no usual domesticity for her. "I'm afraid you've caught me. I've been making a scarf for you, but I didn't get it done in time for Christmas, drat it, so I'm finishing it up for New Year's and——What is it? Neil! Why are you standing there? Oh! Neil! No! It hasn't come out?"

"Rod Aldwick made such an attack on Negroes that I had to tell them—publicly—I'm one. Sounds curious to say 'I'm a Negro'!"

"Curious. Yes. Yes, it does sound curious. It sounds curious to say that I'm the wife of a colored man. That Biddy is colored—and damned forever now. Yes. Curious. And we have to do something quick, to make up for your delightful public confession. I don't know what."

She was at the telephone, calling Dr. Kenneth, begging him to meet them at Morton Beehouse's. She called her father and Brother Robert at the Federal Club. As she dressed, upstairs, with Neil blankly watching, she moaned, "If you just won't say anything!"

"I'm not saying anything!"

She tried to smile. "Well then, if you just won't not say anything, or *something*! I think I'm going to stand by you—or maybe you don't want me to, any longer? Maybe I'm not even good enough to be a colored man's wife."

"Don't be silly."

"What can I think? You could do this to me. I'm pretty tough, or I thought I was, but to Biddy—"

"Vestal, there's no use. I guess it's simple. If I'm a Negro, then I'm a Negro. And Judd Browler—probably a lot of others, too—back me in wanting to be honest about it."

"I could hate you, I believe, if I put my mind to it, and yet I don't, not now, and when I look at you, just as ruddy and red-headed and decent as ever, I don't seem to have any revulsion, and yet——Suppose Uncle Oliver could prove that there's been some mistake—you're not even a tiny bit Negro?"

"Then I'd volunteer. I prefer Ash and Evan and Phil and Sophie and the Woolcapes to Rod Aldwick and Doc Drover and Oliver Beehouse."

"Who are all these weird people? Coons?"

Surely it was impossible that she should not know these, the most important persons living. "They are Negroes whom I prize for their kindness and courage and intelligence and—"

"Oh nuts! You've become impossible!"

The residence of Mr. Morton Beehouse needs only one word: Solidity.

Thirty thoughtful years had been devoted to selecting the final place for his slippers, and to finding a buffet of the right solidity. In this fortress, where the air seemed composed of the same oak as the panels of the walls, Dr. Kenneth, with a suit and a plaid overcoat over his pajamas, was waiting like a fluttering stork when Neil trailed in, while Brother Robert was a bumptious bull, and their host was altogether motionless, except for his eyes.

Robert proclaimed, "Neil, I've been talking to Mother on the phone, and she absolutely denies the whole story. She insists on your getting the Federal Club members together again, and telling them you had a stroke."

Morton Beehouse said, "That would be very much like a private citizen ordering Congress to reassemble. It's too late. After all, I was there, and I may tell you, Neil, that you might better have murdered my daughter than have done this obscene thing to her. She will, of course, leave you immediately, in mere self-respect."

"I will not," said Vestal.

"Think so? Wait till Lorraine Wargate and Janet Aldwick cut you on the street," her father said solidly.

"I won't wait. I'll cut them first."

Morton was calm. "Go ahead, my dear. Get it out of your system. I would expect you to be loyal. The Beehouses are a loyal folk. But when you have done enough for honor, you will agree with me that this fellow, your husband—temporarily—is the most unspeakable, selfish, exhibitionistic, vile, brawling sot and bounder that ever disgraced this city!"

Robert was frightened, but he was a decent clansman, and he rumbled at Morton, "We've had enough of your sauce, Beehouse!"

"We certainly have!" said Dr. Kenneth, and Robert kept it up with, "My father and I love this boy, even if he is as crazy as a loon, and I guess maybe your daughter does, and seems like there's nothing more to say."

But there was, oh, there was, and Neil and Vestal were not home till after three. When they came in, Biddy awoke, crying. They wretchedly tried to comfort her, and crawled to their sleepless twin beds. Vestal vowed, "I do love you very much and I'm going to stand by you—as long as I can. I'm not a professional martyr, though. Apparently I'm not even intellectual enough to be one of your fancy niggers."

"Don't!"

"How can I help it?"

Till dawn, a dawn of sleet and metallic gray.

The next day, the courteous Verne Avondene, secretary of the Federal Club, telephoned to Neil that a committee had met that noon and "accepted his resignation." Verne hoped that "your good lady and Miss Elizabeth are having joyful holidays."

"Not half!" said Vestal, who had been eavesdropping on the extension phone.

———

As husbands do, he believed that his victory had been easy and sure, that she had forgiven him for the bad taste of being born a Negro. As wives do, even very good wives, she let him drop his guard and then she hit. Late in the dim December afternoon, a defenseless time, when they had cheerfully agreed that, yes, they'd better not go to Norton Trock's party, she turned on him with:

"And don't think, because I'm not kicking and screaming, that I don't resent not being allowed to go anywhere, nowheres again ever, because of this idiotic stand of yours. Sometimes I begin to see the Negro in you—I hope I'll forget it again, but I see you shambling and grinning foolishly——"

"Is that really the way you think you see all Negroes?"

"That's the way I *know* I see them, *all* of 'em. And I imagine a kind of horrible shadow over your face. Oh, I've always hated all darkies, and their beastly simpering, that gives them away. They know they're inferior!"

He demanded, not too cherubically, "Did you ever know any Negro, besides Belfreda?"

"Yes! You and your dumb brother, Robert, and your sisters—— Oh, I'm sorry, dear, I'm truly sorry. I'm upset. I could slap myself for saying that."

"Saying what? It's true, isn't it?"

"Honestly, Neil, I'll endure anything except your getting calm and strong and wise on me! I can't stand that."

But they escaped—this time—from the more ardent tortures of quarreling.

———

The Federal Club Smoker had been on Thursday, December 27th. Neil's bank was open all day Friday and half of Saturday; it was also open on Monday, the day before New Year's. An automaton called Our Mr. Kingsblood was in busy attendance upon those days, sitting in at a teller's window, giving advice to veterans whose advice to himself he would have been afraid to hear, talking to Mr. Prutt about the window-cleaning service.

Prutt did a lot of throat-clearing and quick, unnecessary smiling during their talk, and Neil wondered if the miracle had come: if Prutt was going to be so heroic as to decide that this Negro myth was none of his business. He saw Prutt's glance craftily hitch-hiking all over the place, and he realized that the good man was trying to look down at his fingernails ... to see if the halfmoons were blue.

He sat as chilly as a palace guard at whom the dictator peeps too meditatively. There was the smell of death in the air. But he was safe until some customer should complain about having to do business with this colored fellow Kingsblood.

At the annual bonus-giving, when all the employees were supposed to be surprised and pleased by the bank's fatherliness (and once in a while some of them were considerably surprised), when they were all lined up like a daisy-chain in the president's office, Neil seemed to be still on the payroll. But just before Mr. Prutt should have handed him his envelope and his cliché, Prutt coughed, "I'll be back, just a minute," and Neil received the annual gilded leg-chain not from the pale, aseptic hand of the president but from the broad fist of Mr. S. Ashiel Denver.

——I'm still working here, but I begin to get an idea I'm not going to be first vice-president.

———

Of course it got out. Though slowly.

Of course every one present at the Federal Club's Scandal in High Life had promised to keep silence; and of course every one of them confided in someone else. In New Year's week there was nothing in print, but Radio Station KICH, the property of the highly disaffected Mr. Harold W. Whittick, on its chatty Home News Hour promised that within a few days it would be able to give to its far-flung audience—the KICH staff were among the most horrible far-flungers in the country—the details of a shameful incident which had revealed that a well-known financier in the North Middlewest had been leading a shocking double life.

Neil and Vestal listened and looked at each other and were scared.

The day before New Year's, Judd Browler telephoned, "Look, old man, I'm in kind of an embarrassing position. My wife and my dad are simply raising Cain about my wanting to publicly stand back of you for—you know. So I guess you better not come here for dinner tomorrow evening. Might be uncomfortable for you. But *privately,* I agree with you. I'll call you for lunch, this week."

Judd did not call again.

———

They had planned gaily to go to the big New Year's Eve Party at the Heather Country Club. They stayed home and were reasonably bleak. Neil worried, "I don't think I could lose my job, could I? What would we do, if I did?"

"I don't know. We've always been so sort of sure of a decent living. You don't suppose Papa Morton, the old clubman, would cut off my pocket-money, do you?"

"Oh, what if he does! We'll get along somehow." It did not sound like a bugle-call of courage.

"I suppose," she speculated, startled by the revolutionary observation, "that there's quite a proportion of American families that, every New Year's Eve, worry about whether their jobs will hold up through the coming year."

"Yes, I doubt if my friend John Woolcape, the janitor, is spending this New Year's Eve wondering whether he'll switch his investments from General Motors to real estate."

"Oh, don't be so damned smug! You and your crusading friends! I don't see that it took any special virtue in you to get yourself born colored. Can't you forget it, while you're with me? I'm trying hard enough to!"

"You're right. I'll probably become as self-righteous as Corinne Brewster."

"And just who may Miss Corinne be? I don't know any of these new people you seem to have been seeing. Neil, you're drifting pretty far away from me. I say!" Her wistfulness turned to sharpness. "Was she that extremely good-looking colored woman that sneaked in here to see you, one evening?"

"No, that was another girl. I'm very popular. Are you paying me the compliment of being jealous, puss?"

He tried to make it airy and domestic.

All of New Year's Eve, the only person who came in was Pat Saxinar, and she was so profusely enthusiastic about being colored—she had just discovered Harriet Tubman and the National Association for the Advancement of Colored People—that she annoyed that veteran race-crusader, Neil, as much as he had ever annoyed Corinne Brewster.

At one minute after midnight, Dr. Kenneth telephoned to them, and his voice was very old. "My dear boy, I do hope everything will go all right with you and yours, this coming year. I'm trying to get things straight, and God bless you, anyway!"

——It would be hard on Dad and his practice if his hand got shaky. Maybe I shouldn't—— Too late.

——

Vestal was carefully careless with Biddy, these days; everything in her manner said breezily, "Oh, yes, dear, Mother is ever so happy." But the child caught something of the shadow of horror that was moving through the house, and with it some notion that Negroes were aggravatingly important here. With the innocent hellishness of all Dear Little Ones, she restored Prince's name, and went through the house calling "Nigger, Nigger, Nigger!"

Vestal was trembling with something like fury when she whispered to Neil, "Suppose Curtiss Havock heard that from next door? He probably knows, from his father. But if I try to shut the baby up, I'll just make her worse."

Late on a January night they heard that thin wailing, "Nigger, Nigger, Nigger" woven with the snow-wind.

"I *am* going up and make her stop that," sighed Vestal.

Neil said, "Are you sure that was Biddy?"

38

It broke suddenly.

Neil was at his desk in the bank on Tuesday, a week after New Year's, when honest Judd Browler, whose house was well within sight of Neil's but whom he mysteriously never seemed to encounter now, marched up and said, "Neil, as you know, I haven't got any prejudices myself, but everybody seems to think I ought to protect my wife and daughter, so maybe it would look better if you and I just didn't see each other from now on, when we can avoid it." And lumped off without waiting for an answer.

Then, while Neil was chafed by Prutt's constant watching, all the old friends attacked. Curtiss Havock shouted to his wife, when he saw Neil in the yard, twenty feet away, "Christ, there's that nigger!" Elegant Eliot Hansen telephoned to Vestal a message that, translated from hints into English, meant that when she got tired of the shame of living with a colored man, he would gladly take her out for cocktails and see what he could do. (She told Neil.)

But the worst was passing Rodney Aldwick and having him croon like an Easter benediction, "*Good* morn-ing, Neil!"

Then, like a cold drizzle, came certainty that the news was slipping all through the city. A stranger, dark and dramatic, bent over Neil's lonely table at the cafeteria which he frequented these days and muttered, "You don't know me; I'm supposed to be a Greek fruit-dealer, but I'm part colored, like you. But I've kept my mouth shut about it. You take my tip and do the same, Brother."

The openest insult came from Ed Fleeron, who was now mayor of Grand Republic, in succession to William Stopple. He owned a big cut-rate drugstore which sold sandwiches, rubber bathing-caps, gritty candy, velocipedes, electric fans, and some drugs, all in dirty piles incompetently attended by girls who should have been back on the farm.

Mayor Fleeron came like a one-man parade into Neil's living-room, when Vestal was away, and blurted, "I'm the mayor of this city, and a neighbor of yours—unfortunately!"

Neil was adequately angry. "Oh, are you, Ed? I thought you lived in Swede Hollow."

"I don't want any of your lip, Kingsblood! I'm the mayor of this city——"

"Still?"

"——and I tell you we don't want any of you niggers horning into decent white neighborhoods, corrupting the kids and frightening the women."

"And bringing down real-estate values? That's the usual line, Ed."

"Yes, and it's a damn good line, too, and you'll hear a lot more about it, and if my policemen get awful interested in you and your actions, don't come bellyaching to me, as mayor!"

"Before I'd come to you for——Oh, all right. Get out!"

Mayor Fleeron's chronic rival, Ex-Mayor Stopple, who as agent for Berthold Eisenherz had been the original developer of Sylvan Park, came calling the next evening. But his was the affable racket.

He did not mention Negroes; he chirped, "Neil—Mrs. Kingsblood—I've got a customer that's crazy to move out here to the Park and likes the look of your house, and same time, I have a lovely little house in Canoe Heights, right near that wonderful fellow, Lucian Firelock." He did not suggest that this would also make it near to Dr. Ash Davis, and not far from Sugar Gowse. "While it isn't as elaborate as this house, it has a much better view—talk about your magic beauty, why, say, that view across the South End is simply breath-taking. If I could persuade you folks to think about a swap, with something to boot, I could get you a nice offer for this place, and I guess you like to make a profit 'bout as much as most folks, ha, ha, ha."

Neil said, "No. This is our home."

Vestal said, "Certainly not. It's a silly idea. Why Canoe Heights? There's a terrible mixed population there—Jews and Italians and even——Oh. I see."

Mr. Stopple put it gently: "Do you think this is a time for you to be haughty, Mrs. Kingsblood? And the price won't be anything like so good, next time. But I'll hold the offer open for a few days. Good night."

———

Neil said, "He knows."

Vestal said, "Of course he does, my good man. Maybe everybody does, by now.... Do all the high-toned darkies live on Canoe Heights? Like this Dr. Melody?"

"I have no idea."

"Don't any of your—don't you know *any* Negroes on Canoe Heights?"

"I didn't say that! I didn't say anything of the kind! I didn't say I didn't know *any* Negroes on Canoe Heights! I just said—all I said was that I didn't know where Dr. Melody lives, and I don't!"

"Oh, Neil, you never used to talk to me like that!"

"I know, and—— I'm sorry. Yes, let's not squabble." (He realized that superhumanly she was refraining from saying, "*I* wasn't squabbling," and that encouraged him.) "Let's not let Them beat us by dividing us."

"We won't! ... I don't think we will."

They wondered, then and every evening, how many of Them knew and what They were saying. It was a gasping relief to Vestal that as yet the neighborhood children were not taking it out on

Biddy but continuing to see her only as the charming and ingenious imp who had always led them in producing incredible amounts of noise. All but Peggy Havock, next door. She had been Biddy's acolyte, but now she rarely came out when Biddy clamored, and Vestal was sick as she watched Biddy, after yelling for Peggy, stand puzzled, slowly tracing a circle with her small red boot in the snow, staring at the Havock house, vainly waiting.

Most of the neighbors were extra cordial, and extra brief, on the street. From their look it was evident that they were finding something new and objectionable in Neil, even in Vestal. The frankest was their gentle neighbor, Mr. Topman, who at over fifty was still a teller in the Merchants & Miners Bank.

He stopped Neil, to say humbly, "I am told that you have Negro blood, Neil. I must say I was surprised. I always thought that all Negroes were big and black and did a lot of thieving. Could I have been wrong?"

He spoke as to a tremendous authority, and authoritatively Neil put it, "You could be."

"Now isn't that interesting! Tell me, do the Negroes like it, when they go back to Africa?"

"I don't suppose they go back."

"They don't? I never realized that. But I know a Swedish fellow that went back to the Old Country."

"I think that's different."

"Is it? I just wanted to know. Tell me, Neil, do you know a Negro preacher down in Atlanta, Georgia—I read about him—his name was—well, I don't recall it exactly, but it was something like George Brown—do you know who I mean?"

"I'm afraid I don't."

"Or it might have been Thomas. I thought you might know about him. Say, tell me—here's something I've always been curious about. How much do these top-notch colored orchestra-leaders, say like Duke Ellington—how much do they make a year, net?"

"I'm afraid I can't tell you *that.*"

"Oh, don't you know? Well say, do all Negroes want to marry white women?"

"I doubt it very much, but I couldn't say definitely."

"That's funny! I thought all you colored fellows knew all about such subjects like that."

If there was anything comic in Mr. Topman's effort to find a common ground with this Ethiopian, Kingsblood (whom he had known for only thirty-one years), the comedy faltered when he so-licitously asked:

"If Vestal and you have another child, is there very much danger that it will be coal-black?"

———

Considering Biddy's pellucidness, the question was funny, then, and slightly exasperating, but later, when he had heard it put half a dozen times and hinted at a hundred times, it was extremely exasperating and not funny at all. Neil had asked Ash Davis for the exact genetic facts, and learned, as definite, that with the union of a "colored" and a "white" person, the children will not have one chance in ten thousand of being darker than the darker parent. But he was to find that the universal folk belief, among such peasants as college-presidents and sewing-machine salesmen and popular lecturers, was that if anyone with .000001 per cent. of Negro genes married anyone fair as alabaster (which is notoriously fair), their children were more than likely to be all of them as black as the heart of a dictator. The fact that none of these civic worriers had ever heard of such a case was unimportant, because they all had heard of somebody who *had* heard of it!

Not for a time did it come to Neil that if such parents could have such an ebon child, it would still be their child to love.

———

Orlo Vay said to W. S. Vander, a fellow pillar of Sylvan Park, "He's a sap, but he's always been a good neighbor of mine, right across the street, and I'm not sure you could really call him a nigger, if he's only one thirty-second."

Mr. Vander growled, "My definition of a nigger is a fellow that publicly admits it and means it and so kicks himself right out of the human race, even if he ain't but one-hundred and thirty-second part black."

"I guess maybe you're right," admitted Orlo, not unwillingly.

Presently, throughout Grand Republic, the belief was fixed that Neil was—"if you want to know exactly"—one-quarter Negro.

—

Now, when he fled to the Davises and the Woolcapes, he pleasantly felt that he need not lie to Vestal about them. By grapevine, all of Mayo Street knew of his testimony at the club smoker, and they loved him—or just laughed. Without realizing how often, he was in a way of slipping out to John and Mary's late in the afternoon, before he went home. And often, in an uneasy friendliness, as though he was waiting for something, he saw Sophie at Ash's.

He needed their comfort, for no day in late January went by without someone, with a feeling of being very original about it, reminding him that he was "colored."

Tom Crenway, as he could not think of anything reproving to say, just looked it. Cedric Staubermeyer tried to stare like a white man staring at a Negro. But Rose Pennloss, in the next block, waved her hand with a timid cordiality. Shirley Pzort, in the kitchen, got a little mixed-up and thought it was Vestal who was the Negro, and was extra friendly to her, as to a fellow immigrant. Dr. Cope Anderson, a chemist colleague of Ash, came calling, with the Reverend Lloyd Gadd, liberal clergyman; while in the bank, Lucian Firelock went out of his way to be seen shaking hands with Neil in public.

Then he saw the person who for years had been known to the household only as "the little man who comes to the back door." He frequently showed up with a basket in the early evening, to sell them a juicy chicken, cherry marmalade, eggs, or a rococo coffee cake that his wife had made at their farm, out beyond Dead Squaw Lake. This time his fumbling ring at the back door came after eleven, and they heard it anxiously, thinking of Curtiss Havock drunk, of the hostile Mayor Fleeron and his policemen. Vestal went to the door with Neil, as stoutly as though she were two bodyguards with automatics.

The Little Man, standing in half-darkness on the cement back porch, piped, "Mr. Kingsblood—Neil—I haven't brought anything to sell tonight, but I've just heard about how much nerve you showed, and I want to thank you."

But again: on a bus, a small and unknown old woman flared at Neil, "My young nigger friend, do you know what God is going to do to you for having set yourself up against His plain commandment that Ethiopia shall stay in perpetual bondage in the kitchen and not go riding in no public buses with no decent white folks? Oh, he that heedeth not the words of God, he shall go down to hell and gnashing, and that's the Bible-truth, that's God's truth, praise His merciful name!"

That was the prelude to the letters.

Grandfather Edgar Saxinar wrote from Minneapolis that Neil was a lying ingrate, that there never had been a Xavier Pic.

Berthold Eisenherz, lord of the manor, wrote from his winter villa at Palm Beach that while he prized his acquaintanceship, he could make it to Neil's financial advantage if he would move away.

Drexel Greenshaw wrote regretting that a white gentleman like Mr. Kingsblood should call any attention at all to his unfortunate race, and so merely make it the harder for them.

Then the anonymous letters, those wry tributes to glory, written in painful ecstasy by neurotics who spend the rest of their time in sneaking along back alleys, after midnight, poisoning small cats.

They began with a sheet of ruled tablet-paper, inscribed in a rheumatic hand, mailed in a characterless envelope, with the name and address clumsily lettered.

Dear Mister Smart Nigger Kingsblood:

I guess you never thought I would here about how you come out and admitted all these years you been pertending to be a decent white man and now they caught you with your pants down and you are nothing but a nigger and you are trying to get away with it and claim where niggers are just as good as white men and if you red your Bible you would know different it says there plane God made niggers to be white man's servants and if God had intentioned to have niggers same as us white men and become doctors and lawyers and so on and so forth would he made them different color of course he wouldnt. He gave them that disgusting black color like yours to show they inferior dont you see that now you just never thought about that.

The trouble with you fellows you never try and use your so-called branes and if you would stop and think once you would see what I mean and go back to the cabin where God intended you to be.

Well thats a good joke on you, Mr. Dinge, and come now be a good sport and see how ridiculous you make yourself when you open your mouth and show your ignorance and so I had a good laugh and if you admit now that the joke is on you I will forgive you and let byguns be byguns. I freely grant just my luck I had good education while you niggers are all igorant but dont you ever dare say anything about the Mississippi & Louisiana senators they are fine gentlemen and black beggars like you are not fit to black their boots and so you can just put that in your pipe and smoke it, Mister Educated Nigger and thank

An unknown Friend

P.S. The next time you wont get off so easy we dont give you coons a second chants trying to look like a white man you better watch your step you dont know how many people got there eye on you and you never know beforehand when blow will fall.

Vestal received only one anonymous letter, to Neil's dozen, but hers was accurately typed, on linen paper, scented:

Dear Vestal (or Virgin):

This socially impoverished community owes a *great deal* to you and your handsome "hubby" for providing it with a scandal that will amuse us all for *years* to come. But please do let us know whether your *darling* spouse will run for Congress, as a Colored Gempman, and thus enable you to flaunt your "charms" and your fifty-dollar hats in the higher (colored) circles in Washington as you have in G.R. Your fairy daughter, so "superior" to all the normal brats—we have long found her childish swank and parading *very* funny—will in Washington be able to associate with infants *worthy* of her, the precocious offspring of Negro professors, Jewish "experts" and Haitian ambassadors.

Doubtless any failure now on the part of your "better half" to earn a living will, as hitherto, be compensated for by the charity handed out by your impressive, even if slightly dreary, Papa.

You might tell your husband—did you ever chance to think of what a pretty "chorus boy" he would make?—that we are *fed up* with the arrogance of the niggers. The deah boy could not have picked a *worse* time to have allied himself with these gentry. So the niggers now *demand* the *right* to mix with the D.A.R., and the nigger wenches will not work in kitchens or laundries, because they are all *ex-lieutenants,* forsooth!

The Negroes—tell your *delightful* but singularly unalphabet sweetie—will not get along until they perceive that we are not one bit "prejudiced" against their enchanting complexions and noses, but against their preventable diseases, their parasites, their idleness and utter filth and abysmal *ignorance.* Of course all of us know that you appreciate all this about that ilk, and we are duly impressed by your loyalty in sticking to a member of that Neanderthal tribe. Gracious, what a *good time* he must give you when you cuddle and scream!!

Oh, don't *mention* it, my dear Mrs. K., and I hope—and the numerous ladies whom I have heard discussing it *all* hope—that the interest which dear Mr. Eliot Hansen has always shown in you will develop into another "interesting situation." We are all really very *jealous* of the neat arts and wrigglings you employ to attract these dubious types of males, and we shall observe your dual activities with *impressment.*

Or will Neilly and you get *wise* to yourselves and get out of town? The voice of Thersites is the voice of Truth.

A Friend Indeed

As she handed this case-history to Neil, Vestal said wildly, "Is there any chance of my proving that I have decent Negro blood, too?"

39

New Year's Day prophecy and hangovers were finished with, and Neil was primarily a man with a job, at the bank, in the realistic world of bonds and marble and Pruttery.

On Friday morning, ten days after New Year's, Mr. Prutt called him into his office.

Mr. Prutt was a virtuous and thrifty man, though an Episcopalian, and he was motherly in his manner of saying, "Neil, sit down, my boy." He made a tent of his fingers, and looked over the ridgepole.

"I have concluded that your statement about your ancestry, at the club smoker, was not a joke—that you were not drunk, as I had hoped. Of course you regret having made it, and you see how shockingly it will affect your career, but what I don't know is whether you comprehend how seriously it affects *me,* since I am responsible for the credit and stability of this bank.

"As a born Yankee, I have always had great commiseration for you colored people, and have always maintained that it would be more charitable not to educate you beyond the fourth grade, so that you will not get false ideas and realize how unhappy you are. But in your case, I suppose your white blood outweighs any inferior stock, so I imagine that you have always been truly loyal to this Institution, as certainly this Institution has always been loyal to its employees.

"In this unfortunate situation, and you will note that I do not pry unduly into your motives, we shall underwrite you to the limit, and try our best to find out if there is any way in which we can keep from letting you go. BUT.

"For a time, as you will appreciate, it will be much better if the public don't come into contact with you directly. We can scarcely afford to be known as an Institution that employs a lot of colored people when so many of our white veterans are beginning to look for work.

"So I am afraid I shall have to make other arrangements about

the managership of our Veterans' Center, and I'll find book-work
for you, inside, where none of our customers need see you and mis-
understand. People are so inconsiderate! But I shall try to get our
Board of Directors not to reduce your salary ... yet.

"Now, Neilly," very brightly, "I'm sure you see my philosophy!"

"Yes."

And that was all that this colored man contributed to helping out
poor Mr. Prutt.

———

He had gone back to his desk in the Veterans' Center, which he had
planned and organized, and he was gathering up his private sou-
venirs, the photograph of Vestal and Biddy, and his pipe and an
Italian coin he had found on a battlefield.

The telephone called him. It was Dr. Norman Kamber.

"Neil, can you come right over to your father's office? I am phon-
ing from there. Your father dropped dead, just a few minutes
ago."

———

He thought, "This is just silly. This is just melodrama." There was
even a not unpleasurable excitement at so much happening. It was
only slowly that he took in the heavy fact that he would never be
able to talk with his father again; never see his anxious, sandy smile
or hear his chirping little jokes; never be able to make it right with
him for having become a Negro.

He remembered that his father had wanted to live on to be the
founder of a line of kings; remembered how handy around the
house his father had been; and wondered whether the funeral
would be on Sunday or on Monday; and if it was to be on Monday,
would he be expected to come back to the bank that afternoon? The
Veterans' Center would certainly need him.

And remembered that his Center would never need him again.

These distractions were gone in tenderness for his mother, who
would be so alone now. No, she would not be alone. She would have
Joan with her. And he had just seen fit to turn them both into Negroes, with the loneliness that all Negroes have in a white community.

He plodded out of the bank in a vision of his mother alone, not daring to talk to her closest neighbor, even in this urgency of death.

40

The office of Dr. Kenneth Kingsblood was on Chippewa Avenue, only a block from the Second National, in the Professional and Arts Building, known as the P. & A.

The lobby was so crowded with men on crutches, men with bandaged arms, blank-faced mothers with babies in their arms, that he had to wait for a third elevator. The elevator girl was pretty. She flirted with a young man in a white coat, but she smiled at Neil and said "Fifth floor—*your* floor," caressingly. He marveled that she probably did not know what was awaiting him on that floor, a few feet from her cage.

It was shocking to go into the neat triviality of Dr. Kenneth's waiting-room—the two ruddy maple chairs with tartan cushions, the maple table with a stack of picture-magazines and the always-lighted electric lamp with a shade picturing a frigate in full sail—and to see, on the maple couch with the tartan cushions, his father lying dead. His stilled head was in the shadow of the table, on which lay his engagement book, open to this morning, with a name neatly set down for half an hour from now. On the book rested his old spectacles, idle. The righthand ear-piece of the spectacles was mended with adhesive tape grown gray now, and Neil remembered that, looking gaily at him through those streaky lenses, his father had promised to step down the hall in the P. & A. and have the frame mended.

The girl assistant was looking down at the lax thin body and crying, her face red with amazement and loss.

As Neil turned to Dr. Kamber for the comfort of the medicine man, Brother Robert bumbled in, with, "Good thing you caught me at the bank, Doc. I was just going to leave for the bakery and maybe I wouldn't of been able to get here for a long time and——Oh, Pop, Pop! I can't believe it, Pop! That you won't be with us now!"

He turned on Neil: "And you killed him! Your crazy lies were too much for him. You're responsible for his death, and I won't forget it!"

Dr. Kamber ordered, "Chuck it, Bob. Your dad apparently died of a coronary. Neil had nothing to do with it. Your dad was probably proud of Neil's courage."

Dr. Roy Drover, president of the Federal Club, and Dr. Cortez Kelly, duck-hunting neighbor of Neil, who both had their offices in the P. & A., seemed to have crowded into that small room now, and Drover, after a good strong look of dislike at Neil, commented to Kamber, "Well, you can't tell now, Doctor. The way Neil was cutting up may have had a bad effect on the old man. How can we be sure?"

Dr. Kelly protested, "Oh, for Pete's sake, quit it, Roy. Neil is a fool, and I hope to see him driven out of my neighborhood, like any other nigger, but he didn't kill the old man. Come on, Roy, let's scram."

The two medical gentlemen argued off down the hall, and Neil and Robert and Dr. Kamber and the shaky girl assistant silently gazed down at the unnatural silence of the man on the couch.

Neil thought of his father happily raking the leaves, last October, and prosing, "The fall is the best time of the year. It's so peaceful. I've always been a busy man, even if collections are so bad, and I look forward to a lot of peace and enjoyment in the autumn of my life. I like it when I can be peaceful."

But not peaceful like this, lying in a waiting-room, nervous hands rigid.

——Am I his murderer? He'll never know about the Catherine of Aragon line now, and maybe it was true. Did I kill that for him, too?

Dr. Kamber's hand was on his shoulder, but Neil wished that Vestal were here.... And Sophie. And Mary Woolcape.

Robert was blubbering. Oldest of Dr. Kenneth's children, he was yet the most childish and most likely to run to his father with troubles, even after he had himself become a father. He was an overgrown farm-boy, awed and afraid now, and Neil realized what his announcement of Negro kinship must have done to this simple, loving and mercenary family-man.

Then Robert Hearth, the undertaker, arrived, and from that second till the coffin sank in the January earth, the two Roberts took charge of everything. They were so much alike: equally solemn, equally efficient in the superb accomplishment of utterly childish ends, equally sure that it must be a comfort to Dr. Kenneth in the coffin to have a little, clean soft pillow under his head.

And equally certain that Neil had killed him.

—

The once lean and hearty face of his father at the funeral had been painted to a horrible semblance of a waxwork pretty-boy. Neil edgily wondered if the dainty padding of the coffin, displayed through the open trapdoor at the top, thriftily stopped there, and he hated the whole sparkling business of death without annoyance to friends & family; hated the two whispering Roberts, whose stately manner said, "Grieve not—see how bravely *we* take it—costs surprisingly low—24 hr. service."

They both managed to make Neil feel like a stranger, here in his father's house.

His mother was only a wisp of fog, she was quiet, she did not sob, she would not take advantage of her one great day and show off. She humbly did whatever the two Roberts told her. They were so manly with her, and so obliging in their butterfingered offers to take from her a burden of sorrow that neither of them could understand.

What most flattered the two Roberts was the attendance of both Mayor Fleeron and Ex-Mayor Bill Stopple, hats in hands, looking politically at Neil with an unworded leering promise that they would let him off for today.

And the coffin lay in the center of the parlor, and there were strangers all around, people who, Neil could have sworn, had never seen Dr. Kenneth before, and the frescoed figure in the coffin seemed waiting, and they all seemed waiting, sitting around on hired chairs, and there was a stink of improbable massed flowers, and over Dr. Kenneth's crayon portrait hung a black pall hastily cut out of an old air-raid curtain. But the two Roberts had failed to put away Dr. Kenneth's corncob pipe, which still rested on top of the piano, the only thing there that was honest and not waiting.

Robert Hearth pontifically raised his hand, and Robert Kingsblood raised his hand, and turned to his mother, who now first sobbed. The pall-bearers looked self-conscious as they moved in like automata. Among them were Cedric Staubermeyer and W. S. Vander, the neighbors who most hated the reborn Neil.

At no time did any of the attendants speak to him, and they only bowed to the blank, polite Vestal and the interested Biddy.

The coffin, sloping as it passed down the front steps, slowly moved out of the house. Then Neil first understood how final was death. This was the last time when his father would ever use these steps, up and down which he had trotted, so fussily, so happily, for so many years; and on this last passage, he could not go by himself. He had to be carried, and he could not look back at the house one last time.

Hearth ushered them to their proper places in the funeral cars, in a complicated order of court precedence as though Death were a monarch touchy and demanding of propriety. There were words between Alice Whittick Kingsblood and Kitty Kingsblood Sayward as to which of them ought to sit with Mother. Robert Hearth solved it soothingly, with a brisk bland piety that said, This too shall pass away and you will be surprised and gratified by the reasonableness of my bill.

The cars, when they started, all had their lights on, to indicate that this was a funeral. It was by state law an offense punishable by fine to cross the line of the procession, lest Dr. Kenneth's feelings be hurt.

Then the coffin was swaying up the steps into the Sylvan Park Baptist Church, and Dr. Shelley Buncer, in Geneva gown, was waiting as though he had never played rummy, but always in shadowy cloisters had meditated upon the resurrection. His sermon was consoling, and he promised all of them that they would soon see their friend again, but he did not seem excited about it.

Neil wondered again at the strangers who had come to mourn

his father. Who were they all? Patients? Perhaps some of them knew his father better than he did now. He felt lonely, and suddenly Vestal's intelligent hand was reassuring him.

He realized how many were staring at him rather than at the pastor; he remembered that to half of them he was a masquerading black man who had been caught and was going to be driven out of town. Then he noticed two unexpected guests whose eyes, as they sat in the back row, tried to tell him their enduring friendship— Evan Brewster, and Dr. Emerson Woolcape, a fellow-dentist to whom Dr. Kenneth had never spoken.

———

It was cold at the grave, out at Forest Lawn Cemetery on Ottawa Heights, and over the shivering few who had stayed, Dr. Buncer's brave words seemed to hang and tremble like gray snowflakes.

Then they all turned away and left his father there alone.

———

When they were home, the Vestal who had been so patient became sharp.

"Oh, quit being sentimental about your father. There's nothing you can do for him now. But it occurs to me that there's a lot of things you can do for me and our child. Do you ever stop and think that she is very much your child, too, and so like you in her thoughtlessness? Now that your notorious love of truth and justice has inspired you to turn us into Negroes, just what are your plans for us outcasts? I wasn't consulted about your public exhibit of yourself, and now I'm waiting to be told what to do!"

"Why, Ves, when you were so wonderful at the funeral———"

"Maybe I've been too wonderful. Just what do you intend to do, if that old horsehair sofa, Prutt, turns you out of the bank?"

"I don't know."

"Don't you think you better begin to know?"

He nodded.

41

They were alone in the evening, sadly reading. At the doorbell's sound, Vestal speculated, "After ten—what gives? It's probably Brother Robert, come over to enjoy a little knitting and worry. I better go. I'll tell him we're just off to bed."

There was a jangle of voices when the door opened, and high laughter, rough and derisive. Neil rose, ready for battle, but he heard Vestal, like a flute too shrill, inviting, "Certainly, come right in. Enchanted to see you.... Now that was very thoughtful of you!"

At the living-room door there were three black faces and one plastered dead-white, all maliciously merry, and they were Borus Bugdoll of the Jumpin' Jive, Hack Riley, a dark ex-soldier, a white Polish girl called Faydis—surname forever unknown—and the black rose, Belfreda Gray, bubbling, "I always swore I'd come in the front door here, and by God, I have!"

"And, by God, so you have!" Vestal said sweetly.

Self-assured yet languid, hard as a flyer, his thin nose dark and bold above a race-track tie, a black hawk that liked to kill little birds, Borus winked at Vestal, glanced derisively at the jangled Neil, and said smoothly, "Good evening. My name is Bugdoll. I am a saloon-keeper. I heard there was a new mixed couple in town, and I always call and welcome them to our gang."

Faydis crowed, "Yeh, him and me are mixed. He used to go with Bel, but her and Hack have clicked, and Borus is my fellow, and I'm just as white as you folks, maybe more so, but do I love my little brown dumpling! Yeh, I'm just like you, Vestal, living with a colored boy, and is it good cuddling—I'll say!"

Neil drew the breath of one about to repel boarders, but Vestal's voice, clear, low, only to be caught by a husband, insisted, "No. I want you to see what your intellectual friends are like!" Then, cheerily, "Do sit down, everybody. Belfreda—if I'm not being too intimate—how is everything going?"

She was so placid, so merry, that already she had taken the fuse out of their joke. Borus, an expert in social relations, stood easily, a little taller than Vestal, and he condescended, "You know, you're a good guy, lady."

He stared at her with such amusement, as though he knew all her thoughts and snobbishnesses and generosities, knew her in ball-gown or bathing suit, that she flushed and lost the lead. She said hastily, "Neil, I'll get some drinks for your friends. Will you make them at home?"

He thought how taut, quick, knife-sliding, Borus looked, and he said carefully, with the expectation of trouble. "What do you mean by butting in here?"

"Maybe just to needle you, and maybe to see whether you're an honest-to-God raceman or another gravy-sermon, race-relations highbrow. We was wondering if you can take it with us coalheavers, Neil?"

He felt that properly he ought to be offended, and found that he was not at all offended; that a lot of fine, high social fences which he had supposed to exist between Captain Kingsblood (of the Kings-bloods) and Borus the black bartender had been shadows, and that he might be lucky to have the friendship of a Borus, when all the Featherings set upon him.

"I hope so, Borus," he said, very gravely. "But I'm green. I'll have to count on you, if I can."

"You bet!" said Hack Riley, and Borus drawled, "Maybe you can," as one who meant it, or would mean it some day, or would very nearly mean it.

Vestal came in with a huge maple tray with drinks and ice and soda. Hack clumsily rose, reaching out his hands to take it, but the deft Borus was ahead of him, and he began to mix, while Hack and Faydis looked shyly about the serenity and assurance of the room. They all had highballs, and everything was changed, and these were no longer black invaders resented by lofty whites, but just six young people, fond of ribaldry and laughter, having a surprisingly good time together. They laughed at Borus's stories of greedy white policemen, at Hack's opinion of white sergeants, at Vestal's first surprise at their entrance.

Belfreda wanted to know, "How's Biddy?"

"Getting so big now!" said Mother Vestal.

"You ought to give her more broccoli."

"That's so."

"And how is Nigger—Prince, I mean!" said Belfreda.

There was a trace, inevitably, of race-talk.

Borus agreed completely with Mr. Feathering about Negro cul-ture. "What does a smoke want of drayma when he can get a bankroll and a nice piece—pink or tan?" he scoffed.

Hack Riley offered, "I meant to kid the pants off you, Cap, but you're all right. I guess you'll have a mean time with the ofays. So what? I've had one, all my life! I'd like to see you stowing cargo, or pearl-diving!"

It is almost certain that Vestal supposed "pearl-diving" to mean diving for pearls. She replied firmly, "I'm sure he'll do it splendidly. He's such a wonderful swimmer."

She wondered why they laughed so flatteringly.

They stayed not an hour. At farewell, Belfreda patted Vestal's hand, and the troop of the gay enchanted went sliding off in Borus's sumptuous car, with shrieks of "You two guys are okay! Come see us at the Jive." Once, their people had plodded the Carolina roads while Massa galloped, but a Negro in a car goes as fast as a white man.

Neil crowed, "They're roughnecks, but they're fun. They'd be swell friends, if you ever needed them. Can't you see why I take them seriously?"

Vestal examined him coldly. "Those clowns? My dear boy, have you gone quite mad?"

"I thought you rather liked them."

"Well, I didn't want our throats cut."

"Oh, nonsense!" Neil protested. "They're much decenter than Curtiss Havock, and much smarter."

"Who isn't! You mean to say you could ever tolerate the way that horrible Bugdoll leers? I could have him whipped! I'm not South-ern, but I'm awful white."

"Oh, I liked it as much as I do the way Eliot Hansen simpers at you and always manages to touch you! And Borus has courage. Some day we might be very glad to have a house next to him."

"You might. Not me. I won't be there!"

"No? Well, I think I'll walk a few blocks before I turn in."

He rather wanted to be unfaithful to his oppressive wife, as regularized young husbands often do when they are sorely puzzled, when they feel that new and surprising caresses of warmer arms might provide a rational explanation of everything. He very much wanted to telephone to Sophie Concord.

And so, after five minutes of cold air and loneliness, he came home and argued with Vestal till midnight.

February had come in, and the sidewalks were perilously icy under the shifty covering of snow. Cars stalled and slipped backward when they tried to run up the hills, and the chains about the tires as they hit the fenders flapped all day long in an irritable chorus.

In the Capital of the Nation, a few Southern Senators refused to let their fellow Titans even vote upon a bill to prevent employers from refusing jobs on the grounds of an applicant's color.

Fort Sumter had been fired on again, and the Deep South had again seceded from the American Constitution, and this time they were supported by more Northern Copperheads. The new Jefferson Davis was yet to be chosen, but a clear statement of Southern ideals and a bugle-call to armed rebellion had been issued by that aristocratic old planter, Mr. David L. Cohn, who in the obliging *Atlantic Monthly* had recently stated:

"There are whites and Negroes who would attempt to break down segregation in the South by Federal fiat. Let them beware. I have no doubt that in such an event every Southern white man would spring to arms and the country would be swept by civil war."

There was no Lincoln now to call for troops and, eighty-five years after it had started, the War Between the States was won by the South. And in a small frozen city in the North Central States, a Negro named Neil Kingsblood was having trouble in keeping his job, not because of any incompetence or incivility but because of his color—even though he did not have that color, and God still reigned and everything was mysterious in its wondrous lack of any sense whatever.

42

"Considering the British, French, Dutch, Spanish, Portuguese and their excursions in the shadier portions of their empires and the handmaidens they brought home, considering the wanderings of the Moors southward in Africa and north in Europe, considering human nature on warm evenings in the South, it is probable that every 'white person' in Europe and the Americas, from British dukes up to Georgia politicians, has some trace of 'Negro blood.'"

It was Clement Brazenstar holding forth, back in town and staying at the Woolcapes'. Neil was delighted to see that dark clown face again, but at this outrageous theory, he was offended. What would happen to the whole careful structure of his unhappiness if Vestal and John William Prutt and Wilbur Feathering and Rodney Aldwick could also be denounced as "colored"?

That evening, Clem had a few other bombs:

If the whites in such portions of the South as have seventy or eighty per cent. of colored population are disturbed by being so outnumbered, there is one thing they might do besides rig all law and government in order to keep control. They might take the same privilege they have often and generously granted to discontented Negroes, and move away.

With mechanical cotton-pickers and rice-cultivators, four or five million Negro farmhands will probably move to the North in the next fifteen years, and the righteous citizens of the North will have a chance to see whether they constitute a White Problem.

Whenever Negroes break loose and viciously start fighting white merchants and policemen, their viciousness is in exact ratio to the viciousness with which they have been treated. This is an ancient rule from the biology of revolutions.

Prejudice is the most precious birthright of the ignorant, and if the seven wisest men in the world, in person and sober, were for seven straight hours to argue that a Negro like Ash Davis is as admirable a voter and dinner-companion as the average white boot-legger, and properly reared Southerner, particularly if a woman, would at the end only smile politely and answer, "You boys don't understand the Nigras like I do, and how would you like to have Nigras marry your seven daughters?"

So Clem laughed jovially.

———

Neil had to leave at midnight, which is merely tuning-up time in a race-discussion. When he came out of the Woolcapes' little house, he found Wilbur Feathering strolling by, unabashed.

Wilbur said genially, "How are you, Kingsblood? Have a good time tonight? I see you're like me; you enjoy coming down here and studying the downtrodden blacks."

It was from Feathering, then, that Rod Aldwick had his information about the "agitators"?

Neil grunted, and left him.

Next morning, in the bank, he saw Mr. Feathering talking to S. Ashiel Denver. Afterward, Mr. Denver summoned him.

"Neil, I want you to do your best to please Mr. Prutt. He's a very fine man, and *the* most correct moral code. He told me how, when he was a boy in Maine, he once had no penny to put in the Sunday-school collection, and as soon as he got one, by raking a lawn, he tramped five miles to give it to the Sunday-school superintendent, a shoe-dealer, who was so moved by the little fellow's piety that he gave him a pair of rubber boots, only slightly shopworn! And of course Mr. Prutt's fidelity to those of us who are his fellow-servants in the bank is unimpeachable."

"What's the trouble, S.A.?"

"Well, there have been complaints from certain of our substantial depositors about our employing a non-Caucasian. But you know us, Neil. Mr. Prutt and I will do our best for you. But."

One depositor seemed unoffended by Neil's presence, and that was Lucian Firelock, who sent word to him, in his isolated coop, that he would like to take him out to lunch. Neil was pleased. For two weeks now he had been creeping off to lunch alone, at some dog-wagon.

They went to the pretentious Oscar's Montparnasse, a resort of fashion and of wit which was even more elegant than the Fiesole Room. As they walked in, Neil thought that the patrons were staring at him with contempt or hostility, and he felt more uncomfortable for Lucian than for himself.

They were amiably received, and shown to an excellent table, but he immediately saw Randy Spruce and Boone Havock peep at him and speak to the headwaiter. Was he imagining it, or did their own waiter become impertinent now? He was standing on one foot and sucking his teeth, and he threw at them, "How's about some veal chops?"

"That would be all right," said Lucian, while Neil found himself not liking to answer. The waiter demanded of him, "What about you, Brother?"

"All right."

"You boys ought to like 'em. Our best customers do!"

Or was the waiter merely friendly and untrained? Lucian looked annoyed, and Neil resolved:

——I wouldn't care, if I were alone. But I'll never go with any of my white friends to a restaurant again and subject them to this embarrassment. And you can't even explain it to them. They wouldn't understand. They'd say "Why don't you complain?"

———

They did not talk, till the end of lunch, of Negro lore, but of Diantha, consort of the newspaper-owner, Gregory Marl. With singular force and simplicity, Diantha tried to dominate all the polite arts in town, from the little theater to the Foreign Policy Association, and she might have succeeded if she could only have stopped after three cocktails.

(It is a fact that Neil found himself wondering if it was proper for *him* to discuss a white lady like this.)

Then Lucian blurted, "I know you've been avoiding the Federal Club. Why don't you march right in there?"

"I'm not a member!"

"They couldn't throw you out."

"What would it prove?"

"I don't know," Lucian admitted. "Maybe it would prove something right against my whole argument for segregation, which is that there is an inherent difference between Nigras and whites. Oh, Neil, my good friend, you have led me into strange heresies, even though I scarcely know you. Maybe it's just as well I don't know you better. I might find myself a Rosicrucian or a sun-worshipper!"

Neil returned to the bank stepping high.

In mid-afternoon, Mr. Prutt called him in and said, with no fond fussing this time, "I don't want you to ever cause talk again by going to lunch publicly with a white man. Will you give me your promise to that effect?"

"What? No! Certainly not!"

"I have been very generous, Neil, keeping you on, after the complaints from our depositors. And have you appreciated it? The other evening you went to the house of a colored man named Woolcape and met a group of Negro trouble-makers who are plotting to destroy our entire business system."

Neil stood up. "If you believe that, you'll believe anything. I resign."

"That will be rather of a relief all round, Kingsblood, and I shall try to bear you no ill will for having taken advantage of our tolerance." Mr. Prutt held out a dry hand to be shaken, but Neil sighed:

"That's quite all right, sir, but I don't like to shake hands with white men. Good day, sir."

He looked for S. Ashiel Denver, to say good-bye. He saw him hiding in the vault.

So, with the silver-framed photograph of Vestal and Biddy under his arm, Neil walked out of the bank, a Negro out of a job.

The final payment on his house was due, but this would be only a couple of hundred dollars, and he had a bank-balance of $1127.79, and a loyal wife.

He was sure about the bank-balance.

43

Vestal, as the heir of a thousand Beehouses, had no more experience with the men of her family looking for work than with their turning into Chippewas and Hottentots. But she had been fifteen years old in the Panic of 1929, and she could remember quite respectable men, graduates of Yale and Dartmouth, who had lost brokerage houses and courageously gone on facing life on income of less than ten thousand a year.

She was not worried about Neil's lack of income. It was only a question of whether he would accept a position, probably a better salary, in the Blue Ox National Bank, or favor the smaller Merchants & Miners.

Nor, except when he was a schoolboy and had borrowed a lawn-mower from Uncle Emery Saxinar and set up in the jobbing-gardener business (over the summer he got three lawns to do, at thirty-five cents apiece, but there was no future in it, because he squandered his gains on black-and-white sodas), had Neil himself ever looked for work. His appointment to the Second National, after college, had come as naturally as the wrist-watch that was his father's Commencement gift.

He did not understand that the world simply does not care what happens to cautious rebels, once they have ceased to play the safe game of Pruttery. It does not persecute them; it merely sends out word that it is not at home, when they call to say that they are starving.

Neil would not gratify the Blue Ox National by offering to join it, not he, for he disapproved of the Havocks. No, he would go help out the Merchants & Miners and his mousy teller friend, Mr. Topman. But Vestal said that he must do it grandly; he must take the car. No, no, she was only going to the women's club for a little bridge, and she could *just* as well take the bus.

He breezed into the brown diminutiveness of the Merchants & Miners, but Mr. Topman, behind the bars, jerked back as though Neil was known to bite. He reluctantly took Neil to the bank's president, who once had praised his tennis at a Heather Club tournament but could not quite recall him now, and mumbled, "Sorry, doesn't seem to be any kind of opening."

Less confidently—less and less confidently—Neil went on to the other banks, to a brokerage house, to Scott Zago's Northern Insurance Brokerage.

Mr. Zago was grievously busy, or so Neil was informed by Verne Avondene, the office manager, a courtly old man who had once been rich himself. Mr. Avondene's lawn had been one of those mowed by the enterprising young firm of Neil & Co., and Mr. Avondene had then said to him, "What great thing in life do you intend to discover? The golden fleece or the cabin at Innisfree?"

"I'm not sure if I'm going to be a doctor or an aviator," Neil had said.

It had been Verne Avondene who, as secretary of the Federal Club, had telephoned to Neil a few days ago that he was resignated. Now, listening to Neil's fumbling hints about wanting a job, he looked at Neil as at a light colored man whose effrontery was amusing. He did not take the trouble to say No. He just smiled it.

At the Emporium, Levi Tarr said that the accounting and credit departments were already overstaffed, but would Neil care to be a salesman? "I wish you'd try it. The pay isn't much, but you might work up to a position as buyer, fairly quickly. I'd like to have you, both as an intelligent man and because I want to get my father to let me use some Negro clerks. You'd be a wedge."

Neil was very polite, and lied about "other openings."

——Me a wedge! Me waiting on old women! Selling 'em ribbons or whatever it is you do sell 'em.

He went reluctantly to the Power & Light Company, to his father-in-law, Morton Beehouse, whom he had stringently not seen since New Year's and who had stopped the intermittent income he had given to Vestal. To that oak façade he stated, "I don't want a job as charity. I think I'm a fairly good executive."

"And no doubt you also think that you can support my daughter adequately, after you have antagonized every decent businessman in town. Well, let me tell you, if you get any job whatever with this organization, it will be nothing *but* charity!"

"Okay," said Neil as he went.

This was on his second sleety day of job-hunting, and in the afternoon he drove down to the South End, to talk with a Home Loan Association. The streets were slippery enough for chains, and he drove into a garage to have them put on. On the wet floor, gouging the ice off a fender, was a greasy Negro car-washer in torn overalls, who grinned at him and half waved his hand. Slowly, aghast, Neil recognized in this gnome the Captain Philip Windeck whom he had seen at the Jumpin' Jive, precise and authoritative in his uniform as a flyer.

"Phil!" he cried, with an affection that surprised both of them.

"How are you, Captain—Neil?" the grub hesitated.

When they had trudged over the necessary bridge-approaches of conversation, Neil wanted to know: "How about engineering school? Going to be able to go back?"

"I haven't had the nerve to tackle it—to start all over again on that magnificent career that works up through study to officer-and-gentleman to chamois-rag. I feel too segregated. When I started to look for a job, I found that my having been an officer was against me. The white engineers said it had been an impertinence.

"So I took the long trail of the Negroes. I hope you never have to follow it: city to city—Omaha to Dallas to Seattle to Pittsburgh—always hearing that in the next town they're hiring the brownskins, hustling there by boxcar and finding that they aren't. I got lonely for Garnet and the home town. You know it's my home, too, and I love the hills and the rivers. So I'm back, and I'll save up a few dollars and start off again—school or the trail.

"You know, in every machine shop I had one test demand: will you give me the chance to set up any job you pick out on a turret lathe? And they always said the same thing: do you think we're going to ruin an expensive rig like that to please a nigger garageman? Oh, well, *so geht's*."

He was looking at Neil resentfully, but when Neil said simply, "Phil, I'm also a Negro, and I've also been fired for it," the defiance went out of him and, after most carefully wiping his hand on a piece of waste, Phil shook hands with his fellow captain, his fellow penniless job-hunter, his friend.

After work-hours, after Neil had been refused another job, Phil and he went out for a cup of coffee at an Automobile Row diner, where the proprietor, with so many greasy-faced customers, had given up trying to decide which of them were "colored" and which were "white."

Phil said, "You must have seen my dad, old Cloat Windeck, running an elevator at the Blue Ox National Building. The poor old boy is broken-hearted about my decline and fall. He always insisted that I inherited my flying technique from him—running his elevator up to a twelve-story altitude."

And, "I had one fine week in Denver, on my trek. Monday, I got a job hacking, lovely new purple cab, and I was good. I taught myself to say 'Yes, sir' and 'Yes, ma'am' perfectly and to take tips just as cheerfully as I'd taken an officer's pay. No accidents or rows or anything, not even a cop looking cross-eyed, but on Tuesday some white friend kicked to the office about having been driven by an ignorant colored man, and so I was fired on Wednesday. On Thursday, I got a job driving a truck. Four white drivers waylaid me and beat me up and set fire to my truck, and you know, it just didn't seem worth while reporting to the office, so I climbed a freight for Cheyenne. 'America, I love thy friendships, strong men, camerados, aid each to each in labors.' Whitman."

Neil pondered, "I must meet some white people some day. Phil, when you get very mad, do you think about machine-guns?"

"I start to, and then I won't let myself. God, these whites will never know the patience the colored peoples have shown, all over the world. It's like the patience of God himself."

Neil had never been able to talk thus, freely, passionately, romantically, profanely, with Judd Browler or Elegant Eliot Hansen. But he realized, as he drove home, that his Vestal would welcome Judd or Eliot, but not Phil Windeck, not the dripping car-washer, not a man called "Hey you, boy!"

—

He had made the last payment on their house.

"It's sure-enough ours, forever!" he rejoiced, and they danced through the blue and maroon living-room, the sunporch, the small crystal and mahogany dining-room.

"Honestly, Neil, wouldn't you think it was a perfectly charming house, even if you had no idea who it belonged to?" she cried with loving enthusiasm.

"I certainly would!"

It did not seem the moment to inform her that they now had only $761.61 in the bank, with his war pension not large enough to make a vast difference, and that his masquerade, as a young white gentleman pretending to be a job-hunting Negro, was losing its romance with rapidity.

But he had to tell her, in a few days, that he had no prospects of work whatever.

"I guess you'll have to help me find something—anything," he confessed.

Vestal went into action. She let Shirley go, but so gracefully that Shirley left with a kiss for Biddy and a warm farewell to Vestal as to a fellow-victim of them guys in Wall Street.

Vestal cut down on their food, rejected the almost obligatory movie, menacingly eyed Prince's undiminished appetite, and abruptly told Biddy that, no, she could not have a pony.

Then they sold the car. In the United States, that is the same as saying, "Then they sold their four daughters into slavery."

They got a satisfactory price, in the post-war shortage. But not to own any sort of car was an acknowledgment of social death, for a Prosperous American Business Man, for a Busy and Popular Young Matron who was trying to keep up her rank while her oldest friends were staring at her as though they had just met her and didn't think they liked her.

As a substitute for the other gifts which Biddy wanted from moment to moment, Vestal had bought for her a fifteen-cent book of "comic strips." Looking through this enterprising literature, which in America had replaced the Brothers Grimm and *The Wind in the Willows,* Neil found that no few of the cartoons dealt with Negro characters, clownish and vile.

But, in weariness with sermons, he said nothing; he merely stole the opus from his own daughter and threw it into the furnace and sat down to a season of agitation about Biddy's future as a Negro. What school, what job, what marriage would she have when It was publicly admitted?

He could hear Vestal reprimanding him, "You should have thought of all this before you went off half-cocked."

He could hear Wilbur Feathering wallow, "H.w.y.l.y.d.t.m.a.N.?" And how, he interrogated himself, *would* he like to have Biddy marry a boy like Winthrop Brewster?

——Why not, if Win would stand for anything so dictatorial and bouncing as Biddy! He's the most charming and intelligent boy I know.

——How incorrigibly the white man I am—Nature's most devastating freak, after the earthquake and the bubonic plague; debating whether Winthrop is as good as his obvious inferiors, and thinking I'm such a courageous soul for debating it!

Of that debate he did not tell Vestal.

———

When Orlo Vay started off for his optical shop in the morning in his well-heated car and saw that nigger, Kingsblood, a beggar who hadn't even a car or a hired girl, crawl off down the windy street to start his daily search for a job, and when the fellow stumbled on the snow-upholstered ice and danced and waved his arms like a human top in his effort to keep his balance, then Orlo laughed with moral joy.

But Virga, Mrs. Orlo Vay, nervously brought a maple-layer cake across the street to Vestal who, as she furiously vacuumed and dusted the house, did not know whether to feel touched or insulted. For Mrs. Vay had belonged to a distinctly lower layer in that creamy social cake that was Sylvan Park—till now she had.

44

Vestal did not care for this hermit business. She loved parties, all kinds of parties. She did not hold with sitting around at home and having noble principles.

Her father, who was one of the most high-minded inventors of civic duties, who believed that both matrimonial and electric-lighting contracts are drawn up in Heaven, was nevertheless urging her to leave her wedded husband, come home, and be divorced. Then she would again be able to go, panoplied in Caucasian superiority, to evening carnivals where you ate lobster Newburgh and played "Who am I?" If it did not work out, he promised, he would send her off to live in some scenic locality where the taint in Biddy was unknown.

When she dropped in to see her father, he looked up from his desk as though the desk itself were looking up, and said steadily, "Why duck your fate, Vessy? I have talked it over with your Uncle Oliver and with Reverend Yarrow, than whom there are no greater believers in the sanctity of marriage—when it's a real marriage. But they agree with me that you cannot look at it as a genuine bond when you were betrayed into wedlock with a homicidal maniac, a degenerate, or a Negro, and when a man is more or less all three—— We don't want a divorce from this fella Kingsblood; we want an annulment."

"Nuts."

"What did you say?"

"I said 'Nuts.' "

"Do you think that's respectful?"

"I'm extremely fond of Neil. He's good fun—or he used to be, before he became a mass-meeting. Besides, I don't want to let him down."

"You're letting me down, aren't you?"

"Could be."

"Then you certainly can't expect me——"

"We don't. We won't. We won't take another cent from you. Besides, Neil has the refusal of the most wonderful position in—— I won't tell you anything about it, till it's made public. Oh, Dad, you don't want to persecute me, do you?"

"No, I want to save you."

Repeat.

———

Elegant Eliot Hansen, whatever he might think of Neil Kingsblood, the traitor to his class and race, made it clear to Neil's wife that he, Eliot, was merely the more loyal to her, and that he stood humbly ready to serve her with advice, sympathy, petty cash, discussion of the opera, brotherly handshakes, or anything of his that she could use. That resourceful willingness, combined with Eliot's fresh, thin good looks and his habit of tilting his head at her like a worshipping dachshund, made him a more dangerous escape for Vestal than you would have thought.

Except for Eliot and Curtiss Havock, the men in what, till a few weeks ago, had been Neil and Vestal's "bunch" were not a lecherous lot. They were solid homecomers who would have been embarrassed in strange bedrooms and impotent at the sight of a pink valence. They would have defined "venery" (if they had ever tried to define any words besides trade-balance, torque, and this-here-Fascism) as "sports of the hunting-field," not as "sports of the boudoir." But Eliot made up for the timidity of his peers. He was the specialist in goatishness as Judd Browler was the master of trout flies and Tom Crenway of salad-dressing. Just to be seen smiling privily with Eliot was enough to give a bored wife a secondary thrill and an interesting reputation. In the cosmos of Grand Republic, you can find everything, even if in miniature, and Eliot Hansen was Casanova and Solomon and the purer parts of the Marquis de Sade as condensed for newsstand sale in a reprint magazine.

Even to be in Eliot's house, alone with his wife Daisy, was considered suggestive, and Vestal found herself there only because she was on the flower committee of the church, along with Daisy, Pomona Browler and Violet Crenway. They had tea at Daisy's and, to their fury, were given tea at the tea, and as they all disliked one another, they concentrated on Vestal and hinted that they would be glad to receive any confidences about her troubles with Neil.

"What's this I hear—that Neil is going to a bigger bank?" chirruped Violet, obviously meaning (or so the agitated Vestal suspected), "What's the poor zany going to do, now that he's fired?"

"Is Neil's leg going to be strong enough for him to play tennis, next summer?" soothed Pomona, probably meaning "Will he dare to poke his nose into our dear little club and take a chance on having big, strong, indignantly family-protective aristocrats like my husband smash that black, flat, intrusive snout?"

Daisy Hansen probed, "I declare, I'm crazy about your husband. When you see so much of him, can he possibly go on being just as wonnerful as the rest of us girls think he is?" and Vestal interpreted this one as "Come on and tell us about refusing to sleep with that horrible swindler, now that you've found out he's a—you know."

Vestal answered all of them with nothing more than a modest presentation of Neil as the new Apollo with touches of Ajax and St. Sebastian.

Whether the things they said did have these secret meanings, whether their glee in her tragedy was real or a sick imagining, made no difference in Vestal's uneasiness at being investigated, being the eccentric wife of a Negro, and she felt relieved when Eliot came in with a humming-bird sound of "What, you girls not getting any cocktails? Come on, Ves, help me make one."

The well-appointed butler's pantry in that select modern residence, with its special white-enamel miniature refrigerator for ice-cubes, was Eliot's private café on the boulevards, and scene of the inception of many of his happiest seductions, over the swizzle-stick and the slightly gummy bottle of Italian vermouth. Solemnly pumping up and down the silver-plated shaker, which had a dent in it from the time Daisy had thrown it at him, he looked up at Vestal, who was half an inch taller, and purred, "Have you heard the story yet about the pilot that had a studio-couch put in his plane?"

"No—I mean yes—I mean I don't want to hear it!"

"No? You're missing something good, baby. Say, you remember Bradd Criley, the lawyer that used to live here—moved to New York?"

"Yes, I knew him."

"Doc Kelly was in New York here recently, and he says Criley has a real, sure-enough New York actress for girl-friend now, and does he give her a good time! He blew her to a bed six feet wide with a sponge-rubber mattress—baby!"

Eliot referred, with no greater relevance, to soldiers and their amours in Europe, to a cabin that he owned up the Big Eagle River and that was, among his friends, in the appalling argot of the day, referred to as a "love nest." Vestal concluded that he was trying, with all the subtlety inherent in the ice-cream business (wholesale), to get over to her the news that people were still doing it, so why not?

She wanted to choke on a mixture of finding it funny and finding it atrocious.

——He'd never dare to hint this way if I weren't married to a colored gentleman. Now I know Eliot's regular approach, how he goes to work when the love-bells tinkle in that boy-sized brain.... Mr. Hansen, if you touch my wrist again, I'm going to sock you over the head with your own cocktail-shaker.

——You know what's funny? Borus Bugdoll would do this so much better. He's a swine, Borus is, but he's much more educated than this amateur barkeep; he's lived in Harlem.

——I *will* have this out with Neil—things like this happening all because of him. I haven't complained much, but I've got to go to town on the whole business. We've got to move away and change our name and I'd see to it that Neil never pulled the brave-Negro-pioneer junk again. And this morning I woke up confused and tried to think what crime I'd committed and then I realized that I'm married to a Negro, that I'm up against it. Oh, dear God!

Thus, while the delightful Eliot shook and tasted and babbled and smiled.

45

He had not known that to a great many people job-hunting was a heavier part of life than job-holding; more nervous, more humiliating and entirely unpaid.

On foot, to save bus fares, he trudged from office building to factory to warehouse, slipping on the glassy pavements. It had been so cold, this late February, that the First Duty of the high-minded citizen and householder—to clean his walks—was reversed, for if he shoveled them off instead of leaving them in soft lumps of snow for a footing, after the slightest melting of the snow-banks along them the walks became sheets of clear ice through which you could see the cement, and on them everybody in town, practically, broke an ankle or at least sat down hard and looked around indignant.

As the thermometer was depressed to fifteen below, seventeen below, twenty-five below, the citizens appeared in voluminous buckled overshoes, and earmuffs below felt hats, and wished that they had not yielded to fashion and given away the scrofulous sealskin caps they had inherited from their warmer and worthier sires.

Chippewa Avenue, the Corso of the town, which had seemed busy and almost stately in October, was floored with streaky ice, and at each curb was a low wall of caked and dirty snow turning to a gray barrier over which you had to climb, after you had unhappily left the warm bus. There were no crimson awnings now, nor window-displays of summery dresses and red canoes, but just stoves and flannel and cough-medicine. Grand Republic had lost the air of a brisk and confidently growing city, and the buildings seemed low and shabby and scattered, under a drained sky that would never shine blue again. There were sleds and skiis and healthy children in red caps, but not in the dolorous industrial districts where Neil looked for work.

Never had he so longed for spring to come again, for the soft air, the friendly sun. He was like an old man wondering how many more times he will see the blessed summer.

As he plodded through this limbo of unrelieved gray, from door to unwelcoming door, he did now and then have an offer of work, but always of such lowly clerical labor that (or so he thought) to take it would prejudice his future. "I'm no longer ashamed of any kind of work, but this would be a bad precedent," he assured himself, as he trudged on.

Job-hunt—job-hunt—job-hunt—two blocks—cold blocks—job-hunt.

No longer grandly willing-to-accept-an-appointment. No longer seeking-a-position-with-suitable-advancement. No longer salary-no-object. Salary a whale of an object! Salary. Money coming in again—money every week!

Job-hunt, job-hunt, job-hunt, all day, pound the pavements, through the slush, through the cold, feet sore on lumps of ice, blackening ice, feet tired in overshoes, tired feet that squushed in snow, to a wretched tune of job-hunt, job-hunt, job-hunt.

And job-hunt no more as a banker but as a tired Negro who assumed that he had to live.

When he had warned himself, a month ago, that to be a penniless Negro in this Christian land would be difficult, that just to get through one day of the threat and actuality of snubs would be hard, he had not quite known that it would be hell in the cold, hell in the employers' insults, hell in the pocketbook so flat that you took coffee *or* soup at your grubby lunch, hell in the screaming tendons of the lame, jarring leg he had almost lost in defending the freedom of white Americans to refuse jobs to black Americans.

Even if some day the Government should give him a vastly larger allowance for having been wounded, he did not think that he could endure settling down as an idle pensioner, with all life a dreary poor-farm, and Vestal and Biddy a cautious meagerness beside an ambitionless loafer.

He asked himself, "Would I have been so brash and announced myself as a Negro if I had known how hard it would be to get a job without concealing my race?"

The doubt made him stubbornly angry.

"I couldn't do anything else. I had to come out. Job-*hunt*. I had to come out. Job-*hunt*. I had to … This leg hurts so, and I am so cold!"

But with it all, whenever he had to fill out an application blank with the query "Race?" he put down "colored."

———

He had, inevitably, asked for work at Wargate's, but he would not bother Lucian Firelock, and the stranger in the employment office had nothing for him but a place as timekeeper at twenty-six dollars a week—an old man's post.

The stories that Vestal's friend, Mrs. Timberlane, had told about

Fliegend, the toy-maker, sent Neil there, and the old man welcomed him, but there seemed to be nothing in the toy-factory that he could do. He realized that though he had been assuming that he was a well-trained and valuable member of society, he had no skills outside of camping and organizing golf-tournaments and working in a bank. Even in the bank, he had no knowledge outside of routine tasks, and he had been an ornament in the Second National chiefly because he had a smile and was the son-in-law of Morton Beehouse and was so unquestionably conservative and Gentile and white.

He could, he considered, steer a canoe, but not so well as any Indian; he could handle a car, but not so well as any taxi-driver; and while his technique in cooking muskalonge steaks on an open fire was sound, it was not commercial.

He had a new view of Sophie and Ash. With all his fondness for them, he had been a little condescending. He admitted now that while he might conceivably starve, Sophie was very competent, thank you, even in a white world, as nurse and as singer, and Ash Davis could serenely make some sort of rough way not only as chemist but as a packer, musician, waiter, cook, linguist, teacher, and probably, Neil sighed, as a Shakespearean actor or the chairman of the board of a steel company.

When he next saw Sophie, with Ash and Martha, it was with noticeably increased humility that this simple child of midwestern nature asked these sophisticated big-city dwellers where he could get a job.

"Child, I've got to take you in hand. You'd do all right for yourself if you'd ever been around," sighed Sophie. "You go down to Mayo Street and grab off a fat job with Vanderbilt Litch. He's an undertaker and an insurance-man and a money-lender and a very smart egg, and the only spy and tattler in our Bronzeville, and maybe he'd pay big to have a high yalla who is kin to the local squirearchy working for him."

"Oh—I—don't—think—so," said Neil.

To himself he vowed, "I won't go down that far," and then, considerably shocked, understood that Mayo Street and Negro business men still *were* far-down, to him, and that Hack Riley had been right in scolding that he was playing at being a Negro.

But he was not playing, even if he was slightly confused as to what he wanted to do, in the unceasing job-hunt.

———

He had tried the printing-plant of his neighbor, Tom Crenway, who brushed him off. At the Laverick Flour Mills, his old poker companion, Jay Laverick, offered him a drink and inquired whether there was any good love-making to be had on Mayo Street, but when Neil asked for work, Jay shouted, "You? A job here? Hell, no! Matter of principle not to hire you folks."

Then he was employed by the Beaux Arts, but that was all chance.

He was about to walk past that stylish and expensive "women's specialty shop"—dresses, perfume in gold and crystal flasks, costume jewelry, sweaters like the breath of a virtuous baby—when it occurred to him to go in and try his former golf partner, Harley Bozard, the proprietor, a plump, active, eyeglassed man who was proud of being recognized at the 21 Club in New York, and who knew something about pictures.

Neil had refused to take a salesman's job from Levi Tarr, but he was still naive enough to suppose that it would be more soothing to sell Nylon stockings to the wives of large lumbermen, on the fawn-colored carpets of the Beaux Arts, than to gingham-clad housewives on the clattering bare floors of Tarr's Emporium.

Grand Republic was small enough so that, except at factories like Wargate's, the owner of a business did his own hiring instead of leaving it to a Ph.D. with aptitude tests instead of eyes. Harley Bozard welcomed Neil in his silk-paneled office, with greetings manly but strictly refined:

"How are you, how are you, old man? Haven't seen you in a month of Sundays. What are you doing now?"

"That's what I'd like to find out, Harley. You know I'm fairly good at figures——"

"Wait, wait, wait, wait, wait!"

Harley waved his china cigarette-holder in a magic circle and closed his eyes in holy dread, for he on honey dew had fed and been demoniacally possessed of an Idea. He looked like an advertising man, like an interior decorator. "Neil! I've never developed my sports department adequately; always been waiting for a big Idea-Man, and maybe you could be him! Put the department in charge of a great golfer, great tennis-player, great skier, great fisherman, with a record as a high-class war hero—oh, boy! 'Captain Kingsblood brings you the breath of the great outdoors—his expert sports-advice at your service!' It's a natural! I see you as buyer and head, expanding the department to suit yourself, but I suppose you'd better start in learning the technique of selling, and during your apprenticeship I don't know that I could pay you over forty a week—no, we'll raise it to forty-five! But I don't see why you shouldn't be making two hundred a week before long, and maybe a partner! Neil, it's a go!"

Neil said, yes, it was a go, and went out to telephone to Vestal, "I've got it—I've got a job!"

"Oh, darling, I am so pleased. You have had the hardest time and—— What is the job?"

"Sort of reorganizing the sports department for Harley Bozard."

"Oh."

"Of course, just at first, I'll have to start in as a sort of clerk——"

"Oh."

It was the flattest sound he had ever heard. Not much more buoyant was her query, "What did he say about hiring—uh—colored help?"

"What? By golly, he never spoke of it, and I plumb forgot I *was* 'colored help.'"

"And you aren't, either! You're the wonderful Captain K. and my only love, and I'm sorry I sounded unenthusiastic. I was a bit surprised, that was all. Harley is such a back-slapper and shoulder-blade tickler. But I'm sure it will be splendid."

Neil was not at all sure of that, now. He remembered that he had never particularly liked Harley. The man had been to him only a mass of tweeds bending over an ill-conducted mashie. And Neil realized that he was not a great-enough soldier or explorer to be sought out by a congregation of worshipping virgins for inspired counsel about lunch-baskets.

——Not on the level? I should worry about that. I'm at work again. That's important!

——

He went to work on Monday. In the newspaper on Sunday there had been a box in the Beaux Arts page-advertisement confiding that Mr. Harley Bozard had the honor of announcing that Captain Neil Kingsblood, the famous soldier and sportsman, had consented to associate himself with the distinguished Beaux Arts English Games & Sports Shop, and would be pleased to give all lovers of out-o'-doors the benefit of his experience in many lands.

On Sunday evening, Cope Anderson, the chemist, and the Reverend Lloyd Gadd, Congregational minister, telephoned to Neil that Harley Bozard and his chiefs of staff were buzzing about town, whispering, "Come in and get waited on by our Gentleman Negro and see the fun. Ask him any questions you want to."

On his first morning at the Beaux Arts, Neil was not received in any office by any Harley, but at the damp, slaty employees' entrance, by a greasy-haired misanthrope in an alpaca coat, who said bitterly, "You got to check in on time and punch the clock same as anybody else, Kingsblood. Report to the sports department and Miss Garr will show you how to make out a sales-slip and try to teach you, if you can learn it, how to be respectful to the customers. Now here's your locker, and for God's sake keep it locked. And stay strictly away from other folks' lockers. And how the hell they ever let one of you dinges dress with decent people is beyond me, but don't you for one minute think that if the management has gone haywire, we boys have!"

His look dared Neil to hit him.

Miss Garr, Neil's instructor, was a thin and indignant lady, and she kept Neil waiting for ten minutes while she finished her conversation with three other salesladies. They peeped at Neil and giggled, and he heard the word "nigger." When Miss Garr came to tutor him in the higher mathematics of sales-slips and the art of distinguishing a canoe-cushion from a tennis-ball, she kept shrink-ing back from his contaminating touch.

Negroes do learn silence.

———

If the sales-force did not welcome Neil's starred expertness, that monster known as the Female Buying Public welcomed him with writhing and with humorous squeals. It seemed to him that every woman in Grand Republic, including a few that he knew, dashed in to peer at him and to say things that ostensibly had to do with sports but that actually signified, "Are you really a Negro and do you really have these superior sex-powers that I've heard about and is there anything I can do besides look skittish and be ready to yell for help?" Their panting bosoms, their fixed looks, their hor-rible little wriggling shoulders spoke a superstitious and obscene language.

They stared at his Negro hair (sorrel-red), at his Negro face (of winter-tanned morocco), his big Negro hands (terracotta and freckled-sown), his long Negro legs and his powerful Negro mid-dle. And since a Negro is always thick-witted and enjoys being laughed at, they discussed his funny traits not too far from his hear-ing.

They asked him a menagerie of questions. Do you use a fly for salmon-fishing in Nova Scotia, and which fly? Could Joe Louis have beaten Jack Dempsey? Did he know anything about the tennis-rating of my cousin, William V. Getch of the South Milwaukee Country Club? Are Chinese checkers anything like Mahjong? How much did a chess set cost—oh, you know—just any chess set. How much would it cost per week for family of self, husband, two boys (aged 9½ and 11), one daughter (6, going on 7), and father-in-law who enjoys pitching horseshoes, at the Nippisag Fishing Camp on Lake Winnigigonabash next summer, and will the rates be higher than in 1939?

But the question that really passed through the guarded portal of his ears was that of a don't-try-to-pull-that-on-*me* matron of forty, who jeered at him in a voice like a cow-bell, "I suppose all you colored G.I.'s were just crazy to get at them little French girls!"

And one old young woman, not of reasonable architecture, insisted on his showing sweaters to her, though they were not in his department, and leered at him as she smoothed an astragal which he now suspected to be partly constructed of handkerchiefs. Still he did not vomit.

When he had been a white banker, a person to be careful with, he had never encountered women who reeked like these. He warned himself that they were not normal; they were only the sort who skittered to see the dark house of a murder. But he was not hopeful about his future as a freak attraction.

A good many of them pressed too close to him, and a good many more flinched away when he merely held out a croquet mallet. Whatever their physical currents, they agreed in never calling him Mister. He was Captain, he was Uh, he was, in Chinese fashion, Say Look.

As dismaying as the women were their infrequent husbands, who could distinctly be heard protesting, "No, I don't want to talk to the bastard," and worse than these was dear old friend Harley Bozard, hovering, mentally hand-rubbing. And more disheartening than Harley were the ex-privates with their girls, rejoicing in the abasement of a former officer and gloating, "Say, Cap, you know anything about fitting the girl-friend here with a pair of ski-pants? I want you to be doggone careful about the fit around her fanny, get me?"

At various painful times he saw Violet Crenway, Rose Pennloss and Diantha Marl, curving round the crowd to avoid his department and holding up their spiritual skirts as they sniffed past. And when he was looking after Diantha, he saw Major Rodney Aldwick, standing by one of the big white pillars, erect, arms folded, watching him, not sneering but just amused. Neil knew then the knee-loosening inferiority that comes to the virtuous slave and turns him to raging murder.

But his rage faded into gray. Sell sweaters and fishing-lines all his life? He was not angry but only washed-out when, at home, Vestal met him with a frigid "Well?"

—

The sensation-licking crowd did not continue all week. After two days, Neil had to spend a good deal of his time leaning against a counter, which was sharp against his legs.

Saturday morning, Harley Bozard came to fuss, "Can't you do a little better selling your customers? I notice a lot of 'em came in, thanks to the generous way in which we supported you by our advertising, but your sales-report is most unsatisfactory. You got to think less about how handsome you are, Kingsblood, and more about getting the sales-message over to the public."

Neil went home to a Vestal who was not fretful now, but savage.

"I hear you're thoroughly enjoying chumming up to a lot of loud-mouthed young women at the store, laughing with them and humiliating me by talking to them about me!" she observed.

"Now who——"

"Somebody we both know perfectly well told me. I won't tell you who. She was sorry for me. She saw you in the store, all right."

"But *you* didn't come to see how I was getting along."

"I most certainly did not!"

"It didn't occur to you that it may not be easy for me to learn how——"

"Oh, for Heaven's sake, don't go getting high-minded on me about the social injustices of sock-selling, too!"

He walked out, with no words. He did not come home for dinner. He headed for the arms of Sophie Concord.

He walked through the cold to Mayo Street, and a good deal of his exile's fury against Vestal was softened.

——It's been hard on her. She really cares for what she calls "social position." As I guess I did, once. Maybe it would be better for her if she quit me and took Biddy and went back to her father. He'd retire, and move to California with her, maybe, and nobody would know. Why should she and Biddy have to take up my fight? It might be better so, before Vestal gets any more irritated, says anything worse. Dear Vestal, I did love you a lot!

——

Sophie's tenement-house was like a cheerful little hotel, with whole Negro families camped out in one room and making merry over a pot of gumbo. In a hall-room, preaching aloud to an audience of himself, was Elder Mies, a black and meaty freelance prophet who was at once a cobbler and the proprietor of The Inspiration Temple of the Divine Assembly of High Holiness, which did not happen to have any meeting-place just now. Along the hall, as Neil came in at six, airy gamblers of the eventide, who by day were porters and grain-loaders, were displaying their fawn overcoats and green hats with feathers.

When Sophie sang out "Come in" to his knock, he lumbered into her one lone housekeeping-room. He had been there before, but only for uneasy moments at parting.

The room was square, on a corner, a mixture of poverty and reminiscent luxury. The studio couch was a rickety cot covered with a scarlet-dyed deerskin, edged with worn and somewhat ratty shreds of leopard, taken from a defunct theatrical costume. A two-burner kerosene stove, a nurse's cap, a miniature city of cosmetic bottles, and the major writings of John Dewey were on a long table. On the wall were a Vermont valley painted by Lucioni, a quite outrageous abstractionism, the photograph of a Negro girl, naked and shameless and shining, and a huge calendar presenting the portrait of a kitten in a basket, with the days of the month marked with a nurse's notations. In the midst of this litter of a woman too busy for housewifery, too interested in everything alive to arrange her surroundings so that they would set off her own loveliness, Sophie sat buffing her nails, at a dressing-table made out of a golden-oak filing-cabinet.

She rose to look at Neil, serene, unafraid, as tall as Vestal, a loose robe of gold-shot purple open on her autumnal brown bosom. She glanced at him more sharply as she saw how he swayed; she murmured, "Ah, poor baby!" and held out her arms, and he rested his cheek on the smoothness of her breast.

As they sat trustingly on the couch, arms about each other, she spoke tenderly: "Sweet, it's been hell, at that goldfish shop, hasn't it! I stayed away, for fear I'd make it worse for you. But you're as far down now as you'll ever go. It's the first time you've had to face the evil-eyes. They won't be able to hurt you again. Oh, I could love you, now. But—you said it yourself. There isn't enough jungle left in me.

"I've sold all that, to be a missionary. But so have you. So kiss me and go home. Oh, I do get so tired of being so blasted virtuous and hard-working. So tired!"

It had not occurred to this quite typical male that Sophie could also be discouraged. With a certain surprise, he put her head on his shoulder instead of collapsing on hers, and petted her, "You're all in."

She changed from divine mother to child. She whimpered, "Why wouldn't I be? ... Why do you love that woman so much?"

"Oh, well, for one thing, she's so beautiful—you said it yourself—like a race horse."

"She hasn't got legs like that!" Sophie spoke demurely, and stretched out one bronze, bright, stockingless leg like a ballet-dancer, curling her toes.

"She does all right!"

"Seriously, why?"

"The word I think of for Vestal is 'gallant.' She's square; she tried to give everybody a square deal."

"Including herself!"

"Why not?"

"Listen, my sturdy little man, I'm not complaining because you cherish Vestal. If she's going to take you away from me, as she apparently goes right on doing, I *want* her to be good. I don't want to be frozen out by an absolute marmoset." Sophie nestled against his shoulder. "All right, all right. She's the wonder of the ages. The only trouble with her is, she went to school instead of getting educated. She's never delivered a baby in a taxicab, or had to chase a café-owner out of her room without losing the café job. Maybe she'll be all right for you and——"

Sophie paused; her voice then was, at first, almost timid.

"Neil, I'd really like to know her, some day. I don't suppose that'll be possible, but bless her and bless you, and you stick to her ... you congenital white banker! ... *you Yale man!*"

"Why, I didn't go to Yale."

"Oh God!"

"But Sophie, suppose she won't stay with me?"

"Then make her stay, damn it! Don't come to old Aunty Concord for advice to the love-lorn! There's too much of that highly inflammable girl Sophie around this place. Go on back to your Pilgrim mother, Vestal, and may you be elected to the Sons of the American Revolution, you *schlemiehl!*"

He kissed her with quietness and propriety. As he walked home he most ungratefully did not think of Sophie or Vestal or any other woman, but of a good, clean, dirty fight with men like Harley Bozard and Wilbur Feathering and Major Rodney Aldwick, D.S.C.

When he came in, Vestal said gravely, "I think I behaved very badly to you, and I'm sorry—I think I am. But I don't like the way things are going. There has to be some change."

The newly grown-up Neil answered her with an unemphasized kiss and no chatter. He had to be about his business of swords and trumpets.

46

All Sunday he brooded on his Beaux Arts job, his week of humiliation as a large crested bird in a very small gilded cage surrounded by tittering bird-fanciers. He determined that as a Negro worker he would neither drift nor put up with insolence. He would look for the pattern and learn it.

He did not punch the time-clock on Monday morning, but walked into Harley's private office and said breezily, "That certainly was a phony job, Harley. Let me know, next summer, anything I can do to improve your golf, and good luck till then!"

It was a time for a Negro, even one so newly born, to be defiant or be broken. The first considerable race-riot since the end of World War II had exploded, in Tennessee; the typical war of uniformed policemen against terrified plain tanned citizens and their women and children.

It seemed to Neil that he would have considerable solace if he could have one more good lunch before he started the cold job-hunt again. He marched into the Fiesole Room at the Pineland, stating to himself, "I'm not looking for any trouble here, none at all; I'm just standing on my rights." In other words, he was looking for trouble, and doing a dance on his rights.

Drexel Greenshaw seemed to hesitate about admitting him to that Pompeian sanctity but, merely nodding, he escorted Neil to a third-rate table by a back pillar, the kind that was reserved for farmers, small-town ministers, saints, and such riffraff. But the colored waiter served Neil quickly and politely, and Neil contentedly thought about ordering a large cigar. Then Glenn Tartan, manager of the hotel, had materialized out of some garlanded Orient jar, and was standing beside him, pleasantly inquiring, "Was everything all right? Service all right?"

Neil said heartily, "Why, fine, Glenn, just fine."

"Then please note that we have fully complied with the law. Our regular clientele complain vigorously about you colored gentlemen coming in here and spoiling their lunch, but we have served you. And now may I ask you never to come in here again?"

Glenn went away quickly.

While Neil was still gasping, the Drexel Greenshaw who had so recently been so humble to the young banker, Mr. Kingsblood, moved up and said blankly, "Let me give you a little friendly advice, Neil. You ought to get a steady job and be humble to white folks and know your place and not step out of it, and stay away from exclusive places like this. The whites have the power, and it's much wiser not to antagonize them. I know exactly how to get along with them; I never have the slightest trouble. I'll never lose my job—as you did, at the Beaux Arts."

"How did you know that?"

"We Negroes have to know everything, in order to get along in a mean white world. So get wise to yourself, boy, and stay where you belong. Maybe, in time, if you get a reputation as a sensible darky, your daughter will go ahead of you, as my daughters have, and be able to get a nice clean job. There's certainly got to be a change in the colored position, *but this isn't the time for it.* All this revolution talk is wicked and foolish—and by the way, I want you to quit putting a lot of rebellious ideas in Phil Windeck's head. He's to be my son-in-law, and I don't want you corrupting him!"

"Me cor——"

"Yes, sure. You been acting very bad. Neil, it don't make no difference what you were *once*. Now, you're nothing but another colored man. Play safe, like me. Now scram. I'm taking a chance on even being seen talking to you."

——My daughter, my shining, light-footed Biddy, in a "nice, clean job"—maybe in Rod Aldwick's kitchen!

—

On Sophie's insistence, he finally went down to Mayo Street, to see Mr. Vanderbilt Litch, who was a Prominent Colored Elk and who did very well with undertaking, insurance and roulette. Mr. Litch, in a scarlet-and-chromium office with a smart colored stenographer, frigidly explained that he did not care to employ a white man who only pretended to be a Negro in order to get in on the policy racket.

——Well, I'm glad to know that some of the colored boys have reached such a high point of culture that they can snub you just as quietly as Uncle Oliver Beehouse!

He did find, in the Five Points, enough spare-time bookkeeping to keep him from starving, and that with the most successful two Negro businessmen in town: Axel Skagstrom of the Gunflint Trail Canoe Corporation, and Albert Woolcape of the Ne Plus Ultra Laundry, men who did not belong in the Feathering picture of the Shiftless Darky.

Mr. Skagstrom, who was married to a white Finnish woman and who was half Swede, quarter Negro, quarter Chinese, with traces of Choctaw and Mexican—which made him one hundred per cent. African—manufactured excellent canoes. He was a pious Lutheran and he disapproved of what he called "all this vice and laziness that you find among so many colored folks." He felt pretty well about his generosity in employing as many Negroes as whites in his factory. He was a typical American businessman, except that he was less interested in race-questions than most of them, and he was glad to have Neil step into his accounting-room every Friday—at cut rates.

Albert Woolcape was the brother of John, the uncle of Ryan, but no friend of either. They were too radical for him. In his busy laundry on Chicago Avenue, he was willing to employ Negroes, but as most of his customers were white, he insisted that all of his drivers and collectors be white also. When he took on Neil for part-time accounting, Albert granted, "I guess maybe this race-ideal stuff is all right, but a fellow has got to think of himself first, ain't he? Look at the difference between my bank-account and John's! And that Ryan, with all his education, got nothing but a job on a farm!"

Working on Albert's and Skagstrom's books, with the telephone always querulous just behind him and the light never quite right, Neil felt exactly as he had in his hours of book-work at the Second National, except that his two employers were more anxious to please him, as one who, after all, might be "white." He was not sure but that he preferred the suspiciousness of Mr. Vanderbilt Litch.

When he indignantly reported his employers' distrust of Negroes to Ash and Martha, they laughed. Said Ash, "You're a promising ethnologist. The only thing you've missed is the whole point. We've told you right along that there isn't any difference. It's only you and radical Harlem who insist that everything in ebony must be better than anything in birchwood. Quit being a race-fancier! Besides, there's a lot of our race and a lot of our white friends who believe that the way for us to be popular and urged to join the Federal Club is to have a conspicuous number of our boys who become rich and own apartment houses. True, the Irish and Jews have tried the method for centuries and failed at it, but what of that!"

—

Neil had had only a month of job-hunting, but he had stumped his way to so many places that it seemed a year. Through it all, they had their home, sacred and secure—and paid for! To Neil it was the more important, now that he had no office, no club, no houses of old-time friends where he could be sure of welcome, and he did not think that, without it, Vestal would have been able to stand by him.

On most evenings, they stayed home, and when they did not, they usually regretted it. As:

Louise Wargate, Mrs. Webb Wargate, had always seemed to Neil traditionally the Great Lady; gentle, literate, thoughtful, not altogether human. (She was born an Osthoek of Utica, and met Webb when he was in Harvard. Her position was so ducal that she could afford to look like a farm-wife: in gardening-gloves, freckled, without lipstick. We are on a high plane here, and know nothing of Nurse Concord or Albert the Laundryman or white cottages bought on the installment-plan.) As the mother of his old playmate, Ackley, Mrs. Wargate had been to Neil an even smile, a cool hand, and chocolate peppermints in a silver box, but never singing or cookies or sliding down hill, never.

Now, when Neil and Vestal were in a social concentration camp, they had from Mrs. Wargate a civil invitation to dinner, the first they had ever had from her. Neil, after a false dawn of exultation, decided that they had been invited because Louise Wargate felt guilty over not having done for the Negroes all that she had intended when she had first encouraged Webb to hire more of them at the plant. Neil was beginning to see a good deal of that uncomfortable guilt among the worthier clergy and legal gentlemen.

Vestal said, "I don't think I'm very crazy to go."

"I'm not, either. It'll be like tea at the morgue. But I do think we ought to recognize her effort. I do know it's been hell on you, getting dropped out of everything that we used to consider decent society——"

"*Used* to?"

"——and having to become a hermit. Won't you believe that I've suffered about you, in my dumb way?"

"Oh, I know. And I don't want to be a Christian martyr chanting. I'll learn to take it. Only sometimes I wonder if it wouldn't be better for you if—— Neil, isn't there some awfully nice colored gal that could help you more than I can?"

"Conceivably, but I have dedicated my life to you, and I'd like to try and keep that dedication straight."

She beamed, though what she said, since this was Grand Republic, was "Okay, Romeo, let's go!"

———

The Webb Wargate house, on Varennes Boulevard overlooking the Sorshay Valley, was a red-roofed Touraine chateau, larger than Bertie Eisenherz's manorial Hillhouse, and with more el's, eaves, gables, ornamental chimneys, portes cochères, near-marble near-fauns, fountains containing nothing but old hand-bills, flying buttresses, stationary buttresses, raped intaglios, hanging gardens, weather vanes, xats, and Keep-er-Klosed Kasement Windows, but with less books and less pictures. Altogether high-class and European, with pioneer Yankee-lumberman trimmings.

Neil and Vestal were received with gray-silk courtesy by Mrs. Wargate and with jittery incredulity by Webb, who as usual looked like the Second Bookkeeper and Gravedigger, like a saver of paper clips and rubber bands—inquiring but mute, and always apprehensive lest somebody take it away from him.

They had cocktails in the Small Drawing Room, and as Webb passed them to the guests, he was a little taut, as though he were not at all sure but that these ravening black fieldhands might bite him. He had played bridge with Vestal's father for centuries, but he seemed to be saying, "I know so little about you colored people that I don't even know whether it is considered etiquette to offer you a cocktail."

The Wargate dining-room was vast, with exposed beams painted in gold and crimson, and a flooring of figured tiles. They were waited upon by an aged Swedish woman who evidently had been prewarned and held out platters to Vestal and Neil as though she were handling baskets of hot coals. The food was all hardnesses covered with floury sauces. And there were no other guests. Son Ackley and his consort were so conspicuously absent and unmentioned that they were overwhelmingly present.

The talk tried to keep itself away from the subject of Negroes. It was Vestal who deliberately yanked up the curtain.

"You know, it's been funny, the number of confused people who assume that somehow I have magically become a Lady of Color—oh, yes, people we all know, who are bright enough to sign checks and go round in eighty-four. The poor Junior Leaguers are in a quandary, one of the deepest quandaries this side of the Grand Canyon. They don't like to kick out the daughter of Morton the Magnificent, and maybe the easiest thing for the poor darlings would be to disband the League. Don't you think so, Mr. Wargate?"

"Yes—yes—I see how you mean," faltered Webb.

He had a suspicion that she was being humorous, and however powerful Webb Wargate was at selling wallboard and plastic brushes in Chicago and Venice and on Mount Kaimakischalan, he always had vertigo and pains behind the eyeballs in the presence of humor. But he also had his duty as a leading member of the National Association of Manufacturers, and now that these guinea pigs had themselves brought up the embarrassing subject of vivisection, he felt that he ought to encourage them, he ought to Get in Touch with Changing Conditions. He turned quackingly to Neil:

"Tell me—I'm perhaps inexcusably ignorant—but is the desire for political participation making much headway among the, uh, colored population?"

"I haven't much information on it, sir, but I imagine so."

"You mean, from your own personal experience, you would, on the whole, be inclined to think so?"

"Yes, I—well—I might say that I think I have been somewhat aware of it."

The conversation never rose again to such dramatic heights.

As they drooped down the Italian marble front steps, Vestal sighed to Neil, "Well, there's another place we'll never go again."

"Looks that way."

"Who cares? Webb's grandfather used to saw wood for my grandfather, back in Maine."

"Is that so?"

"No, but it might be."

"I wonder how the Wargates ever made so much money and got such a big house?" said Neil.

"I don't. I wonder what makes them think Brussels sprouts are a food.... Oh, sweet, Webb wasn't trying to highhat you. He's just a smug, ignorant man. He doesn't matter—none of them matter—just you and me."

47

He was alone in the house, after the daily job-hunt. Vestal and Biddy and Prince were out at the Timberlanes', one of the houses where they would not be resented nor yet greased with the tactful kindness that was worse than jeering. He stood at the western window of the sunroom, meditating.

Why not flee to a metropolis or to the wilderness, and seek anonymity? No. Vestal and Biddy (and Prince) were too gregarious for any forest clearing, and New York or Chicago would be too hard and rectangular and grim. A flat would seem too constricted, after this house where there was space to dance and freedom to yell and this view up Eisenherz Hill in the last forgiving light of the frozen March afternoon.

Against the gold-leaf of the sunset, Hillhouse was a proud brick hulk with limestone-framed Tudor windows, and a flat, balustraded roof instead of the swoops of the Wargates' roofs and rooflets. The pines on the hillside were against an apple-green strip of sky with a tapestry of apricot and purple draped above it. Pines and sunset recalled to him old canoe journeys on the Northern lakes so near to this, his own city. If his one-time friends here seemed to hate him, at least they gave him that much attention, while in Megalopolis there would be no one even to wish him bad luck. No, they would brave it out in Grand Republic.

He remembered that once he had longed to be able to buy Hillhouse. Then, he was to have become a super-banker. Biddy would be coming home from Farmington and Bryn Mawr, and Hillhouse would be full of her young set, Wargates and Sparrocks and Prutts and Drovers. Yes, he marveled, once he had longed for all this! Well, he had a livelier fight now. He would be lucky if he could keep the cottage. But to guarding that, he swore, he would devote the patience and ferocity of his Chippewa ancestors, whose bark lodges must have stood up on that hillside, only a hundred years ago.

Vestal came in gaily, started supper. They were well content. Neil informed Biddy, after supper, that once upon a time there were some extraordinary people called the Ojibways, or Chippe-was, who used to camp right up there on our hill, and right here where we're sitting, maybe they used to fight with bows and arrows among the rocks. Biddy was so entranced that she brought all her dolls and her velocipede and the slightly mutinous Prince to sit in a half-circle and listen to him.

While Vestal was putting Biddy to bed, under martial law, he wandered again into the sunroom. In the bold moonlight, the shadows of branches were inky on the snow-patches that were webbed with Biddy's tracks. It was all his, his and Vestal's and Bid's. Here they would stay, every evening, all their lives.

Yet they did venture out once more, to an interracial and toler-ant and fiercely intellectual party given by Diantha Marl, at Brian Angle's studio. After that, they really did stay home.

Diantha, as the wife of Gregory Marl, who owned both of the newspapers in Grand Republic, was a social leader. But all on her own she was, at forty-five, an authority on China, which she had never seen, James Joyce, whom she had never read, the qualifica-tions of all political candidates, particularly of those who were en-tirely unqualified, and the sulfa drugs, which she ever so faintly mixed up with vitamins. As a Talking Woman, she could curry-comb a private audience as violently as any leaderess in New York or Washington.

On Race-Relations, she was tremendous. She had once sat down at the same luncheon table with a colored woman, and had been so kind to her that the poor soul had talked up just like a human being. (There had been sixteen other people at that table, and the object of Diantha's charity had been a professional lecturer for the Niger-ian Anthropological Foundation.) Whenever Negroes were men-tioned, Diantha always told this story of her own tolerance; a hundred times she had told it.

Her husband's papers were very liberal about Negroes, and stated editorially that there was no reason why they should not be employed at any work whatsoever, provided they could do it as well as any white man.

These newspapers had never employed any Negro.

Diantha was giving the party to show that whites and Negroes can mix socially without any harm, but she was not so reckless as to have it right in her own home. She had borrowed the studio of Brian Angle, who was the local art-world and who still went on believing that Diantha was really going to order that portrait of herself.

Nor was she so offensive to the social code as to invite any such ill-conditioned Negroes as John Woolcape, who was merely janitor in this same Mermaid Tavern Building in which was Mr. Angle's studio. The Mermaid was half-timbered, or anyway it looked half-timbered, and it contained a photographer's establishment, a music shop, a twittering of voice teachers, and Rita Kamber's Vanguard Bookshop.

The Negroes whom Diantha did decide to invite could be counted upon for fairly civil conduct. They were Ash Davis and Neil Kingsblood.

She had also summoned Martha Davis, whom she had never met. But, by refusing to come, the woman had shown how ungrateful these darkies really are. Diantha bore up gallantly and explained to everybody who was interested, "Probably it's just as well she's not coming. You never know what kind of illiterate hoydens these half-educated colored climbers like this Davis will have picked up along the way."

Diantha was surprisingly cordial in the social *habeas corpus* which she issued to Neil, by whom, when he had been a white banker, she had been bored, but who had now become as interesting as Gargantua the gorilla, and in the same way. Neil had not wanted to go, but Diantha had insisted with pretty petulance, "Don't be silly! Don't tell me you're going to miss this chance to do something for your race. Why, you'll meet the best people in town, Kingsblood!"

Vestal said, "You bet I'm going with you, Neil! Think I'd have Diantha probing into what she'd call our 'love-life' without being there to protect you?"

———

In the long studio, which was furnished chiefly with stacks of unsold pictures, there were sixty guests. They who did not know Neil and Ash made several unfortunate errors in picking out the Negroes at whom they were to stare, and caused Colonel Crenway to go home early and indignant.

Their host-by-pressure, Brian Angle, was a young man with a tentative beard and too much mother, who was nevertheless not a bad painter. He considered Neil undistinguished, but he told Ash that he looked like a stern and youthful doge. Lorenzo Gristad, a dark and nervous little man, a photographer, whispered to Ash, "These white guys can't do a thing in the world for you except give you a job, can they?"

Dr. Cope Anderson, the chemist, and Peace, his wife, astonished the slummers, the rich illiterates, by talking to Neil and Ash as they would to any other reasonable human beings, and so did Dr. and Mrs. Kamber and Lloyd Gadd, the Congregational minister, though they still thought of Negroes as people whom you meet on committees. But fifty out of the sixty guests just watched Ash and Neil and waited for them to do something dirty or funny.

Nor was Neil cheered by Vestal's first meeting with Ash.

She had never encountered him; she had heard of him only as a man whom Neil respected. All she saw now, in the man with whom Neil shook hands so affectionately, was what she described to herself as "a quite nice-looking darky, very neatly dressed, maybe an expert valet." She gaped when Neil glowed, "Vestal, this is my great friend, Dr. Davis."

She reflected, "A doctor? Could be. I've heard there are some colored doctors."

She observed, "How d' you do," and she made it extraordinarily plain to Ash that she did not really care how he did, and did not want to hear how he did, and why introduce *her* to colored chiropractors?

Ash bowed, not too deep, and that was all of the joyous meeting of Neil's wife and Neil's friend.

———

There was a quantity of whisky and a fair supply of chicken salad, but the tourists got tired of looking at the exhibits. The party had not been going at all, and what made it go now and go vigorously and go very badly was Wilfrid Spode.

There is a name and a talent to mark: Wilfrid Spode, known to thousands, and most unhappily, as Friddy Spode: a man who has been intimate with all the most devastating geniuses, the most obscene drunks, and the most determined Lesbians in Taos, Taxco, Woodstock, Minorca, Munich, Carmel, Chelsea, Greenwich Village, and the Left Bank of the Seine. There is a man as alien to Grand Republic as an ornithorhynchus, a man who by contrast makes Curtiss Havock seem decent and Dr. Drover gentle.

Friddy Spode was born in Kansas City, but he was an author. Nor, mind you, was he an unpublished author. His novels, which were catalogs of fornication, in style very much like mail-order catalogs, with the four-letter words all spelled out, had, till World War II, been privately published in Paris and paid for by his wife.

Friddy had a seamed and rather dirty face, the face of an evil old horse; his neck was always dirty and his nails an exhibit of dirt and his hair not so much worn long as always needing to be cut. He usually wore a corduroy jacket that was rather on the boyish side for a man of forty, and the only reason he did not wear the traditional Rive Gauche broad black hat was that people expected it of him, and he loved to disappoint them. He did better. He wore a cap— very dirty.

Yet his wife, Susan, half a dozen years younger, was as plump and clean a little pigeon as you could find outside a pot-pie. She was a painter, except that she did not paint and could not paint. And she was Vestal Kingsblood's own cousin. She was the legitimate daughter of Counselor Oliver Beehouse.

When she met Friddy, she had been doing something exciting but phony which she called "studying art in Paris." She was lonely there, and she could speak no French and not much of anything else. Friddy picked her up at the Café Select. He lived by borrowing money; he was as painstaking at begging as he was sloppy in composition; no sum was too large to whine for and none too small to take. He asked visiting American businessmen for five hundred dollars and accepted fifty; he asked little students of singing for ten francs and got fifteen.

He borrowed a hundred francs from Sue, on sight, and that night he negligently seduced her. He found out that her father was rich, and yawningly he married her. He never had any interest in her afterward, nor any especial aversion to her, while she adored him and never noticed the dirt, and believed his sour jealousies to be wit and his lore of the privy to be literature.

When the Germans were about to enter Paris, the Spodes fled, and since then they had been able to live in California by black-mailing Oliver Beehouse with the threat that if he did not come through, they would come home. Sometimes, as now, they did come, just to show how distressing it would be if they remained in Grand Republic.

For a month they had had a studio-flat in the Mermaid Tavern Building. Sue cheerfully did the cooking and the financing and made their bed whenever she could get Friddy out of it.

It had been the existence of Friddy as his own son-in-law that had caused Oliver to be so agitated when his brother Morton found that he had a Negro for son-in-law. To Oliver's classic legal mind, Negroes and Hindus and American Indians and criminals were all alike, and the only worse menace than Friddy was Neil.

As soon as the food got better, Friddy and Sue would be back in Paris. Meantime they endured the bestial American tiled bathroom by finding their fun where they could. They found a lot of it tonight, in taking over the management of the helpless black barbarians, Neil and Ash.

It was not that Friddy cared a hang about Negroes, but he got a lot of innocent pleasure out of annoying Diantha's friends.

He was in superb, international form, tonight. He had a drink and hailed Vestal as his cousin and tried to kiss her on the cheek. He had a drink and most audibly congratulated his happy and humming wife, Sue, on having in the Negro Neil one connection who was not a fool. Then he had another drink, a lot more drinks, and delivered an unscheduled public lecture.

He stated that all Negro music, sculpture, acting, pugilism and sexual hypnosis were superior to the accomplishments of the whites, and he wound up, "If you'll all shut your traps, maybe I can get one of our colored guests to explain why it is that his race is so much subtler and more sensitive than you white bourgeois."

Ash muttered to Neil, "That jackass knows his business. Usually, it's a woman who does this to us. The only absolutely guaranteed way to ruin us is for some exhibitionist to overpraise us. He's making me anti-Negro myself!"

But Friddy Spode was not forever to take over the bedeviling of the guests. The hostess, Mrs. Marl, may not have been trained on the Left Bank, but her natural capacity for making reasonableness sound disgusting was even greater than Friddy's. It was just that she had been slow in starting, tonight, but, after enough drinks, she caught up.

In Grand Republic we do not say that a lady is a notorious drunkard. We say that she "enjoys a little nip now and then." Diantha had enjoyed a number of nips, big and little, and she suddenly took the lead over Friddy.

She managed to annoy the two guests, Judge Cass Timberlane and Mrs. Shelley Buncer, who, by talking together in a corner and not listening to Friddy, had escaped going mad. Diantha came up to them and mourned, with all the woe of the world in her voice, "Really, I did think I could count on *you* two to show a little common courtesy to our poor guests of honor! There's Mr. Kingsblood and poor Dr. Dash having to stand up, while you two monopolize these chairs!"

Cass got his wife and went home at once. Mrs. Buncer beat him by two stairs and one yelp.

Then Diantha got Ash to herself, and cozily complained to him, for the benefit of twenty onlisteners, "Dr. Dash, I have a bone to pick with you! Why don't you tell these colored women not to try and talk like *us*? It's too confusing. When I got your wife on the phone—and I must say she took her own sweet time answering it!—I thought she must be some white lady, and I got all balled up. Of course you know I adore Negresses and think they're very artistic, but honest-lee, they haven't got any right to throw us off like that!"

She took in Neil then:

"All you colored people sing spirituals so beautifully. It's the high point of American art. So now you two boys go ahead and sing us some spirituals.... Shut up everybody, will you! These colored fellows are going to do some spirituals."

"Don't know any," growled Neil.

Ash Davis had a wistful love for spirituals, and he did not intend to parade them for drunken whites. To him they meant that half of his ancestors who had been Negro and Indian limping on the old trail of thirst and horror, singing low that they might not whimper. He said, "Thank you, but I'm rather ignorant of them, and I'm afraid I'll have to slip away now, Mrs. Marl."

Diantha broke into a vast and alcoholic pity for herself, and her cultured accent slipped back into the ancestral shanty across the tracks, as she wept, "I wonner if you preshate what I—tried—oh— tried s' hard do f' you darkies, sevenin'?"

———

Lucian Firelock and his wife were there, and it was she who fluttered, "I'm a real Southern woman, Mr. Kingsblood, but I want to shout right out that Dr. Davis has been our best neighbor in Grand Republic, the nicest to our children, and I'm just mad—I'm not sure what I'm apologizing about, but I sure am doing it!"

What worried Neil was that after their introduction, Vestal and Ash had not spoken again. On the way home, he said anxiously to Vestal, "What did you think of Dr. Davis?"

"Who? Dr. Davis? Which one was he?"

If there was any sequel at all to the Case of the Drunken Hostess, it was that Neil was driven into violently embracing his crusade. It was his bride, his sword, his crown, his scourge, his victory, his defeat. It was his busy little fad and it was his prayer and his madness, his crucifixion and his glory.

48

They were at home, snug against the evening of March winds, and Biddy was singing herself to sleep upstairs, when the Neighborhood Committee rang and marched in. They were four solid citizens and their resolute look indicated that they preferred to be courteous, but they were going to be hard.

They were Former Mayor Stopple, Former Friends Don Pennloss and Judd Browler, and Mr. W. S. Vander, ex-lumberjack, who had carried into his wholesale lumber-business the good old methods of eye-gouging and spiked boot, and who was as harsh and honest as Bill Stopple was slick and crooked.

All of them arranged their grins and, except the tough Mr. Vander, sat on the edges of their chairs. In that cheerful room, they seemed as out of place as so many shiny-black bull-fish. Neil stood by the fireplace and Vestal, at her small white desk, frigidly played with a lavender quill-pen.

As Gruppenführer, Honorable Stopple emitted, between throat-struggles, "Folks, some time ago I told you about a dandy little house I could show you on Canoe Heights. My, is that a view!"

"What do you want? Come to the point!" Vestal snapped.

"At your service, Ma'am, and may I say that there is no one who has a greater admiration for your father than I have?"

"You may, if you feel you have to."

Honorable Stopple was becoming irritated by this ingratitude. Was he not here unselfishly, on behalf of the public weal? Nobody loved a public weal more than Honorable Stopple, but he did want a little credit for it. On the surface, however, he still held that noble calm of a man who is always looking for votes and quick turnovers.

"I shall always accept your judgment, Ma'am. Now I have been somewhat concerned over the thought that you folks may not be altogether happy here." Vander grunted. "I think we may call Sylvan Park the highest type of residential addition, without excessive valuations, but I must say, regretfully, that there is a lot of social prejudice here. Personally, my motto is live and let live. Whether the cause of this local prejudice is some lack in our religious training, I would not presume to say. As a layman, I feel that it is impossible for us to comprehend the task of the clergyman, and it ill behooves us——"

"Will you please stop admiring your philosophy, and get to work?" Vestal was snarling now. Neil was looking appraisingly at a large and chunky vase.

"I certainly will, Ma'am! Lots of folks around here don't want colored neighbors, and that's the clux or the clue or whatever it is of the whole matter! They can't understand that it isn't Neil's fault that he's colored. But there you are: a sort of what you might call a growing resentment against you folks. And so maybe you would be happier in some other neighborhood ... and a whole lot safer!"

He was too level-voiced for Vestal to go on being pert, and he continued more blandly:

"Mr. Berthold Eisenherz, who once owned all this property, a very fine man, is willing to take your place back at just what Neil paid for it, figuring that depreciation on the house and any appreciation on the lot will just about balance. This seems to me a very generous offer, very, and may I venture to advise you——"

"Mr. Stopple, we had this all out before," said Vestal. "You don't seriously expect us to listen, do you?"

Don Pennloss came in. "Look, Vestal, we are here more as friends of yours than as authorized representatives of the property-holders. But we are that, too."

Judd Browler blurted, "Neil, you got no idea how we've worked to keep certain neighbors from—well—demonstrating. They're fed up. You can't go on fooling with them. They simply will not tolerate a non-Caucasian living here and lowering the social tone of the community."

Honorable Stopple said, "I hate to think of what some of the hotheads might do—charivaris that would scare your sweet little girl—and worse."

"Mayor, I just don't like blackmail. Or blackmailers," said Neil, and Vestal nodded.

Then Vander got to work. Mr. Vander had not gone to school with dear Neil nor gone to parties nor played hockey with him. He was twenty years older, and all his salad days had been pork-and-beans days and he had been in the Big Woods, freezing half the time and getting warm by fighting with axe-handles the other half. He loved both his family and his investments and he did not love Negroes or anybody who was not a Vander. He had a flat head, a stormy jaw, a steady, blue eye, and no sentimental objections to clubs, ropes, fire, or splinters under the nails. He was a good wholesale-lumber dealer, but he might have been a good sea captain, prime minister, executioner or lieutenant-general, and he barked now as one with authority, so that Prince woke up, under the couch, and barked back, and Vestal rose, to walk across the room and stand beside Neil.

"Blackmail, hell!" said Mr. Vander. "It's going to be a lot worse than blackmail. You folks apparently got no idea how sore people are at having niggers right in their front yard. I know I am! I get damn sick and tired of paying my taxes right on the dot and then finding some Christ-forsaken Spig or Wop or Kike or Dinge——"

"Careful of the language, ol' man!" tittered Stopple.

"Oh, these niggers are used to any kind of language."

Vestal, her hand on Neil's arm, restrained him, and now she laughed at a certain wistfulness in Mr. Vander:

"Honestly, I'm getting fed to the gills on having the boys downtown rib me all the time! 'So you're living in a nigger neighborhood, now—ain't a nigger yourself, are you?' they say—you know, kidding. One time in Chicago, I heard a workman—some kind of city work he was on, where they had some shines doing clerical work, and he was grousing, 'It just naturally makes me sore to see a nigger sitting at a desk while *I* have to stand up with a shovel.' Say, I know just how he felt! Makes me sore and it ain't right to see you darkies living as nice as I do myself, after all the hard work I put in to get where I am. By God, that ain't justice and by God I ain't going to have it!"

Stopple ballooned up again, lovely silken pear-shape, glittering and yellow, full of gas, always going up and collapsing and surprised about it. "Now, now, Brother Vander, you must of got out of bed on the wrong side, this morning. But Neil, it was pretty foolish of you to talk about 'blackmail.' I must say, I never heard of a blackmailer that did the paying!

"Nothing could be more friendly than we are. I said to my wife, 'Pauline, I never expected Mr. Eisenherz to be that generous. He's a diplomat and a swell,' I told her, 'but just the same,' I said, 'you scratch an Eisenherz and you find a tightwad, no matter how many French paintings he buys, or what have you,' I said, and to tell you the truth, Neil, I was simply astonished, and I hope my influence may have had something to do with it, when he come right out and was willing to refund the full purchase-price, cash on the nail, and no if and or but about it. So, if you take his offer, you won't be one cent out of pocket. But mind you, the next time a committee calls on you, maybe it won't be this same committee, and maybe they won't be so friendly, and maybe you'll be only too glad to sell for one whale of a lot less dough."

Vander growled, "Maybe you'll be glad to get away with a whole hide, and no dough at all!"

"I *am* going to hit him!" Neil stated to Vestal.

"No! That's what this fellow wants!"

Vander chuckled. "Sure, let's have a little hitting, Kingsblood, a little action!"

Vestal's hand was firm on Neil's arm.

Stopple oiled them, "Now, now, you boys be good. We're talking business! So, Neil, after another twenty-four hours, my offer will be lower, a lot lower, but meanwhile you can get me on the phone any time, night or day.... Well, gentlemen, I think it's all perfectly clear now, but I don't want to go without assuring Neil and his good lady that they have our heartiest good wishes. Good night—good night! This way, gentlemen."

———

Vestal embraced him. "Oh, my darling, darling Neil! I'm getting it through my thick head now what it's all about. Never mind those shirttail Nazis. We'll stick right here."

"You realize tough things could happen?"

"Hallelujah!"

The ghost of Sophie Concord smiled on Neil with a wistful benediction and was gone.

He complained, "Why didn't you let me hit Vander?"

"They'd have had you arrested, and that would get in the papers and make a lovely case against us. Besides," judiciously, "I think probably Mr. Vander would have licked you, and I don't want to have you beaten up. I need you around. Oh, Neil, we'll live now, even if we die from it!"

49

But next morning Neil felt low and cold as he tramped the streets, trying not to slip on the ice. He could not afford to break his legs now; they had to carry him until he could find a job.

And suddenly, that March day, he had a job.

He had gone into the establishment of Brandl: The Beltrami Avenue Florist to see if he could buy a crocus or two for Vestal. The little old Bavarian, Ulrich Brandl, who in grander days had sold him orchids (white scarf and white kid gloves and Vestal's smile and glitter and all the white man's memories), hailed him cozily:

"Ah, Captain, let me have the pleasure to give you this small bunch of crocuses. I have heard about your braveness. I understand it, for I was born a German and, though I hated Hitler and all oppression, and though I have been a good American for thirty-five years, when I come in a saloon for my glass of beer, I hear certain fellows say, 'The only good German is a dead German.' All prejudice is one. Could I shake your hand?"

"You wouldn't happen to have a job for me, would you?"

"That also, perhaps. I would be flattered if you worked for me."

So Neil became a florist's clerk, probably knowing less about flowers and the freshening of them and their packing than anybody except Hack Riley of Mayo Street. But he was zealous, and the customers did not indicate that they were undergoing any horrors in being waited upon by a Negro. The jungle dampness of the shop, the gilded tinfoil, the piles of unwrinkled tissue paper, were relaxing, after miles of factories and the hard chairs outside the boss's office.

All day long he argued mildly with Mr. Brandl, who inveighed against all prejudices and superstitions, and himself, it proved, was prejudiced against nothing except Englishmen, Jews, Brazilians, Irishmen, Presbyterians, Mormons, chewing-gum, sunflowers, Heinrich Heine, and two-door coupés.

But Neil could not, on his pension and his tentative salary at

Brandl's, keep up the home which had become his extreme symbol of dignity and independence. He must turn to—what?

Then he was betrayed from inside.

———

He had never, of late, quite known what to do about his family, and he regarded them with a wry mixture of humor and deepest guilt. He dropped in to see his mother and Joan two or three times a week and found them becoming hermits. He told himself that it was not he but superstition that had made them "Negroes," but the argument did not relieve him much nor relieve them at all.

His sister, Kitty Sayward, had nothing for him now but a "Yes, what is it?" One member of the family, Cousin Pat Saxinar, had taken the whole business adventurously, perhaps gladly. She had gone to live in a settlement-house in the Southwest End, and was busy there and seemingly content—a good woman as only a good woman can be good.

But Neil had to avoid Brother Robert's house, because of the resentment of his sister-in-law, Alice, backed by her brother Harold W. Whittick. She was a bad woman as only a good woman can be bad. In March, she sued Robert for divorce, for cruelty, humiliation, and deceit in not having, before their marriage, told her that he was "colored."

When Neil brought the news to Vestal, she hesitated. She did not look so disgusted as a man would have liked, but finally she achieved:

"Oh, well, Alice always was one of these what-do-I-get-out-of-it wives. And all her relatives were hammering at her to leave him. I know. My father and sister act as if I were a traitor to them because I don't leave you. But so far, I've pounded them down. I can't seem to get you out of my heart and soul and flesh. Oh, Neil!"

It was like one of the moments early in marriage when, without preliminary, they had suddenly wanted each other. He could feel the intensity in her, and while her eyes were smiling on him, utterly concentrated on him, she panted and her lips were slightly open. He moved close to her, and the two bodies pressed together, as though they had wills of their own.

He knew that she had unconsciously eaten up the myth that all Negroes, even deskmen and strained and nervous scholars, are superior sexual animals and that her renewed passion was all self-deception, that she was being violated by a son of Xavier Pic who did not really exist. But he could not feel that this was the moment for disquisitions on psychology, as he kissed her and she slowly sighed.

———

If she was going to be loyal, he thought, she must take her place with Martha Davis and Corinne Brewster. With a complete wife, an adoring child, a friend like Ash, and with Vestal and Martha become friends, what more could a man have?

He advanced his desire to have Ash and Martha here for dinner. Vestal moved uneasily. "Do you think that would be wise? I have no doubt they're very fine people, but wouldn't they be embarrassed? Would it be kind to them?"

"Ash is a distinguished chemist, and after dining with Sorbonne professors at the Ritz, in Paris, I guess they won't wilt before the luxuries of this house!"

"Don't roar at me! By all means have them, if you insist. But how do you know they ever dined with any professors at any Ritz? Do they boast of things like that?"

"Ash and Martha have never boasted about anything! About the Ritz—I'm just imagining——"

"Why should your Sorbonne professors want to dine with Dr. Davis? Is he that big a chemist? And if he is, why should he want to dine with us? All the chemistry we know is that salt isn't any good in coffee."

"I tell you, I'm not thinking of him as a chemist."

"You didn't tell me, but never mind that."

"I think of him as about the most charming man I know."

"You forget that I met him. He seemed a nice, civil person, but I didn't notice that he was so reeking with charm."

"Well, maybe you would have, if you'd looked at him carefully."

"N' doubt, n' doubt. Well, we'll have them here, and I'll look at 'em both carefully!"

No, the augury was not good. And Ash said, when he was invited by telephone, "Are you certain that Mrs. Kingsblood would like to have us?"

———

The Davises came, well-dressed, soft-voiced, attentive, everything perfect except that they never were really there. Most of the time, they spoke only in response to whatever Vestal might offer, and as there was very little offering, there was very little responding. Neil had to make talk for all of them, but he was not especially inventive.

Vestal was dreadful. She was too polite; she agreed with everything, without listening to what she was agreeing with.

"I guess the President is having quite a little trouble with all these strikes," Neil tried.

"Yes, that's so and——Strikes, did you say?" mumbled Vestal.

"Oh, yes—strikes," Ash achieved.

Before dinner, Ash and Martha had obediently taken cocktails, but they never quite finished them. "Just like poor relations—conciliatory," Vestal spitefully muttered to Neil. He had done the ordering and laid the table, but she had cooked the dinner herself and, not listening to Martha's shy offer to help, she served it, with a look which said to Neil, "Are you satisfied, my lord, now that you see me humbly waiting on these dark intruders?"

When the conversation had almost swooned and died, and no one took up any of Neil's remarks about airplane service and the Junior College basketball team, Ash straightened up and began to talk, as an expert, about the future of plastics.

"They're almost too practical," he said. "We shall have bedrooms for a fairy princess, with concealed lights and transparent beds and cupboards—it will make all the previous conspicuous waste look utilitarian."

"I take it you don't approve of people having pretty things," said Vestal, and that killed that.

When they were drinking coffee in the living-room and everybody was suffering and waiting for the end of the bad farce, Biddy came down in pajamas, quite illicitly. She stood in front of Ash, looked polite and solicitous, and chanted, "Oh, your face is dirty!"

Even Vestal was shocked, but Ash smiled, with "No, that's just my tan, young lady."

"Did you go to Florida and get tanned? My dolls have just been to Florida. They stayed at Palm Beach and they said it was very expensive. Or did you drink too much coffee? My mummy says if I drink coffee before I'm sixteen, I'll get all brown, too. My, I wouldn't like to be all brown. Don't you mind being all brown?"

She said it with the liveliest interest and, ignoring the signals from her mother's shaking head, she crawled into Martha's lap and rested her head against Martha's shoulder.

So Vestal was altogether too bright and jolly about it.

Ash looked at her more steadily than before, then glanced at Biddy with a quality of pure love, and Ash said, "No, baby, I wouldn't mind being permanently tanned if there weren't so many people that can't seem to stand the sun. They like cellars and anemia better."

"What's denemia?" demanded Biddy.

Vestal did a Viennese operetta in the jocundity with which she caroled, "Now dearest, you skip up to bed and don't bother Dr. and Mrs.—uh—Davis."

———

The guests managed to get away without violence.

Vestal sobbed, "Oh, I know, I know I was horrid, but Neil, I just can't do it. I don't mind your being a Negro—because I don't think you really *are*—I think there's a trick in it. But I can't stand *them,* or any other colored people, and there's no use my trying."

"You listen here!"

"Don't scream."

"How can I help it? Nobody could have been more well bred and intelligent than Ash and Martha, if you'd given them a chance——"

"That's the trouble! I've been brought up to believe that darkies are funny people, dancing and laughing and saying, 'Oh, thank you, Miss Vestal, ma'am, you white folks is sure wonderful to us poor coons.' But this Davis sketch thinks I'm just another female that's dumb about chemistry and economics. Cellar and anemia indeed!

Oh, I know I'm unreasonable, but my heart isn't in it. And my heart has to be in anything I do now, because I'm going to have another baby."

———

When Neil had thoroughly betrayed all his anxiety by trying to sound delighted, Vestal said gravely, "Let's not have any guff about welcoming *this* little stranger. I hate it, oh, I simply hate it! I've been longing all day to escape somewhere where nobody knows me. I can't stand giving birth to a Negro baby! Somehow Biddy doesn't seem like one—I'm sure she isn't. But now to have a black baby—I can't do it. I want an abortion, and I don't want one and I won't have one, and I'm nearly crazy!"

She sobbed all night. Biddy came anxiously in to see "what she could do for poor Mummy," and Neil lay on the other bed and stared at the rolling films of light thrown on the ceiling by passing cars.

50

She was the Little Woman of the Ages, very pleasant and kind, helpful to the ambitions of her husband and the boys, and many of them were very bad ambitions. She made cookies for the neighborhood children and listened fondly to foolish serials on the radio; she was a good church-worker and a willing neighbor. She believed everything that her minister, her congressman and the secret anarch who invents the fashions in shoes and cosmetics told her, and it is she who has licensed and justified all the ravenous armies, all the pompous churches and courts and universities and good society, all the wars and misery since time was.

The Little Woman of the Ages spoke, and she said, "I don't know anything about anthropology and ethnology and biology and all that silly highbrow junk, and you can say what you like and quote all these long books, but I tell you there's a darky family lives right down the alley from us where they keep goats, and I know and I'm telling you that the darkies *are* inferior to us, and I'm not going to have 'em working in any store or bank or office where I have to go.

I'm sure I wish 'em all the good luck in the world, as long as they stay in their places. And folks that say the colored folks are just like you and me—why should I pay any attention to ignorant talk like that—they don't really believe a word they say.

"I am the Little Woman of the Ages, and my dainty foot is upon all thrones and swords and mitres; for my nice little voice are all songs made, and for my delight on lonely evenings all stories told; nations shall not assemble nor men and women love nor labor save by such bonds and ceremonies and complexions as are approved in the holy laws that I learned from my father, who was a wonderful man, and if he were alive today, he simply would not stand for all this nonsense that a lot of irresponsible people seem to be spreading around, and who learned the laws from his mother who had them from her pastor who had them from his bishop who had them from his mother who had them from her spiritualist medium to whom they were handed during a trance in which the medium talked with God in person.

"You can say what you like, but Italians are tricky and Okies are shiftless and Negroes are lazy and Jews are too smart and a world-government is against human nature and against all the principles laid down by George Washington, and I don't want to hear any more such wicked nonsense, and I, who am Hertha and Isis and Astaroth and the recording secretary of the D.A.R., proclaim that when all civilization flattens out in the universal propriety of death, then everything will be nice and respectable everywhere, and there won't be any more of this trying to be smart and show off with such silly talk, and now let's have another nice cup of coffee and say nothing more about it."

51

Ash said on the telephone, "No, I thought your wife was very pleasant, last evening—trying her best to be natural with us. You must expect her to take a long time before she accepts Negroes as normal. I've tried to do the same thing for forty years, and I'm still a little bewildered to find that I'm not an American citizen or a father or a chemist but a Negro. And now, forget all that, because something very dangerous is starting."

So Ash gave him the first news of the Sant Tabac.

When Neil had rushed home after work, to inquire how Vestal felt—she just felt like Vestal, and she was irritated that he should insist on her feeling any other way—he telephoned to Evan Brewster, to Cope Anderson, and put together his information:

The Sant Tabac was a new organization, founded in Grand Republic and likely to spread to other Northern cities. It was a conspiracy to drive as many Negroes as possible back South. To prospective members who thought that it resembled the Ku Klux Klan, the organizers explained, "No, there is to be no violence whatever. In fact, we want to protect the colored people—from their own leaders, who'd like to get them into riots, to please the Kremlin. We won't stand for any lynchings, or even any beatings—not unless the mokes act nasty and rile the cops. Our policy is entirely benevolent and constructive: to get all the niggers that have grabbed off white men's jobs in the North fired, and no new ones hired."

There was a great deal of wit and archness in this campaign for economic murder. The name Sant Tabac was made from the initial letters in their slogan: "Stop all Negro trouble, take action before any comes." The first set of officers were Mr. Wilbur Feathering, who was "Big Havana," Mr. William Stopple, "Little Havana," Mr. Randy Spruce, "Penatela"—not Panatela—while the treasurer, or "Ole Leather Pouch," was Mr. Norton Trock of the Blue Ox National Bank. Among the directors were Mayor Ed Fleeron, Dr. Cortez Kelly, and the Reverend Dr. Jat Snood.

The Peter the Hermit of the order was Feathering, but the whimsy in the titles and name were from Randy and that advocate of Modern Art in Advertising, Mr. Harold W. Whittick, whose merry notion it had been to invent a Portuguese island called Sant Tabac, where tobacco had been discovered and all colored peoples had been banned.

Many of the crusaders were wearing a button depicting a pipe-smoking monk, but their achievements were less playful than their ritual, for the members were solid men of affairs, and if the local peerage, as incorporated in the Federal Club, were above joining, they did contribute. The leaders were trusty, swift and secretive men, given to strategy. And everything they did was known to the Negro world before it was known to the members. Randy Spruce's office, where the plans were made, was in the Blue Ox Bank Building, and Cloat Windeck, the father of Phil, was head elevator man at that building and in charge of all waste paper.

Evan Brewster suggested to Randy Spruce that the members would save money if Negroes were accepted as workers instead of being expensively jailed or hospitalized, but Randy had no time to waste in listening to a blatherskite preacher.

The Sant Tabac, however earnest, cannot be credited with all the discharges of Negroes in Grand Republic. The return of the white soldiers, the strikes, the conversion of factories from tanks to suspender buckles, and the general conviction, richly cultivated by the radio and the comic strip, that all Negroes are amusing but bungling fools, were greater elements, but all of them worked sweetly together to start the epidemic of firing Negro workers, which began on All Fools Day.

It began at Wargate's, with the letting out of two hundred brown-skin workers.

The management explained to them that they were being sent back to the breadlines solely because, with war manufacture ended, Wargate's had to close several departments entirely.

Some of these departments were opened again in a couple of weeks, with new designations and with all-white workers.

The Five Points was certain that, by the end of the year, all of the Negroes working for Wargate's would be dismissed. The discharged men stood about on corners, not parading, homeless, scared, swapping information about mythical towns in which, "fellow told me they're hiring spooks now."

One of the six hundred Negroes working for Wargate's was a chemist named Ash Davis.

———

Ash said cheerfully to Martha and Neil, "If I get fired, I can probably get twenty a week fronting for some hair-straightener."

The naive Neil marveled, "Wargate's can't let you go. Why, they'll make hundreds of thousands of dollars out of your discoveries."

"They will, but they don't know it. They think I'm just fooling around at pure research. The South made tens of millions out of Carver's discoveries about the lowly peanut, but they still made him use the back door. You whites are idealists. You put principle above mere money-grubbing—the principle of hate of the unknown. However. Wargate's might keep me on as a floor-sweeper. I'm a neat sweeper."

"Or," Martha said cheerfully, "you might become a red cap and carry baggage, like most of our people that finish graduate school."

"Not a chance. The Ph.D.'s that get taken on as red caps have to speak at least seven languages, and I speak only three."

Then Drexel Greenshaw walked in on them. "Heard about the firing at Wargate's?" said Ash.

Drexel was pontifical. "Naturally, but I'm not as worried as you young people. I've seen too many set-backs for our race. And you must ask yourselves if this really is as unfortunate as some say. Remember that the folks who are being let out are mostly these new colored fieldhands that have just come up from the Southern backwoods—lot of ignorant, rude, money-wasting hicks—typical immigrants, I'd call 'em. All the old-timers, like Al Woolcape and me, have suffered a lot from having the white folks think *we're* like those cattle. Oh, I'm sorry for them, but they better go back South, where they belong."

"I'm an immigrant, too," Ash pointed out.

"You're different. You belong."

"To what? I'd like to find out!"

Drexel expanded, "The white folks are only too glad to have colored gentlemen like you and me working for 'em. Mr. Tartan says to me, 'Mister Greenshaw, I don't know how we could ever run the Feesoly Room and satisfy our high-class clienteel without you.' 'I try to do my best,' I says to him, and he says, 'I know you do, and we appreciate it.'

"Why, I figure some of my best friends are white folks. Mind you, I'm no Uncle Tom. They got to treat me dignified. You young peo-

ple don't understand white psychology. If you make yourself valuable to 'em, they'll treat you more than square, and if they been getting kind of prejudiced against us, it's the fault of the black trash.
Why, years ago here, we all got along real nice with the whites. My
girls were brought up to play with real nice white kids, and when I
went to church, I was treated like any other communicant. But the
white folks are disgusted with these rug-cutters and slick-chicks
that try to act like they're the same as white folks. All the whites ask
of us is humility, and that's one of the best Bible virtues, ain't it?"

They did not listen; they had heard it all from Drexel Greenshaw before. They were fond of the erect old man, the father of
their friend Cynthia Woolcape; the gentlemen's gentlemen's
gentleman, the Southern colonels' Southern sergeant.

———

That week a Negro veteran was lynched in the Deep South.

From the Mississippi Delta to the Howard Law School to the
clubs of Harlem ran a shudder and a mutter, "Next time it could be
me," and dark Communist and Fundamentalist were united as they
looked quickly back on the streets at night. Ash Davis as despairingly as Sugar Gowse, Drexel Greenshaw and Dr. Darius Melody
along with Hack Riley, heard the horror within hours after it had
happened, and they cried "How long, O Lord?" and not meekly.
And a Negro named Neil Kingsblood looked at his wife in honest
terror and shivered, "It could be us and here and now."

———

More of the black workers were dismissed every day by Wargate's
and the smaller firms. Every day the Mayo Street corners were
more packed, the grumbling less amiable, and so the canny authorities sent in more policemen—and so the policemen were
stoned now and then—and so they sent in still more policemen—
and so one Negro was shot and four were arrested—and so a
two-by-four was dropped from a third story upon a policeman's
head—and so Feathering said, "I told you so; join the Sant
Tabac"—and so there were accelerated dismissals of Negroes from
Wargate's, from the Aurora Coke Company, from the Kippery
Knitting Works, from the grain-loading gangs at the elevators, from

the railroad car-shops—and so the street-corner gangs became more ugly—and so more policemen were sent in *per omnia saecula saeculorum*.

Among the white labor-union leaders, a third protested, a third said nothing, and a third rejoiced.

And then, with a handsome letter from Duncan Browler about his work, Ash Davis was fired.

There had been no warning. The letter was awaiting him when he came home on a Friday evening. When he had read it, Ash lost, for an hour, his poise as a skeptical man of the world, and became a frightened and belligerent workman out of work.

He wrote to a number of firms in the East which knew his ability. They answered that there were so many white chemists returning from the wars and, besides, maybe their present staff might object to working with a non-Caucasian.

Anyway, chirped he to Martha, he would prefer teaching to working in another commercial house.

He could get no appointment in any white college, including one that had intended to give him an honorary degree. There were a few, an increasing group, of Negroes on university staffs, but Ash did not have that luck. The college presidents lovingly answered— when they answered at all—that while *they* had no "prejudices," not one prejudice, all of their present band of hope and light were likely to object to working with a brownskin.

Months later, after he had gone to New York, Ash was sold down the river to a small Negro college in the Deep South, salary $1800 a year and a house, only there wasn't any house yet.

Then Phil Windeck lost his job at the garage.

Then Drexel Greenshaw lost his job.

52

Glenn Tartan called in Drexel Greenshaw, and tittered, "I've got some bad news to tell you, old man, and I want you to know that it isn't in any way my fault. The owners have decided to change our policy and employ only white help in the dining-rooms and so I'm afraid—— But we all wish you the very best of luck, and I've dictated a letter of recommendation that'll knock your eye out."

If the oratorical Drexel said anything now, it was not heard.

He tried to see the chief owners of the Hotel Pineland, but they were too busy. They were Dr. Henry Sparrock and Mrs. Webb Wargate, who was everywhere known as a Great Friend of the Negro. Dr. Sparrock was busy campaigning for the Red Cross, and Mrs. Wargate for the Suffer the Little Children League.

Drexel sneaked back to the three-room cottage which he shared with his daughter Garnet, and for a week he was ashamed to leave it. The tough boys from Texas and Arkansas, kicked out of Wargate's and loafing around the Bar-B-Q, would have laughed at him.

Garnet said good-bye to Phil Windeck and went off to work in Chicago. Drexel sold his house, and lived with his other daughter, Mrs. Emerson Woolcape.

He tried not to, but he could not help criticizing her cooking, her bed-making, and her care of the baby. He told himself—she did not tell him—that he would have to stay away from her house by day. He got a waiter's job in a very nasty hash-house, from which he was discharged within a week, for criticizing everything in sight, including the overcharges. Albert Woolcape was willing to set him up in a chicken-joint of his own, but Drexel was suddenly afraid of responsibility.

For some months he sat on Emerson's porch, wondering whether the no-count white waiters now at the Fiesole Room would understand that Mr. Randy Spruce had to have four lumps in his coffee—things like that, which only Drexel understood.

Drexel died alone, suddenly, during a summer thunderstorm. Garnet came back for his funeral, and gave up all notion of marrying Phil Windeck, who was running whisky into Oklahoma, in partnership with Sugar Gowse. Garnet is now a civil-service stenographer in Chicago, lonely and chaste, she who was so ripe for love.

When the Fiesole Room had changed to white waiters, Randy Spruce had made another entry in the Sant Tabac books, and chuckled. Poor dear fuzzy Randy, who was some day to be caught in a scandal with a telephone operator and to skip town. He did such a lot of evil, but all so innocently. If he had ever asked himself why he hated Negroes, he would probably have found that he did not hate them. He had never really met one. He meant so well. They say he has a wonderful job now with the Atomic Bomb Perfume Company.

———

Select portions of that April might have been called spring, even in Grand Republic. As he made pyramids of early daffodils in the showcase, Neil whistled, with a feeling that he had never been anything but a devoted florist.

Mr. Brandl looked anxious over his morning mail and over a couple of unexplained telephone calls, during which he answered nothing but "Yes" and "I see." After scratching his hands and worrying his soft gray bush of hair, he trembled, "Neil, I keep hearing where you are a friend of a Dr. Davis, that is a very bad Negro agitator. I would like to stand by you, but I know from the war what tattle and rumor can be like. I could lose all my business, and I have an old wife."

Neil sighed, "Okay, Ulrich, I quit. Tell the Sant Tabac boys that you fired me."

Mr. Brandl mourned, "I want to give you a lovely reference for your next job."

What next job?

———

Vestal was not too astonished when he walked into the house before eleven in the morning, a man out of work. "Cheer up. I knew it would come. Now *I'm* going to get a job myself, and keep it till Booker T. is about ready to arrive."

"How?"

"I've already talked with Levi Tarr, at the Emporium. I won't be on the counter at first, but in the marking-room. And don't go getting proud and uxorious on me, and be offended by my working. We have to have the money."

"I'm not *going* to get proud and what-is-it! I know we do."

After seeing wartime women in uniform, in overalls, he was not so ashamed of letting her go to work as his father would have been, but he still had his young-white-gentleman worries:

"Will it be all right for Booker T.?"

(They had never agreed on this working title for the coming baby, and neither of them really approved of anything so flippant. It had chosen itself and it persisted.)

"Sure, he's a healthy little brute. And they have a doctor's office right in the store."

"The other clerks will plague you, as the wife of a colored man."

"Not me they won't! I'll plague back. I'm not tolerant like you, Captain! And your mother—she does face things, when she has to—she's promised to fetch Biddy from kindergarten and keep her afternoons till I get back. Oh, it won't be so bad. And some day— I've been thinking; all this prejudice against you simply must cease. Isn't this the Land of the Noble Free? I hear so. In a couple years you'll be in the dough again, and I can stay home with Biddy and Booker and recline on my new chaise longue and say to my maid, very languid, 'Bring me my nail-polish, Anzolette, and just pop your head out of the window, will you, and see if little Master Booker is playing around in his helicopter.' Oh, Neil, Neil, he will be white then, when all this is over, he will be white, *won't* he!"

She did go to work at Tarr's. Apparently she was quick and competent, and soon she was selling furniture, on which she was an expert—by a Sylvan Park standard. Apparently no one dared to mock her, twice.

Neil rose before seven, got her breakfast, bullied Biddy into resuming the burdens of life, waved good-bye to the family wage-earner when she hurried off, washed the dishes and swept the house, took Biddy to kindergarten. But instead of feeling degraded and made small, he was pleased that he could do this little for Vestal, and pleased that there was this one place where he could work without rebuke for being black.

It was when he trudged out to look for more virile labor, like making figures in large books and saying, "The discount rate is one and a quarter per cent.," that he was dreary; it was when he abandoned the refuge of home to go and be dutiful to the other members of his family that he was helpless. His brother Robert hated him, had resigned his job and was going off to anonymity in Chicago even before he should be divorced.

Sometimes Neil could work up a little rage in his own defense. Why couldn't his family admit that they were, by the very definitions they had all maintained, Negroes, and face the world with Negro courage, not with the white mythology about the delights of exclusive clubs and polite churches and invitations to dull houses? Was this structure of anxious jealousies, this "good society," so precious that, in losing it, his family had suffered very picturesquely?

Sometimes, aside from his mother, these people seemed not related to him at all. Much closer were not only Ash and Phil and Sophie but a youngster like Winthrop Brewster who, in the university, was studying electricity and manners, teleology and basketball, Sibelius symphonies and dancing with girls of all colors, and who at pipe-fogged "bull sessions" spoke up as briskly as any of the collegians who were the sacred descendants of Norfolk hedgers, Killarney potato-diggers, Welsh miners and French skunk-skinners. Why could Kitty and Charley Sayward not be as realistic as this boy?

It was hard to be so realistic himself as to demand that Vestal accept the fact that her two children would be "colored," and learn to see all "colored" people as human. He was joyful when, on a Sunday morning, Vestal said eagerly, "Know what I'm going to do? I'm going to take Biddy and go call on Dr. and Mrs. Davis." (She never did come to call them Ash and Martha.) "I want to have their little girl come play with Biddy some day."

"But Nora is almost ten years older than Bid."

She was touchy. "Of course if you don't *want* me to call on your——"

"No, no, no, no, I'd be delighted, and I do hope you'll come to like them. You know, don't you, that Ash has been fired?"

"So?"

She had no notion, clearly, that Ash's discharge meant anything more to him than a like embarrassment to a white chemist. Ash was still in town only to sell his house, with a choice between being cheated by Frank Brightwing and gypped by William Stopple. He might not be in a mood to be patronized by Vestal, but she was so pleased with her own resolution that Neil tried to cheer it.

She would not let him go with them. She was full of enterprise and benevolence, though Biddy did ruffle her by a certain over-enthusiasm about going to see "Uncle Ash and Aunt Martha and darling, *darling* Nora." Biddy had made detailed plans for the presentation of a play and a grand opera by herself and Nora (whom she had never seen), this coming summer, and when Neil explained that Nora would no longer be here, Biddy waved all such triviality away, as blithely arrogant as her mother.

——I guess that's all to the good. Bid will be like Winthrop. She'll say, "Certainly I'm colored. I also have one crooked toe. So what!"

On that cold April afternoon, after lunch, Vestal started beamingly off for the bus, with Biddy prancing under the skeleton maple trees. They were to be home at five. At a quarter past four, they returned, silent.

"Don't be such a baby—take your own coat off, and skip upstairs and play," Vestal ordered Biddy, while Neil was rigid. His "Well?" was cautious.

"If you must know, it didn't go so well. Oh, they were just as pleasant as they could be, and they do have a nice house, but—— Maybe it had nothing to do with their being colored, maybe they're just too intelligent for me, but I caught myself wishing that I were at Judd Browler's, talking about vegetable gardens. And Nora was just too darned nice and patronizing to our poor moron child. Neil, are you so sure you really want me to try and feel natural with your highbrow buddies—all these Hindus and Koreans and Zionists and Nigerians? I do get so sick of propaganda. I'm not sure I can do it, my dear. I'm not sure it will go. At all."

Neither was Neil.

———

Ash had not yet found his teaching job (he had given up calling it a college position), but he had sold his house through Frank Brightwing, who was very jovial about "you darkies" and had willingly persuaded the purchaser to pay almost half the value. Ash believed that jobs would be more easily found in the educational slave-market of New York, and he was leaving Grand Republic—probably forever, lamented Neil.

Vestal said abruptly, No, she did not think she wanted to go with him to see the Davises off. Besides, she couldn't run away from her job that way! Whether she meant to or not, it seemed to Neil that she was reminding him that she, the tragic white woman, was toiling to support a vagrant Negro, and that such heroism was too uncomfortable to last.

Grand Republic was proud of its new Union Station and the waiting-room, the Great Hall, of gray limestone with murals of the explorers Radisson and Groseilliers, David Thompson, Le Sueur, Lieutenant Pike, the Sieur Duluht. Neil plumed himself, "Xavier was one of those fellows. Biddy and I belong with them, not with the Prutts and Wargates—those parvenus!"

Not the departing Ash himself had more greeters among the Negro crowd than Neil. How many of them he had come to know on first-name terms in these six months: all the Woolcapes and Davises and Brewsters, Phil Windeck—who was now a bootlegger and overdressed in zoot-suit fanciness, Axel Skagstrom, Borus Bugdoll, Wash, Hack Riley, Dr. Darius Melody, Sugar Gowse. As for Sophie, Neil twined his arm with hers so naturally that he did not know he was doing it.

They were all crying to the Davises, "Gosh, we're going to miss you, Professor," and "Kiss Harlem for me, Ash," and "Oh, Martha, we need you!" and "Oh, come back soon, Nora." But as Ash turned away from them to go through the train gate, the portal through which he would never return, his eyes had no hope in them. He was leaving not only his friends but the one place—in America—where, for a time, the whites had permitted him to pretend that he was a scientist and a responsible citizen.

The last thing Neil saw of Ash, as he started down the stairs to the train-platform below, his hand in Nora's, was the apology in his face as a fat white woman cursed him because she had jostled him.

Behind him Neil heard a white man explaining to a friend, "That guy they were saying good-bye to was this educated nigger that was a draftsman or something at Wargate's. Well, every nigger that leaves here makes this burg just that much better!"

The two men laughed, for they did not hear the earth moving.

—

When the telephone rang, at home that evening, a woman's voice, entirely unknown to him, said "Neilly?"

"Yes?"

"So your friend Ash has sneaked out of town and your friend Dexter got the axe. It'll be your turn soon, sweetie!"

"Who is this?"

"Don't you wish you knew! But I wouldn't want a bunch of niggers and perverts to know my nice name! Say, is it true that Vestal has nigger blood, too, on her mother's side? Why don't you two unspeakable fakes get out of town? Nobody wants you here!"

Neil hung up; he told Vestal nothing.

Later in the evening, when they were reading, he heard Vestal say, low and urgent, "Don't look up, but there's somebody staring in through the window."

He sprang up, he hobbled rapidly outside, but he found no one.

—

Mr. Cedric Staubermeyer demanded of Dr. Cortez Kelly, his neighbor, "Wouldn't you say that Kingsblood absolutely broke his father's heart, and killed him by his misbehavior?"

The Kelly who had once denied that fine theory agreed: "Yuh, you might put it that way."

Long hatred of the Jews had given Mr. Staubermeyer both training and professional delight in the art of Rumorizing. Evening after evening, when other residents of Sylvan Park said, "I don't see anything particularly objectionable about Kingsblood; seems a nice quiet fellow," Mr. Staubermeyer gave forth, "You know he not only got fired from the bank for embezzlement but had a fight with his own father and yelled at him so outrageously that the poor old fellow dropped dead from a heart attack. I heard that from old Doc Kingsblood's own assistant, who was right there at the time."

"What? Is that so? Well!"

53

The epidemic of firing went on, but not everything was evil for the lost people in dark Egypt. Certain returned soldiers said that if a man could die with them in Europe, he could dine with them in Minnesota, and they had Phil Windeck elected to the American Legion.

Yet they were less friendly than their fathers might have been. Thirty years before, the Negroes had seemed to be gaining so much more of what they wanted because they had apparently wanted so much less. They had demanded then only a roof and sidemeat and not to be lynched. Now, they were demanding every human right, and whites who were self-admiringly willing to give them a dish of cold potatoes were sometimes unwilling to give them room at the workbench and the polling-booth, and muttered, "We've been too easy. We got to clamp down on these apes before they claim they can do our job just as good as we can." The black crusade had never seemed so risky as now, but any gain that was made was a real increase in human dignity, not a pink bow tied on inescapable chains.

Neil might have been comforted by Phil's small laurels—he did not know how doubtful Phil himself was about accepting them— but he was suffering from domestic twinges. Vestal was doing so well at Tarr's that she began to see herself not just as husband's little helper but, quite properly, as on her way to a lively career of her own in what she had come to consider "the art of merchandising." She was turning from a Popular Young Matron into a woman. She exulted to Neil that, after Booker T. arrived, she could hire a nurse for him and become a buyer, a department-head, at Tarr's, with her own office, her trips to New York, drawing-room on the train, hotel suite, handsome dinners.

——Maybe some day she'll own a business and give me a job as colored porter. Am I doing her any kindness by sticking to her? Why not give up this house, this way of living? Could I be a man on my own? Can I get the education that enables a Sugar Gowse to live alone? Ought I to go? I will if it seems best for her.

But that mild resolution did not help him a couple of days later when he walked in on the interesting scene of Morton Beehouse, backed by Brother Oliver and by Vestal's sister from Duluth, making his most determined effort to save his poor daughter.

"Ah, good evening, Neil. Do sit down," said Morton—in Neil's own house. "We are faced by no pleasant duty this afternoon, but I give you credit, whatever faults of evasion of responsibility you may have shown, for possessing good intentions. We feel you don't realize how you have permitted Vestal and Biddy to drift into a position of ignominy."

Vestal was merely listening. Either she agreed, or she had promised to keep still.

"If you did realize it," Morton went on, "you would take steps to end it immediately. It isn't their fault, it isn't their doing, that you are a colored man, and I can't see why you should expect them to bear the penalty."

Neil wondered, "You expect me to *encourage* them to leave me?"

Uncle Oliver jumped in, splashing. "My dear boy, isn't that obvious? It still isn't too late to save their reputation, but if you delay much longer——"

"No."

"What?"

"I said No. I'm completely devoted to Vestal; I do realize her discomfort; I shan't try to control her; she must do what she wants—which may not be what *you* want, by the way. I did not marry you."

"Thank God!" said Oliver, with equal vulgarity.

"But I have decided that Biddy and the baby that is to come—if I'm a Negro, then they're Negroes, and no more of this shame about being what we are that you white men have put over on us."

"Quite," said Uncle Oliver. "I see," said Uncle Oliver. "So you intend to visit on these two innocents the—oh, let's call it the mark of——"

"No, let's not call it that. What you don't understand is that I don't any longer think they'd be better off as white children. I don't think my Negro friends *are* inferior to a parchment-head like you. Not to be rude, you know."

"I see. Quite."

———

Now Oliver's firm had represented the Eisenherz estate, and Oliver knew all about Sylvan Park real-estate titles and about "restrictive covenants," those gentlemanly agreements whereby white purchasers of property agreed never to sell to any Negro, not even to Dumas or St. Augustine. All of Grand Republic, except the Five Points, Swede Hollow, Canoe Heights and a few tracts of swampland, was now covered by these restrictive covenants, which have been the most delightful of devices for tactfully saying to all clean and ambitious Negroes that the better whites preferred them to be dirty, unambitious, and distant.

Oliver also knew a great deal about the Sant Tabac, and he went to Boone Havock and Rodney Aldwick to discuss it, though none of the three was on the official roll of Sant Tabac members.

———

Neil and Vestal heard the street door close, that Sunday afternoon, and then, in the dining-room, the sound of Biddy, crying desperately. When they galloped in, she raised her head to stare at them mutinously, her wet eyes red and desolate. She choked, "Mummy, Mrs. Staubermeyer says I'm a nigger."

"Oh——"

"Am I a nigger?"

"Only as much as your father and mother are, and you can see for yourself how much that is," Vestal swore, "and we think we're pretty nice, don't you?"

"Am I a nigger like Little Black Sambo? Or that nasty boy on the shoeblacking can?"

"Not a bit like Little Black Sambo. More like Uncle Ash. Or Nora."

"Oh, I love them!"

"Biddy! Quick! What happened?"

"I was playing with Teddy and Tessie Staubermeyer and Teddy said I was a nigger, and I said no I wasn't, and he said his papa and

mama were all the time laughing at my daddy because he is a nigger and so I'm a nigger, too, Teddy said, and he said I couldn't play
with them any more unless I all undressed, and I didn't want
to——"

"What's all this?" Neil's anger was that of a cold man.

"He said and Tessie said, if I was a nigger, I was a slave, and slaves
aren't good for nothing except to take off their clothes and parade
around in front of their masters, bare-naked. And then Mrs.
Staubermeyer, she was listening to us from the porch——"

"She was?"

"——and she said no, they didn't ought to make me undress, it
was too cold, but it was a good joke on me, though, my daddy was so
high and mighty and he wasn't nothing but a nigger, she said, and I
better get out of there and go home. And I went."

They coaxed Biddy into laughing before she was put to bed, and
she announced that while she was a Negro like Nora Davis, she was
also an Indian princess named Rosemary Kitten Sunshine. She was
already devoted to both of those romantic strains, with a sentimentality her father could never achieve.

Outside her room, Neil growled, "I'm sorry she had to get the
news that way, from a family of degenerates. Come. We're going to
have a talk with the Staubermeyers."

On his way down the hall, he glanced into his "den" and noticed
his favorite Winchester on the wall. He made no particular connection, but he did remember that he was an excellent rifle-shot and
that this form of sport is not hindered by a lame leg.

———

Cedric Staubermeyer, dealer in paints and carpets, was not meaty
and resolute like his neighbor, Mr. W. S. Vander. He was puffy and
pouting and unpunctual, but in his hysteria he was dangerous.
When he found Neil and Vestal at his front door—it was of golden
oak, with net curtain inside a diamond-shaped plate-glass insert—
he looked embarrassed and sulkily muttered, "Come in."

The mantel in the parlor was also of golden oak, with a plate-
glass mirror, and on the more-or-less Oriental table-cover was a
pamphlet by Jat Snood.

Mrs. Staubermeyer was a loftier character than her husband: a vixen with free-running gray hair. She stood with her arms in two sharp V's.

Neil remarked, "I'm not going to talk about calling the police or any of that monkey-business, but if there's any repetition of what happened to my daughter this afternoon, I'm going to start trouble."

"And just how?" demanded Mrs. Staubermeyer.

As that was a challenge hard to meet, Neil was relieved when Cedric started shrieking, "You'll start trouble? You'll get into trouble, more trouble, you mean! Got any idea how glad this neighborhood would be to get rid of all you coons? Including yours truly! I always had an idea you were a nigger or something, Kingsblood, because you got along so well with the kikes and the wops!"

Vestal bored in, "Are you two cultured Gentiles aware that your son suggested that my daughter take off her clothes?"

Mrs. Staubermeyer laughed, like the scratch of a file, and she giggled, "Oh, he's practically a grown man, that way. All the Staubermeyer men mature so early. And let me tell you, madam, that we don't never want your daughter to come into our yard again, so you needn't worry!"

———

For days, Biddy was alternately afraid and slightly proud of her misadventure, and in sleep she trembled. Various more or less horrible versions of what had happened skipped about the neighborhood, and in no few of them, Biddy had been flagrantly indecent. They kept her at home as much as they could, and they rejoiced:

"Anyway, thank Heaven, she always will have a nice yard of her own to play in."

54

It was revealed to Mr. Oliver Beehouse that since Sylvan Park was altogether protected by restrictive covenants, when Neil Kingsblood had contracted to buy his house, back in 1941, he had, by concealing the fact that he was "colored," been guilty of grave crimes against Mr. Eisenherz, Mr. Stopple, the state health code, the Constitution, the Bible, and Magna Carta. Oliver supposed that when his niece, Vestal, saw her husband not only unemployed but houseless, she would leave him. Oliver knew a great deal about corporation taxes but not much about women.

One other person knew as surprisingly little about them, and that was Neil. He assumed that because Vestal backed him in saucing Uncle Oliver, because she let Biddy believe that both her parents were "colored," he could count on her being his true follower all the way.

But one afternoon when she came home from work, not many days after, it was clear that there was no overflowing font of patience and love in her at all. She looked at his clothes with disfavor, and sniffed, "Aren't you letting yourself get kind of sloppy? You've got to try and keep neat, if you ever *are* going to get a decent job."

"I can't afford a new suit, but I've been careful about brushing and pressing this one."

"There's an ick, jam or something, on your tie."

"I'm no fuss-Prutt!"

It was a family phrase which once they had found funny, but Vestal did not smile as she continued the attack: "And another sign of your losing your grip, and it worries me, is the fact that you want to run away from me so often. You spend so much time with these lowdown soap-boxers, like this fellow Brewster—is that the preacher's name?"

"It is, and you know it is. And let me tell you that I don't spend a quarter as much time away from you, with my race—though I ought to—as I used to spend playing poker with Judd's gang or going hunting and generally wasting time. You think my real interest as a boy crusader is a bore, whereas you used to think that my foolin' with games was manly and noble."

"I still do! As compared with these fanatic field-days where you and the other crackpots rearrange the world."

"Vestal!"

"Well, I'm tired of it, tired clean through. I think I'll take a little nap before I get supper. Tired! What really makes it hard for me,

Neil, is that you're two people: the boy I married and a Negro whose interests I don't know at all. Which of them am I married to now?"

In his distress at never being able to chart Vestal's loyalty, he went for counsel to his mother. It was a lively spring afternoon outside, with clouds playing tag with the sun, but his mother sat over solitaire in a room with the shades down, a chill ghost of a woman, like the soul of a baby in limbo.

He begged, "Mom, how can I persuade Vestal that she's no worse off than millions of Negro women?"

"I don't think you can, Boy, and she is worse off, if she thinks she is. I'm not sure but that you ought to tell her to go, go far off, when the new baby comes. You'll be lonely—you got no idea how lonely—as lonely as you've made Joan and me. But I imagine things will get worse with Vestal and you. She's a spirited girl. Maybe you ought to ask her to go before they do get worse."

"Maybe."

———

In late spring, when the snow still filtered down for half an hour now and then and veiled the plum blossoms and lilacs and flowering almond, but when the trees were almost in full leaf, that full-bodied ex-diplomat, Mr. Berthold Eisenherz, left his Florida villa and migrated home as though he were going into exile.

With his eyes fixed on a signed photograph of H.E. the Rt. Hon. Sir Reginald Widescombe, G.C.M.G. on a satinwood table in his library at Hillhouse, with his fingertips together, each of them like a miniature of his polite bald head, Mr. Eisenherz listened while Mr. William Stopple explained that by selling property to this Neil Kingsblood, a notorious Negro agitator, they had been guilty of breaking the covenant and injuring the equity of the innocent white property-holders in Sylvan Park. That they had been ignorant of the fellow's taint was probably no excuse in law and, what was worse than any legal foot-slipping, if they didn't do something at once, Mr. Eisenherz's remaining unsold property in the addition might drop in value.

Had it dropped yet? worried Mr. Eisenherz.

No, not yet, but everybody knew that it would, because everybody knew that all Negroes like this fellow were unbathed and noisy, and while he, Mr. Stopple, had no prejudices, and neither had he, Mr. Eisenherz, still facts were facts. Weren't they?

Bertie Eisenherz had been very fond of the mulatto mistress he had had for two years while he was with the legation in Portugal, and he was irritated by all this insular imbecility, but he needed the money, he always needed the money, for the maintenance of his precarious conviction that he was a great gentleman. And though he was devoted to his Renoir and his autographed set of Henry James, he was legitimately the grandson of Simon Eisenherz, the shrewdest and most resolute pilferer of Indian forest-land titles in Northern Minnesota.

And so:

Neil received from the law-firm in which Rodney Aldwick was a partner a letter bleakly asking him to call.

He went in warily to see Aldwick, who wanted to shake hands and who was altogether on the friendly and jolly side:

"Neil, personally I think this whole matter is picayune nonsense, but unfortunately, under the restrictive-covenant custom, both your neighbors and poor old Bill Stopple's firm could sue you for having purchased your home on fraudulent pretenses, knowing all the while that you were—colored, shall we say?"

He looked at Neil brightly, as if awaiting the pleasure of having him get angry and rave that he had not "known all the while." Neil sat bulkily still and Aldwick, a little disappointed, went on:

"Mr. Eisenherz is still willing to refund what you paid. But he is no longer just offering it; he is insisting. He demands that you hand over the place at once. After all, what is it? Just another house and lot, that's all. If you refuse, he will take legal action, and I imagine that in the settlement, any costs that Mr. Eisenherz may be forced to undergo will be assessed against you. And they will be considerable. I'll see to that! Ha, ha. Well, my dear fellow? After all, you know!"

"It's my house, bought legally, honestly paid for, and I stick."

"Oh, come now, Neil, we're both of us men of the world."

"Not me."

"You know that this has nothing to do with reason or legality, Neil. If the Sylvan Park suburbanites want to keep their tedious neighborhood lily-white, they will, you know, and you'd be happier in a more cosmopolitan district. Same like me."

"You heard me."

"Yes—yes—I heard you, my friend. So in all geniality let me tell you that we shall file suit and chase you out of the house, with speed. If you refuse to go, you will be jailed for contempt of court. So! I'll be seeing you."

Neil took the case to Sweeney Fishberg, which was to proclaim that he had a righteous cause and that he would probably lose it. Sweeney was half Jew and half Irish, half Communist and half Roman Catholic, half propagandist against all prejudice and half cynic about all propaganda. He was St. Francis rewritten by Henry Mencken, Lenin with footnotes by George Schuyler. He liked to talk with Clem Brazenstar, but he preferred to go hunting with Boone Havock.

He estimated, "You could fight on the ground that they can't prove you're a Negro at all, or on the ground that in this state, as small a number of Negro genes as you have don't legally constitute you a Negro."

"No," Neil said stubbornly, "I want to fight out the whole business of restrictive covenants. We'll make 'em illegal. Now that they've forced me to be a Negro, I'm going to *be* one."

"You kind of helped 'em on the forcing, didn't you? So you're another chronic martyr. I thought you were too good a golfer for that. Still fighting to save John Brown from the gallows? Why do all you cranks and abolitionists come to *me?* I'm a Boston Catholic *and* a Republican. The case would cost you a lot of money that you haven't got, with the bumbling Beehouses backing Rod, the young Lord God, and my services will set you back a lot more than you'd think from this ratty office. No, you better grab old Bertie's offer, and sneak up and paint swastikas on his house at night and——All right, all right, all right! Don't badger me! I'll take it, and I'll twist Aldwick's powdered neck off!"

—

Slipping under Rod's vigilant arm, Sweeney Fishberg went directly to Bertie Eisenherz and got his consent to having the case postponed till fall, in the hope, eternal among radicals like Sweeney, that God would awaken in the next three or four months and see what His children on earth were doing to one another.

The news of the postponement, the news that they would have to endure the dreadful Kingsbloods for another season, started a combustion in Sylvan Park. W. S. Vander and Cedric Staubermeyer, shuddering at being contaminated by Biddy, were heard screaming, "We're not going to wait for no court action! We're going to drive those niggers out of here before our property is ruined!"

Since their zeal was not directed that way, none of them even thought of Neil's mother, who may have had more "Negro blood" than her son.

—

That warm evening, Prince dashed up and down the yard, a happy dog and, for one of middle age, full of romance. They heard him singing a small, contented, doggy song of love. But something made him uneasy, and presently he came to the screened open window with low barks of inquiry. Neil went out to the yard to reassure him, and when he patted that sleek head, Prince mooned up with adoration, and rolled away again, to look into the unusual matter of a night-roistering squirrel.

When Neil had settled with his newspaper, he heard, from just outside, the astonishing crash of a shotgun. He leaped up and, despite Vestal's wail of "Don't go—don't!" he slipped out to the stoop.

Prince lay near the sidewalk, a mass of raw meat, already stiffening. As Neil gaped, he felt something brush by him like a breeze, and Biddy, in pajamas, had run out and was kneeling beside the stilled dog, her one only remaining playmate. In the dusk, Neil thought he saw the dog's head lift in a reproachful look.

Vestal moaned, "Oh, the cowards! Neil! It could be you, next time—or Biddy!"

Two evenings later, he found their carrier-brought newspaper on the lawn, torn to pieces, and next morning, a straggling sign

"Nigger get out" had been painted on the side of their garage. That day, though the organization was supposed to be dead in Grand Republic, he got a full-dress Ku Klux Klan warning: "You better get out of this neighborhood quick don't think we are fooling this is sent to you in the name of the cross of Christ, decent womanhood and American civilization."

All they could do, in the still and listening evenings, was to sit and wait, sit and listen, waiting.

—

Mr. Josephus Lovejoy Smith—but he signed it "Jos L. Smith"—was born in Upper New York State, and he affirmed, "No, I'm not related to Joseph Smith, the Mormon, though he used to talk with the angels right near where I was born. But I am distant kin to Gerrit Smith, who raised abolitionist hell and teetotaler hell, and continued to be a respectable land-promoter."

He was a fat, immobile, gentle man of sixty who had a book and toy and stationery shop of merit, just off Chippewa Avenue. He was a lowchurchman, a right-of-center Republican, but his abolitionist tradition, and a regret that Gerrit Smith had denied his ally, John Brown, at the last, had always made him feel guilty that he had not "done more for the poor darkies." But he did not know what to do, except to be indignant over newspaper accounts of lynchings and to sell as many books by Myrdal and Cayton and Du Bois as he could.

Neil and Vestal had bought magazines and Christmas cards in his shop. His brown house, which resembled a large sitting hen, was not far from theirs, and they had seen him taking walks, under an umbrella, in the rain. But they had never said anything more to him than "Good morning" or "Have you any water-color sets?"

When he came calling and sat down breathless in their living-room, they were perplexed.

He puffed, "You might not be interested, but my father was in the last year of the Civil War, as a boy. My mother's father was a colonel in a Vermont regiment and he was related to Owen Lovejoy, who was, I believe, a desperate anti-slavery man. But—I hope I'm not intruding, but I felt that I must come and tell you that I have been hearing—in fact, I was approached to join the gang—there is a plan among some of the folks around here to mob your house and drive you out."

"They really mean it?" from Neil.

"May I ask if you will defend your house—if you will fight?"

Neil looked inquiringly at Vestal, and she answered, "To the limit!" Neil droned, "I would rather they didn't start anything, but if they do, I have some guns here."

Mr. Smith considered, "I don't believe I hold with violence or the use of firearms in general. I don't even hunt pa'tridges more than once a year. But I don't like this mob rule. If you can use some ten-gauge shotgun shells, I'd be glad to lend them to you. It's quite an old gun that I have. By the way, the fellow that came to enlist me, I tried to get out of him—he was Curtiss Havock, your next-door neighbor—I asked him what night they plan it for, but he wouldn't tell me. And incidentally, Mr. Kingsblood—Neil—would you like to go to work for me in my store—starting tomorrow, if you'd care to?"

———

"You know," said Vestal afterwards, "there *is* something to race differences. No gang of Negroes, however mean they are, could be as hideous as Curtiss and Feathering and the Staubermeyers. I'm beginning to get annoyed."

———

His day at Smith's Book Store was disappointingly casual. No one stared at him, no one objected to receiving 1 doz. bl. pencils #2 from his black hand. Vestal came over from Tarr's to have lunch with him, and they took the bus home together, and nobody paid any attention to them, and they felt silly—and then they did not feel silly at all, but frightened all over again. For one Mr. Matozas, a man with an 1890 cyclist's mustache, a detective on the Special Squad of the Safety Commissioner (which meant chief of police), came calling that evening, slyly making with his derby hat.

"Just kind of on some routine inquiries for the Commissioner," he gurgled.

Vestal—she did not like him nor his derby nor the leather-covered billy visible in his side pocket—snapped, "Tell the Commissioner that you found this family acting suspiciously: staying home in their own house, listening to 'This Land of Freedom' program on the radio, and reading a speech by President Truman."

Matozas was a great laugher, chronic, though his red knuckles had been split. He laughed, and he said, "Yuh, I'll sure tell the Commissioner that. He'll be glad *one* family is behaving itself, in this gin-hoisting town! That's a fine little girl you got."

"Yes. We've noticed that. But when did you ever see her? She's been in bed for half an hour now."

"Oh, I get around. The Special Squad gets around quite a lot."

Neil took charge. "What do you want?"

"The Commissioner thought there's something you folks ought to know. Of course ordinarily, with your wife related to Counselor Beehouse, the Commissioner would come to see you himself, but Judge Beehouse has come out flatfooted and told us that he doesn't want any part of this business, and the law will have to take its course."

"What law? What course? I wish you'd make your threats a little clearer!" said Neil.

"Threats? And me coming here to tip you off that if you want to pack up and move out right away, our Squad will give you any help we can! But if you don't—— Mind you, I don't know nothing about no mobs, but it would be just too bad if a mob assembled, illegal, and we got here too late! Good night, folks."

Neil said then, "The Commissioner, this fellow's boss, isn't only an appointee of Mayor Fleeron but a great friend of his, and of Wilbur Feathering and, curiously enough, of Rod Aldwick. I think we better get Biddy out of here, quick."

They picked up the baby and dressed her without her ever quite awakening, and Neil carried her to Mother Kingsblood's, Vestal stalking beside him like Diana in a camel's-hair topcoat. They almost ran on the way back, so apprehensive were they.

From the darkened living-room they kept watch on the street. Neil brought his favorite rifle down from his den. His fingers felt cool on the barrel. The evening was pleasant, tempting the strollers out after the long imprisonment of the Northern winter, yet there were rather too many people ambling by, neighbors and strangers, and Neil fancied that everybody halted slightly and stared at the house.

And among the strollers, quite separate and casual, they noticed Detective Matozas, Mayor Fleeron, and Mr. Wilbur Feathering.

And nothing happened, nothing at all, and they went to bed. They did not sleep well, and Neil kept rising, to look out. There was nothing suspicious . . . except that Detective Matozas was standing by a cottonwood tree in Curtiss Havock's yard, smoking cigarettes, all night long. Perhaps he just liked cottonwood trees and cigarettes.

At breakfast, when Neil said "It'll be tonight, sure," she nodded, and he pleaded, "Don't you want to quit?"

"Never!"

"I can get some of the boys to come in—say, a colored captain I know, Captain Windeck. Why don't you go to your father's for tonight, and not bother us?"

"Do you want me to go?"

"Yes, I think I do."

"Well, I'm not going! I stick," said Vestal.

———

Pat Saxinar left the Marxian nunnery of her settlement-house that day and came to see Neil in the Smith store. From her father, the alienated Uncle Emery, she had rumors that Neil's house was to be bombed.

Neil telephoned to Phil Windeck at the garage where Phil had a new job, virtuous and underpaid, and to Evan Brewster, but neither of them knew anything clearly. He wished that Ash and Ryan Woolcape were in town. He tried to reach Dr. Cope Anderson, for that bulky chemist, to whom his Negro friends were exactly like his white friends, only slightly more so, would be a competent bruiser in a fight. But Cope and Peace Anderson were in Milwaukee.

At the store, Mr. Smith brought him two boxes of shotgun shells, but Mr. Smith said only, "Uh—some shells I happened to come across. You might want to go hunting, next fall." To Neil these shells were of value only as antiques and symbols of faith. They were ten-gauge, and he hadn't seen a ten-gauge shotgun since the Civil War.

Vestal and he again returned together on the bus. They had the nervous calmness of before-the-battle, and they did not feel moved to prepare anything for their dinner beyond sandwiches and coffee. He no longer suggested that Vestal desert. It was not that she said anything in particular, but she had the look of battle.

They hastened over to Mother Kingsblood's to see Biddy, hastened back. Neil began to bring his guns and ammunition down to the living-room.

From that room, which they again kept dark, they could watch the small, semi-circular stoop, and when the bell rang they saw Pat Saxinar out there, and admitted her with enthusiasm.

Three minutes later, at another bell-ring, the sentry Vestal called out, "It's a nice-looking young man, some kind of a soldier, in what I think is an American Legion uniform. Hot stuff. Golly, I think he's colored."

She let in Phil Windeck, soldierly again and trim, with a .45 automatic in his pocket. She was as casual with him as with Pat—more easy and casual than with the next recruit, who was Sweeney Fishberg.

That grumbler was bushy-haired and tart, and about as soldierly as Professor Einstein. He was growling, "This is a service we give all our clients, and most of 'em need it." He disapproved of Phil's automatic; it was illegal, useless and tended to violence. But he handed it back.

Then, fat and stooped, walking slowly down the middle of the street, concealing nothing from anybody, carrying his enormous shotgun unsportingly over his shoulder, his nose like a rabbit's but his eyes like an aged hawk's, came Josephus Lovejoy Smith, formerly of the Republican County Committee. And right after him, walking nervously and looking down as if he was thinking hard, carrying a Marlin repeating-rifle in a neat case, appeared Lucian Firelock, who said to Pat, at the door, "Good evening. Is Mr. Kingsblood at home? Oh, good evening, Neil. Good evening, Nurse."

The Nurse, following him, was Sophie Concord, in uniform with a dark cape over it.

She merely nodded to Neil, but to Vestal she said cheerily, "I thought I might be able to help you, Mrs. Kingsblood, if there's any cooking to do—or any nursing."

Last of all, in the clerical collar and black waistcoat that he rarely wore, with a rifle under his arm, was the Reverend Evan Brewster, S.T.D.

Lucian Firelock said to him, "Have you any information about the primaries in Mississippi, Mr. Brewster?"

It had been harder for him to call Evan "Mister" than to call him "General" or "Eminence."

Jos. L. Smith was introduced to Phil Windeck and Evan. He shook hands firmly, and afterward said to Neil, "I don't think I have met any colored gentlemen socially before. They seem to have scarcely any accent."

The party became cheerful. It was a Sylvan Park evening of early summer, with birds and the sound of playing children and peace over everything, with plenty of guns and ammunition, and hot coffee by courtesy of Vestal and Sophie. Neil gave a lesson in the handling of guns to Sophie, who had the unprejudiced idea of closing both eyes when she pulled the trigger, and Vestal laughed with them. Since most of them had not dined, she started to cook ham and eggs, but Evan took it away from her, and showed how a dining-car cook can turn a fried egg by flipping it in air.

"This whole combination of party and firearms," said Evan, "makes me think of when I first studied Greek, with a Congregational minister in Massachusetts. He had a shack for his study, in the garden, and he used to sit with his Greek Testament on a card-table in front of him, and a .22 rifle ready to pot the rabbits that ate his carrots——"

They heard a rock smashing through the sun-room window. They slipped to the front of the house, to see people gathered across the street, in the thin darkness.... But Evan carefully turned off the gas in the kitchen before he turned to war, and brought out a plate of the eggs that had already been cooked. The besieged picked them up in their hands and ate, while Neil turned off all the lights. The people in the neighboring yards were moving about, shadowy, not laughing. It was absurd to think of them as dangerous. But Neil posted his guards sharply.

Vestal insisted, "Phone the police, Neil."

"Don't think it'll do any good."

"Possibly have a legal value," said Fishberg.

When Neil reached the desk sergeant at police headquarters by telephone, the sergeant was evasive. "People round your house, Mister? Whaddayuh got? A menagerie?"

"They're threatening us. I'm a, well, a Negro, and they're trying to run us out."

"Ain't that mean of 'em! Nigger, eh? Where yuh say you live? Mayo Street?"

"I told you before."

"Sure, I know all about you, Kingsblood. We have information there's a few kids roughhousing around there. What the hell are you? An old maid? I always heard you zigs were scared of your own shadows. Can't you stand a little good-natured charivariing without bothering the police force? We—" A yawn. "—got something more important to do."

Neil reported to his army, "That's interesting. The police knew all about this, even before it started. And Mayor Fleeron is one of the neighbors that want to drive me away. Fine fellows, the police."

"And how!" said Sweeney Fishberg. "You've never been on a picket-line."

There was no more laughter. Neil had chosen for his own firing-post one window of the living-room, had stationed Phil Windeck at the other. He fretted at Vestal, "You stand back in the dining-room, way back. You got to be careful about the new baby."

It occurred to Sweeney to telephone the office of Sheriff Alex Snowflower, who was not dominated by Fleeron. Sweeney worked the hook up and down, in the dimness, and said uncomfortably, "The phone wire has just been cut."

Lucian Firelock was annoyed and bewildered that he should be on this side of the barricade. But he turned decisively to Phil with,

"Mr. Windeck, where should you hit a man if you want to stop him but not kill him, not hurt him badly, Phil?"

The background of suburban street could not have been more placid, with the branches in a gently moving screen across the cool lamplighted windows over the way. But against this background, the menace grew rapidly. Dozens and then scores of men and excited women filled the yards opposite, oozed into the street. Aggressive men pushed forward in the center, men whose killer faces were the more grotesque above their pert ties, their near-gentlemanly tweed jackets.

They ceased to be human beings; they became bubbles on a dark cataract of hate. Rigid in the living-room, Neil saw that the leaders of the mob were Wilbur Feathering, the Reverend Dr. Jat Snood, Harold W. Whittick and Cedric Staubermeyer, with the flat-headed but sturdy W. S. Vander as war-chief. Following them were seventy or eighty face-screwed, hot-voiced maniacs: poor neighbors, prosperous neighbors, a blot of toughs whom Neil had never seen, with irate pietists from Snood's tabernacle.

But he could also make out a good many people who were flapping their arms and bobbing up and down in protest: Charley Sayward, S. Ashiel Denver, Norman and Rita Kamber, and the lovely Violet Crenway, who worked up the general homicidal tension by screaming, "Oh, be careful, everybody be careful!" while her delicate face was rosy with the joys of horror. And a fortress of five clerics—Buncer, Gadd, Lenstra, Father Pardon and Rabbi Sarouk—stood together, their hands flung high, warning back the crowd—twenty years too late.

Through all the assembling, Sweeney Fishberg, by the light of a pocket torch, was casually noting down their names, as future witnesses. Neither Randy Spruce nor Mayor Fleeron nor Rodney Aldwick was to be seen, but there were unrecognizable people up on Judd Browler's roof.

At first the crowd stayed in the streets at Neil's corner, or in the yards of Curtiss Havock and Orlo Vay, with no perceptible objections from the owners. But they were edging up on the sidewalks at the front and side of Neil's yard, and the protesting ministers had been pushed back into the tree-thick darkness.

"You heard he killed his father!" cried an unknown, and a dozen unknowns answered, "Sure, and we'll get him for it!"

There was a diversion then, and for a time Neil did not see what it meant. Swinging into the crowd, headed for his front door, three men marched like the Continentals of 1776: John Woolcape, Albert Woolcape, and Borus Bugdoll. There was nothing to choose among the scholar, the haggling laundryman and the racketeer for pure, high fury, but it was Albert, who had tried so hard not to be a Negro belligerent, who could be heard shrieking, "You let us pass!"

The crowd realized, from Borus's color, what they were, and eddied about them. Neil did not see them again. He saw only the bulk of the crowd, saw the clubs rising, and heard one scream.

Now, like a slow tide of mud, the crowd moved into Neil's own yard. Not thinking, not much afraid, outraged at their trespass, Neil stumped to the front door, unlocked and opened it, and stood in the doorway, rifle on his arm. He was conscious of how fresh and pleasant the air was, and conscious that behind him were Phil, and Vestal with an absurdly large automatic pistol.

He called out, "I'm going to kill the next fellow that takes a step." They froze.

From the front of the crowd, his voice rough and resolute, Vander the lumberjack croaked, "Don't talk like a fool! You're going to move out of this neighborhood tonight, or we'll tear the house down and take care of every damn nigger in it!"

Neil said with chilliness, "Mr. Vander?"

"Yuh?"

"We ordinarily say 'Negro,' not 'nigger.' "

Jat Snood let loose. "Come on, brethren! Get going! It's the work of the Lord! Let's go!"

Neil nuzzled his rifle at his shoulder, and Feathering yelped, "Look out for him!" But Vander snarled, "He don't dare!"

So Vander and Snood and Feathering swayed toward Neil together. As they did, there was a shot from the crowd, and a bullet, passing over Neil's shoulder, got Vestal. He heard her gasp; for a second turned his head toward her. She snapped, "It's nothing. Just touched m' arm. Let 'em have it!"

But Neil took his time, because he was a target shot, and because he was meticulously choosing among Vander, Snood, Feathering. Really, Vander should come first, but the missionary from hell had his merits——

Then he fired. His first shot caught the Reverend Dr. Jat Snood in his right thigh, and he went down. The second got Feathering's right knee, but unfortunately the third—perhaps Neil was nervous by now—missed Vander, nipped off a toe of Cedric Staubermeyer, and sent him home howling.

The crowd stumbled backward, beginning to shoot. Then Mr. Jos. L. Smith, from an upstairs window—that of Biddy's pink-and-white little room—let go with his ten-gauge cannon, and sprinkled quail shot over the whole brigade, and they broke, screaming for aid.

The policemen in their patrol-wagon must have been waiting not two blocks away. As Mr. Smith's artillery roared, the gong was heard, the patrol wagon pushed politely through the retreating crowd, and the policemen leaped out and trotted toward Neil and Phil and Vestal in the doorway.

At their head was Detective Matozas. He and his gallants must have had careful orders. They seized Neil and Phil, but at Vestal, who stood just inside the door with Sophie beginning to bandage her arm, Matozas growled, "Get back in the house there, you. We don't want you. We just want these niggers—starting all this riot, shooting prominent citizens!"

Vestal put aside Sophie's ministrations with an affectionate pat, and spoke to Mr. Matozas clearly: "Then you'll have to take me. Didn't you know I'm a Negro, too?"

One policeman muttered to another, "I didn't know she was a tar-baby," and his mate revealed, "Don't be so dumb. Can't you see it by her jaw?"

Matozas commanded, "Well, we're not *going* to take you, no such a damn thing, and you get back in there and quit trying to work up sympathy!"

He reached for her arm.

"Oh, you'll take me!" said Vestal, quite sweetly, and brought the butt of her automatic down on the detective's head.

As she was herded with Neil toward the patrol wagon, she squeezed his arm. "Are you as scared as I am? Will you hold my hand in the wagon? It looks so dark in there, but if you hold my hand, I shan't be too frightened. What a wonderful start this is for little Booker T.! Neil! Listen! Listen to Josephus Smith bawling out the policemen. There must be lots of good white men, aren't there?"

"Keep moving," said a policeman.

"We're moving," said Vestal.

READING GROUP GUIDE

1. When *Kingsblood Royal* was first published, in 1947, Sinclair Lewis was one of America's leading writers (in 1930 he became the first American to be awarded the Nobel Prize in literature), and the novel was an immediate sensation, offering a powerful, in-depth look at race relations in America in ways that were eye-opening and controversial for much of mainstream America. It was widely reviewed, garnering praise from the likes of Clifton Fadiman, and was often compared to another important book about race in America: *Uncle Tom's Cabin*. However, soon after it was published, the book sank into obscurity and was ignored, even as other novels by Lewis, such as *Main Street* and *Babbitt*, became entrenched in the canon of great American novels. How might we account for the long-term critical neglect of what is arguably Lewis's most politically charged and incendiary novel, his only major work to put issues of race center stage?

2. At the beginning of *Kingsblood Royal*, the novel's central character, Neil, seems to hold many of the racial attitudes in circulation in the middle-American community in which he lives, a community that Lewis clearly intends to serve as a microcosm of American society; the name of Neil's town, Grand Republic, is a not-so-subtle reference to America itself. As the novel progresses and Neil embarks upon his "conversion," his consciousness changes radically, and he comes to look upon his own world—that of middle-American white society—very differently. Discuss how Neil's ideas about white society and "whiteness" in general change, and how *Kingsblood Royal* puts that society into stark relief.

3. Throughout the novel, Neil is by turns shocked and enlightened by how alike black and white individuals and attitudes are, but also by the differences between black and white perceptions and outlooks. Discuss the ways in which *Kingsblood Royal* works to challenge and re-

define our sense of the differences *and* similarities between black and white communities in America.

4. In chapter 25 Neil has what he considers "the most critical evening in his history." Why is this the case? Discuss the events of this evening, and the ideas and discussions that make it up.

5. Two of the novel's significant characters—Ash and Drexel Greenshaw—mirror each other in interesting ways. Discuss these two characters—their backgrounds, careers, and fates. What do they share? How are they different? In what ways are they illustrative of black life in America in the 1940s?

6. How does Neil's relationship with Vestal change as the novel progresses? Does Vestal herself change, along with Neil? Do you see Vestal as victimized by the events of the novel? As heroic? What role does she play in the narrative of *Kingsblood Royal*? What can she be said to represent?

7. At numerous points in the novel, Neil "comes out," or speaks the truth about himself, a series of episodes that culminates at the Federals Club. At the same time, Neil is warned throughout—by both black and white friends and colleagues—to remain silent, advice that he finds himself unable to follow. Why is it important for Neil to announce what he knows about himself in a public manner, even if it should lead to ruin?

8. Throughout Neil's journey toward ostracization after "coming out," he is shunned by his wife, by friends, and by colleagues, as if his "blackness" seems a polluting or contaminating influence to the white people around him. Discuss this theme—racism as fear of contamination—as it is played out throughout this work, from the Kingsbloods' initial "servant trouble" (their anxiety about their maid Belfreda) to the expulsion of the Kingsbloods themselves from Sylvan Park at the novel's end.

9. Lewis's description of the gathering mob near the novel's conclusion underscores a sense of contrast present throughout the novel: on one hand the quiet world of middle America, and on the other the hypocrisies and violence fueled by racism. Here is a passage that illustrates this contrast in a particularly vivid way:

The background of suburban street could not have been more placid, with the branches in a gently moving screen across the cool lamplighted windows over the way. But against this background, the menace grew rapidly. Dozens and then scores of men and excited women filled the yards opposite, oozed into the street. Aggressive men pushed forward in the center, men whose killer faces were the more grotesque above their pert ties, their near-gentlemanly tweed jackets. They ceased to be human beings; they became bubbles on a dark cataract of hate.

Explore and examine this sense of contrast—the violence lurking within the "civilized" and calm world of Grand Republic—in *Kingsblood Royal*.

10. Sinclair Lewis is widely considered to be one of America's greatest satirists. Discuss how *Kingsblood Royal* makes use of satire, and its close cousin, irony, to illuminate and condemn the hypocrisies of American society with regard to issues of race.

11. How, in your view, have the perceptions and the realities of how race is "lived" and experienced in America changed since this novel was published? What contemporary issues or debates do you see reflected in *Kingsblood Royal*?

A Note on the Type

The principal text of this Modern Library edition
was set in a digitized version of Janson,
a typeface that dates from about 1690 and was cut by Nicholas Kis,
a Hungarian working in Amsterdam. The original matrices have
survived and are held by the Stempel foundry in Germany.
Hermann Zapf redesigned some of the weights and sizes for Stempel,
basing his revisions on the original design.